Seasons

Seasons

Deanna Lynette

authorHOUSE®

AuthorHouse™
1663 Liberty Drive
Bloomington, IN 47403
www.authorhouse.com
Phone: 1-800-839-8640

© 2011 Deanna Lynette. All rights reserved.

No part of this book may be reproduced, stored in a retrieval system, or transmitted by any means without the written permission of the author.

First published by AuthorHouse 1/24/2011

ISBN: 978-1-4520-2349-6 (e)
ISBN: 978-1-4520-2348-9 (sc)
ISBN: 978-1-4520-2347-2 (hc)

Library of Congress Control Number: 2010906563

Printed in the United States of America

Any people depicted in stock imagery provided by Thinkstock are models, and such images are being used for illustrative purposes only. Certain stock imagery © Thinkstock.

This book is printed on acid-free paper.

Because of the dynamic nature of the Internet, any web addresses or links contained in this book may have changed since publication and may no longer be valid. The views expressed in this work are solely those of the author and do not necessarily reflect the views of the publisher, and the publisher hereby disclaims any responsibility for them.

Unpublished Work © 2007 Deanna L. Peaks

Along life's journey seasons change.
Life can become cold like the winter.
Sometimes you fall like autumn.
The tears you cry are like the showers of spring.
Sometimes the sun never stops shinning, like the summer.

But we know the reason the seasons change,
is because God's hand is on the world.
Turning it at just the right angle, at just the right time;
so nothing stays in the dark for too long;
or burns up in the light.

So just like life, God knows when to put you in a season
and when to take you out.
Seasons change, but love remains because God stays the same.

~Brianna R. Wright

1
Kennede

"God you guys, it's been so long since we've rung in the New Year together," Brandi said smiling as she turned back around from looking in the backseat at her twin sister Brianna and our cousin Summer. "I mean, even though all we did was go to church, it just feels so good to be around my girls again."

"I know," I said pulling into my driveway, "we really should make it a point to spend more time with each other." I looked over at Brandi whose mocha complexion seemed to be glowing before I said, "no boyfriends," while pointing to her and Summer. Then I turned and looked at Brianna after I put the car in park. "No doctors!" I said that because the guy Brianna is dating is a doctor that she works with; she looked at me with a smart aleck smirk, "and no—"

"No kids!" Summer spoke up before I could finish speaking, she pointed to my daughter who was asleep sitting in between her and Brianna. "I don't know why ya'll keep making me sit back here. Ya'll know my thighs and butt are way too big to sit in the backseat every time we go somewhere."

"Oh hush," I waved at Summer, it seemed that she was always complaining about her plus size figure. "Somebody just grab my child, please." I stated.

"I've got her," Brianna offered as we were about to walk into my house.

"So Ken, is church always like that?" Summer asked while we were walking through the door, "because if church was like that a few years ago, I would have never stopped going. I think I might try this church thing again."

"You should," I said. "Since I've started attending church again, I have truly been trying to change. And did you see the look on our mother's faces when they saw *all* of us in church together again?" Our mothers were the reason that we had this close bond, that's because our mother's are sisters that come from a very close knit *Christian* family. Grand-daddy, whose real name was William Spencer, was a devote Christian and family man. He was a deacon at First Baptist Church, and he was also lead singer of the churches male chorus. While Granddaddy was doing some kind of *deacon duty* at the church, or rehearsing with the male chorus, our grandmother, Lillian, was working with the youth choir. She's not as active with the youth choir now as she was about seven years ago, before Grand-daddy passed away.

About forty plus years ago the pastor of First Baptist, whom at time was Reverend Robinson, decided to make Grandmother the head of that choir, after she spent so many years of dedication in the music department. As a matter of fact, I think it because most of the youth choir was made up of her and Granddaddy's six kids may have been another reason she became the leader. They had two boys, William Jr. (but we called him Uncle Bill), and Uncle Marvin, then four girls, Aunt Julie (Summer's mother), Aunt Lisa (the twins mother), Karen (my mother), and Aunt Regina is the baby out of the group. At the time Grandmother was appointed the head of the choir, her kids ages ranged from fifteen down to the age of three; the oldest being Uncle Bill as we called him growing up. Even though we were all raised in the church it didn't mean we were exempt from the troubles of this world. Everyone in our family has gone through something that wouldn't be classified as "Christian like," but the difference with us is we knew how to go back to the Lord.

"Here Ken, please take your big child," Brianna handed RaeLynn to me. "I swear that child gets bigger every time I see her."

I took RaeLynn to her room to take off her jacket and clothes. "Bri, she is not that big, she's supposed to be that size for four." I said as I walked back into the living room.

"So, back to this church business," Summer said sitting on my couch then leaning forward. "Are the New Year's Eve services that good all the time?"

"To tell you the truth this was my first time going," I admitted.

"Mine too," Brandi stated. "Well, I've been before but it was a long time ago with Granddaddy and Grandmother at their church, and it wasn't like it was tonight." Our mothers no longer attended their childhood church; they now belong to Genesis Christian Church, which is a lot bigger than First Baptist. I would say Genesis has about four-thousand plus members, where First Baptist has about two-hundred members strong. I was kind of skeptical of visiting such a large church at first, but everyone at Genesis made me feel so welcomed that it felt like it was only two-hundred members because the members made it feel so close and loving. Plus the pastor, Dr. Williams, has a way of preaching that will make you think that he's been listening in on your conversations with Jesus. "Girl, that was them old men and women singing those tired songs with no feeling back in the day."

"No feeling and no drums!" Brianna added to her sister's statement. "I like to feel the music," she stood up and began to wind her hips.

We all laughed as Brianna continued to dance with no music, then stopping suddenly before she sat back down in her seat.

"Okay, now changing the subject," Brandi said laughing, "Does anyone have any New Year's resolutions?"

We all sat silently. "I'll be the first one to start," Summer spoke up. "First off, I'm going to get more involved in church again. I realized what's missing in my life is God."

"Well, we all need God in our lives," Brianna started, "some of us more than others, but we need Him to help us through…"

"Right," Summer said. "Maybe then everything with me and Damon will be alright. I could probably even change him."

Everyone sat quietly with doubtful looks on our faces. "Change him?" Brandi questioned. "You can't change no man, Summer."

Summer spun around to face Brandi, "Why can't I?" She asked very seriously. "Aren't you trying to change Jayson?"

"That's totally different," Brandi said defensively. "Jayson's not like Damon at all. The only thing wrong with Jay is his choice of occupation; Damon's just a dog."

Summer's caramel colored face twisted with an attitude, "A dog…how are you just gonna call him out like that?" she questioned in disbelief.

"Okay ladies," I said standing; I could see that this conversation was going to lead into an argument. I love my cousins, but they weren't about to start nothing in my house while my daughter was trying to sleep. "Let's move on to the next resolution. I'll…"

"No, we're going to finish this," Summer said cutting me off, pointing her finger back and forth from her to Brandi. "So how is Damon a dog, Brandi?"

"Don't play dumb Summer," Brandi said as she kept a straight face. "How many times have you run to us crying because Damon has been cheating on you, or he tried to k—" Brandi stopped talking and Summer's eyes got big like someone surprised her.

Brianna and I looked at each other puzzled, then back at Summer and Brandi before I said, "He tried to do what?" I looked at Brandi first then turned back toward Summer. "Kick you? Because I know he better not have tried to kill you. As matter of fact he better not have tried to kick you either."

I could see the tears forming in Summer's eyes as she faced Brandi. "I thought you said you wouldn't say anything?"

"I didn't say anything to anyone before tonight," Brandi said looking at Summer with concern as Brianna and I looked on confused. "Summer, you can't keep letting this go on. Maybe I should have said something sooner."

"Say anything about what?" Brianna asked as if she was getting fed up of not knowing what was going on like I was. "Would somebody please tell me and Kennede what's going on!"

"A few months ago," Summer exhaled hard as a tear rolled down her face. "Damon and I were arguing about some girl that called his phone. So I had slapped him, and he pushed me up against the wall and tried to strangle me." Tears were flowing as Brianna, Brandi and I went to hug Summer, "I know it's my fault the reason why he—"

"No Summer, there is no excuse!" Brandi cut Summer off. "No man has a right to hit a woman and you know it. You were raised better than that." Brandi continued shaking her head from side to side.

"Honey, why do you stay?" Brianna asked. Summer shook her head and shrugged her shoulders. "There is so much more out there for you. I mean— you will be graduating college in May, then off to law school. So why waste your time?"

"You don't understand," Summer replied.

"Please make me understand, please," Brianna said. "I don't know what it's like to be in that type of relationship, but we were raised watching our father beat the crap out of our mother." She glanced at Brandi who was looking down at the floor with this strange look on her face, as if she were remembering the times her sister was speaking of at the moment. "So yes, please make me understand why you would put yourself through this," she said folding her arms and looking Summer in the face.

"Bri, I'm not like you," she said wiping away tears. "I can't live as long as you do without a man." Brianna gave her a "girl please" look. "Besides, Damon's my first love. We have been together since I was sixteen, six years is a long time to just throw everything away."

"Oh come on," I said to her breaking the "hug circle" we made. "Raymond and I met when I was fourteen; he was my first love too and my husband. We even have a child," I pointed toward RaeLynn's room. "But where is he now? And as much as I loved him… No, let me be honest, I *still* love him, but I couldn't hold on to something that was over. I couldn't put myself through that. Better yet, I couldn't let my daughter see me that way."

"We're not like you and Raymond," she sniffed then wiped her face again. "Damon and I are going to make it."

"Okay Summer." I looked up to the ceiling, *Lord please help this girl;* I said a quick silent prayer. "One thing I'm gonna say though, I pray that we don't end up burying you because these *arguments* went too far. That would be unfair if you ended up dead and one of us would be in jail for killing him." Summer plastered a fake smile on her face and shook her head in disagreement. No one else tried to protest and we left the conversation at that.

* * *

Who in the world is calling me so late? I thought as the phone rang while I was walking back into my bedroom from seeing my cousins off. "Hello?" I answered the phone.

"Happy New Year lady," the familiar voice said.

"Malik?" I questioned.

"Yeah, it's me," he said.

"Why are you calling so late?" I inquired. "Did you just assume that I wasn't asleep?"

"Were you sleeping?" he asked. "I apologize if I woke you."

"No, my cousins were just leaving," I said settling in the bed. "It's not all the time that my phone rings at two forty-five in the morning."

"I'm sorry," he said. "I just wanted to see how my best friend was and to tell you Happy New Year."

"Happy New Year to you too Malik," I said in a soft spoken tone.

"What do you got up for tomorrow?" he asked.

"I think Mama's cooking, so I'll probably be over there. Why?"

"Oh no reason," he said. "I was going to come by and see my favorite girl."

A smile came across my face, "Oh, you want to see me?"

"Naw, I was talking about RaeLynn," he laughed.

"Forget you Malik," I held a half smile on my face.

"You know you my girl too." Malik said still laughing.

"Why don't you just come by Mama's," I said to him. "Are you going to see your parents tomorrow?"

"Yeah, I guess I could slide over there," he replied.

"Cool, I guess I'll see you tomorrow then," I said.

"Later."

I hung the phone up picturing Malik's chocolate frame in my mind. *"No, that's your best friend,"* I said aloud to myself. Malik and I grew up together, but that doesn't mean that I have to deny how fine he is, with his milk chocolate skin, close cut hair, a little taller than me with a small muscular body. He was there with me through all of my troubles with Raymond and he hasn't left me yet. Surprisingly in the twelve years we've known each other, we've only kissed once. Okay, let me be honest, we've kissed more than once. After Ray and I divorced, I felt very vulnerable and Malik was always around, so we kissed.

Actually, we came very close to sleeping together; I mean *very* close. It was to the point that clothes were on the floor and skin was touching. I just couldn't go through with it, so that's why I consider that kiss when I was young the only kiss because I try to forget that moment in our friendship. I was twelve years old that summer we kissed for the first time, and it happened to be the best summer of my life. That was also my first kiss ever and with the finest thirteen year old on the block. The girls on our block already hated me for no reason, but for the longest I thought it was because I'm mixed and my daddy is white. We grew up in a predominately white neighborhood. This meant most of the neighborhood kids were white too.

Malik's family and half of my immediate family were the only black people on the block. Then a few years later Raymond's family added to the black population around there. My little sister, Kayla, started to have the same problem with the girls her age on our block when she got older too, but they seemed to accept my little brother Robert Jr. (although we call him R.J.). That's probably because they wanted his little cute butt looking like he could be Chris Brown's stunt double or twin. My kissing Malik just one time made those girls ready to declare war on me, and only because they wanted him too.

Thank God that was just a little summer thing. If I had been with Malik, I never would have met Raymond, fell in love, married, had a baby, and learned a huge crash lesson in *Heartbreak 101*. Even though our relationship ended in divorce, there is still a big piece of my heart that belongs *only* to Mr. Raymond A. Collins. I don't think I will ever stop loving my first love. My feelings aren't as strong as they were when I married him, but he still has a huge piece of me forever. Our daughter is the spitting image of him--so beautiful and lively just like he was when we were growing up.

I walked into her bedroom to make sure she was ok, she laid there stretched out across her twin size Dora the Explorer bed sound asleep. I smiled looking at the perfect gift that God gave me and Raymond. Every time I look at RaeLynn, I'm reminded of the good times her father and I had that resulted in her being here. I could never regret being married to Ray because through our marriage, even though we didn't last, we were able to bring life into this world, a beautiful one at that. I guess God knows what He's doing when He allows certain things to happen in your life and how some things just fall right into place at the right time.

Still smiling I walked back into my room, this time I was finally going to get some sleep. As I was about to get in the bed I noticed the red light on my cordless phone stand was flashing, indicating that there was a voicemail message. *"I don't remember hearing the phone ring again,"* I said aloud picking up the phone to check my voicemail.

"You have one unheard message," the voicemail lady said. *"Hey Ken,"* Raymond's baritone voice said softly in my ear, my heart dropped as shockwaves went through my body, like he was sitting right next to me. *"It seems like your line is busy, or maybe you're just busy,"* he chuckled; I twisted my mouth because I knew what he was trying to imply. *"But uh, I just wanted to tell you and RaeLynn Happy New Year and I love you both. Hope to talk to you all soon."* I looked at the phone then pressed the number two, "message will be saved," the voicemail lady said.

I continued to stare at the phone wanting so bad to call Raymond back and let him know that I received his message. I started to dial his number then quickly hung up, *"dang I can't call him,"* I put the phone back on the stand. "He *is* remarried." I sat there in my bed wondering why he took the time to call at two in the morning to wish me and RaeLynn a Happy New Year. First of all, he knows good and well RaeLynn would be sleep, and knowing his wife was probably in the other room.

"I love you both," I kept replaying that part of his message in my mind and a smile came across my face. *"Yeah, I love you too, Raymond."*

Brandi

When I finally got home it was around two fifty-five in the morning. Brianna dropped me off because I didn't feel like driving tonight. Also, I didn't want to come home alone. For the last few years I've been scared to be by myself in fear that someone would follow me home and try to hurt me. As soon as I walked in the house I reset the alarm because of this fear, and the fact that I knew Jay probably wouldn't be home until much later, so I had to be safe. I was walking upstairs when I realized the light in my bedroom was on, I became scared because when I left the house earlier I'm sure that it was off. Terrified of what might be up there, I ran back downstairs to get one of Jay's guns that he kept on the top shelf in the back of the closet.

"Babe," I heard Jay say from the top of the steps and I felt relief as I closed the closet door. "Is that you?"

"Jayson Darnell Hill!" I yelled walking over to the bottom of the steps. "Boy I was about to bust a cap in your butt."

"Yeah right you wasn't about to do nothing girl," he laughed.

"I was," I laughed too. "I thought you were spending New Year's with your family?"

"I did, but I wanted to be with you for the rest of the night." He walked down the stairs. "Happy New Years Boo."

I walked up the stairs meeting him halfway. "Happy New Years to you too." Jayson wrapped his muscular arms around me, and we kissed long and passionately. *God I love this man.* As we continued our lip locking he put one hand around the back of my neck, while the other one rested in the middle of my back, but it didn't stay there. With every tongue wrestle his hands would move. Eventually his hands were holding on for dear life to my ample backside. Even after all these years, every time Jay kisses or touches me, I always feel like I am about to melt. He looked into my eyes then I said, "I love you so much."

"I love you too," he said licking his lips showing the silver ball in the center of his tongue. "C'mon let's go upstairs and get comfortable," he said as he gently slapped my behind while still holding me in hug formation.

"There's only one thing that could make me comfortable right now," I said as he turned to walk up the stairs. I followed him with my arms around him from behind when I noticed that our son wasn't at home with us. I asked, "Hey, where's Jordan?"

"Oh, he stayed with Mama and Dad," he said laying his six foot one frame on our king size bed. "They wanted their baby to spend the night with them so I was like it's cool with me."

"Cool with me too," I said standing in our bathroom taking off my jeans and sweater. I washed my face removing what little makeup that I had on, I also freshen up in "other" areas before putting on a light blue silk nightgown. I walked over to Jay who was now bare chest, showing off his beautiful six packs, but still wearing his baggy dark colored jeans that showed the top of his boxer briefs. This man is so fine to me and his thug appeal made him look even better, it is so sexy. He was making me want to jump in the bed and give him *every* part of me. "Hmm…hmm, you are so…uhm," I said not finding the words to describe my light brown skin man, as he cracked a seductive smile.

"Come here," he motioned to me with his index finger, licking his lips slow and sexy. I smiled and he smiled back with a devious grin, now playing with the tongue ring in his mouth, "I think I want some of my chocolate tonight." He said about my mocha complexion which he referred to as chocolate.

I walked over to the bottom of the bed, and then eased up to Jay's neatly shaved face. He wore a thin mustache that connects to his thinly shaped up beard and sideburns. I used my tongue to trace the outline of his lips, he then stuck out his tongue and our tongues met to perform a kiss as I played with his shoulder length cornrows. I could feel him responding to my actions as I rested near his pelvic region.

"Babe, can I tell you something?" Jay asked sitting up with me still in his lap facing him. I wrapped my long legs around him. Well, at least I like to think that my legs are long. I guess you could say that my sister and I were taller than the average woman, both of us standing about five foot eight and a half or five foot nine, if you want to round it up, which I like to do so I can *appear* taller.

"What's up baby?" I said with my arms around his neck scratching his back with my short French manicured nails. I am a nurse now so I can't have my nails as long as I used to wear them, so now I keep them short enough so I can do my job, but believe me I get them manicured on a regular basis.

"Brandi you are so beautiful," he said looking into my eyes as I smiled at his statement. "I mean, I love you with all my heart and soul, I just love you so much," he exhaled and ran his index finger along the side of my face moving the hair that was hanging there out of the way.

"I love you too," I said to him looking into his eyes, then I looked down at my arm around his neck and began to admire the differences in our complexions that started to remind me of my grandparents. Granddaddy was about my complexion, maybe a shade darker with both of his parents being black and Indian. Grandmother and Jay have about the same complexion, but she's a shade or two lighter because she is mixed. Her father was white and Indian, while her mother was a mixture of black, white and Indian, which makes the Spencer family one big rainbow of races, a beautiful rainbow though. Not to brag on my family, but I think everyone that's born into this family is beautiful and some of us are so attractive that some of us could have had a career in modeling.

"Let me finish girl," he smiled at me.

"My bad go ahead." I smiled back.

"I'm ready to change," he said very seriously. "This lifestyle was good for awhile, but it's getting old. I'm getting too old to be doing this even though I'm only twenty-three years old, I'm tired of this game. I'm ready to change for you and Jordan. You both deserve far more than all of this, you especially B. You've put up with a lot from me and there's no woman I know that does what you've done. I really appreciate that, thank you babe for being there for me. I hope that you'll always be there for me," he continued to look at me with a serious face which seemed so sexy, but the way I was feeling there's not much he would have to do to make me think he wasn't sexy.

"I will baby, and you know it," I said kissing his cheek, "I can't even see myself with no one but you," I looked into his eyes and he smiled at my statement.

"One more thing," he said taking one of his arms and wrapping it tightly around my waist while the other one he was using his fingers to gently glide up and down my thighs. I was so ready to end this conversation and start another one that only consisted of our bodies talking, "I have a New Year's resolution that I want to share with you."

"What?" I questioned.

"By the end of this year I plan on first finishing up school, then getting a *real* job," he said using the same fingers that were just visiting my thighs to start playing with my long mane. I knew that Jay had attended realtor school, but I assumed he finished and all he needed was his license. Maybe that's what he meant by finishing school, "then my next resolution is to make you Mrs. Brandi Renee Hill."

"You want to get married this year?" I questioned with wide eyes. Jay and I always talked about getting married although I didn't intend on it being so soon, but I am ready. Hell, we already live together. As a matter of fact, it's been almost two years since we moved into this house together, which Grandmother can't stand.

"Yeah babe," he smiled at me, "by this time next year we'll be husband and wife," I kissed him on his lips. Thank God, then that means what we were about to do we can do anytime without guilt. Surprisingly the guilt didn't even come from me; he was always the one that mentioned maybe we shouldn't do this right now. To change his mind all I would have to do is hit his spot by sucking on his earlobe and the side of his neck, then I'd have him hooked.

"I like that idea," I said, "but I've got another one in mind."

"Uh no I've got one too," he raised his eyebrows with the sexiest seductive look on his face, along with sexiest grin.

"Tell me," I said.

"Uh-uh," he shook his head, "this is a show rather than tell."

"Well show me," Jay turned me over on my back and he kissed my lips, then moved down to my neck where I could feel the sensation of his tongue ring moving in circles. Jay took off my nightgown as he began to gently kiss on my breast then moved slowly down to my navel. "Jaaaay," I moaned closing my eyes loving every touch this man was applying to my body.

"You like that?" he asked then he resumed to kissing me, this time below my navel as he continued to move south of my body.

"Ummm," I moaned again, turning my head to the side. My face was greeted by one of our many pillows that we had on the bed. I began to moan louder when Jay used his teeth to take off my panties. Once they were off, he started licking and kissing me from my feet, up my leg, and then to my thighs where he stopped so he could take his time. He started sucking on my inner thighs being a gentleman and giving each thigh equal amounts of satisfaction. My body was getting more and more excited when he started licking the other thigh again slowly before he moved in between them giving me a new meaning for a *happy* New Year.

* * *

The sun shining through the blinds woke me around nine-thirty in the morning. I rolled over and felt an empty space where Jay should have been laying, but instead I saw a note on the pillow.

B,

I had to make a run real quick. I didn't want to wake u.

I promise real soon it will all be over. Luv u.

I hope and pray. I've been dealing with all this for five years, but that's just the half of what we've been through. We knew each other years before we got together because we went to the same high school. During our senior year we decided to get together, that's when all the drama started. Around the time Jay and I made it official as a couple, my parents were ending their marriage of twenty-one years. My dad just up and left one day without saying a word, or shall I say after he beat my mother damn near to death leaving her to take care of my older brother Donte, Brianna and I without any kind of help. During the time our parents divorced Donte was away at college down in Florida attending FAMU on a full scholarship. He had decided to go to school so far away because of all the drama that went down with our parents when we were growing up, although sometimes he relied on them for money to get food and other things he might need while he was away from home.

When Daddy left and after the divorce was finalized, Mama was having a hard time making ends meet, that's when Brianna, Donte, and I decided we were going to help our mother out since we were all over eighteen years old now. Bri found a job working in an office part-time because she had the experience from a previous summer job. Donte began to work part-time at the book store on campus at his college. All I could do was dance, because that's what I loved to do. Instead of getting a job the previous summer, (before my parents' divorce drama) like everyone else, I went away to New York with my dance group to study what I loved. So, that's why I ended up working at a strip club. None of my family knew about me working there except for Ken, Summer, and of course Bri. They hated the choice I made settling to work at a strip club as much I hated working there. Even though

I only worked there for three and a half months, that little time changed the course of my relationship with Jay for the rest of our lives.

Jay had found out about me dancing at a strip club and we didn't talk for about a month maybe two. Within the time that we didn't talk, he met and impregnated this sixteen year old girl named Lacy. By the time I found out about the pregnancy we were back together and I had quit working at the club because of an incident that Jay still doesn't know about and something I wish I could forget. When all of this took place, Lacy was already three months pregnant, that's how Jordan came. Of course I was upset, but I loved Jay much more than the anger that I felt toward him at the time. So on November 21, 2003 Lacy Moss gave birth to Jordan Deion Hill, but due to the complications during the birth, she fell into a coma. Three days after the delivery Jordan was released from the hospital, but Lacy died. Soon after she was laid to rest, actually it was two weeks later, her parents then moved to California. They don't even acknowledge Jordan or Jay, because to them those two are a constant reminder of what killed their daughter. I guess they forgot that Jordan is a part of her and their grandchild. Jordan knows nothing about the whole situation with Lacy and his grandparents. I'm the only mother that he has ever known which is why he calls me momma now. Even though Jordan is a reminder of the breakup between me and Jay, deep down I've forgiven him and accepted his son as my own.

The ringing from the house phone broke my thoughts causing me to jump out of fear, "Hello?" I answered hesitantly.

"Babe it's me," Jay said on the other end.

"Hey, what's up?" I smiled with relief that it was him, then I began running my fingers through my hair trying to do a quick fix, as if he could see me over the phone.

"I was calling to say I love you," he said, "I'm sorry for leaving you this morning. I'll be home in a minute to make it up to you."

"I'll be waiting," I hung up the phone and went downstairs to greet my man.

3
Summer

"Damon, this is the third time I've called," I said speaking to his voicemail. "I wish you would call me, I'm worried about you. You know how negros act crazy on New Year's. Please call me back, I love you." I hung up the phone and laid there in bed wondering why Damon hadn't called. The conversation with my cousin's started to resurface in my mind. I know that Damon can be a dog, but I hate to hear it from them, because they just don't know the man I know.

The man I know is a smooth talking, fine milk chocolate brotha I've known since I was fifteen years old. I will never forget that day we met because it was a week before Christmas. I was with my best friend and current roommate Chyna, at the movies. Damon and I talked for almost three months before we became a couple, by that time I had turned sixteen and he was eighteen years old with his own apartment. He had graduated high school the previous year, he didn't go to college so he began working which was the reason he had his own place. It was the first night of my spring break when we decided to be a couple. It was also the first night I spent with him at his apartment. That night I lost my virginity to him and from that moment on I've been sprung, but it was more than just sex though. It's because it seemed that Damon was the only man that showed interest in me--a "big girl." Things were going good for almost two years, we had our arguments like any other couple, but we always made up. By the time I graduated high school Damon and I were fighting to keep this relationship alive, but my freshman year of college I was a single woman. It was hard letting go, but I was able to do it and right into the arms of this guy that was in one of my classes named Lamont. He was average looking meaning he was kind of cute, not *hella* fine though, he was a few inches taller than my five foot three height with a small frame. For a year and a half while I was in school at Tennessee State that small frame was mine. When Lamont and I stopped talking I began to talk to Damon again, since that moment we've been back together.

I got out of the bed to get something to drink when the phone rang, "Hello?"

"Hey there," Damon's sexy voice said on the other end. "I'm sorry I hadn't called."

"Damon, I've been worried sick about you," I took a sip of orange drink, "where have you been?"

"I do believe I am a grown man," he said already starting to sound annoyed by my question.

"Look let's not start this New Year off this way," I said.

"If you must know," he started, "I've been out with Amir."

My eyebrows rose, "Amir's back?" Amir and I lived two houses from each other. Damon came into the equation later on down the road because he and Amir went to school together.

"Yeah he's back," he said, "and he got his stuff together too, pushing a new Lexus and about to buy a house here too."

"Really?" I asked, thinking maybe I got the wrong one, "what's he doing now?'

"You know he's an engineer," he said, "and he's making some serious bank, oh yeah he asked about you too."

"He did?" I asked with excitement. I remember Amir being this cute Asian and Black guy with the most beautiful green eyes I've ever seen. Honestly, I had a small crush on him when we were teenagers. I soon got over it when he ended up with a girlfriend then soon after that I ended up Damon.

"Why you sounding like that?" he asked replying to my question.

"Like what?" I questioned.

"Like you are all excited to see him or something," he replied.

"I mean, we all grew up together," I said trying to calm down the excitement in my voice. "That's my dawg too."

"Well, get some clothes on cause we on our way," he said before hanging up the phone.

I ran to put on some clothes. Actually, I took a quick shower and put on some white leggings with a Tennessee Titans jersey. I got that jersey while I was attending school in Nashville at TSU, but I'll be graduating this year from the University of Louisville. I went back to the bathroom to unwrap my hair which has grown out past my shoulders. I had cut it in a short bob at the beginning of last year, but since then I've let it grow back. Damon said he liked my hair being long even though I liked my hair in the bob. One day I'm going to get bold enough to get my hair cut like Kennede's. She has the Eva Marcille (Pigford) brownish blonde natural curly thing going on.

I heard the doorbell ringing frantically, "excuse-" I stopped talking as I opened the door to a much finer Amir than I expected. "Amir?" I called his name as if it was a question, because I was shocked by him looking as good as he did. He had always been nice looking to me, but now he just looked so grown up with his sexy green eyes, caramel skin, and medium build. The way Amir was looking now he reminds me of the NFL player Will Demps who is just absolutely gorgeous.

"Dang girl don't look so surprised, it's too cold out here for all of that," he said and I moved out of the doorway so Amir could step into the apartment and out of the cold weather. After I closed the door he started reaching out for me, "give me some love girl," he opened his arms.

I leaned into him wrapping my arms a little above his waist putting my head on his chest. I closed my eyes and inhaled his intoxicating cologne. *My God this man is too close to perfect*, I thought, *I wonder if I could trade Damon in for Amir*. I swear there is nothing like a man that looks and smells good.

"You uhm, you are looking good," I managed to say as I pulled away checking out his clothes. He was wearing khaki pants with a white turtleneck sweater and a brown leather coat, looking like he was a male model ready to be on the cover of *GQ Magazine*.

"You look good too," he said looking me up and down with approval, "*really* good."

"Thanks," I said twisting my hair around my finger as butterflies took over my stomach. I started to feel like the shy girl who was finally talking to the man of her dreams, but I soon snapped back into reality, "uh where's Damon?"

"Oh he's on his way up, I think he was on the phone," he said then his face showed concern, "I really need to ask you something before he gets up here."

"Okay what's up?" I asked having no idea what Amir was about to ask. "Here let's sit down," we sat then I looked over at Amir and we locked eyes which I didn't mind looking into those beautiful emeralds. "I just—" he began to talk, but was cut off by Damon's entrance that also broke my gazing into Amir's eyes. His tall lanky frame shadowed my doorway. Damon is about six feet even, and one hundred-thirty pounds soak and wet while Amir whose frame is much bigger has to be about six foot two and two hundred plus pounds all muscle.

"You just what?" Damon asked Amir as he walked over toward me.

"I just uhm," Amir stumbled for words, "I just wanted to tell Summer that I love what she has done to her apartment."

"Well, I have a roommate," I said trying to play along because I had a feeling that what Amir had just said wasn't the *important thing* he needed to ask me. "Yeah she's out of town right now. You remember my best friend?"

"Who Chyna?" I shook my head in agreement. "You gonna have to give me your number so I can holla at her. Man, I haven't seen her in years."

"That's who you betta be hollering at," Damon said talking to Amir who just looked at him and then start laughing sarcastically. "Let me holla at you in the bedroom for a minute," he said now talking to me.

"Okay," I said standing up from the couch as I started to follow Damon into my bedroom. "We'll be back," I said to Amir before stepping into my room.

I shut the door and Damon was standing right in front of me. "What the hell was all that about?" He pushed me up against the wall.

"What are you talking about?" I asked with confusion, having no idea what I had done or said to make him upset with me all of a sudden.

He put his hand around my neck and said, "You know damn well what I'm talking about." He started choking me. "You were trying to push up on my boy?"

"No," I gasped, "you're hurting me, please...stop!" He loosens his grip from my neck, but pushed me up against the wall grabbing my shoulders. He shook me so hard that it caused my head to hit the wall, "Damon please quit!" I pleaded with tears filling my eyes.

At that moment I heard a cell phone ring on the other side of the door. "Just tell me the truth," he said still holding on to my shoulders. "You want Amir?"

"We were just talking!" I shouted as tears began to fall heavily down my face, "I swear Damon, why are you doing this to me?" I asked and he squeezed tighter to my shoulders before throwing me on my bed. "Please stop, please don't hurt me," I begged again while I was moving slowly to the other side of the bed.

"Whatever," he said walking over to the bed. "I should beat the hell out of you." He raised his hand like he was about to slap me, and I covered my face getting ready for the hit.

"Hey yo Damon," Amir said from the other side of the door as he lightly tapped it, I exhaled with relief but I still kept my hands over my face just in case he decided to try to hit me. "We've got to go man I just got an important call, let's roll."

"You better be glad," Damon stood over me then turned around and walked out of my bedroom leaving me in the bed curled up with a headache. *I can't keep going through this with him*, I thought, *I wish I could just get the courage to leave him alone.* I lay in bed still curled up in a fetal position holding on to my pillow as I cried myself to sleep.

The phone ringing woke me up. "Yeah?" I answered softly.

"Summer, are you okay?" an unfamiliar male voice asked on the other end.

"Who is this?" I questioned.

"It's me Amir," he answered. "Are you okay? I heard what was going on in there."

"How did you get my number?"

"Do you remember the important phone call I got when we was at your place?" he chuckled.

"You used my phone," I smiled. "That was smooth."

"Yeah, well you know," he said. I could hear the smile in his voice. "I had to do something to try and stop him. I couldn't stand hearing what was going on in that room anymore."

Tears started to form once again "So, what did you have to ask me earlier?" I asked trying to change the subject.

"Oh yeah," he said, "why do you stay with Damon?" he asked now in a serious tone.

"That's the question of the new year," I said sarcastically as the tears silently fell down my face.

"I'm not trying to get in your business," he started, "but you are too beautiful to put up with that." More tears began to fall. "Are you alright?" Amir asked. "Look, I'm so sorry."

"No, no," I said wiping away my tears. "Do you remember how to get over here?"

"Yeah."

"Can you come back over here?" I asked. "I'd rather talk to you about this face to face."

"I'm on my way," Amir hung up the phone. I needed some time to think about Amir's question. *Why do I stay with Damon?*

I continued to lie in the bed thinking about the question that everyone seemed to be asking me. I guess I should have seen the signs of physical abuse coming because it started with verbal abuse. *"You look fat; you betta lose some weight before you lose me; or why did you cut your hair, that's ugly on you, women shouldn't be bald; you betta not cut it no more; sometimes you can act so stupid; yep, you act like a stupid ugly fat bitch."* If my older brother Malachi knew about this, Damon would be a dead man. If *any* of my family members other than my girls knew he'd be dead, but Malachi would go nuts. I am the apple of my big brother's eye, because it was just the two of us when were growing up even though we had our mother and stepfather of course. Now that he makes good money playing in the NBA, he spoils me, which is part of the reason I am able to attend school full time and maintain an apartment.

"Hey Summer, just wanted to let you know it's me, Amir." He said knocking on my door.

I wiped my eyes and went to the door, my little trip down memory lane made me cry at some of the hurtful things Damon has said to me. "Hey Amir." I opened the door and then I walked over and sat in my living room chair with the ottoman. I love this chair because it was so big almost made for two. "Thanks for coming back." I put my feet on the ottoman thinking back to when I bought this chair, how I expected me and Damon to cuddle up in it together to watch a movie or something.

"Summer let me just start off by saying this, I am a real man." He sat on the couch next to my chair, actually the end table separated the chair and couch. "I am also a real friend and I really care for you Summer," he paused and looked over at me, even with a serious face he looked so good.

"Thanks Amir," I felt tears begin to form once again. I thought my tear ducts were dried out, but I guess not. "I really appreciate you being a real friend too."

"So Summer I'm going to stop beating around the bush," he leaned forward and looked at me again. "Baby girl, when did all this happen? Hell, tell me what happen?" I started crying then exhaled loud and hard. "Look, I know this may be hard for you, but I'm not stupid Summer he's abusing you isn't he?" he asked.

I shook my head in agreement, "it started with him talking down to me," I said barely over a whisper.

"Talking down to you like what?" Amir got up from the couch and sat on the edge of the ottoman.

"Well it started with him telling me I'm fat," I started wiping my face as I was talking, "then I was stupid, soon after that I was a fat ugly stupid bitch. He was always telling me that I can't do anything right, how in the hell are you gonna be a lawyer he'd say. Then he told me because I cut my hair I was a bald ugly bitch and no man other than him would put up with me."

"Whoa, whoa, whoa," Amir shock his head then looked at me with confusion and disbelief. "Summer you know you aren't any of those things right?" I began crying harder, Amir grabbed my hand, "baby girl you are beautiful, smart, and you are not at all fat."

I looked up at him with one eyebrow raised, "now I can except you saying I'm smart and beautiful, but now you just flat out lying about me not being fat," I smacked one of my thighs. "Look at me, I wear a size twenty and I'm only five foot three, honey that's fat."

"Trust me I've seen fat, and my definition of fat is someone that's not carrying themselves with any pride and being just flat out sloppy," he pointed to me in admiration, "that's not you at all. You carry yourself so well, and truth be told, there are some women who wear a size two that can look sloppy and fat based off the way they carry themselves. You aren't fat at all Summer, thick maybe, but trust me you work it well," he looked at me in a way that made me believe him like he was being truthful. "You look beautiful, but it's no good for me to keep saying it if you don't believe it," he grabbed my hand, "but regardless you don't deserve to be beat."

My eyes began to swell again, "I mean, I understand I don't deserve that," I started to get chocked up, "but sometimes I make Damon so mad and he doesn't know any other way to express his anger. I just have to watch what I say around him so he won't—"

"Summer that's some straight up bull!" Amir cut me off and let go of my hand. I could see the anger in his face so I leaned back. "I'm not trying to scare you I promise, I'm sorry, but it doesn't matter how mad he gets he has no right to put his hands on you. I understand that's my boy and all but a real man doesn't beat his woman. So because Damon is beating you and verbally abusing you, I'm sorry in my opinion, he's not a *real* man."

"But I love him," I cried harder half believing my own words. "Besides, Damon's the only man that wants me. When things are good between us, it's good. I'm never going to find a man like him. Like I said when we're not fighting, he loves me like no man has and I'm not like Chyna or my cousins. They're beautiful enough to get any man they want, my choices are limited."

"Uh," Amir laughed sarcastically, "just because Chyna and Kennede are light skin or the rest of them taller than you and smaller in size means they deserve better?" Amir shook his head, then took his hand and cuffed my chin in his palm. "Summer Parker, I wish you could see what I see. A beautiful woman who's smart and intelligent that deserves a man who is going to treat you like the queen you are. And you're right, you will never find a man that treats you like Damon, because no *real* man will treat you like dirt one day, then try to make it up by saying how much he loves you, then goes back to beating you the next," he grabbed both my hands. "Summer, I pray that you realize that you are a queen that deserves the world. The only man that can fit a queen is a king. I pray that you get all that and more, but mostly I pray that you love yourself better, then love God better." He gripped my hands tighter. "Do you mind if I pray with you now?" he asked.

I smiled through my tears. "Sure, I really need that." Damon never offered to pray with me. He never did anything like Amir was doing now by showing that he cared. Amir's prayer wasn't long at all. He asked the Lord to reveal some things to me and to deliver me from the way I thought of myself; he also asked God to bless me and protect me… "Amen," I said at the conclusion of Amir's prayer.

"I hope you feel better in every way," he said giving me a hug. "You deserve *true* happiness."

"Uhm I know this might sound crazy, but do you mind just holding me for a while?" Amir looked at me with a funny look. "No, no I don't mean in any sexual way. I mean I feel safe with you and I just want you to hold me until I fall asleep."

He didn't say a word, but he pulled me up a little so he could position himself behind me in the chair. The way I envisioned Damon and I laying in the chair together, is how Amir and I ended up, with me sitting in between his long legs and his arms wrapped around me. I rested my head on his chest and sniffed intoxication again. "Thank you." I felt so comfortable that immediately I feel asleep.

"Hey Summer," I heard Amir say behind me. "Hey sleepy head I need to get out of here it's kind of late, well it's rather early." he said and kissed me on the cheek.

"Okay that's cool," I got up then looked at my clock on the wall. It was 6:45 a.m. and the sun would be up soon. "Thank you again and I'm sorry I kept you out so late."

"No," he grabbed my shoulders gently and looked me in the eyes, "you're worth it. I'll give you a call a little later." He kissed me on the forehead and I walked him to the door. "Later baby girl," he walked out of my door toward his car.

"Later," I waved at Amir as he was getting in his car. I stayed at the door until he pulled away despite the cold January morning air. Just as Amir was almost out of sight, I saw a car off in the distance that turned its headlights on and slowly crept behind him. "*Oh my God, is that Damon's car?*" I whispered to myself and hurried to close my door, "*I've gotta call Amir.*"

4
Brianna

I can't believe this, I thought to myself looking down at the pregnancy test. "I must have done something wrong." I said shaking my head in disbelief. The knock on the door startled me, "uh yes?"

"Brianna is everything alright?" a female voice asked.

"Uh yeah," I wrapped the test in toilet paper and put it in the trash. "What's going on?"

"Dr. Hamilton has been looking for you," Connie my co-worker, said on the other side of the door. "He says it's about the patient in room 316." Connie is about my age; she is a white girl though, a cool one too. Sometimes she tends to think that she is black just because she has a couple of kids by a black dude. That's when I have to put her in check.

I opened the door swiftly. "Okay, I'll be right there, thank you." I said to her.

I walked down the hall in what seemed to be slow motion, holding my stomach. *I can't have this baby. Everything is just moving way too fast. I don't know what I'm going to do. What will he say?* All of these questions ran through my mind as I walked in room 316. "How are you doing today Ms. Lansing?"

"I'm feeling much better," she said sitting in the reclining chair instead of lying in the hospital bed. "Dr. Hamilton said I can go home today." She stated with a huge smile.

I smiled back while checking her vitals. "Well if that's what the doctor ordered then that's what we'll be serving."

She continued to smile while staring at me. "You know I think that Dr. Hamilton likes you." I gave her a why-would-you-say-that-look. "Oh don't be fooled."

"I don't think so Ms. Lansing, because Doctor Hamilton is very much married." I said.

"So what, I can tell by the way he looks at you," she said casually. "He looks at you different from everyone else around here."

"Okay Ms. Lansing, your blood pressure is normal and as soon as I get those orders from the doctor, I'll take out your IV so you can be on your way," I said trying to change the subject hoping this little old black woman would get out of my business. "Do you have someone to pick you up?"

She stared at me. "I can see that you are trying to change the subject because you know it's true," she stated with her arms folded, "but my daughter is on her way."

"Okay, I'll be right back with those orders." I walked out of her room rolling my eyes. *If she only knew*, I thought. "Did Dr. Hamilton write the orders for room 316?"

"Yes I did," a man's voice said behind me. I turned to see Dr. Hamilton standing in front of me. "I see you got my message."

"Doctor Hamilton, I need the orders for room 316 so I can get this woman home," I said in a serious tone--not looking in his direction.

"Bri," he leaned down and whispered in my ear, "do we need to talk? What's up with you?" I looked up into his brown eyes and held a gaze. "What's wrong?" he repeated half smiling showing one dimple. God this man is just too fine for words. With his peanut butter brown skin, he stood about six foot three and I'd say he was maybe two hundred pounds of pure fineness.

"Can you just give me the orders please?" I questioned while reaching for the papers in his hand, but he grabbed and held onto my hand instead.

"No, not until you tell me what's going on with you." He said not letting go of my hand.

"We'll talk after I finish with this patient," I snatched my hand back along with the papers that were in his hand. "Or we can just talk after I get off, besides my shift ends in thirty minutes."

"So, you want to talk after your shift ends?" he asked with one of his eyebrows raised as he was stroking the hairs on his chin.

Seasons

"I don't want to talk about this here, maybe you could come by later." I said looking around as if someone were listening to us.

"Oh I see," he smiled now showing both dimples perfectly placed in his cheeks, "you want to make this an *all night* kind of thing?"

I shot him a look that could have killed. "No, I'd rather talk to you about this face to face. I don't want to talk about it while we are here." I said looking in his eyes then quickly looking away not wanting to lose focus on the task at hand. "Look, I've got to finish up so just come by my place in about an hour, if you can."

"Yeah," he smiled reminding me how much he resembled the rapper Common, just too fine. "I can probably get away." I rolled my eyes at him then I turned around and made my way back to Ms. Lansing's room. *I wonder what he is going to say and think when I tell him about this baby.*

*   *   *

When I walked through the door of my apartment I threw my bag and purse on the couch. After I did that I ended up just throwing myself on the couch, coat and all still on. *God I can't believe this is happening to me. What am I going do?* That was the question I kept asking myself.

If I would have just kept my mouth quiet and my legs closed, I wouldn't be in this position now. But I just *had* to let Dr. Lance Hamilton know how fine he was if he already didn't know. It didn't help that he never wore his wedding band which made me approach him the way I did. If I would have seen that ring, I would have never said anything other than hello to him, because during that time of my life I was sick and tired of always being "the chick on the side."

It was my first day working on the fourth floor of Mercy Hospital when I met Lance. I saw him standing on the other side of the nurse's station looking over some papers when he looked up and saw me staring. He smiled, then began to walk over to where I was sitting. "Hello," he extended his hand, "I'm Doctor Lance Hamilton, and are you new?"

"Uh yes," I staggered for words as he held on to my hand; I was so mesmerized at how fine this man was standing before me. "Well, I'm new to this department; my name is Brianna Wright."

"It's nice to meet you Ms. Wright," he continued to give me this hypnotizing smile. "You look really familiar, are you sure that I haven't met you before?"

"Well, my twin sister Brandi works in this department too," I said to him smiling back.

"Oh okay," he said still smiling also, but he stopped to look down at his beeper. "I have to run now, but I hope this won't be the last time I see you."

"You can see me whenever, wherever, you want," I said before I realized.

His eyebrows rose, "I'll hold you to that," he gave me a smirk and walked off. From that moment on we've been talking, then eventually dating.

It wasn't until after the third date and the second time we slept together that I found out the truth. I knew that Lance was over thirty, because when we met he told me he was thirty-two which at the time would have been ten years older than I was. That night after our third date, he reveals to me while still laying butt naked in my bed, that he's knocking hard on forty's door. Well, it wasn't exactly in my bed, but we were on the living room floor wrapped in a sheet. Yes I am a freak, which is probably the reason Lance loved having sex with me, because to me any place goes, and sometimes we just couldn't make it to the bedroom like that night.

Not that the news of him lying about his age wasn't enough to handle, he proceeds to drop the bomb of the century on me. He then tells me that he's married with two kids, leaving me in total shock and disbelief. I didn't want to believe it because Lance was one of the finest men I've ever had. The man made me feel like I was the most beautiful woman in the world with his words, and the way he used to make love to me. It was like he gave me one hundred-ten percent every time we had sex. At that moment after he revealed his dirt, I kicked him out of my apartment and told him never to call me again, forgetting that I would see him at work the next day. I did everything I could to try and avoid Lance, but it didn't work.

We ran into each other close to his office. He begged for me to hear his side of the story, so I went into his office with him. As soon as I sat down he gave me this sad story of how he and his wife have been unhappy for several years and the only reason they were staying together was because of his ten year old son and eight year old daughter. Stupid me fell for his story and vowed if his wife couldn't make him happy, *I* would. And I started right there in his office, we had sex on his desk after I made that vow to him. I thought I was satisfying him by giving him my time and my body, not realizing I was taking away from his family.

This has been going on a little over a year and now it's starting to get old. I'm tired of the sneaking around and playing these mind games. Telling me he's going to leave his wife and marry me, and like a fool I believed him. I wanted to believe him. My heart wanted to trust him. Now that I've decided to end this, I get pregnant of all things!

A knock at the door made me awake from my sleep. I walked over to answer it. "Did you just get in?" Lance asked walking in the apartment.

"Oh no," I said taking off my coat. "I just fell asleep on the couch, I guess I forgot about it."

Lance walked toward me saying, "What did you want to talk to me about?" He tried to hug me, but I backed away. "What's wrong Bri? Did I do something to make you angry?"

"Look Lance," I pushed him away then sighed. "There is so much I need to say to you."

"Okay baby," Lance said standing by the end of the couch while I was standing at the opposite end, "what's on your mind?

I exhaled hard then sat on the couch. "Okay, first I think we should end this," I said not looking at him.

"What do you mean end this?" He asked sounding like he was hurt. I looked up at him and he looked at me puzzled, "I don't understand, I thought everything was going good between us."

I began to laugh, but it was more like an *are-you-serious* sarcastic laugh. "Going good? I mean the sex is good yes," I stated, "but how could things be good when you're still married?"

"Bri, you know you're the only good thing that's in my life besides my kids right now, please don't do this to me." he pleaded.

"What about me?" I said looking over at him pointing at myself, "I'm twenty-three years old in love with *and* pregnant by a forty year old married man."

His already distant look went even further, he took a seat on the couch, "wha- what do you mean pregnant?"

I looked into his face, trying not to get caught up in the way he was looking at me. "I took a pregnancy test and it was positive," I looked down at my hands, "I'm pregnant with your baby."

"It could be an error or something," he looked over at me, but I kept looking straight. "Maybe you should take another one that one was probably wrong, it has to be wrong."

"No, it wasn't wrong or an error," I said glancing over at him. "I took two of them. Lance how could two pregnancy tests come up with the same result?" he looked at me with a blank stare, "we just have to face the fact that I have a baby on the way."

"Well," he blew into his hands as if he were trying to keep them warm. "I guess you know what you have to do huh?"

I turned toward him, "what?" I began to get angry because of what he might be implying. "I hope you are referring to my responsibility toward this child."

He chuckled, "Seriously, you can't be considering having this baby." I gave him a why-not-are-you-serious-look. "Don't do this to me Bri. I do still have a wife and a family, please don't do this me." He had the nerve to give me a puppy dog face. He must have learned that from his daughter.

"Are you serious, now you're concerned about your *family?*" I asked laughing, but actually crying on the inside. "You didn't give a damn about *your wife* and your family when you were busy impregnating me, and what do you mean don't do this to you? Baby, you did this to yourself."

"Bri, I can't tell my wife that I have another child on the way," he tried to plead his case. "She'd leave me, or try to kill me...that's why you can't have this baby now."

I shook my head in disbelief, "So, you're telling me I have to kill my child so you won't get caught by your wife?" I started to get angry as tears were beginning to form in my eyes. "But Lance you said you were leaving her anyway, to be with me. This is your best shot at leaving her now," I said almost to the point of begging, something I never thought I'd be doing over a man. I was raised better than that, which made the tears swell up in my eyes even more to think what Grandmother or Mama would say if they saw what I was doing now especially for a married man.

"Brianna, it's not that simple," he said. "I am going to leave her one day so I can be with you, but right now it's not a good time. If you would have got pregnant at the right time for me I'd be more than happy to leave her, but the time is just not right. You can't have this baby, not now."

I shook my head again, this time in disappointment. Mostly I was disappointed in myself for falling so hard for this married man. "You never had any intentions of leaving her anytime soon did you?" He looked down in shame. He was about to speak, but I raised my hand. "You know what, get out. I'll take care of *my* baby by myself."

I got up and walked toward the door. He got up and followed me without a word. I moved aside so he could open the door himself. As he opened the door he turned around like he was about to say something. "There is nothing more you can say to me, now leave, please just leave!" I said as I walked over slightly pushed him out, and closed the door then leaned against it. "God, please help me," I said aloud sliding down to the floor with tears now flowing down my face.

Normally during times like these I'd like to write down my feelings that would turn into poetry, but the way I was feeling now I couldn't come up with the right words. Only prayers came out of my mouth and my thoughts were about trying to gain God's attention. "God, I know I'm the last person that needs to be asking for your forgiveness, but I'm so sorry God I really need you."

5
Brandi

"Ma, have you talked to her?" I asked my mother over my cell phone as I was driving to get my hair done. That's another thing I started after "the incident" either on the phone when I'm alone or always being around somebody. I was just that scared to be alone since that happened.

"Yeah yesterday, but she didn't say much," Mama said. "She was acting kind of funny."

"I know," I said turning into the parking lot of Kennede's shop. "I saw her at work and she was *really* quiet, and you know that ain't her at all."

"Who knows what's wrong with that girl," she said. "But hopefully she will be alright. I just hope whatever is going on it isn't real serious."

"Ma, I'll find out, she's supposed to be at the beauty shop tonight." I turned off the engine.

"That's right; you all get your hair done at the same time." Mama said.

"Yep, and that's when the truth comes out," I said walking into the shop, "I'll call you a little later okay?"

"Alright baby, bye now." Mama hung up before I could give a response.

"What's up girl?" I said walking toward Ken's station.

"Hey B," Kennede looked at her clock as she was curling this girl's hair. "Aren't you a little early?"

"What, I can't come talk to my cousin?" I asked pulling a chair closer to Ken's station. "I also wanted you to start on me first, since you know how long it takes my hair to dry."

"After I finish Lena let me sit down and rest," she said combing out Lena's hair, "then I'll start on you after my breather."

"Have you eaten?" I asked picking up a magazine, "I can go pick up something while you're resting."

"Naw girl that's okay," she took the cape off Lena. "Here you go Miss Lena I hope you like it."

"Kennede don't play," Lena said reaching into her purse, "you know you always lay my hair. Thanks Kennede."

"Well, you take care then Lena." Ken said to Lena then sat in her styling chair. "I ordered a pizza earlier that I haven't *even* eaten yet," she said to me now sitting up, "you want a piece?"

"Sure," I got up and followed her into the back of the shop. "So, how's RaeLynn?"

"Bad as ever," she handed me a slice of pizza, "but she's spending the weekend with her daddy."

We went back to her station before I asked. "What's up with you two now?"

"Girl, it's just," she said taking a bite of pizza, "have you ever felt so stupid about doing something, then you see something or *someone* that reminds you of what you did?"

"Don't I know," I said referring to the horrible days that I spent stripping, including that awful night that ended those days and now has me paranoid, thinking that someone is always following me.

"That's the way I feel about Raymond sometimes," she confessed. "Almost every time I'm near him, it reminds me of all the stuff he put me through. Girl but the crazy thing is I've forgiven him, but I can't forget. I pray that God will work with me on that, then sometimes it's like," she paused and a smile came across her face.

"What?" I smiled too wanting to know what it was that my cousin was about to admit to, "it's like what Ken? Don't leave me hanging."

"No I'm not gonna leave you hanging," she smiled even more. "It's just," she let out a sigh, "even with all that's gone on with us and all the drama, I still can't forget those good times, which actually seemed to outweigh the bad sometimes."

"Well Ken that's normal," I explained while sipping some ice tea. "I mean you two were married at one point and time, then ya'll was together for what seemed to be forever. Honestly, I never thought that you and Ray would break up, it just seemed that you two were perfect together."

She sat there looking off like she was thinking about something, "I know, I never thought that either," she looked at me. "But I think that I'm still attracted to him, girl you know yourself that Ray is fine."

I shook my head in agreement, because fine he was, looking like L.L. Cool J's little brother. I looked at her with both eyebrows raised, "could this be?" I questioned. "Are you thinking about hooking back up with him Ken?" she twisted her face. "Come on Ken you can be honest with me, you want Raymond back don't you?"

"Well," she hesitated. "I mean yeah, but I think it's just in those lonely times, and trust me they have been getting to be more and more as the days pass," she looked down at her hands, "but I can't have him, he's married and he seemed to move on so, as much as I would love to have him back, I just can't."

"Yeah that's true he does have a wife, well hell do what my sister's doing," I said to her jokingly. "Speaking of Brianna, she is still coming in right?"

"She hasn't called to cancel," Ken said, "what's going on there?"

"I don't know," I got up and Ken motioned for me to go to the shampoo bowl so she could wash my hair. "I'm hoping to find out what's going on with her tonight. You know she can't keep quiet too long."

"So she is still messing with that doctor at your job?" Ken asked whispering while she was putting shampoo in my wet hair.

"You know," I said looking up at Ken, "they use to hang around each other all the time, but here lately they don't even seem to speak. So I believe something went down between them."

"I hope she leaves him alone," Ken stated, "I mean he's married and I would hate for her soul to go to hell over some good sex."

"Pray," I said. It was the only word that I could think to say at the moment.

"I do all the time for all my girls," Ken put a plastic cap on my head, "so how are you and Jayson?"

A smile as big as Texas came across my face, "well I was gonna wait 'til all of us were together," I reached into my pocket and pulled out the two and a half carat platinum diamond engagement ring, "Jay and I are getting married!"

"Oh my God!" Kennede grabbed my hand and then pulled me close to give me a hug, "congratulations girl!"

"What are you two heifers hugging and stuff about?" Summer said sneaking up behind us with Brianna in tow.

"I know what ya'll so *happy* about?" That was Brianna

"Because your sister is getting married!" Ken said with so much excitement in her voice.

Brianna looked disappointed, "I thought I was your sister, why didn't I know first?" she asked with an attitude.

"Oh don't start Bri," Kennede said, "she just told me and I had to drag it out of her. Besides she was gonna tell all of us at the same time anyway."

"I'm sorry ya'll," she broke her frown with a slight smile; "I've just been real stressed," she looked down.

"We all have been stressed out," Summer stated. "Daddy's been working me like crazy at the office, and school is kicking my butt." *And not to mention Damon's probably kicking her butt too*, I thought. Summer worked at stepfather's law firm. Her real father died before she was born. Uncle Charles is the only man she and her older brother Malachi can remember as their father.

"Well my stress is far crazier than that," Brianna said.

"Okay," Summer stated, "so spill it."

"Hold up let me get started on your head first," Ken said, "then we'll get down and dirty."

We were all sitting around as Kennede was finishing up Summer's hair. She had hooked me up with body waves; and Brianna's hair was in a straw set. We all looked fit to be put on a cover of a magazine. Everybody in the shop was gone except us and the other beautician, Kandi.

"So what's been going on Bri?" Kennede asked while flat ironing Summer's hair. "I mean you said that you been stressed."

"Well," she let out a deep sigh, "I broke it off with Lance."

Our eyes widened. Even though that man was married, Brianna was totally in love with him. "Good," Kennede spoke up, "honey he was just sending your soul to hell." Brianna rolled her eyes at Kennede.

"Anyway, that's not all," she sighed again. "A couple of days ago I found out that I am four weeks pregnant."

Kennede dropped the comb on the floor. Summer almost broke her neck trying to turn to face Bri, and I just held my mouth open so wide you could probably see my tonsils. "Pregnant? Are you serious?" I questioned with concern.

"As a heart attack," she said calmly, "but that's not the worst part. He wants me to have an abortion."

"Ah hell to the naw!" I jumped up scaring Bri and Ken. "You are not going to kill *my* niece or nephew just because he wants to cover his tracks."

"Is he crazy?" Summer questioned. "Did he even ask you what you wanted to do?"

"He probably volunteered to do it himself," Kennede spoke up. "I can't believe he had the nerve to say something like that."

"Ya'll, I'm not going to do it," we all gathered around Bri and gave her what she needed, a hug from family, people who really cared. "I couldn't do that to this child, it's not their fault that their parents are irresponsible."

"I know you better not kill that baby," Summer said. "That child has *too* much family, on his or her mother's side for that to go down."

"Right," Kennede agreed with Summer. "We love you *and* that child too much to let anything like that happen."

Brianna began to cry, "I love you guys too." My eyes started to become moist, then I looked over at Ken who had glossy eyes right along with Summer. "I love you all so much. I don't know what I would do without all of you." That's when the full waterworks began to flow among the four of us. This bond that we share is far deeper than just cousins, although Bri and I are already sisters. We are like a group of four best friends.

"Okay ladies," Ken said wiping the tears from her face, "now ya'll are looking too good to just be sitting here crying and laying around in the house." Even though Ken didn't get her hair done when the rest of us did, it looked like someone had already hooked her up with some fresh flips. It was different from her usual naturally curly do.

"Ooh yeah," Summer yelled out first with excitement, "let's go out."

"Go out where?" Brianna asked. "Wherever we go I'll be the driver, because I can't drink right now."

"Ahhh!" we sighed together like she was a child that had just said something real cute. "What about bowling?" I suggested.

"Bowling?" Summer repeated what I said like she didn't understand the first time I said it. "Girl, we just spent all this time getting *beautified*, we don't need to do anything that's gonna sweat these hairdo's out." I shook my head in agreement. "How about dinner and a movie?" Summer now suggested.

"Yeah," Brianna, Kennede and I said in unison. "We haven't been out to eat dinner or went to see a movie together in a long time." Kennede stated.

"Alright ladies," I said, "it looks like we're going for dinner and a movie. Now the next thing is, where do we go for dinner?"

"Let's keep it simple and cheap, how about O'Charley's or Chili's? I could really go for some strawberry lemonade and some southwestern egg rolls." Brianna suggested.

"You have my mouth watering already," that was Summer who seemed to be glued to her reflection, playing with her straight shoulder length hair. "I am so hungry let's hurry up and go!"

"Let me clean up my station and finish some things in the back," Kennede said as she was sweeping away the hair that she had trimmed from me and Brianna's hair. "Then we can be on our way. Oh, can somebody help me out by straighten up the front waiting room please?" Kennede turned around and asked before she went into the back to the office. "The more help I have the sooner we will be to eating those Southwestern egg rolls."

"Oh yes," Brianna jumped up and began to moving the chairs we had placed around Ken's station back into the waiting room where they belonged. "I will clean up in the waiting area so I can go get my food, I can hear it calling me."

I walked into the waiting area to help Brianna clean in that room, "Hey sis," I said setting one of the chairs in its correct place as Bri placed the magazines in order. "You know I love you and I will be there not only for that baby, but I'm here for you too."

"You don't look at me any different do you?" Brianna asked me looking into to my eyes as if she were trying to find an answer to her situation. "I don't want any of you to think of me in any other way, not any bad way."

"Look Bri," I put my arm around her. "We're all human; we all mess up and make mistakes, some more than others. I know I've made plenty of them, but we just have to ask God to forgive us, and He will."

"I know," she started, "but God probably hates me for being with Lance."

"He loves us even when we mess up," I said trying my best to speak to my sister on a subject that was still kind of new to me. Of course we grew up in church, but it had been so long since we were *made* to go, and now I go freely because I need Him. We all need Him. "Just ask Him to forgive you and He will. That's all you have to do, ask for forgiveness and He'll forgive *and* forget."

She grabbed and held onto me tightly, "I love you so much sis," she said.

I kept one arm around Brianna then looked into her face with a smile before saying, "I love you too Bri."

6
Kennede

Peace at last! RaeLynn was with her father and now I am finally able to catch up on some much needed rest. Between RaeLynn and work, I hardly get to have anytime alone or any peace and quiet. I also needed to meditate on the word Pastor Williams preached this morning. I now attended the church that my mother, all my aunts and their husbands belong to, Genesis Christian Church. Our pastor, Dr. Walter Williams is a preaching machine. I would say that Pastor Williams in around the same age as my mother and her sisters, mid to late forties. But this morning pastor preached from 1 Chronicles 4 verses 9 and 10; *The Jabez Prayer*, better known as enlarge my territory. It was like pastor was speaking to me, the way he explained it not enlarging my "physical house," but enlarging my thinking, and enlarging my faith. And I needed an increase in my faith. I was also happy that Brandi decided to come with me along with Jayson and Brianna. Although my cousins and I are extremely close, Brandi and I were like best friends; actually that's what I called her because we didn't have very many friends outside of each other.

After I came from Mama's house after church, I just needed to relax, so I lit some candles and decided to take a long hot bubble bath. I had lit so many candles around my house; and in my bathroom and the bedroom, someone would have thought that my lights were cut off. I went to the bathroom to start my bath water; while the water ran I went back into my room to remove my clothes and put on a robe. Once I finally settled in the warm bath, I laid my head back and closed my eyes. As soon as I did that a crazy thing happened, I started to think about Raymond.

It's been close to four years since we've divorced, and the negro is already remarried with other kids. I won't lie, it hurt like hell to find out he was remarried with another child. It killed me even more to find out he was married three days after my birthday, which was the same date our divorce was final. So much for a *happy* birthday that year. Raymond and I married the day of my senior prom. Instead of going to get my hair done right after getting out of school early, we went down to the courthouse to get married. Nobody knew what we were going to do; actually it was a last minute decision. We knew we wanted to get married before I started hair school, and we were already engaged; everybody knew that. I will never forget that day when he picked me up.

"Raymond, where are we going?" I asked. "You know Ms. Ada's shop is the other way."

He looked me in the eyes, "I want to marry you."

"I know Raymond," I looked at him, "but what does that have to do with me going to Ms. Ada's shop now?"

"Kennede Marie Johnson," he sighed and reached into the glove compartment pulling out a velvet ring box, he handed it to me, "I want to marry you *today*."

"What?" I said excited and confused, there was no doubt that I wanted to marry the finest, educated, wealthiest young black man in Louisville. "Ray, I- I'm, what about prom? What about my family?" I stumbled over my words, and he with his gorgeous self kept staring at me with sincerity, then pulling the car over.

If I didn't mention it before I will say it again, Raymond is so fine from head to toe. He's tall, about six foot three, with a medium muscular size body, peanut butter complexion, almost putting you in the mind of a young L.L. Cool J. Around the time of my prom, Raymond was a junior at the University of Louisville majoring in business. His wealth, well that came from his parents. His father owned one of the most successful *and* largest (Black owned) Mercedes dealerships in Kentucky, and his mother not only was lawyer, but she was now a senator as well. But it wasn't like my family didn't have money though.

My father is vice president of the local appliance company that has national merit. My mother started off working at the same appliance company with Daddy in the warehouse, but she quit after having R.J. and at the suggestion of Daddy who had gotten promoted to his current position around the time that Kayla was born.

Raymond turned to me and opened the box that I still held onto which revealed a white gold wedding band that matched my three carat engagement ring. "I'm still taking you to prom," he looked into my eyes with his brown eyes glistening from the sun. "But I can't wait any longer; I want you to be my wife *today*. I love you so much Ken."

There was so much truth in his face, "we can't just walk into the courthouse," I stated, but I was really asking because I wasn't too sure on how those things went, "we have to make an appointment, don't we?"

"No baby we don't need any appointments," he kissed the back of hand, "we can just walk right in there and we can become husband and wife today, please." he began to beg.

"Nobody knows about this?" I questioned as fear began to sit in. I knew that he had an uncle that was also a judge and I didn't want him to tell his family without even considering mine.

"No baby," he began to drive toward the courthouse. "I know how you are with your family, so it wouldn't be fair if my family knew and yours didn't. So what we will do is just tell all of them tonight." We pulled up to the courthouse, he jumped out and came to my door, "plus my parents will be over your folk's house tonight anyway."

"Okay Raymond Alex Collins," I said hugging him, then looking him in his eyes, "I trust in you completely. I love you."

I was so nervous while I was getting dressed for the prom that night. Everyone thought it was because it was the first time I was going to a formal event like this, but little did they know I had a bomb to drop on them.

"Ken what's up with you?" Brandi asked as she was applying my eye shadow, "you just have this natural glow."

I started to smile, as I was thinking about Raymond. "She's in love," Brianna spoke up before I could respond to her sisters question, "plus tonight Raymond's gonna turn her into a woman." She added.

"Shut up," I threw a bottle of fingernail polish at her, "I'm already a woman."

Everybody's eyes lit up and open wide, "you two haven't done *it* yet, have you?" Summer rushed from across the room and stood in front of me with her hands on her hips.

"No," I said hating the fact that I couldn't tell my cousins that I was a married woman, "but I'm already a woman without having to do that. That doesn't make you a woman."

"But girl its all of that," Summer said. Being that she was the first out of the four of us to have sex, even though she was the youngest in the group. "Now it's going to hurt at first, but afterwards its feels too good." She lay across my bed putting one of my throw pillows between her legs at the knees.

I was smiling and laughing at my cousins, but my stomach was in knots. Not because it was my prom night, but it was because of the announcement I was about to make to my family and Raymond's parents in a few minutes.

"Kennede?" my mother knocked on the door, "can I come in baby?"

"Yes ma'am," I stood up from my vanity, "come in Mama."

"Raymond is here," she walked over to me gently touching my face, "Brandi you did a wonderful job on her makeup."

"Thank you Aunt Karen," Brandi said heading toward the door, "I'll see you downstairs," Brianna and Summer followed Brandi out of my bedroom.

"Baby you look beautiful," Mama said, "I'm so proud and happy for you. And that Raymond, he's such a nice young man. He's going to make a wonderful husband for you someday."

He's already my husband, I thought. "I know, I am so in love with him."

"I know you probably won't be home tonight," she sat on my bed, "just don't forget to keep the promise. Baby promise you'll wait until you are married."

"I promise Mama," I said kissing her full almond colored cheek, I looked at my mother for a second admiring her beauty. "Now let me finish up so I can make my grand entrance." I smiled.

"Okay sweetie," Mama walked out of my room.

I walked to my full length mirror then removed my robe that revealed my dress. This dress was off white with diamond spaghetti straps. Ironically it looked like it could resemble a wedding dress. "Here goes nothing, Mrs. Collins." I put on my engagement ring and wedding band, then proceeded downstairs.

"Oh my God Ken, you look so good," Aunt Lisa gasped.

"Kennede you look gorgeous," Raymond's mother exclaimed with her hands over her mouth.

"Go on girl," that was Summer who seemed to be grinning from ear to ear.

Raymond rushed up the stairs to grab my hand and help me down the rest of the stairs. We paused on the steps to take some pictures. "My little girl has grown up so fast," Daddy said smiling and turning red, I think I even saw him shed a tear.

"Raymond," Mama began to say with her light brown eyes glossy as well, "I must say that you and Ken are such a beautiful couple."

"Thank you," we said in unison then laughed, "Wow Ken you look… breathtaking," Ray whispered in my ear.

"Are you ready to tell them?" I asked him looking fearful.

"Let's do it," he said walking down the last step. "Excuse me everybody, but Ken and I have an announcement to make."

Everyone quieted down, some sat down then Ray and I looked at each other then back at our families. "Well, first thank you all for being here with us this evening." I started smiling nervously.

"We're family Ken," Aunt Julie said, "you know we'd be here."

"Right," I said, "but that's not all we have to say," I looked back up at Raymond who was still smiling, then nodded as to say to continue, "this afternoon Raymond and I went to the courthouse and got married." I let out a huge sigh of relief, but everyone else took in the air I just let out.

"What?" Mama said slowly, it seemed like that was the only word that she could get out at the moment. Her face appeared to have disappointment all over it too.

"Kennede and I are married now," Ray raised our hands to show our wedding bands. "we did it this afternoon at the courthouse," he repeated my statement although no one else said a word either because of shock or disappointment or a combination of both. The house seemed to be quiet for at least two minutes before anyone decided they could talk again.

"Ray…I um," Mrs. Collins, Ray's mother tried to speak. "Why didn't you all say anything to us? This isn't the kind of thing you just spring on the family before you're supposed to head off to Kennede's prom."

"I agree," Mama finally chimed in. "I wish that you two could have had a wedding, you two could have waited to have a wedding so your families could be included. There wasn't a reason you two decided to get married so soon?" Mama looked down at my stomach then raised her eyebrows.

"Oh no ma'am," I let go of Raymond's hand and walked over to Mama then grabbed her hand, "Mama I made you a promise not to do anything like that until I was married, and I meant that, I'm still a virgin, but not for long." I smiled and looked back at Ray, "but I'm married now so it's ok Mama."

"Well," Mama stood up with our hands still together, then walked me back over to Raymond, "welcome to the family." She said with a solemn face while hugging him.

"Thank you," he looked Mama in the face; "I promise that I will do everything in my power to make Kennede a happy woman."

"You better," Daddy finally said getting up, he stood next to Ray waiting to hug him also, "I would have loved to give my baby girl to you the right way Raymond," he hugged Daddy, "I guess now its son-in-law." Daddy laughed and Raymond smiled in relief as well. Even though Daddy was a tall medium size white man that looked like he wouldn't harm a fly, Raymond still feared him because he knew that Daddy owned guns. I believe Daddy wasn't shy about showing them to Ray when we first started dating.

"I'm happy for you two," Ray's mother hugged me; "I always loved you like my own daughter."

"Thank you Mrs. Collins," I said to her smiling. That night turned out to be the best night of my life. Ray and I went to the prom and afterwards he took my virginity. Instead of going to a hotel, like many of my other classmates, we went to his condo. He had it setup so romantic, roses and rose pedals were all throughout the condo. That night our relationship was taken to another level. I was really in love with that man. The way I felt for him seem to intensify after we made love over and over again on our wedding/prom night. It seemed like we repeated the act a hundred times all through the night, needless to say I was very sore by the next morning.

That following Monday after prom, I moved into Ray's condo. I graduated two weeks later, and that's when we went on our honeymoon. He took me to the Bahamas, where we made love on the beach almost every night we were there. Once we returned to the states, Ray gave me my wedding/graduation gift, a 2002 S500 Mercedes, which I still have to this day, but I'm thinking of upgrading it soon. I was so excited and thrilled, first off because it was a Mercedes, but second because it was only May 30, 2001 and I was *already* rolling in a 2002 Mercedes. On top of everything else it was fully loaded, CD player, navigation system, and it was black with black leather interior. So when it was time for me to enter hair school I had haters lined up to hate on me.

Some of the girls at the hair school made my eighteen months there a living hell. . On top of being hated because of the car I drove, the husband I had, (Ray would come visit me at the school, those heifers couldn't stand it because he was so fine and had money, and he was with me; a mixed rich wanna be black girl), then on top of all that stupid stress, I get pregnant. That's when Ray and I started to fall apart. It wasn't until after I graduated school and my ninth month of pregnancy, things began to change. He stopped the romantic gestures, plus started staying out late and leaving home early. I thought that after RaeLynn was born that he'd start staying at home with me and his daughter more often, but I was wrong. He loved his daughter dearly, but I felt when it came to me he didn't care at all, causing me to feel depressed.

Bizarre thoughts started to set in my mind, which now I believe was nothing but the devil speaking to me through my depression. One particular night, while Ray was out of town on business, "the devil" really began to make me have even more crazy thoughts. The main thought was that I should kill RaeLynn as well as myself to make Raymond feel bad. And I had it all planned because I wanted him to feel the loneliness that I felt. I was going to drown RaeLynn, who was only three months at the time, and I was going to take an overdose of painkillers. The day came, and I wasn't myself, I wasn't thinking right because I was actually going to take my own child's life. I had started the bath water, and I prepared RaeLynn for what was supposed to be her death. Just as I stepped into the bathroom, the doorbell rang. A blend of frustration and relief set in, so I rushed to the door.

"Kennede what's going on?" Mama ran into my house taking RaeLynn out of my arms. As she took her, I fell to the floor, "baby don't do this, God doesn't want it."

"What are you talking about Mama?" I said still on the floor with tears flowing down my face.

Mama laid her hand on my head and demanded the devil to come out of me at once. "In the name of Jesus, come out!" She continued to yell. When she spoke those words it was as if whatever was in me came out, and that left my body faint.

After I regained consciousness I started to talk to Mama, "Ma, how did you know?"

"Girl, I could tell something wasn't right with you," she patted my head, "and I was sitting at home when something told me that Kennede needs you. I started to call, but it was like God was telling me not to call, but to come over here. I didn't question it all, I just came on over. I know how it can be when you just had a baby and your husband's not around."

I looked up at Mama, "thank you Mama for saving our lives."

She shook her head, "no baby, thank God. All I did was what He told me to do," I began to cry even harder. "Sweetie you need to talk to Ray. Obviously there is something going on that you two need to work out. As soon as your husband comes home, you two need to have a serious conversation. I'll even take RaeLynn with me."

"I know we need to talk Mama," I kept crying, laying there with my head in Mama's lap, I heard Ray's car pull up in the driveway, "what do I say?"

"Let God use you," Mama closed her eyes and started to pray. "Lord, in the name of Jesus, do whatever you need to do in this relationship. Give my daughter the words to say. But God, whatever is in your will for this marriage let it be done, in Jesus name, Amen."

"Amen," I said, "but Mama, what if Ray and I aren't meant to be married anymore?" I questioned.

"Honey I'm going to tell you something that I should have told you a long time ago," she started, "you should have consulted with God first before you two just jumped into this marriage."

Her realness sparked something in my mind and tears started to flow again. Just as I was about to respond, Ray came through the door. "Baby what's wrong?" he rushed to my side.

"I tried to kill myself and RaeLynn," I sobbed. "I wanted you to feel the loneliness I felt. I wanted you to hurt the way you were making me hurt."

Ray grabbed me and pulled me into him for a hug. "Well, I'll go back in here with RaeLynn. Did you want me to go on and take her home with me?" Mama asked.

"No, you don't have to do that Mrs. Johnson," Ray answered, while Mama was still holding on to me tightly. Once he pulled away, I saw the tears in his eyes. "Kennede, I never meant to hurt you. I never wanted that to happen, I love you." He hugged me again.

After that moment, the romance started again, but it wasn't sincere. So after a year and a half, I decided that we should just break up, and I filed for a divorce. During the divorce process, I found out that Ray had been cheating with this woman during our marriage. And after our divorce was final, he married her.

*   *   *

"Hello?" I ran to answer the phone that was interrupting my bath time and my thoughts.

"Hey girl," Ray said on the other end of the phone, "what took you so long to answer the phone?"

"I was taking a bath," I answered, wondering why he was calling, "is everything alright with RaeLynn?"

"Oh yeah, yeah she's fine, she's asleep right now," he said, then he became quiet for a minute before he said, "uhm, I need to talk to you."

"Okay," I said now putting some lotion on my legs, "what's on your mind?"

"Actually could I speak to you in person?" he asked.

"Uh, in person?" I asked in surprise, "what's so important that you can't say it over the phone?"

"Look Ken," he sighed, "I'd rather tell you in person. Can I come over to talk to you, please?"

I finally gave in, "you want to meet somewhere tomorrow?" I questioned.

"Well no," he replied.

"No? Then how are we going to talk?" I questioned in frustration.

"Ken, I'm outside," he said, as my eyebrows raised then I heard my doorbell ring. "Can you come open the door please?"

I tied my robe tighter and went to open my front door still in shock that he was probably sitting in my driveway the entire time we were on the phone. When I saw Raymond standing on my doorstep the only word that came to mind was woo! No matter how bad that man hurt me, I can't deny that he is *still* the finest man in this city to me. The man has style too; he's the best male dresser I've ever seen. When I opened the door he was wearing blue jean pants with a white collar shirt and oversized leather jacket and a dark blue baseball cap that had a white "P" on the front, cocked slightly to the side. He looked at me like he was surprised to see me, or he liked what he saw. "Ken I'm sorry I came over on such short notice," he said giving me a hug, "I'm sorry for interrupting your bath too," he kept looking me up and down like I was the main dish on a menu.

I tighten my robe, "it's okay, have a seat," I said sitting on the couch while he sat on the love seat.

"Your lights aren't out are they?" he asked looking around at my candles. "I mean you have candles lit all over the place."

"Oh no, you know how I like to relax with candles and stuff," I smiled and he was smiling back at me, looking so dang sexy. "So, what's so important that you had to talk to me in person at this hour?" I asked calmly.

He looked down, exhaled, and then looked into my eyes. I quickly looked away, "please don't do that Ken." *No don't you do that*, I thought. When we were married and every time before we had sex there was never any words needed with Ray. All he would have to do is walk in the room and give me that look like the one he just gave me, and it would be on. He got up from the couch, I backed up like he was gonna hit me or something, but he sat on the couch next to me then gently grabbed my face, "I want you to look me in the face, so you'll know what I'm saying is real."

"Okay," I sighed, feeling something I hadn't felt since the day I married Ray, which was strange. If he would have asked me to marry him again, at that very moment I probably would have.

He moved his hand from my face down to my hand, grazing my body with his fingers in the process, sending chills down my back. I was trying so hard not to show what I was really feeling, very weak. "Ken," he said my name so soft, and I started the melting process, "I just want to apologize for everything I put you through," he said as he removed his cap revealing his freshly cut faded wavy hair, but shockwaves went through my body because of his apology. Raymond Alex Collins *never* admitted when he was wrong. I was about to speak when he put his finger on my lips, "please let me finish." Honestly, I wanted to put his finger in my mouth. *Okay Lord, uhm you need to take over now, because **right** now my flesh wants to gladly do the job*, I thought. I motioned for him to continue, "I know now that I put you through hell. And it's sad that it took me to go through what I put you through in order for me to realize it."

"What?" I asked with concern, "so, what's going on?"

"My son," he looked as if he had tears in his eyes, "my son might not be mine," I held my chest as if I felt his pain, "Shaundie trapped me."

"How do you know that Rashaun isn't or might not be yours?" I asked, knowing all along that his wife Shaundie was no good. She was your typical "hood rat" that he just had to have.

"Shaundie confessed to me that when we messed around, she was still messing with her ex. And when she got pregnant, she and I weren't even having sex yet," he set up, "so when we finally had sex, she was already a month pregnant, I should have known. I thought he was just premature, but he looked and was completely healthy."

"I mean," I sighed, "at that time you were still *legally* married to me, so—"

"I know," he cut me off, "but that's not when the cheating took place. Rashaun may not be mine but," he exhaled and rolled his eyes, "but Shaundie's pregnant again, and we *know* for sure it's not mine."

"How do you know this new baby isn't yours?" I asked.

"Because the baby was conceived in November," my face showed puzzlement because Ray was hardly in town for most of that month. "Exactly, I wasn't even here from November second to the twenty-fifth. Even when I got back we didn't do anything, because I was jetlagged. From Louisville to China and back is a long flight."

"I know," I said agreeing with him, "so, what are you feeling?"

"Ken, honestly I feel God is punishing me for what I did to you," he said, "I mean, I asked for forgiveness, but I guess He didn't want to hear that from me."

I shook my head, "God doesn't work like that at all and you know it," I started. "If you asked Him for forgiveness, then that's the end of it," Ray just looked at me like I was a teacher and he was a student eager to learn. "Ray, God doesn't work like us, God forgave you the moment you asked. And I have to."

Ray turned back around to face me with the look of amazement on his face, "you forgave me?" I bobbed my head up and down. "I thought you probably hated me and was just being nice to me because of RaeLynn."

"Ray, I forgave you but wasn't easy," I looked at him with sincerity. "It wasn't easy and it didn't happen overnight."

Ray stood up then pulled me up, my heart raced because I didn't know what his next move would be as he looked down at me and stared into my eyes. Like I mentioned before, Ray was about six foot three about two hundred-twenty-five pounds, so he was kind of towering over my five foot five, one hundred-fifty pound frame.

He grabbed my waist and pulled me into him for a hug. "Thank you," he whispered in my ear as he was still holding on to me like his life depended on it. "I wish I could go back and fix all of the bad I did to you. I miss you as my wife Ken."

I quickly pushed him away, "uh…well we can't go back, what's done is done." I sat back down on the couch, "it was just in God's will, please don't say that again."

He sat back down too, "please don't say it like that," he looked as if he wanted to kiss me as he moved in closer. "Don't say what's done is done, like you don't want us again."

"Ray I don't," I said nonchalantly lying, "I mean, if it's in God's will then it's in His will, but we're not together, so I don't think it's His will."

A tear rolled down his face, "Ken, I never loved her," he confessed before he looked into my eyes. *Oh no here we go again, alright stay strong girl*, I said to myself before he could finish his statement, trying to do a little inner pep talk. "I never had a chance to love her because I was always still in love with you," another tear began to fall, which made my eyes swell because he's never showed this magnitude of emotion toward me. "I've always loved you Ken, I never stopped loving you. I just want my *real* family back. Me, you, and RaeLynn. I need you Ken," he finally stopped begging then he held a gaze that would make my panties drop, if I had some on.

Ray then took his index finger and went down the side of my face; *here goes my flesh again Lord*, I thought. "Look Ray, don't do this, uhm...I—" he cut me off by moving closer and kissing me. After the shock wore off, which was about five seconds later, I pushed him back, because I was kissing another woman's husband. "Okay, you really need to go home to your *wife*, I'm sorry but is not me."

"I wish it was though," he looked away. "The thing is...I'm not staying with *my wife*, I'm staying with my parents for the moment. Me and RaeLynn have been there the whole weekend."

"Oh," I said running my fingers through my slightly flipped but damp hair, "why didn't you tell me earlier?"

"Because I didn't want you to, hell I don't know Ken, I'm sorry," he said throwing up his hands, "I can't win for losing."

"No, I didn't mean it that way," I reached over to his face. "Although I'm not *in* love with you anymore, I still have much love for you," I lied. I was still madly in love with that man. Ray is in my system forever. He's like an infection that has no cure, and even if there was a cure, I don't think I'd want it. I know I wouldn't want it.

"That works for me," he grabbed my face again. "Just to hear you say you don't hate me and you have love for me makes me feel like I did when I first married you." He began to kiss me again, and this time I didn't stop him. I let him kiss on my neck as I closed my eyes and a moan escaped my lips.

He moved my robe slightly over and revealed my breast, he then tried to untie my belt, "okay now," I pushed him away, "we really need to stop." I said aloud, but my body wanted to jump all over him. I know that I'm saved now and this is wrong, doubly wrong because he's somebody else's husband now, but that didn't stop the urges from coming.

He got up from the couch. "Yeah," he began to walk toward the door, "thank you though for being there."

I tighten my robe and walked toward him giving him a hug, "anytime you need me, I'm here."

"I need you now," he pulled me close. "I want you now." He bent down and allowed his lips to cover mine again; this time taking my breath completely away. He pushed me up against the door still kissing me and caressing my body through my robe. "I want you," he said again very soft, yet stern while sucking on my earlobes.

My eyes rolled in the back of my head, as another moan escaped my lips. "I want you too," I continued to moan as he was now sucking on my neck.

"Well," he untied my robe with no protest from me this time, I tell you the flesh really is weak and now it was winning big time, "let's do it."

Ah what the hell. *It's been almost, if not three years since I've had some*, I thought. The last time was with this guy I met two weeks after my divorce, I don't even remember his name because at the time names weren't needed. We only had one night together, but we had sex all over his house. Soon after that night, I got saved, then made a vow the next man I would sleep with would be my husband, not my ex-husband who was now somebody else's husband. *But they were separated, it wouldn't hurt, just this one time with Ray and that's all I need. But he is still legally married*, I kept debating with myself.

"I just don't know about—" Ray covered my mouth with his while touching my body with his hands as I tried to protest, in a not so forceful way. I felt like putty. My legs were becoming weak, and just leaning against the door was a task, all because of Ray's touch. *Forgive me Father for I am about to sin.*

Brianna

"Look Bri, I...uhm, I'm sorry. I didn't mean to say the stuff that I said the other day. I--uh, I guess I was being a little selfish," Lance sang into my voicemail. "I hope you don't think you can avoid me, we do still work together. Come on Bri." Silence, "I, I love you. Please call me."

I hit seven, "message deleted," the voicemail said back to me. I sat there looking at the phone with a grin, how dare he say he loves me when he has a wife at home? He was just so full of it. I hung up the phone completely then went into the kitchen to get some rocky road ice cream I bought earlier.

"God," I began to speak out loud, "why do I always get the men that already are in relationships?" I asked the Lord, but stating the truth. In the last five years I've been a magnet for other women's men, no lie, almost every man that I've talked to or "messed" with has had some form of commitment to another woman. Be it a wife or a girlfriend, for the last few years I've been the chick on the side. Honestly speaking, I'm sick and tired of it. I want to be the number one sometimes, I want to say that this is my man in public and not have to worry about his wife or girlfriend coming to bust me up. All this started with Ty Williams. He was average, about five foot eleven medium build, light skinned, because at the time I despised dark skin men, even though I am a chocolate sister myself. Why do or did I despise dark skin men? One answer: my daddy.

Daddy was as dark as they come; he was so mean and evil, and living with him was pure **HELL**! I'm pretty sure that my siblings would agree with me as well. Although Daddy worked, he was an alcoholic; I like to call him a "functioning alcoholic." On top of the fact that he was a "functioning alcoholic," he was also was an army veteran. He was sent to serve in Desert Storm in the early '90's, and ever since he came back he's been a crazy dominating fool. Ironically, it was Daddy's craziness that drove all of us in to different outlets of expressions. Brandi always loved dancing her problems and troubles away, while Donte would be hanging with the kids on the basketball courts trying to negotiate deals for the winner, (which would later help in his career as a sports agent). I loved to write my problems away, because that was my favorite thing to do, and it would help with the issues that Daddy brought home.

I remember that I would sit outside using my imagination to get me out of the "hellhole" that I called home. Writing short stories and poetry was my escape. So, I guess I could thank Daddy for giving me a reason to find one of my gifts. Speaking of Daddy, here's a quick version of how Donald Albert Wright came to be my father. First of all, let me mention how intimidating he was just on appearance alone. He was six foot four and two hundred-eighty pounds with a strong facial structure and dark chocolate in color. Mama is only about five foot five between one hundred-seventy to one hundred-eighty pounds. Okay when my parents met, Mama was sixteen and Daddy was a nineteen year old Army Reserve. Well, Mama was kind of hot in her young age, and a year later after meeting Daddy, she was pregnant with Donte.

When she gave birth to Donte, Daddy was already stationed in Georgia, but because he wanted his new family with him, he came back to Louisville to get them. He returned on Sunday, proposed to Mama on Monday, they were married by Wednesday, and by Friday Mama and Donte were moving to their new home in Rome, Georgia. According to Mama, the entire time she spent in Georgia she hated it, because her family wasn't there and neither was my father. She said she couldn't go to work because she really didn't trust anybody to watch Donte. By the time he was almost old enough to start preschool or head start she ended up pregnant with me and Brandi. Her plans of trying to work then went out the window. She then depended on Daddy who began to feel the strain of trying to support a family of five by himself. He started to act like he was in total control of my mother and began to be abusive toward her.

By the time their relationship came to blows, Daddy had to be stationed in Fort Knox, which was basically right outside of Louisville. At that time Brandi and I were five years old and Donte was eight, and the best part is that Mama was glad she was near her family again. She started to work part time in Louisville while we were in school at Fort Knox. We lived on the army base for almost a year and half before Daddy was deployed to the Middle East. Mama still decided to continue to live in Fort Knox even though Daddy had been shipped out. A year later he returned with an injury. He was shot in the knee, which caused him to have to retire from active duty, but he continued to work an office type job on the base. The dangerous combination of painkillers and alcohol started to turn my father into a monster.

Daddy would start to just beat on everybody in the house because we may have been looking at him wrong or if we shut the door too loud, or just about anything crazy. Mama was getting fed up. By now, Donte had just turned thirteen, we were nine about to turn ten later that year, and already because of Daddy's behavior, Mama sent Donte to live with Grandmother and Granddaddy. Mama decided to send him to live with them because Donte was about to kill Daddy for him beating Mama almost unconscious. A few months later Mama left too, with Brandi and I in tow.

Mama, Brandi, and I moved in with my grandparents along with Donte, but it didn't last long. We stayed with them for about six months before my father wormed his way back into Mama's heart, or rather in her head. Then there we were moving back in with my father—all but Donte of course. He continued to stay with my grandparents up until he graduated in 1999. When Mama went back to Daddy, instead of us moving back to Fort Knox on the army base, Daddy bought a house that was only two blocks from Mama's parents.

For the next five years after that, Daddy did nothing but become more unbearable and more controlling. He and I fought every other day, I mean we FOUGHT! He used treat me like I was just another nigga from the street. On the days he wasn't fighting me, he was arguing and fighting with Brandi. It seemed poor Mama got it every day though; I never understood why she would continue to let it happen. Now, Mama never just let him beat her up, she had a lot of fight in her too; she was a Spencer and we don't back down easy. I remember a couple of weeks before Daddy's final disappearing act, he and Mama was having a huge fight, I still don't know what it was about to this day.

I remember hearing all this yelling, glass breaking, things being thrown, *bodies* being thrown… Even though I was three days shy of my eighteenth birthday on October 25th, I was still terrified like I was eight years old. I was the only sibling at home that day because Brandi stayed after school to work on an upcoming ballet and she was the star dancer. Donte had already gone back to school starting his second year at Florida A&M. He wanted to move as far away from Daddy as he could, or move as far as his money would allow him to go without being too far from his mama. I called the police, and by the time they finally showed up, Daddy was gone. I walked in my parent's bedroom when the police arrived, you would have thought that a tornado had hit that room with the way things were all over the room. Clothes were hanging from the ceiling fan, the mattress was no longer on the bed, but up against the opposite side of the wall, the full length mirror on Mama's closet door was shattered along with the dresser mirror, it was just total destruction. Then there Mama was in the corner balled up into the fetal position almost completely covered in blood. Her almond complexion face was tarnished with shades of black and blue. She had a busted lip, cuts and bruises from the glass and probably from Daddy beating and throwing her around the room. The police got an ambulance for Mama and rushed her to the emergency room. We later found out that along with the visible scars, she had a few bruised ribs, a broken nose, and a concussion which resulted in her staying in the hospital for little over a week.

While she was recovering in the hospital, our family helped us to move out of our house and we were set up in a house that my Uncle Bill, Mama's older brother owned. He, along with his wife, Aunt Katie, their two kids, who are also twins, Demond and Danyelle, and the rest of my family helped me and Brandi move while Ma recovered. Of course charges were filed and a warrant was out for the arrest of Donald A. Wright. When he was *finally* caught, arrested, and jailed, Mama filed for a divorce. Nobody has seen him since the day he stormed out of the house after causing a storm that almost killed my mother. I wouldn't even know what to say if I saw him today, because he is the reason that I have a hard time with men that are very dark skinned. I know it sounds a little weird, but the damage my father did was internal, and it cut that deep.

Anyway, back to the reason I ended up talking about Daddy, Ty Williams. I know I can ramble on and go off course, but I can't just tell half of the story. Ty was the first guy that started this cycle of men already being in relationships while they were with me. He wasn't married, but he had a girlfriend that he had been with for three years. The funny thing though is how I found out about this girl. Although we didn't have sex, we engaged in *other* activities of the oral nature, if you know what I mean! It was about two weeks after our "last engagement" when he arrived for our date.

"Okay," Ty began to speak. "Now where do you want to go?" he asked.

"I don't care, what about bowling, or something fun," I replied.

"You're driving so you pick the place," he stated; that's right he didn't even have a car. I had to drive everywhere, but at that time I was so excited to have a man interested in me and willing to take me away from my home life (even if it was for a temporary moment), I would do anything.

"Well," I twisted my face thinking of a place that we could possibly go, "how about the fair?"

His face dropped, "naw, we can't go there," he answered quickly without any hesitation.

"Why not?!" I was about to protest. "I haven't been to the fair since I was a little bitty girl. Come on that's where *I* want to go," I walked toward the door with my keys in my hand.

"Brianna, we can't go to the fair," he said firmly. "Let's go play laser tag or something like that." He tried to change the subject or at least try to offer another activity to get my mind off of what I wanted to do even though I was the one who was driving.

"No, I want to go to the fair," I said pouting like a seven-year-old instead of a seventeen-year-old. "You said I could decide where we can go." I neglected to mention that once again that it was *my car* that was taking us and that *I* was the one driving, because he was very sensitive to the fact he didn't have a car.

"Look Bri, we can't go there ok," he opened the door and pushed me out of it, "ride up to the store so I can get something real quick."

I looked at him with confusion, *was that suppose to be a question? I thought. What happen to can and please?* "So are you asking me to take you to the store or was that some kind of demand?"

"Please can you take me to the store?" He asked as I stood on the driver's side of my car and he stood at the passenger's side.

"Now, why is it that we can't go to the fair?" I asked starting the car and beginning to pull away from the house.

"Brianna," he sighed loudly, "look I didn't want to tell you like this, but my girl works up there," he said very nonchalant.

My eyes grew big and I almost crashed the car trying to look over at him. "Girl... as in girlfriend?" I asked and he just shook his head. "What... when, did this happen?" I asked getting upset.

"We've been together for about three years," he replied calmly as I pulled up to the gas station. "Do you want anything?" He asked unbuckling his seatbelt about to get out of the car.

"Yeah, an explanation," I said facing him. "So, when were you going to tell me that you had a girlfriend?" He just looked down like he was ashamed. "Hell, I've known you for only six months, but I should have been told about this girl."

"Brianna I," he started to say while he was blowing into the air, "I mean you never asked me if I had anybody when we first met."

I laughed sarcastically. "You mean to tell me I had to ask?" I questioned. "I thought *'I have a girlfriend'* would be voluntary information, I shouldn't have to ask that."

"Look I'm sorry," he looked down then back over at me, I just looked away in disgust, "so do you want anything?"

I laughed again, *this nigga is crazy, he is seriously not going act like nothing just happened here.* "Yeah, get me a soda please."

"I'll be back," he said getting out of the car, before he closed the door he leaned down and said, "I really do like you though," I rolled my eyes. "I will be right back." He said again then closed the door.

"You might be back, but I won't be here," I said waiting for Ty to go into the store. As soon as he was out of sight, so was I. I don't remember where I ended up going, but I didn't go home in fear Ty would be there waiting. When I got home, he had left four messages on my voicemail saying how messed up it was what I did by leaving him stranded at the gas station.

Ty wasn't the only person with somebody either, but he was the most interesting until Lance came along. After Ty was dismissed, Sean came *back* into the picture. Now Sean had a girlfriend that I knew about prior to our involvement. Actually, I had been talking to Sean before I even met Ty. Sean is Raymond's younger brother, and we met through Kennede. I knew Sean's girl from school, and even then she didn't like me. Once she found out about me and Sean messing around, she hated my guts. Sean and I messed around off and on for two and a half years. He was the one who took my virginity when I was nineteen years old. Shortly after giving away some of my precious jewels with him, he moved out of Louisville and we just lost touch. I must admit that I do miss Sean a lot. Other than him having a committed relationship with another woman, he really is a good guy, or at least one of the best guys I've ever messed with so far.

Next on my list was K.D., which I later found out stood for Kindred Davis, but he was upfront about his girl. By this time, I really didn't care anymore. Having another woman's man started as an accident, but it ended up being something I looked for in a man, strange I know. K.D. and I didn't even last a year, but after that I just kind of laid low with my childhood friend Brian, until I met Lance, which was a year after the whole K.D. situation. I had met Brian back in Fort Knox, both of his parents were in the military. Actually it was his mother and his stepfather, his real father did the same number mine did but his exit was when Brian was only two years old. He lived on the base next door to us along with his two older sisters Janie and Samantha and his step brother Royal, who was only a year younger him. The way I met Brian was through his sister Janie, who was sixteen at the time she started to baby-sit Brandi and I after Donte moved in with our grandparents. Once we moved from Fort Knox, Brian and I lost touch for a few years, but we ended up going to the same high school.

I hardly even talk to Brian now since the whole Lance situation started. We talk maybe twice a year, three times if I'm lucky. I kind of pushed him to side when Doctor Hamilton came along. However, I did call and apologize to him for the way I acted when the *good Doctor* started making house visits. He said he understood and there was no love lost. He also confessed to me that he was in love with me, and would never stop loving me. I guess I should have left Lance alone and went on with Brian, but he just wasn't my type. Brian was kind of cute I guess, with a milk chocolate complexion like myself, and he stood about six foot four. He has a large frame, not fat, but not in shape either. He was a lot bigger than my five foot eight and a half size nine frame.

"Oh my God," I jumped up after looking at the clock. I forgot to go to the pharmacy to pick up the medicine my doctor called in for nausea. I rushed to Walgreen's, because first thing in the morning I will be running to the bathroom, falling on my knees to worship the porcelain god. When I pulled up to the drive thru, everybody and their mama was there. I decided to just go inside the store. I whipped my Mustang that I just bought brand new at the beginning of last year into a parking space. Once I stepped in the store the first person I saw oddly enough was Brian. He noticed me instantly and came over to greet me.

"Brianna," Brian said spinning me around, "wow you are looking good."

"This is so funny," I said looking at him thinking he looks more attractive than I remember. "I was just thinking about you."

"Oh really," he raised an eyebrow. "I've *never* stopped thinking about you," I felt nervous for some reason. "What brings you here?"

"Well, I'm here to pick up a prescription," I looked down, then slowly looked back at Brian. "I'm pregnant."

A look of disappointment swept his face. "So, I guess that means you have a man."

"No," I said firmly pulling him to the side. "Its Lance's baby," I whispered.

"*The married dude?*" He whispered back and I nodded. "Damn, I didn't know you two were still kicking it."

"Well, not anymore," I said in an as-matter-of-fact-tone. "I'm gonna be raising my baby by myself."

"Not if you don't want to," he said walking a half step away, as I looked at him bewildered.

"What?" I asked taking the same half step. "What does that suppose to mean?" I inquired.

"It means I'm your friend and as your friend, I'm going to be there for you in *any way* that I can," he grabbed my hand.

"Thank you Brian," I hugged him still kind of shocked by his statement, "you really don't have to do that. I mean, with the family I have plus with God, I think that I'll be alright."

"And you will have me there too," he said looking me in the eyes. "I want to be there for you Bri, I love you girl, and I would do anything for you."

My eyes began to water. I knew that everything Brian was saying he meant, he was never all talk and no action. He walked in what he believed and talked about. It's just hard to believe that he'd still be there after I basically kicked him to the curb for Lance. "I love you too boy," I smiled. "Here, take my number and give me a call."

"Brianna I never forgot your number," he said then recited my cell phone number. "You're in here," he pointed to his heart.

I smiled, "you're in mine too," I said touching my chest. "Oh by the way, you wouldn't happen to have a girlfriend would you?" I asked as precaution. Even though at the moment I didn't want any kind of relationship, I just wanted to make sure that if I wanted one with him, it wouldn't be that type of obstacle in my way.

"No," he replied. "What makes you ask that?"

I breathed a sigh of relief. "Oh just making sure," I said not wanting to take those roads again. "Don't forget to call me."

"I wouldn't dare forget to do that," Brian said smiling then walking away. Okay, here we go, let's try this again.

8
Summer

"*Summer, Summer!*" I heard Chyna calling my name, but I had the worst headache and I didn't want to move from the spot I was in on the floor. "Oh my God Summer," Chyna rushed over to me.

"Chy-na," I whined, trying to cover my face that she obviously already saw. "You shouldn't have come in here," I said softly trying to turn away so she wouldn't see any more of my black eye and bruised face. I tried to get up from the corner that I was sitting in, or rather the corner that Damon left me in, but when I tried to move my side ached. I then bent over and screamed out in pain.

"Summer, what in the hell happened?" She asked trying to help me up, "Look, I'm taking you to the hospital."

"No!" I said loudly out of fear. I tried to move around like I normally do, trying to convince her that I didn't need to go to the hospital. "Please don't...oh," I grabbed my side from the severe pain. It was sharp and felt like I was getting punched all over again.

"I don't care what you say," Chyna said moving around my room, first getting my tennis shoes then getting my purse like she didn't even hear what I had just told her about not going to the hospital. "We are going to the emergency room right now Summer. So I suggest you go on and let me help you get your shoes and stuff on so we can go, or would you rather I call the ambulance? It looks like enough damage has been done for me to call one."

I leaned over slowly trying to get my shoes that she put next to me, but I still felt those sharp intense pains that now seemed to invade my entire body. "There's no need to call the ambulance, just let me change my clothes first," I got up slowly so I could go to my dresser.

Chyna moved closer to the bedroom door. "Okay I'll let you change, then you're gonna tell me the reason that I'm taking you the hospital." She said with her hand on her hip. "I know the obvious, that your *punk ass* boyfriend beat the hell out of you, but I wanna know why." She continued to fuss while I was changing my clothes. I didn't mind changing in front of her because we were like sisters and I felt comfortable doing that in front of her without any kind of weird feelings or feeling insecure about my size. "Chyna please," I said softly through my swollen lips, I didn't have to look in the mirror either to know. I could feel it, and I've had them so many times that now I just know the feeling.

"No Summer, don't '*Chyna please*' me," she continued to stand in my doorway with both hands now on her hips. "I'm sick and tired of this nigga feeling like he can use you for his own personal punching bag. If you're not tired of it then *I am,* and I'm going to do something about it even if you won't."

I stood up grabbing my purse and walking closer to the door. "Don't go doing anything crazy please, and whatever you do, please don't say anything to my family right now, because they will go looking for Damon with *guns*. Trust me, if they know anything about this I *guarantee* that Damon won't be living by tomorrow."

"That's not such a bad idea," Chyna said very seriously. "That nigga needs to pay for putting his hands on you like this Summer." She put her arm around me as we proceeded out the door. "It needs to stop now before you end up dead, then I'd end up in jail because I would straight clock that fool. Maybe your family needs to know, this just needs to stop and right now," she kept repeating as she was helping me into the passenger seat of her small size S.U.V.

"I know Chyna," I said trying to buckle my seatbelt. A tear started to roll down my face, I don't know if it was from pain or from the fact that the words that my friend was saying to me were ringing true. I think it was a combination of both, and she was right, this was the last straw, this is the worst I have *ever* felt after one of the many fights Damon and I got into. Like she just said, this has to end, and *tonight.*

We pulled out of our apartment complex and proceeded to the nearest emergency room. "Now, I hate to even ask this because it really doesn't matter why," she started, "but what was the reason *this time* for Damon to beat you damn near to death?"

"Well," I sighed letting more tears fall, "its crazy how it started because this all stems from another fight we had at the beginning of the year. So, this fight is the result of a fight we had on New Year's."

Chyna slowed the car down as we were approaching a stoplight. "Wait a minute," she glanced at me, "you mean to tell me that you fought with this… that… him over a fight ya'll had almost two weeks ago?"

"Kind of," I replied. "Ok, here's what happened. After I came from church with my cousins on New Years, I had called Damon and he didn't answer his phone. As a matter of fact, I had called him several times and he never answered." I took a deep breath which also hurt in my side as well. "So, when he finally called back he told me that he was with Amir."

"Oh yeah," Chyna said like she just remembered something, "I thought I saw him the other day in the old neighborhood." Chyna and I were neighbors growing up along with Amir who lived two doors down from me on one side and Chyna was one house over on the other side. Amir, Chyna, and I were pretty much together from birth since neither of our families moved from their homes since all of us were born and all of our parents still live in those same houses to this day.

"Yep, that was probably him," I said about to go into the real reason I am on my way to the hospital. "Well, both of them came over. Amir came right into the apartment while Damon stayed behind in the car on the phone, so Amir and I were talking when Damon came in. I guess we were too close or something because the negro started going off," I looked over at Chyna who was shaking her head, "so he took me in the room and started to strangle me."

"Summer," Chyna said with disappointment as she glanced over at me. "Uh girl…I don't know… just finish the story."

"Well," I sighed again. "Amir must have heard what was going on, and he made up an excuse so they would have to leave and it could stop Damon from doing any further damage." I paused again to look at a couple that was standing on the corner keeping each other warm in thirty-five degree weather. I wanted to cry even more because I started to feel that true love like that was something I would never get to experience. I shook my head vaguely and started to finish telling my best friend the rest of this *crazy* story that is called my life. "After about thirty minutes, I get a call from Amir and we began talking, then I invited him to come back over and talk to him face to face."

"Hold up," Chyna was now stopped at yet another light. "Don't tell me that you slept with Amir? That's not what all this is about is it?" Her mouth was opened wide as well as her eyes, "if so, I'd knew it would be a matter of time."

"No, that's not what happened though," I said trying to answer that question for her but wanting to get back to what she meant by *she knew it would be a matter of time.* "So, Amir came over and we talked, I cried and talked, he made me feel really good, but we didn't sleep together. We fell asleep in each other's arms in the big chair though."

Chyna's eyes grew as wide. "Word?"

"Yeah," I kind of smirked myself thinking about how comfortable I was in that man's arms; it was a security I've never felt before with a man. Don't get me wrong, I felt security with Daddy, but this was different, something a daddy can't give you, not unless you live somewhere that incest is ok, but that's just disgusting anywhere. "Well, Amir didn't leave until a little after six in the morning. Hell it was damn near seven in the morning before he left," I could tell Chyna wanted to say something, but I held up my hand. "Hold up there's more. When I was watching Amir leave, I saw a car off in the distance that followed Amir, and it was Damon.

"That fool is even more crazy than I thought," Chyna just had to comment as we pulled into the emergency room entrance. "And this is the result of two weeks ago?"

"Yes and no," I stated as I was trying to get out of my seatbelt. "Actually, I haven't really seen Damon since that night, well until tonight. Of course he brought that up and proceeded to whip my butt." I opened the door about to step out.

"Let's make this the last time this happens Summer," Chyna said to me. I nodded my head in agreement then closed the door. "I'll be in there in a minute, I'm going to go park," she said after rolling down the window. I just turned around and went into the emergency room.

* * *

"Miss Parker, after looking at this x-ray, it looks as if you have a few bruised ribs. Your nose isn't broken, but it is fractured," the E.R. doctor, whose name was Dr. Gill, came into the room and announced.

I nodded, "you aren't going to admit me are you?" I asked hoping not, I can remember when Aunt Lisa was admitted to the hospital pretty much for this same reason.

"Oh no," Dr. Gill sat on the stool and Chyna leaned forward like she was about to say something as she sat in the chair next to the stretcher. "But there is an officer outside the door if you wanted to press charges on the person that did this to you."

"Yes she does," Chyna quickly answered before I could even process in my mind what the man had just said, "where is he, I'll do it for her," she stood from her chair and was on her way out of the door.

"Doctor Gill you called the police?" I questioned as I tried to rise up from the stretcher, but when I tried to do that a sharp pain went through my side, "oh God!" I yelled out.

"Are you okay?" Doctor Gill asked as he put one hand on my back and I nodded my head lightly before returning to a less painful position, "but to answer your question I didn't contact the police, there was an accident that involved them and I thought I could just grab one of them to come talk to you if that's what you wanted."

"Can you please bring the officer in here please," Chyna spoke up sounding very demanding.

"Okay," the doctor was walking out of the room, when Amir appeared in the doorway, and my heart dropped. I didn't expect to see him walking through the door, but when he did come in the room I got the feeling that his arrival at the hospital was more than likely Chyna's doing.

"Girl what happen to you?" He asked walking over to the side of the stretcher kissing the cheek that wasn't bruised.

Once again before I could answer for myself, my best friend/newly self appointed spokeswoman answered for me, "she let Damon use her face and body as a punching bag."

"Only part of that's true," I finally spoke up for myself, "but we were fighting and he did beat me up," I paused then looked up at Amir, "and it was because of you."

Amir shook his head, "because of me?" He repeated in the form of a question while pointing to himself with a baffled look on his face, after a few seconds his face went from baffled to one that said he found his answer, "oh was it about the whole New Year's thing, when I stayed over there late, or early?"

"Yeah," I shook my head in agreement, "remember when I called you after you left to see if you were being followed by him?" He bobbed his head, "I saw his car off in the distance and when you pulled off I saw the car follow you. I was concerned and hoping that he wouldn't do anything crazy to you."

"You know what," Amir grabbed his chin like he was thinking, "he called me too, right after you, but he didn't do anything just asked me some crazy questions. Dang, I should have known something was up."

"I'm sorry Amir for dragging you in the middle of our drama," he came close to me and gently hugged me, "I'm just glad his crazy butt didn't try anything with you."

"You don't have to apologize for Damon's action, that's not your fault at all." he said still holding on to me, "but like I said before Summer, you are too beautiful to put up with this," he stroked the side of my face with the back of his finger. "Why don't you let me show you how a *real* man treats a *real* woman?" he asked, but it sounded more like a statement as he gazed into my eyes with those spellbinding green eyes.

I could see Chyna smiling out of the corner of my eyes, "I would love to, but—"

"But what?" Chyna asked in a very loud voice, making both Amir and I jump. "Forget Damon! Summer, he doesn't even care about you so *why* should you give him the time of day?"

"It's true," Amir said in agreement with Chyna, "the only time he seems to spend with you is to beat you," I gave him the evil eye, "look I'm sorry, but you know it's the truth."

A light tap at the door stopped me from responding to Amir's comment, "excuse me, but are you, you Miss Summer Parker?" The black police officer came into the room looking down at his pad, and I nodded. "Doctor Gill said you wanted to talk to me?"

"Yes I did," I said to the officer, "the person that did this to me, his name is Damon Lott," I exhaled hard.

His eyes traveled down to his pad once again, and then he looked up at me with bewilderment, "did you just say *Damon Lott?*" He questioned me like I was slow or something, or perhaps he was just slow.

"Yeah, that's what I said," I responded now getting annoyed, "is there something wrong with that name or something?"

The officer then put his pad away, "is this an African American male, who is about twenty-four to twenty-five years of age?" He asked looking at me with a wrinkled up forehead.

"Yes sir," my face grew concerned, then his wrinkles went away, he now looked as if someone had died, "come on now, is there something wrong?" I asked once again.

"Well ma'am," he cleared his throat, "it seems Mister Lott was also just brought into this emergency room," my heart dropped as he continued, "he was ejected from his car, and they don't think he's going to make it through the night."

Tears swelled up in my eyes, "where is he?" I asked slowly getting up from the stretcher.

"Why do you care Summer?" Chyna asked with an attitude, "girl what's wrong with you? He just beat the hell out of you, remember?" I could tell she was obviously aggravated with my sudden concern for this man's wellbeing.

I walked to the door where the officer was standing and said to him, "just tell me where he is please."

"Follow me," I went behind him as Chyna and Amir followed me. As we approached the room there was a young woman who was positioned up against the wall next the entrance, crying. The woman looked like she's a Latina, about a size six with long black wavy hair that came to the middle of her back. Also she looked like she was about the same height as Chyna, who is five foot five and very pretty. "Miss Parker that is Mister Lott's wife, Linda."

"His what?" my heart plunged into my stomach and it seemed to be breaking too as I asked the officer thinking maybe I heard him wrong. "No, you didn't just say his wife, no that's not his wife," I said in disbelief and now crying once again.

"*Wife?*" Amir also questioned. "Are you sure officer? Because this is his girl- excuse me, ex-girlfriend."

The officer looked down at his handy dandy pad again as if to double check the information he was telling us, "yes young man, it seems that the woman over there is Mrs. Lott."

"Hello," the woman approached us, "are you all friends of Damon?" She asked sniffing from all of the apparent crying she had been doing.

"Uh, yeah," Amir said before I could say anything, "my name is Amir," he extended his hand for her to shake.

"Oh I've heard so much about you," she began to say, "I'm Linda, Damon and I have only been married for a little over six months now. I wish I could have met you all under better circumstances."

"I wish I would've known about you," Amir said under his breath, but I heard him, "Likewise," he said aloud, "this is Summer and Chyna."

"Oh, so *you're* Summer," she hugged me while my arms stayed at my side with her long hair all in my face. "I'm so glad to finally meet his sister. Oh my God were you in an accident too? Are you okay, because it looks like your face swollen too?"

I tried to stay poised even though I was crying on the outside, but not as much as I was on the inside. The way that I felt on the inside it was like I was on the floor rolling around crying hysterically, I don't know if it was because I had just met Damon's wife or if it was because he lied to her and said that I was his sister. I think it was a mixture of the two. "Can I see him?" Was all I could get out of my mouth. Chyna was speechless for the first time, because she didn't say a word, but her face showed what she was feeling, shock with extreme repulsion. The same thing I was dealing with internally.

"Sure go on in there," she said to me. "I'm going to the cafeteria, I need to try and eat something. Being pregnant I shouldn't go without eating," another stab to the heart.

"You're pregnant too?" I laughed sarcastically. "Well it seems that Damon has kept so much from us, his *family*."

"Oh I'm sorry," she said. "Maybe he wanted to surprise you all. I'm only a little over a month or so pregnant. Well, I'm going on to the cafeteria."

I walked into the room that Damon was in without another word to *his wife*. His wife! How could he do that to me? And on top of everything else she's pregnant too! Damon was lying on the stretcher with tubes all over the place, and his face seemed to match mine, bloody and bruised.

"I can't believe you." I started to say standing over him knowing he probably couldn't hear me; both of his eyes were closed. "I know it's not the right place for me to do this, but right now, I don't even care anymore," I wiped away some of the tears that were falling. "You lied to me; you hurt me, emotionally *and* physically. I know this is wrong, Lord forgive me. Damon, I am so glad you're suffering. You deserve everything you are getting." More tears began to fall. "I really loved you, but now I hate you." I turned to walk out of the room, then I looked back at him again, "you know what? I hope you burn in hell!"

Later That Evening:

"How are you feeling?" Chyna asked me as she was about to sit down on my bed next to me, "can I get you anything?"

"No, I'm fine right now," I sat up so I could talk to her. "Honestly Chyna, I don't know how to feel. I just can't believe that Damon lied and hurt me like that, I really did love him," I said as Chyna rolled her eyes at the mention of Damon's name. I knew she couldn't stand him before, but since everything that went down tonight, I know she was probably ready to kill him with her own hands, even if he wasn't already on his deathbed. "I mean, why do I get the jacked up men? Is *'all dogs who are no good apply here'* written on my forehead?"

"I mean," Chyna paused like she was trying to select her words carefully, "well Summer, we did try to tell you—"

"Look, I don't want to hear that," I said cutting her off. "I knew he had no business beating me, but sometimes I felt I deserved it." she looked at me like she was taken aback by my statement. "Especially after he saw Amir leaving our apartment at close to seven in the morning. If the shoe was on the other foot I probably would have clocked like he did too."

"Come on now girl, no woman deserves that," she said touching my hand then she started to give me a grin. "But you always have Amir."

"I'm not trying to do anything with that boy," I said right before the doorbell started to ring, "that's probably him now with my medicine," I was removing the covers and about to put on my house shoes so I could answer the door.

"No, you just stay here," Chyna got up from the bed to get the door. "Look who I found at our doorstep," Chyna returned to my bedroom with Amir behind her, "he was just so cute I couldn't tell him to go away."

We all laughed at Chyna's statement as they both made themselves comfortable on my bed, "hey baby girl, how are you feeling now?" he sat next to me.

"Okay," I responded trying to sit up a little more than I was before Chyna answered the door, then the pain hit me once again, "I think I'll feel a lot better once you give me that medicine."

I reached for the Walgreen's bag that was still in Amir's hands. "Hold up," he pulled the bag away. "I've read that you have to eat when you take this kind of medicine," he said looking at the information sheet that came with prescription. "So, Ms. Summer, I'm not giving you anything until you eat." He smiled at me with that beautiful smile to go along with those beautiful eyes and even more beautiful body. Good Lord! That man was just all around fine, and an ideal man for any woman.

Amir is saved and not just the guy that wears the cross chain and that is as far as his relationship with God goes; he is actually on speaking terms with God and isn't ashamed of it. Again, he is fine, with a good job, and fine, with a body to die for, intelligent, plus he's fine, owns his own house without living with his mother, has his own car (which is a Lexus at that), no kids, and did I mention FINE!!!

"Hey guys," Chyna said, that's when I remembered she was still sitting there. "I'm going to my room for a minute then I'm going to leave, cause it looks like you're in good hands now Summer."

"Oh she is," Amir smiled at me before looking back at Chyna who was standing in the doorway. "Don't worry I'll take good care of the patient."

"Well alright I'm out," she waved and I waved back at her.

"Amir," I whined playfully, "so are you going to get me something to eat then?" I asked him with my arms folded, but smiling back at him.

"Nope," he said still giving me that beautiful smile, "I'm going to cook for you."

All I could do was keep smiling, "what, you are going to cook for me?" I asked.

"I mean it's nothing really big," he said looking in the other grocery bag he had with him, "I was just going to whip up some spaghetti if that's alright with you?"

"Yeah that's fine but," I said not able to stop smiling, "I've never had a man cook *anything* for me before, this is a first for me."

"Okay guys," Chyna yelled from the living room, "I'm about to go see *my* man. You sure you don't want me to stay Summer?"

"No, I've got her," Amir answered before I could even get the words out, "I told you she's in good hands."

"Alright, see ya'll later," she said and I soon heard the front door closing then locking.

I turned to Amir still smiling, "you are a trip," I unfolded my arms, "you just gonna send my best friend away, then you're about to cook for me, what's next, a marriage proposal?"

"In the near future," he said smiling then getting up and walking toward the bedroom door.

"What?" I questioned with a confused look on my face as he walked out of the bedroom going toward the kitchen. "I was just playing about the whole marriage thing you know." I said getting out of the bed to follow Amir.

"I wasn't," he said calmly removing the items from his grocery bag, he began to go through my kitchen like he already knew where everything was so he could prepare the spaghetti. "Summer, I'm not playing about the marriage," he glanced over at me as he was filling a pot with water. "I would love to marry you one of these days, because you deserve to know what it's like to be treated like a queen from a *real man*. And I want to be *that man* to show you what it's like."

"Amir," was all I could say. Everything that he was saying at this time was coming out of left field. I mean, what woman doesn't want to be treated that way? I know that Amir is capable of doing just that. I've been around when he was dating other woman. When he dated a woman, she was the one and only, it's never been one here, one there, one everywhere. So, I know that if we ever did get together, that would be the least of my worries. I sat down at the kitchen table. "How can you marry someone you don't know in relationship way? We're not even a couple."

"I'm not saying I want to marry you tomorrow," he said. He was standing over the stove, hard at work cooking dinner for us. "I'm talking about maybe a year or two from now. I want to make you feel so good, that you'll forget about all the bad things Damon has ever done to you." He stopped his work long enough to look at me with all sincerity.

All I could do was smile at the thought; I knew that Amir's words were genuine. "Well, actions speak louder than words; many people have made *plenty* of promises to me with words, and no action." I stated.

Amir came over to the table and kneeled down in front of me, "first off, I'm not everybody," he started as he grabbed my hand and looked up into my eyes. "Secondly, this right here is just the beginning of what you'll be receiving for the rest of your life, *if* you want it."

"Okay Amir," I put both of my hands into his as I kept looking intently into those green eyes. "I'm going to trust you, but you have to give me some time to get over this whole thing," I said like I was giving in. "But please, *please* don't let me down or break my heart. I don't think that I could ever go through something like that again."

"Summer," he said with so much authenticity in his eyes and voice, "I plan on putting your heart back together." Tears of joy started to form in my eyes at his words, he gripped my hands tighter. "Then I would *never ever* even think about trying to break it, I want to love you. I want to make you the happiest woman in the world, and with God's help, *I will.*"

"I...huh," I said sighing. "What is left for me to say?"

"Not a word," Amir rose from the floor and gently pulled me up with him, he stared into my eyes then he bent down to place his lips on mine. Oh my God! His kisses were so soft and so...I can't even explain how *good* it felt. All I know is what I felt in that moment is something I've never felt in my twenty-two, a few days shy of twenty-three years on this earth. After our kiss we gazed into each other eyes yet again, "this is only the beginning."

9
Brandi

Waterfront Park was packed with people trying to enjoy the seventy degree weather, which was abnormally warm for the first few days of April. It had been so long since we've had warm weather like this in the city. Especially after a few weeks ago when we were snowed in; it seemed that everybody and their mama was out here today soaking in all of this nice weather. So many people being in the park today gave me a sense of security, but it also scared me in a way too. It was a couple of times that I would look up to check on Jordan while he ran through the playground and I could have sworn I saw something lurking across the other side as if it were watching me. I shook my head and looked back in that direction, and the dark figure was gone. *I'm tripping big time*, I thought.

I shook my head again trying to put it out of my mind and get back to my reason for coming down to the park in the first place, the wonderful spring day. After I got off work I picked up Jordan from daycare then we made our way to down to the park so he could enjoy this gorgeous weather too. I then looked down at the engagement ring that Jay had given me about three months ago, it seemed to be sparkling so bright in the evening sun.

"*I'm ready to change for you and Jordan,*" I thought of the words Jay said to me on New Year's. *Changing, yeah right.* I rolled my eyes at my thoughts. Here it is April and nothing has changed at all. I mean for awhile he was out there looking for a job or so I thought, but he must have given up because now he's not even trying to look anymore. I've tried to be patient with him because I do understand the way our country is going economically right now. I'm trying to be the supportive, *loving fiancée* that I should be in the situation, but now I can't take it anymore. It seems that he's gone more than he ever was before, leaving Jordan and I at home alone, and you know I'm *not* comfortable at all with that idea. Although I've never been the jealous type or one of those girls who just because their man isn't around, he's with someone else. I know Jay would never cheat on me, hell he has no reason to cheat. But the *"game"* is taking the man I love away from me; I just pray that it doesn't take him away forever, either through death or jail.

"Mommy, mommy," Jordan ran up to me, "I'm hungry, can we get something from over there?" He pointed to the hotdog stand just steps away from us.

"Baby no," I said wiping off his dirty hands and face with an antibacterial wipe, "once we get home Mama's gonna cook some hamburgers and fries okay?"

"Yeah, yeah," he began to jump up and down, "can my have cheese on my hamburger?" I laughed at my son's grammar, "please Mommy?"

"Its can *I* have," I corrected his English. "And yes baby you can have whatever you want on your hamburger, but first we have to go home and give you a bath." I said hugging him.

"Okay," Jordan ran ahead of me.

"Jordan slow down," I said to him running trying to keep up with him. Just as I was putting Jordan in his car seat, my cell phone went off, indicating that I had a text message. I pulled out my phone to read it.

```
'Hey B, just wanted to say I luv u,
I'll be home earlier than usual. See u
later.'
```

I rolled my eyes at the message as I got in the driver's seat of my S.U.V. See that's the stuff I'm talking about, *he'll be home earlier than usual.* Hell, that could mean he'll be home around ten or eleven; hell it could even be around midnight. Most times, or should I say here lately, Jay doesn't seem to walk through our bedroom doors until two or three in the morning. This is really driving me crazy. If it wasn't for Ken taking me to church with her, I think I would have lost my mind by now. I've been trying to get closer to God in hopes that Jay would see my change and would decide that he really wants to change too. I started making my way home thinking about what may happen whenever he gets home. If I could just get home to call Ken so I can ask her what she thinks about the whole situation.

"Think about it B," Ken was saying to me over the phone, "it seems like it's gonna take something to happen either to Jayson or around him in order for him to realize he wants to stop selling."

"But Ken," I started, "he promised he was gonna stop, for me and Jordan, I thought that his son and I would be motive enough to get out of such a dangerous occupation." I said now patting out hamburgers.

"Yeah his future wife and son are a good reason, but its gonna take a life changing experience that will make Jay stop," she paused, "I don't mean to bring up your past, but you remember what made you stop stripping?" A chill went down my spine at the mention of my past with stripping. Yes the money was fast and sometimes easy to get, but what happened to me, made me want to crawl up somewhere and die, or kill somebody. And the aftershocks was worse than the actually act. "Brandi, girl I'm sorry for bringing that up." Ken apologized.

"No, no girl, that's okay," I came back to reality. "It's funny that you mention that though, because Jay *still* doesn't know what happen. He thinks I stopped because we got back together."

"You've never told him?" Ken questioned.

"Girl, Jay would... never mind," I said wanting to change the subject all together, "Kennede let me finish cooking, I'll talk to you later though."

"Okay," she exhaled, "I'll talk to you later."

I put the cordless phone on the stand then went back to cooking. I held my once growling stomach which is feeling nausea now. It looks like now I'm gonna have to force myself to eat so Jordan wouldn't have to eat dinner alone. I finished cooking, putting the extra burgers on a platter so whenever Jay decided to come home, he could eat too. Jordan and I sat down a kitchen table, then ate together;. Well, Jordan was the one that ate mostly, I only ate half of my burger. The conversation that Ken and I had earlier took away my appetite.

"Mommy I'm finished," Jordan pushed his plate away with two fries and a small piece of hamburger still left.

"Okay sweetie," I said to him glad he was finally finished eating because I couldn't fake it anymore. "Let's go upstairs to get a bath and then its bedtime," I said to him. When we got home from the park, my mind was elsewhere, so I forgot to give him a bath before I started cooking.

"Oh man," he marched to the garbage can then toward the stairs. "Is Daddy coming home?" He turned around and asked me before he went up the steps.

"Yes baby, he'll be home," I just didn't know what to think or to say. Things had gotten that bad that now Jordan was beginning to pick up on it.

"I miss Daddy, I wish he would come home before I go to sleep," he marched up the rest of the stairs with his little head lowered.

"I do too baby," I said under my breath with tears trying to escape the brims. I turned my back toward the steps, hoping that Jordan wouldn't turn around to see the tears that now made their way to my face.

*   *   *

"God," I exhaled hard as I was starting off my prayer while I lay across the bed, "Lord I uhm, I really need you um," I stumbled over my words, "I'm new to this, but please hear me Lord and please change Jay. I mean, just change his outlook on life and this whole drug thing," I said aloud, "then God change me," I continued my prayer with tears now falling down my face. "And please God help me to forget my past," I sobbed. "Lord I really want to get over this. Jesus please help me to move on from this fear that I have. I think I've forgiven...I want to forgive him. Well I've tried to forgive him, but God just help me. I love you, Amen."

I spun around and set on the edge of the bed wiping my face only to allow more tears to fall. I picked up a magazine that was sitting on the nightstand and pretended to read it. Although I was turning the pages my mind was on the night that I decided I wasn't stripping anymore. Let me start off by saying that I hated working at that place with a passion anyway. If it weren't for the fact that my family needed the money, I would have stopped a long time ago. The club was called The Black Foxx Gentlemen's Club. It was named after it's owners Lester Black and J.B. Foxx, but trust me there wasn't a single *'gentlemen'* that walked into that hellhole. The only half decent part of the job was this girl I befriended named Shayla Love, but everyone always called her by her stage name, Lovely. She wasn't from Louisville; she had moved here from Paducah, Kentucky to attend the University of Louisville.

The story she told me of how she ended up at 'The Black Foxx' was that she had fell on hard times while she was in school and her family couldn't afford to send her any extra money. Then to add insult to injury she was unable to find work anywhere else that would fit into her class schedule so she began stripping at the club when she was only eighteen. By the time I got there three years later, she had just turned twenty-one years old and was only a few months from getting her degree. Basically, when I started she took me under her wing which meant I spent a lot of time with her and her boyfriend, co-owner Lester Black. (Around the club he was known simply as Black). Not only was that his last name, but he was black as hell in complexion, and his demeanor was black, giving me a weird feeling every time I was around him, and those were the times that Shayla would be around too. So, you can imagine the way I felt that night when he basically cornered me in the hallway after I finished my set on stage.

That night I was in a big rush to take my butt home after I saw Black lurking in the corners of the club as if he were waiting for me. Like I said before, I hated being in that place anyway, and by that time Shayla had pretty much disappeared. She hadn't showed up to the club in almost two weeks without calling or sending an email or anything. Each night I walked in that club I dreaded it ten times more, because Shayla wasn't there to go through this with me.

"Hey Cocoa," Black said to me calling me by a name I never want to be known as ever again. "You did a good job tonight," he smiled, touching on the side of my arm. I moved it trying to give him a hint that I didn't want his slimy hands touching any part of my body even if it was only my arm.

"Thank you," I said annoyed, trying to pick up the pace so I could get my clothes on and get as far away from this place as I could. "Look Black, I'm trying to get home, I have a really bad headache."

He moved closer towering over me with his tall slender frame, reminding me of my crazy father and how he used to bully us. "I got something that can help that headache," he chuckled with this evil grin plastered on his face, "come on Cocoa let me help you out with that headache," he grabbed me then began to caress my arm.

"Look, let me go," I said trying to plead with him, "I just wanna go home please," I said now begging him trying to break lose from the grip he had on my arm.

He began pulling my arm then grabbed me around the waist as he dragged me, unwillingly, into this closet. "Don't fight me Cocoa," he said pushing me up against the wall. "Just relax I'm not gonna hurt you if you just calm down," he said in a soft voice as he was using what seemed to be all of his strength to keep me from moving. "You know you want me," he continued to talk as I continued to squirm trying to break free from the hold he had on me. With each squirm I made, he would grip tighter to my body causing me to fear him even more with each grip.

"I don't want you," I said with tear-filled eyes, trying my best to get loose from the hold that he seemed to have on me. "I'm going to get my boyfriend to—" **SLAP!** He cut off my statement with a backhand to my face which made the tears now fall. "Why are you doing this to me?" I questioned wondering what it was that made him just snap.

SMACK! He hit me again, "you not gonna tell no one a damn thing," he said now covering my mouth with his huge hands. **THUMP!** He used his free hand to wrap around my throat while he pushed his body up against mine so I couldn't move anymore, that's when fear *completely* overtook me. "You betta' not tell anybody, I swear I'll kill you," he said removing the hand that was around my neck, "I wouldn't want to kill someone as fine as you, but if you try anything I swear I'll do it, I mean it," he said with this evil sounding voice. Even though it was dark in that closet I could still see the whites of Black's eyes that were filled with something unnatural sending chills down my back, and not in a good way. Tears started to fall down my face heavily as he used the hand that was just around my throat to rip off the bikini style panties I was wearing. Once they were off he proceeded to rape me.

When he pushed himself inside me without permission the pain and the reality of the situation set in making me want to scream as loud as I could for someone to rescue me. I tried to cry out, but Black still had my mouth covered with all of his might not even giving me the chance to try and bite him. While tears were falling constantly on the outside, I was screaming bloody murder on the inside. "Why are you doing to this to me?" I whimpered with his hand still over my mouth. I wanted to scream so someone would rescue me, but with the music in the club being so loud, I doubt anyone would hear my cries anyway. I could still hear the music playing; I think it was an Usher and Lil Jon song that played as I feared for my life, "please stop! Please stop!"

SLAP! He removed his hand from my mouth long enough to apply yet another hit to my face. "Will you shut the hell up!" he yelled in my left ear in between the moans, that were making me totally nauseated, "oh, oh yeah," he moaned again followed by his body shuddering while he released his unwanted semen inside of me. I began to gag at this act that no man willingly has ever done, but here this sick bastard had violated my body and proceeded to do something I thought only my husband would do. With that thought in mind, I started to taste the vomit in my mouth as he threw my limp body on the floor like I was nothing more than garbage. That's exactly how I felt too, as if he had just used the bathroom on some day old garbage. It made me feel so dirty and nasty like the trash no one would even bother to clean up to be thrown in the dumpster, but instead someone continued to pile more trash on top it because that person just didn't care.

"Damn that was good," he laughed maliciously. I didn't bother to look up to see his facially expression ,because the way he was laughing let me know that his face probably appeared just as evil as he sounded. "Bitch," he said opening the door. It was the last thing I remember him saying before I blacked out.

Once I regained consciousness I was laying in the dark closet alone, I didn't even remember Black leaving the room. I didn't want to move too quick because I wasn't sure if he would try anything else. That's why I continued to lie on the cold floor of that closet shaking and silently crying. I wasn't sure how long Black had left me there, but the pain hadn't left my body one bit; it actually was hurting worse after the fact than it did during the whole thing. I tried several times to regain my strength so I could get myself up, but it took one of the club's security guards Big Ron, who came to the closet looking for something else to find me laying there on the floor to help me up. He then carried me to the club's office where he called the ambulance even after I begged him not to call one, but he ignored me of course. One thing that I didn't say was who had done this to me, I guess it was out of fear because Black was actually crazy enough to follow through on doing what he already did, I thought he would kill me if I ever pressed charges. So I lied to everyone saying that it was too dark that I couldn't see who the person was that attacked me.

Even with all the drama and the hospital trip, I was able to keep this ordeal from most of my family, everyone except Kennede. Luckily, as my next of kin I had only one person listed and that was Ken. She met me at the hospital by herself, and even without all the details of the attack she still swore never to tell a soul. To this day as far as I know Ken still hasn't told anyone. Then a few months after the attack, Black started stalking me by showing up random places such as the library of my school.

Going through the beating was enough for me to deal with let alone having to deal with the stalking. I guess that's why I am so hard on Summer now, because I know how it is to get beat up and thrown away like you're nothing, and it only took one time for me. I couldn't image having a man to continue to do that to me day in and day out like Damon does Summer.

God why! I kept hearing in my head as I sat on the edge of the bed. "B, what's wrong?" Jay said as he opened the door and rushed to my side.

I looked at the clock, 1:13 a.m. "I'm tired," I sighed.

"Well baby lay down," he said putting his arm around me.

"No, I'm tired of this; I thought you said you were going to stop this stuff." I moved his arm and he looked at me confused.

"Uh Brandi, not this again," he said rolling his eyes, "I thought we've been through this enough?"

"Yes we have Jay, but I was hoping this would have changed by now," I said not trying to yell because I didn't want to wake up Jordan. "You promised me at the beginning of this year that you were gonna change. What happen, uh, what happen to that?"

"Brandi I've told you," he said hanging his head. I could tell he was mad and frustrated because he said my name instead of plainly calling me "B," like he usually calls me. "I've tried this 'simple' life, I've tried to find a job. There's nothing out there for me baby, trust me I've worked my ass off."

"Well, what happen to school?" I quickly asked, he didn't respond, "you were so excited about going back at first, Jay what happened?"

He sat next to me then shook his head, "I don't know," he put his arm around me again, but this time he pulled me close, "I guess I got scared. I've got so use to *this lifestyle*, I don't know how to give it up."

"Just do it," I said to him sounding like a Nike commercial, "it can't be that hard."

"B, I'm working with this dude now," he said looking at me, "I'm hoping to try to own some property you know, maybe open a mini mall or something with salons, barbershops and stuff."

"Ok, there you go right there," I sat up interested in his new found ideas. I remember that maybe about a year ago Jay did go to realtor school; I know that he didn't have that much more to go, or all he needed to do was take the test to get his license.

"But baby I have to fund it some kind of way," he kissed me on my forehead, "don't worry we'll be alright."

I shook my head, *I sure hope so*, I thought as I folded my arms. "Jay it's just," I started moving closer into his arms, "our son said something to me that I could hardly explain to him."

He pushed me back to look into my eyes, "B, what is it?" He asked as if he were expecting the worst.

"It's not that serious," I said but then held up my hand. "Hold up, yes it is that serious. He asked me when you were going to come home because he misses his daddy." Jay let out a huge sigh of disappointment, then moved from me and held his head. "*We* miss his daddy," I said. I grabbed him so he would look at me again, "he went on to say he wish you would stay home," I added that part for my own benefit.

"Sorry," was all he said with his head hung again.

"Do you see what I'm talking about now?" I asked him as he nodded in agreement. "Our son misses his father, and the bad part about it is his father lives under the same roof as he does, but he never sees him, I mean you. *I* never see you."

"I know, I know," he kept shaking his head, "I'm sorry B."

"Stop being sorry and do something about it, let me give you something to think about," I paused, "okay, this lifestyle and the fast money that you think is *so* good, but what's more important to you, the money or your family?" I looked at him very sternly.

He looked at me concerned, "B how could you even ask that?" He questioned, "Baby what are trying to say?"

"Jay," I exhaled with a tear rolling down my face, I took my index finger and stroked the side of his face. "I love you with all of my heart. I want to be your wife, I want to have your kids, but if this doesn't change and *soon*, I'll have to leave."

He pulled me into him and began to hold me tight, "no, no, no," he said in my ear, "B don't leave me. I...I wouldn't know what to do without you. Baby please don't leave."

I pulled away from him, but held his hands. "Baby, I won't leave you if you stop all this," I said looking at his glossy eyes. "Do you realize how much danger you put me and your son in when you do this? That's another reason I want you to end this because I don't want Jordan to ever witness us going to jail."

"*Us?*" Jay questioned.

"You should know when police raid a place there's no questions asked, everybody goes down," I said making my point. "I don't want him to have that on his mind, he shouldn't have to go through that, none of us should."

"I know, B, but you don't have to worry about that because I don't do those kind of transactions in this house," he said as I looked away from him rolling my eyes. "Brandi, at the beginning of the year I promised you that I was going to change and babe that's my word."

"Baby, I understand that you are truthful," I said, "but I need more than *your* word. I need a reality to believe in; I need to know that tomorrow I won't have to wonder if any of this conversation even mattered or meant anything to you."

Jay grabbed my hands and looked into my eyes. "Brandi Wright, you mean the world to me," he paused for a moment before letting out a long drawn out sigh. "I guess...I'll just have to live off of what I have saved up now, so I can go on and get my realtor license."

"Look," I said looking down then back up at him. "I make enough money to support us for a little while, but Jay you're going to have to do something soon, did you already forget?" I put my left hand up for him to see my ring finger.

He smiled, "I could never forget," he grabbed my hand and brought it to his lips. "That's why I'm trying to do something so I can make you my wife then give you the world."

I shook my head in disagreement, "you don't have to give me the world, all I need is you," I kissed him on the lips, "and to be your wife."

"Soon," he smiled and kissed me again, "very soon, as a matter of fact let's set the date now."

"Now?" I questioned with surprise, "but Jay I've always wanted a June wedding, and that's only two months away."

"We could do it," he grabbed my hands with excitement, "it could be a small wedding, family and close friends only," he put my hands up to his lips, "baby let's just do it please?"

I sat speechless, "Jay I uhm," I shrugged my shoulders, "what do I say?"

"Say June fourteenth," he looked into my eyes and held my hands tight, "say that June fourteenth will be the day that you become Mrs. Hill."

I smiled because it sounded reasonable to me. We had already completed the couple's pre-marriage classes at Genesis Church so we could use the church facility for our wedding. Yes I joined there too the Sunday after my second visit with Ken. When I joined I was already engaged and coincidently the class was beginning the following Saturday so I signed Jay and I up for the classes since I already knew we'd be getting married sometime this year. "Okay babe," I exhaled hard like I was giving in or something, "June fourteenth will be the day!" I jumped into his lap then he kissed me.

"Okay," he exhaled too.

"So that means its crunch time," I stood up and began to walk around the room nervously as if we were getting married in a few minutes. "We have to get tuxedos for you and I'll have to hurry to get dresses. Oh God, I'll have to call the church tomorrow to make sure we can use the chapel since we're just gonna have family, we won't need the sanctuary." I put my hand on my forehead.

"Baby, babe calm down B," Jay laughed as he stood up and pulled me into him as he placed a kiss on my forehead, then looked down at me. "We are *finally* going to make this happen okay baby?" He kissed my forehead again. *Yes finally.*

10
Kennede

I sat in my styling chair reading through or rather glancing through a book. My mind wasn't on work or anything else but my ex-husband. Here I am judging my cousin about her relationship with a married man, but how much more different was I? Just because Raymond is my ex doesn't make my situation special.

"Hey Ken," Tammy said breaking my thoughts, "are you alright sugar?" she walked over next to me.

"Yeah," I replied softly, putting the book down on my station, "I've just got a lot on my mind that's all."

"You feel like talking about it?" Tammy asked very concerned. As the owner of the shop, she felt that she had to play the mother to us younger girls here. Honestly though, Tammy has been like a second mother to me since I've been working at *Styles Salon* right out of hair school. I felt that I could talk to her about some of the things that I couldn't talk to my own mother about, but this thing that I'm going through now I don't think that I could even tell her.

"No, not right now," I said hoping to get out of the shop for a minute, "Although I need to get out of here for a little while to clear my head."

"Well," she started, "when is your next appointment?"

I looked down at my watch, it was only eleven forty-five in the morning. "My next client doesn't come in until two-thirty in the afternoon."

"Why don't you go on and get some air," Tammy said, "especially if whatever it is has you this quiet, you just go on and get yourself together."

"Thanks Tammy," I got up and hugged her. "Oh, by the way my next client is Mrs. King, so if she comes in earlier than she's suppose to—"

Tammy held up her hand, "don't worry about it, you just go get some air."

I thanked her again then walked out of the shop and toward my car with my cell phone in hand. "Hey boy, are you busy right now?" I asked Malik, "I could really use a friend right now."

"Na I'm not busy, I just got out of class and about to go find me something to eat." he said.

"Hey lets meet at *4th Street Live* and hit up one of those restaurants for lunch," I suggested, "I *really* need to talk to you, plus I'm hungry too."

He laughed, "Alright girl, I'll see you in a few."

I hung up the phone and proceeded downtown to meet my best friend. I am so thankful I had Malik. No doubt, my cousins and I are like sisters, but I couldn't share this kind of info with them. I would look like a total hypocrite, after all I said to Brianna about her relationship with Lance; I couldn't tell them. Then on top of everything else, here I am claiming to be a Christian, telling my cousins how much I've "changed" then as soon as my ex-husband flashes his gorgeous smile, among other things, here I go doing what one of the *Ten Commandments* says *not* to do, committing adultery. I've asked God for forgiveness, but its still on my mind what took place between me and Raymond. Even though it only happened once, it's been haunting me since that night. I had to break from thoughts for a minute so I could parallel park. I walked toward *4th Street Live* when I felt a tap on my shoulder. Before I could turn around I heard, "hey lady."

"Malik," I turned around and hugged him, "boy you know you can't be walking up on people like that."

"You ain't getting ready to do nothing," he said now walking next to me, "you looking good, though."

"Thanks," I smiled then looked him up and down, "you look like you just came from a hospital."

"Ha, ha," he laughed sarcastically. "You know I have to work after we eat lunch." Malik is in medical school, and worked part time at University Hospital, so he was wearing blue scrubs. "By the way, which restaurant we going to?"

"I was thinking maybe *TGI Friday's*, I've been craving the *Jack Daniels* chicken." I said walking toward the entrance.

"That sounds good to me. Here you go Ms. Johnson," Malik grabbed the door to hold it open.

"Hello, welcome to Friday's, will it be a table for just two today?" the hostess said to us.

"Yes, thank you," Malik said as the hostess walked us to a booth, "so what did you need to talk about?" He asked after we sat down.

"Well," I exhaled hard as I began to tell Malik about the night Ray came over. How he told me about Shaundie cheating on him and his son not being his, then how she is pregnant again and Ray knows for sure it isn't his baby. On top of everything, else Ray and Shaundie are separated and he's staying with his parents.

"Oh wow," Malik said with his eyebrows raised, "this sounds like a soap opera or something. Also sounds like Raymond is trying to get back with his first love."

"But I'm not finished," I said looking down and just as I was about to speak, the waitress came to the table to get our order.

Before the waitress could leave our table good, Malik leaned in and asked, "what do you mean you're not finished?"

"That's not the entire story," I picked up the glass of water to drink, "after Ray told me about he and Shaundie, we began kissing."

Malik nearly spit out his drink, "excuse me? You were kissing your ex-husband who is now Shaundie's husband?" He grinned.

"Calm your voice," I waved my hand at him then looked around to see if someone might have heard him, "but that's just the beginning," I said and twisted my face.

"No way," Malik smiled showing his beautiful straight white teeth, "Ken don't tell me that you slept with him."

I bit my bottom lip and whispered, "Yeah."

"Oh my God!" Malik covered his mouth with his hand. "Kennede Marie Johnson, I can't believe you did that, *you* slept with someone else's husband."

"Dang Malik," I said with my eyes wide open, "why don't you just tell the whole world."

He shook his head in disbelief, "I just…I'm shocked,. Ken, I didn't know that you had it in you girl," he now smiled.

"Whatever," I waved at him, "I was shocked too when it happened, but that's been almost three months ago."

"Excuse me, and you are just now saying something to me?" He questioned as he put his hand on his heart, "I'm hurt Ken, I thought we were tighter than that."

"Malik," I sighed, but before I could speak the waitress brought our food. I blessed the food then continued, "that's why I asked to meet with you, I've been holding all of this inside," I said enjoying my chicken breast.

"Uh," Malik continued to shake his head even while he was eating his shrimp, "I tell you, you think somebody is your friend then they withhold this kind of information from you."

"Shut up and let me finish saying what I was going to say," I said to him, he just kept grinning like *The Grinch*. "But I couldn't tell my cousins because a few weeks before what went down between me and Ray, I was criticizing Brianna for being pregnant by a married man."

Malik dropped his fork then waved his hands, "whoa, whoa, whoa, Bri is pregnant by the doctor dude?" I nodded my head in agreement, "Oh my God, I swear you Spencer girls have more drama going on. I'm going to change my profession from doctor to reality TV producer," he continued to laugh while I looked at him with a smart-aleck look.

"First of all us *Spencer girls* don't have a whole lot of drama," I lied. It seemed every time I turned around, one of the four of us had something going on. "It's just sometimes we choose the wrong men to fall for, that's all."

"Uhm, uh, what would your grandfather, Mr. Spencer, no excuse me, *Deacon* William Spencer say about his beloved granddaughter's?"

I smiled at the mention of Granddaddy's name. "He'd probably be in jail because first he would have killed one of those Negro's for messing with his babies." Even though Grandddaddy was a Christian man, he would literally *kill* for his daughters, and when the grandkids came along he'd kill for us as well. There was one thing that you didn't mess with and that was Deacon Spencer's family. That tradition is still alive today; we don't play about our own. With us talking about Granddaddy made me miss him so much too, all his wisdom and encouragement, but I thank God that Grandmother is still here to give us the wisdom that Grandddaddy can't give us now. "Yeah, Granddaddy wouldn't be having all of this going on."

"Man, your granddad was mad cool too," Malik said smiling, "and your grandmother is too, oh I almost forgot, what would she think if she knew that her precious granddaughter's are out here doing what they doing?"

"Whatever Malik," I said to him not wanting to discuss how bad we would hurt my grandparents. "But there is more in this saga," I said looking at him who was eating like it was either his last meal or it was his first meal ever.

"Oh Lord," he said, "What more could happen, Ken?" He asked as I gave him an evil eye.

"Anyway, Ray told me about a month ago that he has already filed for divorce," I said then Malik started laughing, "what's so funny?" I questioned.

"Because after this man sleeps with you, the next thing he's filing for a divorce," he continued to laugh, "damn Ken you must have really put it on him to have the man leave his wife."

"No it wasn't like that," I tried to defend myself. "He and Shaundie were already separated and on the verge of a divorce anyway. Remember I just told you she cheated on him."

Malik twisted his mouth, "yeah right, Ken. You don't think you had *anything* to do with his decision to file for a divorce?" he asked.

"I don't want to think that I did. That's nothing to be proud of Malik, I don't want that on my conscience."

"I knew it all along," I gave him a puzzled look, "that you two would end up back together."

"Nobody said that we were getting back together," I protested even though I can't say the thought hasn't crossed my mind. Especially after that night, I hate to think about it because I feel so guilty. But I must say it felt so good to be touched, kissed, caressed, and held by Raymond again, I can't deny that. "We only slept together once it doesn't mean anything."

"Yeah it may not, but think about it Ken," he said giving me a serious look to match his even more serious tone. "Just face it, ya'll are meant to be together."

I looked at Malik with a blank expression, then I looked down at my watch. "Oh shoot, I gotta go back to work," I said grabbing my purse to pay for my food.

"Oh now you got to go," Malik said reaching for his pockets and pulling out his wallet, "don't worry, I got this sis."

"Thanks," I got up, gave Malik a hug and kiss on the cheek, "I'll talk to you a little bit later."

"Alright then, Mrs. Collins," Malik said as I was walking away. I turned around and just smiled at him, then turned to walk out the door. *I guess I could be Mrs. Collins again.*

* * *

"Big sis it smells too good up in here. what are you in there cooking?" Robert Jr. asked as he walked through my front door.

"Hey R.J.," I said hugging him. "I'm cooking some pork chops, green beans, and broccoli rice and cheese casserole," I answered his question then looked around. "Uh— where is my daughter?"

Just as I was asking about my child, Kayla walked through the door hand in hand with RaeLynn. "Mommy, Mommy!" She screamed running into my arms as I bent down to hug her.

"Hey boo, I've missed you." I squeezed her.

"Me too," RaeLynn said letting go of me then reaching into her backpack. "Look what Auntie Kayla bought me," she showed me this mini painting set, I'm just glad it was watercolors and not real paint to get all over my beige carpets. "I have a picture for you and one for Daddy."

"Okay," I said to RaeLynn as she started to run toward her room, I looked at my little sister, "what's up girl?"

She came over and hugged me, as she was hugging me RaeLynn came back and hugged Kayla's leg. "Auntie Kayla I forgot to say thank you again," she said then ran off back to her room.

"You're welcome," Kayla yelled to RaeLynn who was already out of sight. "Well to answer your question big sis, I've just been trying to make it through the rest of the school year. You know I've only got six more weeks then I'll be a senior!" she said loudly dancing playfully around my living room.

"Well, I'll be graduating in six weeks," R.J. said joining Kayla in dancing playfully. "Oh and let's not forget the most important, I'll be eighteen next week!"

"Oh God!" Kayla and I said in unison. "Ya'll are making me feel old and I'm only twenty-four, I'm still in my prime." I laughed.

"Oh Ken, you'll be twenty-five next month," Kayla said in a matter-of-fact tone. I looked at her and I felt I was looking at the sixteen year old version of myself. Kayla and I looked a lot alike, golden skin, dimples and thick. Both of us wore a size ten, but Kayla was more athletic and taller than I am, she's about five foot ten. Another difference my sister and I have is that she wore her hair in long layers while you already know I rocked a shorter do. Now my little brother on the other hand takes his height after Daddy, both of them being six foot two.

"Yeah big sis, you getting up there in age," R.J. came over and put his arm around me, "but you still look good girl!" he smiled. This boy was just too cute, that's why he had all those young girls trying to knock my parents door down. Plus he's the star running back for his high school, that makes him more of a target for the young hoochie's.

"Keep talking," I said walking back into the kitchen. "You will not get any food."

"You know I'm just playing," he said following me. "Plus, we don't have time to stay, I've got to get back home to do my workout," he said grabbing a napkin.

"Here boy," I said handing him the food, "you go on and work for that scholarship boy." R.J. had received a full scholarship to Ohio State since he was the best running back in the state that lead his high school team to the state championship. We are so proud of him, and I can't wait until he starts playing so we can travel to Columbus, Ohio for his home games which would only be about a three hour drive.

"Thanks sis," he took the food then kissed me on the cheek, "I holla," R.J. said throwing up the peace sign.

"Bye Ken," that was Kayla.

"Ya'll be careful and lock my door on the way out please," I yelled from the kitchen.

"We got you," R.J. said. "Hey what's up Ray? What's good?" I heard R.J. say, I peeked around the corner and saw Raymond standing at the door with my siblings.

"Hey what's up R.J.?" He shook R.J.'s hand then hugged Kayla, "Miss Kayla, man ya'll have gotten so grown."

"Daddy!" RaeLynn ran from her room into his arms. He picked her up and swung her around.

"Hey baby girl," Ray said still holding RaeLynn.

"See ya'll later, later Ray." Kayla said walking out the door.

"Be easy," Ray closed the door. "Ken I hope you don't mind me coming over without calling."

"Its cool," I said starting to remember the last time he came over without calling what happen. But RaeLynn was home tonight and I didn't even want to do anything else Raymond. "I was just cooking that's all," I said walking back into the kitchen, Ray followed me with RaeLynn still in his arms.

"Daddy I have something for you," she jumped down. "C'mon Daddy let me show you," she pulled his hand.

"RaeLynn why don't you go get it for him," I said looking at my child, "I need to talk to Daddy for a minute, okay."

"Okay Mommy," she ran off to her room. Once she was out of sight Ray caught me off guard by kissing me ever so softly.

I closed my eyes beginning to fall in the trap called Raymond. I had to quickly come to myself and when I did, I pushed him away. "Not now," I said trying regain my composure. "So, what's with the *impromptu* visit?" I asked curious to know why Ray showed up on my doorstep with no phone calls yet again.

He didn't say anything at first, but reached in his back pocket, "I had to show you this," he handed me some paper. "It's officially over."

"Divorce papers," I sighed; feeling mixed emotions as I read through the familiar papers. I just didn't know how to feel. On one hand I wanted to jump around for joy, on the other hand I felt that I was partly responsible for this. "Wow, so it's really over uh?"

"Yeah, you know what this means?" He asked grabbing my shoulders. He looked into my eyes, like he did the day we married; like the countless times we made love, and just like he did a few months ago. "I can be with you again."

Before I could express the way I felt, RaeLynn ran back into the kitchen. "Here Daddy," she handed her father a picture.

"Wow, baby girl," Raymond seemed to light up looking at the picture RaeLynn had painted for him. "This is beautiful," he said to her as I stood back and admired the relationship between the two of them. Ray was like the best father in the world to RaeLynn; he loved his daughter to death and the thought made me smile, thinking of how my daddy was with all of us. He's the best father too.

"RaeLynn its time to eat, so go and wash your hands," she turned around and ran to the bathroom as I returned to the stove. "Ray you're more than welcome to stay and eat," I said to him hoping that he wouldn't turn down my offer.

"Thanks," he said. I turned back toward the stove again, but I could feel Ray creeping up behind me. He was barely touching my body, but his lips were on the back of my neck. I closed my eyes wanting to repeat what we did a little over three or four months ago. I could feel his lips moving as if he were talking, but whatever he said after 'thanks' I honestly don't know. The fact that he was talking on my neck made want to put RaeLynn to bed, skip dinner all together and go straight for desert. "Ken did you hear what I said?" Raymond asked.

"Huh?" I snapped back into reality. "Wh- uh, um I'm sorry, what did you say?" I turned around and he was right in front of me. I looked in his eyes like I was trying to search for words.

He smiled his seductive smile then licked his lips, "I said I was hoping to stay for dinner, then possibly desert," he said slowly, "I want—"

"Daddy," RaeLynn cut him off as she stopped then looked back and forth between me and Raymond then started to grin. "Daddy was you gonna kiss Mommy?"

"Hey now," Ray said sternly as he walked over to her. "What me and Mommy do is our business, *grown folks business*. So I suggest you sit down and get ready for dinner."

RaeLynn looked down, "yes sir, I'm sorry Daddy." She said sitting down at the table; all I could do was smile.

"That's okay," Ray went to the table and sat in the chair next to RaeLynn. "There are some things that's none of a four year olds business, and that was one of them. And it's nobody else's business either," he said referring to her big mouth. I love my child but that girl can talk a mile a minute. Plus she will run down everybody's business if she's around when something is going on. That's how I know when either one of my younger siblings are in trouble or something. RaeLynn stays over my parents house after school only until I get off work. The girl is like the *National Inquirer*, she knows all the business.

"Yes sir," he reached out his arms and she hugged him.

"Well, its time to eat now," I said looking at them and thinking that I could have this again. I could actually have my family back, Raymond, RaeLynn, and me happy again. *God it's in your hands now.*

Brianna

"Ok, there it is." Doctor Michael's said to me as I looked at the monitor, "looks like everything is going good."

"That's good," I sighed relief lying back looking at the heartbeat of my unborn child. "Can you tell what the sex of the child is?" I asked, but knowing in my heart of hearts that it's a girl.

"Sure, give me a moment," she said as she moved the probe around my swollen stomach. "Looks like you're having a girl."

I smiled knowingly, I even think a tear formed. "Thanks Doctor Michaels." I said to her as she removed the probe and wiped the jelly from my stomach. I couldn't believe here I was having a man's child and there might be a possibility my child won't even be able to see her father because of his family. That's probably why the tear was forming, on one hand I was excited to be having a child because I was always told it could never happen, but on the other hand I'm thinking why now, why with him?

"Ms. Wright like I mention before everything is going according to schedule," Dr. Michaels said, "and your due date is September nineteenth."

"September nineteenth?" My smile faded, "now just because you say that date, it doesn't mean that will be *the* actually due date?" I questioned with my lips turned up.

"Well, I'm just using a calculated guess that it will be that day," Dr. Michaels said, "If you have the baby a little bit before you wouldn't be in any danger. But anything after that day, we should be concerned. Is there something wrong?"

"Oh no, its just September nineteenth is the father's birthday," I said looking down at my twiddling thumbs.

"Okay, that's good," she looked at me with concern. My face must have showed what I was *really* feeling, sadness with a touch of distress and resentment. "Or not," she finally said after staring at me.

"It'll be okay," I said grabbing my purse, "thanks again Doctor Michaels."

"Anytime, just remember if you have any problems just call my office," she opened the door for me to walk out.

"Okay," I walked into the waiting room to make my final appointment. As I was walking to my car I began to think about Lance. *I can't believe that this child could be born on his birthday of all days.* Truth be told, Lance had been heavy on my mind anyway. Ever since that day I met back up with Brian, I've been comparing the two even though I know I shouldn't. I can't help it though. I've been trying to have some type of relationship with Brian, but he's just not Lance, or should I say Brian doesn't know how to *do* what Lance does so well. Although Lance is married, he used to treat me like a woman. That's because Lance is a man, Brian isn't, plain and simple. Let's just say that Brian has a lot of growing up to do in every area of his life.

Every time I was with Lance, he would do things to me that no man has ever done, that is with the exception of Sean. He made me feel wanted, beautiful, all those things a woman wants to feel from a man. Lance would make me want to pull out my hair, his hair, hell anybody's hair in excitement. I would never have to tell him what felt good and what didn't. It's like he already knew what would make me climb a wall, or what would make me want to scream, but nothing would come out. Those were the times he would smile and chuckle because he *knew* he was putting it down; afterwards I'd be smiling too. Lance would be a good man if he weren't already married, honestly sometimes I wish he wasn't married to his wife but to me.

Brian on the other hand, he just doesn't make me feel like that. I constantly have to tell him to stop something because he's either hurting me (not in a good way), or telling him to stop because it's just not feeling good period. No doubt Brian is a cool guy, but he just acts so young. Playing video games all day and listening to nothing but rap music and just playing games period at inappropriate times. I know I'm only twenty-three and Brian is twenty , but he just acts like he's ten years old, and that drives me crazy. It's hard to go back to childish games when you've been hanging with grown folks.

Okay, even though I'm pregnant and all which means I'm bigger than my normal size nine, but that doesn't mean I shouldn't be romanced. Well, a few weeks after I met back up Brian, we decided to go on a date, we went out to eat and to a movie. After the movie we came back to my place where unfortunately we had sex, if that's what you want to call it. First of all, there wasn't any foreplay, no excuse me, his idea of foreplay was kissing and gnawing on my neck. Then it happen, all of four minutes, the absolute worst in my history, especially after you've been sexed good by Doctor Hamilton. I think that's why I've been thinking about Lance so much lately. Although he had a degree in medicine his expertise was in love making. I guess that's why even though I haven't talked to him in months, I can't get over him. I've even changed my department so I wouldn't have to run into him, and so far it's worked. I haven't seen him voluntarily since I put him out of my apartment after I told him I was pregnant a little over five months ago. Part of me wanted to go over to his office and talk to him, just to see what's been going on in his world. Also to tell him that we're having a daughter, and that I do want him in our child's life. I was confused about what I should say and needed to talk to either my sister or one of my cousins.

    I was sitting in the parking lot of the doctor's office, mainly because it was right across the street from the hospital I worked. I sat contemplating going inside to talk to Lance, I pulled out my cell and began dialing numbers.

    "Hey sis are you busy?" I asked my twin sister.

    "No, not right now," I heard her eating something, "just on lunch what are you doing?"

    "Across the street," I paused, "I had a doctor's appointment this afternoon."

    "Why don't you come to my floor?" She suggested.

    "Well, I'm on my way," I said getting out of my car. "I'm glad you suggested that, I really need to talk to you."

    "What's up?" She asked.

    "Girl I'm on my way," I said now crossing the street. "We'll talk then and make sure we can go somewhere with some privacy."

    "Just meet me in the 5th floor lounge," she said.

    "Okay, see you in a minute," I closed my phone and made my way to the lounge.

    "Are you working today?" Connie my old co-worker asked as I was entering the elevator.

    "Oh no girl, I only work Monday, Tuesday, and Wednesdays," I told her, "I'm meeting my sister for lunch though."

"We miss you down on the fourth floor," she said as the elevator stopped on her floor, "you should come visit us."

"I might do that today," I said hugging her, "you take care." *Yeah I might be there today to handle some unfinished business.* "Hey I thought you were gonna be in the lounge?" I asked Brandi who was waiting by the elevators as I stepped off of them.

"I decided to meet you here," Brandi said reaching out to my stomach. "Hey little one, I can't wait 'til you get here so I can spoil you rotten."

"Oh Lord," I said rolling my eyes, because she always meant what she said. "I'm not trying to have you spoiling my baby like that."

"Girl please," she waved her hand at me as we walked into the lounge, "so what's up?" we sat down.

"Girl, first off I'm having a girl," I said then Brandi began to grin so hard.

"Oh my God Bri, I'm going to have a niece," she covered her mouth.

"Yep, she's due September nineteenth on Lance's birthday," Brandi's smile faded and her face grew concerned, "yeah that's the same way I looked too when the doctor told me."

"Is that what you want to talk about?" she asked looking at me with a serious expression.

"Yeah," I started, "a part of me wants to let him know because I want him to be in our daughter's life, but he's still married." I leaned on the table and rested my hand on my chin then sighed. "It'll almost be impossible for him to be in her life and maintain his own."

"That's a decision you can't make for him," she stated, "I think you should tell him, give him the option to either be in the baby's life. I mean because he may not want to."

I looked over to the side, "I hadn't thought about that," I twisted my mouth. "I guess the way he is with his kids; I guess I assumed he'd respond the same way to our child."

"Bri, listen to me though," she said, "I never said he'd be flat out against wanting to have a relationship with your child, you just have to have an open mind. Also you need to talk to him."

"Yeah, I'm going to call him." I lowered my head, then pulled out my phone.

"Uhm, that might not be necessary," I looked up and saw Lance walking through the lounge entrance, "talk to him, okay? And I'll just see you later." Brandi got up and hugged me.

"I'll call you later," she walked toward Lance and stopped to say something to him. Immediately he looked at me and I got butterflies, he then proceeded in my direction, "I was just about to call you."

He grabbed my hand, "come with me to my office please." I followed Lance to his office, which had been moved since the last time we saw each other. It was now right around the corner from the 5th floor lounge. As soon as Lance closed the door behind me, he grabbed and embraced me. I closed my eyes then sighed, I didn't realize how much I missed his touch. "Bri I've missed you."

Trying to hold back all my *true* emotions, I backed away, "I wanted to talk to you about something very important."

"Okay," he sat on the edge of his desk as I sat in the chair in front of him, "but can I say that you look amazing. I mean pregnant and all, you are glowing."

"Thank you," I said with a blank look, "well I went to the doctors today and I'm having a girl on your birthday."

Silence swept the room, "a girl on September nineteenth?" He asked after about a minute.

"Yeah," I paused, "I know that you didn't want me to have this baby, but—"

"I was being selfish," he cut me off. "I'm sorry Bri, I was trying to cover my own tracks."

"So what are you saying?" I asked looking up at him then quickly looking away. I can never look at Lance too long without starting to catch even deeper feelings.

"I'm saying I've come to terms with the fact that I'm having another child," he admitted, "and I'm not going to deny it, I mean her."

"I want you to, I'm sorry," I started to rephrase what I was about to say, "do you want to be in your daughter's life?"

"As much as I can," he said looking at me, I looked back with confusion on my face, it must have showed, "Bri I do still have a wife."

"So I'm guessing she still doesn't know?" He got up and sat in the chair next to me. He reached out for my hand, but I folded my arms. "Answer my question, she doesn't know you have another child on the way outside of your marriage does she?"

"No Brianna she doesn't," he said sternly. "I can't tell her that, it would mess everything she and I have."

I began to laugh, but not really thinking the situation was funny, "everything ya'll have?" I shook my head because I couldn't believe for a brief moment, I was going to let him back into my life. "I don't know what I expected from you, I see you still want to have your cake and eat it too."

"What are you talking about?" He looked at me strange, "it's not the way you think."

"Really?" I questioned now standing, "you're just going to say the same thing you said to me when I first told you about this child, that it's not the right time for you." I continued to look at him this time with an attitude, "you want to keep your little security that you have with her, but still have your fun on the side with me. Sleep with whomever you want, oh but don't let her get pregnant cause that'll mess up your "happy little home" that you have with your perfect little wife, or so she thinks, and your perfect little kids." I was fuming as I walked around his office while I spoke. "Screw everybody else including Brianna, because that little dumb girl doesn't really mean anything to me, she's just something to play with when my 'perfect little wife' isn't acting so perfect."

"That's enough!" He raised his voice and stood up in front of me with the angriest face I have ever seen on him. "Brianna that's not true, at all! I do love you."

I shook my head in disagreement, "you can't love me Lance," I raised my hands like I was trying to get him understand by using hand movements. "You are married, it's impossible for you to love me."

"I don't love her like that anymore," he stated and backed away from my face then sat on the corner of his desk. "You don't know how much I want to be with you, but the reason I don't leave her, is because of money."

"Money?" I repeated, "what does—"

"She'll wipe me out," he cut me off. "Especially if she knew about something like this, she'd really hurt me financially, child support, alimony all of that. But once the kids are over eighteen and graduate high school, I think I'd be ok."

"So you mean to tell me, that I'd have to wait ten years until I could be with you if *I* decided to continue this?" I questioned. "You know what?" I grabbed my purse, and walked toward the door. I faced him then said, "you don't have to worry about me anymore. If I'm *still* single in ten years, I *might* give you a call. And that's not a strong possibility either."

"Please don't go Bri," he begged as I opened the door. I looked at his face and for a moment I thought I saw a tear forming in his eyes, "don't go," he said again. I rolled my eyes, turned around, and walked out the door, slamming it behind me.

Bastard, I thought, *maybe I should just teach Brian how to love me the right way instead of trying to wait around for some married man. Uh, ten years? He's not even worth it.*

*   *   *

"Girl you better keep that man," I said talking to the television, I was watching Tyler Perry's movie, *Daddy's Little Girls*. "At least he wants to raise his kids." I spoke those words, then looked down at my stomach rubbing it, "at least they'll have a father they can claim in public." My phone began ringing breaking up my *'pity party,'* "hello?" I answered.

"Hey what's good?" Brian asked on the other end, "I was calling to see how your doctor's appointment went."

"It went cool," I said putting down my lemonade, "I'm having a girl."

"For real? That's cool," he said, "so, are you busy?"

"Na, I just got finished eating," I said to him, I knew where the conversation would end up going, him wanting to come over. Honestly I wasn't trying to deal with him tonight, "it's my Friday night movie time."

"Do you mind if I come watch a movie with you?" He asked and I rolled my eyes, *I knew that was coming.*

"Well," I said very hesitant, "I'm really tired tonight, plus the movie I'm watching is almost over."

"Oh, okay," he started, "so maybe I'll give you a call tomorrow or something?"

"Yeah, yeah that'd be a lot better," I lied, because I really didn't want to be bothered with him tomorrow either, "look, I'm about to turn in now, so I'll talk to you later," I yawned for extra affect.

"Alright then, holla." He said sounding disappointed.

"Bye." I said. After I hung up the phone I started laughing at how I acted my way out of that situation. I was laying back on the couch when I heard a knock on my door. "I know he didn't just ignore what I said and came over anyway," I whispered because if it was Brian, I didn't want him to hear me.

I walked over to the door, looked out the peephole, then exhaled in aggravation. "Please just hear me out," Lance said as I cracked the door opened with the chain still on. "Thank you," he continued as he walked through my doors.

"So, what do want?" I sat back on the couch as he set on the love seat. Lance sat down and looked at me like he was trying to figure something out. "Okay, I know you didn't come over here to just stare at me, so what do you want?" I asked again.

"I want to be with you," he said. I began to laugh looking in the opposite direction. "Now Brianna please listen to me."

"Lance what can you tell me?" I looked back at him. He was now leaning forward looking so good to me for some reason, but I can't fall for that right now, I have to be strong. "You are married, how many times do I have to say that? And I can't do this with you anymore. I'm trying to change my life around and messing with you doesn't help."

"I know, I know it's wrong," he started, "but is it wrong if I'm in love with you? And I know you love me too, is love wrong?" we locked eyes.

"No love isn't wrong but adultery is wrong," I broke the stare.

"Come on Bri," he got up and I got nervous. The wrong touch by this man and I would end up one more time where I didn't want to go again. He sat on the far side of the couch, "we're in love, I love you so much. Just to let you know, I *do* want to be there for our daughter. That's all I've been thinking about since you left my office," I glanced over at him, he was smiling. *Damn, why did he have to do that?* He was looking so good showing those dimples that I seemed to love. "I was thinking you know after she's born, the three of us going to the park or something. I mean, after she's a little older of course, about three or so you know us being a *real* family."

I was beginning to get sucked in his fantasy. The picture he painted was one that I couldn't ignore. I knew that Lance had the potential to be a good father, I mean he was a good one to the kids he had now a whole lot different than what I had. I would have loved to go the park with my father pushing me on the swing or something, us having picnics and being happy. But it didn't happen that way for me, I always vowed that my kids would *never* have to experience what I did with my father. I don't think I could let my daughter go through what I did, because I remember how hurt I used to be in my childhood. I couldn't let Lance make false promises to my daughter like the one he was making now; there's no way we can be a family when he *already* has one that he'll go to once he leaves here.

I snapped back into the real world, "that sounds real nice but uhm, did you forget about the life you have now? The one you told me earlier that you *can't* leave right now."

"Let me explain something," he said reaching out for my hand, but I looked at him like he had ten heads. "When my wife and I began to have problems, she threaten me, told me if I left her and the kids, I would pay. She would clean me out, on top of that hurt me, I got scared. That's why I haven't left her yet."

"But if, I mean are you happy, is she happy?"

"Hell no. We are like strangers in our home, we haven't made love for almost two years." He said sounding upset.

I held up my hand, "please spare me that info," I said. *Is she crazy? I thought. If I was married to him I would be sexing him real good every night. Hell, he isn't even my husband, and I've probably had sex with him more than she has within the last year.*

"Sorry, but the only time we talk is about bills and the kids. We have nothing else to say to each other, but I've finally decided to uhm, leave her for you."

I looked over at him, "are you serious?" Is the only thing I could say as I was feeling mixed emotions. Lance has said he was going to leave before, it's now been almost a year and a half and nothing has changed. I want to believe him because I would love to be with him and not have to hide the love we have for each other anymore.

"Yes," he said without hesitation. He took his hand and began to run his fingers through my hair. Once he reached the end of my mane, which was at the middle of my back, he took his fingers and ran them down my back. I closed my eyes and moaned, "you want me too?"

I bit my bottom lip and looked over at him, he was working the hell out of his bedroom eyes. I pulled him closer to me and kissed him softly, "I've *never* stopped wanting you," I said looking in his eyes as my lips grazed his while I was speaking.

He smiled once again showing his dimples. "I love you, Brianna Raven Wright," he kissed me again with so much passion causing me to get butterflies like it was our first time doing this. I felt a cold chill go through my body as I wrapped my arms around his neck. We started kissing with more aggression, that's when I placed my hand on the back of his head.

The harder he kissed me, the more I felt I was going to go crazy, even this man's kiss was different. Brian could never make me want to have an 'O' just by kissing. Hell he could never make me have one any other way either. When Lance stopped kissing my lips, he moved to my chin then started to kiss my neck just like he was still kissing my lips; he began using his tongue now on my neck. "Lance," I moaned softly. I felt like I was going to explode. Every inch of my body felt like it was on fire, but in a good way. He moved back up to my lips and kissed them once more, but this time softly allowing his tongue to intertwine with mine. "I love you too." I pulled away long enough to say, afterward we were back at it. As we were kissing it seemed that Lance's hands were moving all over my body, tugging at the blue jean button down dress that I had on. Needless to say I ended up damn near naked on my couch, "when did this happen?" I asked after looking down, wondering how I got so into his kisses that I didn't realize him removing my dress from my body. The only thing that wasn't off were my panties, which he would probably take off next.

"I want to make love to you," Lance moaned while I was kissing and licking on his neck. He started to unbutton his shirt showing off his white wife beater. "Bri, I want to make love to you," he repeated as I was trying to unbuckle his pants, but still kissing his neck. He grabbed my shoulders gently and lightly pushed me away from him. He licked his lips slowly while he looked over my naked body with approval. Feeling self conscience of my big pregnant belly, I took my dress and tried to cover myself. "Please don't cover yourself up."

"But Lance I'm too big for you to be looking at me like this," I said trying to hold the dress over my exposed breast and stomach.

"Baby there is nothing wrong with your body, I love looking at you," he pulled the dress from my hand and tossed it across the room. "You're even more beautiful like this, but it doesn't matter because I love you either way." He nonchalantly pushed me back and removed my panties using his fingertips to barely touch my body as he slid them down my legs. I leaned my head back, closed my eyes and let out a loud sigh in satisfaction. Once he threw the panties on the floor he went for my neck yet again. This time he let his tongue move in circles on my neck, sucking it like he was trying to put a hickey on that spot. My body started to shutter to some extent because this was being done right. I moaned once more thinking *this* is the way a woman wants to feel before having sex.

I couldn't take it anymore, I opened my eyes and pushed him on his back so I could get on top of him right there on the couch. I sat on his massive manhood allowing him to enter inside of me as we both let out a loud sigh of pleasure even though we had just got started. I closed my eyes all over again, "Lance I love you so much," I moaned, feeling his hips move underneath me.

He then grunted loudly. I opened my eyes back up and looked at him making the sexiest face I've ever seen him make. It was somewhere between gratification and serious even though his dimples were still showing while his eyes squinted. "Brianna I love you," he moaned when I moved my hips matching his movements, "oh God," he sighed. We continued to move in a rhythm as if we were in sync and our wails of fulfillment being the drum that kept us on beat with each other. "Baby I've missed this," he heaved like he was getting exhausted.

I bit my bottom lip, "I've missed....oh," I let out a soft cry of pleasure not able to finish my sentence, but I was still able to keep up the perfect tempo we were making.

Lance chuckled at me briefly before he went back into his own planet of making pleasure noises. "Did you mean...uhm," he groaned, "you...uh... you missed this too?" I closed my eyes shaking my head in agreement. I heard him chuckle again, but this time in a cocky way because he knew he had me in a vulnerable state; when I couldn't talk, he already knew what the deal was. "I've missed you, Brianna," he moaned my name and I matched his call, "you missed daddy haven't you?" he asked me assertively. Even with my eyes closed I could hear the smile in his voice, I shook my head again, "say you missed it."

"I....uhm....I," I tried to answer, but with each stroke I was becoming more and more speechless. I could tell Lance loved the fact I wasn't able to talk, but if I knew him he was going to keep trying.

"Does it feel good?" he moaned this time still matching each movement I made, I shook my head, "come on baby, tell me how it feels?" I heard his smile as I kept my eyes closed and my mouth opened trying to relay a message through the moans, because the words just weren't forming. "Say it baby, don't it feel good?" he groaned. He then gripped my waist pushing himself deeper inside of me, I moaned louder while digging my nails deeper into his back. "You like that huh?"

He moved more insistently still squeezing my waist while thrusting himself so far inside of me that I could feel him hit my *inner* walls. I finally open my eyes while gripping harder to his back then I let out a loud cry in satisfaction. "Yeeesssss!" I finally screamed as he got louder with his moans. I tossed my head back, closed my eyes again experiencing total bliss as he continued to make my body feel like it was going to burst. He moved his hands from my waist down to my thighs, his hands then glided around to my backside as he slapped it; I screamed out again before I started biting my bottom lip. I begin to think, *I could never go back to Brian after this. There is no way I could ever do that again. I don't think I could even pretend to enjoy sex with him anymore after tonight.* Lance just doesn't know how much deeper I was falling in love with him with each stroke. Why do things that are wrong, feel *so* damn good?

Later That Night:

"Uhm, baby where are you going?" Lance asked still half asleep when I moved his arm from around my waist so I could get out of the bed. "Baby please don't leave me because I just wanna hold you right now."

"Lance I need to go to the bathroom, so go back to sleep." I explained after kissing his lips as he kept his eyes closed. I stared at him admiring his *fineness* even while he was sleeping. Gazing at this man gave me the inspiration for a poem. The thoughts were flowing all through my head so fast that as soon as I got out of the bathroom, I had to find some paper and a pen to write down what I was thinking immediately.

"Baby I thought you were coming back to bed," Lance yelled as I was coming out of the bathroom.

"I am Lance," I waved my hand at him even though he couldn't see me because he still had his eyes closed. "I'm just getting my notebook," I said walking to my dining room table. Once I returned to the bedroom I sat in the desk chair. I moved the desk and chair into my bedroom so I could turn my extra bedroom into a nursery instead of a computer room since the baby was on *her* way. I turned away from the desk and focused my attention toward the bed looking at a naked Lance who was now snoring and laying under part of the sheets. The sheets only covered his pelvic region and one of his legs. That man looked like a beautiful *Black* Greek god statue with every muscle chiseled in the right place making up this perfect body. He is the perfect example of inspiration, putting pen to paper with a vision in full view I began to write:

> *~Irresistible is what he is, otherwise why would I allow myself to get caught up in a situation I've often chastised other women about. But there's something about Dr. Lance Hamilton that won't allow my mind to take the obvious control my heart has over this critical decision to be the other woman...soon to be the only woman, or so he says.*

"It's really not working out" or "We don't even spend time together" and "I just don't love her anymore…" are the titles of the songs he sings daily. Obviously being the tune I want to hear because like my favorite song, it brings joy to my ears as the melody begins to play and the words flow free. But what can I say, <u>I'M CAUGHT UP!</u> Needing to believe every word that proceeds from his mouth which is the only way that would make what we are doing okay. Never choosing to be the other woman, it was a role that was thrust upon me by this man I can't seem to resist. And giving into this temptation is not my fault, so don't blame me. See if you knew Dr. Lance Hamilton you would see the reason for my infatuation, so blame him. And just as soon as he handles his "situation" it will be "us" instead of them, but until then I guess I'll wait patiently and assume the role of "the other woman." ~May 2008

12
Summer

"Congratulations class of 2008!" Dr. Mills the dean of the university said as he closed the graduation. We all screamed in excitement, but for me this meant so much more. I felt like a new woman, and I was new woman. Damon and I are history, especially after that last episode that happened months ago, and Amir and I are getting closer everyday. He has been my best friend since everything went down. We haven't made any kind of boyfriend-girlfriend relationship commitment, but we do take part in kissing every now and then. If someone wanted to put a title to what we are, I'd say that we are openly dating. What that means is if someone was to come along and ask one of us on a date, there wouldn't be any problems because we're not really in a serious type relationship. But the reason we aren't in that kind of relationship is because of me.

The truth of the matter is that I've been learning to love myself. I've finally accepted myself; my big breast, curvy hips, plump booty and all. Amir has also accepted it too, "the new me." With this new me, I began to work out at least three times a week and so far I've lost about twenty-five to thirty pounds. I also even cut my hair again, back in a bob, but eventually I'd get the courage to get it all chopped off. Anyway, it wasn't enough for Amir to keep telling me I was beautiful if I didn't believe, but now I do believe. Another change I made in my life after Damon was going back to church again. I started going to church with Ken, then after a few weeks I found myself walking down the aisle to be saved. That was the best decision that

I've made in a long time. I even talked Amir into visiting my new church, he loved it so much he joined on his first visit. I can't explain how much my life has changed for the better since I let go of what I thought I needed.

"Congrats graduate!" Malachi said as the rest of my family bum rushed me after the ceremony. "Its time to party now," he said as his new flavor of the month sauntered over to his side.

Malachi is a professional basketball player for the Atlanta Hawks. The chick he brought with him this time was a sister, thank God. He has been known to bring a white girl home, like the last chick. She was good and white. This new girl was pretty though. She was about our complexion (caramel); maybe five foot ten because she came to my brother's shoulder and he's six foot six, very tall. She wasn't the typical model type that someone in my brother's profession might date. She could probably be a full figured model though, with her thick hips and big booty. Even though Malachi could probably have a model or any woman for that matter, he knew thick women is were it's at. He's from Louisville, where he grew up surrounded by thickness.

"Oh sis, this is my girlfriend Gabbie," he smiled really hard. Something told me that he was probably serious about this one, he introduced her as his *girlfriend*. The others I barely even knew their names because they were literally here today and gone tomorrow.

"It's nice to finally meet you. Kai has told me so much about you, oh and congratulations." Gabbie said extending her hand toward me.

"Thank you. It's nice to meet you too." I said.

"I'm so proud of you," Mama said hugging me with Daddy next to her and Grandmother standing close behind waiting to congratulate me as well.

"Yes baby, I am so proud of you too." That was Grandmother talking. "If William were here he would be so happy to see this too," she said referring to Granddaddy, and then hugging me. For a soon to be seventy year old, Grandmother moved around like she was as young as me. Her birthday was on the Fourth of July, and my family has already begun to plan a huge 70th birthday celebration for the matriarch of the Spencer's.

"Well it looks like its time to party," Mama said.

"No, its time to work," that was Daddy, "I'm just playing baby," he laughed putting one arm around me.

"Charles," Mama said hitting him playfully on the arm.

"Its time to eat," Malachi said, "ya'll know when I come home I've got to have a home cooked meal."

"Well if ya'll stop your yapping and make your way to the car I can go finish dinner," Aunt Karen spoke up. Although we were having the dinner at my mama's house, Aunt Karen was doing most of the cooking along with the rest of her sisters. "Julie you know I need to get inside your house so I can finish frying my chicken."

"Lord Jesus," Malachi grabbed his heart, "those are my two favorite words fried chicken, especially yours Aunt Karen."

"If your mama doesn't come on, you won't be getting any fried chicken." Aunt Karen looked at my brother smiling, "shoot won't nobody get any if Julie doesn't bring her butt on."

"Mama, your chicken ain't going anywhere," Kennede stated lightly hitting her mother on the shoulder.

"Come on Charles lets hurry up and go before Karen has a fit," Mama said looking up to Daddy, then she hit Aunt Karen's other shoulder. "So are you riding with us?"

"No, Robert and I can follow ya'll," she said.

"I have to go get my degree right now and I'll just meet everybody at the house," I said letting them know they could go on and leave.

"So how are you getting to your mom's?" Brianna asked shuffling toward me with her big belly leading the way. I smirked looking at her belly; *that could have been me; yeah I probably would've been entering my sixth month too.*

"I'll take care of that," Amir said creeping up behind me as he touched my shoulder breaking my thoughts. I quickly turned around, he gave me a hug then kissed my cheek, "hello everybody," he greeted the family.

"Hi Amir," they sang like a choir smiling and Amir smiled back at my family's response to his greeting.

"I'm sorry I didn't see where you guys were seated," Amir began his apology for not sitting with my family as he walked over and hugged Grandmother, "but you all don't have to worry I will take the graduate home."

"That's okay baby," that was Grandmother, "we better get going so we can put the finishing touches on this party, baby you are coming to the party aren't you?" She asked Amir holding on to his hand.

"Yes ma'am," he put his arm around me, "I know how you Spencer's party, I'm not about to miss it at all."

"Well let's get this party on!" Malachi said as my family proceeded to the exit, "we'll see you over Mom's."

I walked with them out the exit but was about to go in the opposite direction to retrieve my degree. "Okay guys see you over there," I waved to my family then looked over at Amir who was staring at me with the biggest smile.

"Congratulations Summer," he hugged me again, this time more flirtatious than the hug he gave me in front of my family. "You just don't understand how proud I am of you," he stepped back like he was checking me out or something.

"Thank you so much for your support, I don't know where I'd be without you and God, I tell you," I exhaled hard, "this year surely has been one of transition." I continued to walk toward the line. "My God hasn't it," he said still holding my hand attracting the attention of people walking by us, but Amir was fine enough to draw attention like that, "but I know your family has fixed a feast."

"Oh my God did they," I said releasing his hand, "I think they cooked everything not only because of my party, but you know we still get together on Sunday's to have dinner." Long before there was a *Soul Food*, my family ate like that every Sunday. Shoot with all those kids, Grandmother and Granddaddy cooked like it was a Sunday everyday. The only difference now is that we eat at a different house each Sunday. I think now they have assigned Sunday's, but the last Sunday of the month is always at Grandmother's house.

"Man I can't wait to get over there," he stated, "I have never known a family that can cook like yours, I swear I love your family."

I smiled at him, "they love you too," I said to Amir, then gave my name to the lady in charge of giving out the degrees. "Shoot you've been around my family since you were little, remember when you used to beg your parents to go with me during our barbeques?"

He put his fist over his mouth laughing, "man do I?" We continued to laugh as I waited for the lady, "but come on now Summer, my family wasn't as big as yours, shoot I'm the only child and we just didn't do stuff like that. Man as a kid I used to wish that I could have been apart of your family."

"For real?" I chuckled, "uh uh that couldn't happen then we would've been related."

"And, what's wrong with that?" He questioned as I just stared at him with a blank look, then his eyebrows rose, "oh so you're saying that if we were cousins or something, I couldn't do this," he bent down and kissed my lips so softly, I closed my eyes almost forgetting that we were around other people.

I stopped him when I felt a tap on my shoulder; the lady rudely shoved a manila envelope in my face. I took it from her, but I truly wasn't giving her a second thought especially after a kiss like that. "See if we were cousins we couldn't do stuff like that," I said as we began walking toward the door that leads to the parking lot.

"We could have been kissing cousins," he laughed bending down in my face before opening the stadium door for me, something I had to get used to, a man other than Daddy opening every door for me to walk out first.

"Eeeelll!" I hit him playfully. "I'm glad things worked out the way they did, you being the best friend I could have ever had during one of the worst moments in my life."

Amir reached over to me, and placed his arm around my neck, "yeah I'm glad things worked out the way they did too," he opened the passenger car door, "but whose to say that I won't end up in your family anyway?" I glanced at him grinning as he closed the door then quickly entered in the driver's side.

"I never said it couldn't happen," I said as I began to open the envelope, "wow, I've finally got it! Thank you Jesus!" I said with the brims of my eyes becoming misty looking down at the paper that read Bachelor of Arts in Political Science.

"Yes thank you Jesus," he agreed with me as he began to pull off, "especially after all you've been through and to accomplish something like this."

"This is just the beginning too," I smiled, "but I'm still not sure on law school anymore though."

"What are you talking about?" He glanced over at me as he drove his Lexus through the streets, "I thought you were so into becoming this world famous lawyer."

"Yeah the old me wanted to have that profession," I started to say as I was looking down at my degree. "But I don't know about this new person. It's like everything is changing inside of me since I made that change a few months ago. Everything in my life is just moving in a new direction, and honestly I like where I'm going even though things seem cloudy right now."

"Just trust Him," Amir pointed upward, "God will never let you down. And obviously He has you in a new place wanting to do new things, man I'm so happy for you Summer, I promise."

I looked over at him, "thanks," I said as he gave the sexiest glance in history, he almost made me ask him to do that again. "I'm so thankful to have you in my life."

"Well you know that I'm here for you," he moved his right hand from the steering wheel to grab my hand, "whatever you need, whatever you want, I'll always be here to help you in anyway that I can, always."

I glanced over at him, "and vice versa, I'll always be here for you too Amir," he brought my hand up to his mouth and kissed the back of it smiling.

"I'm serious Summer, I'll always be here, but uhm," his smile faded and he moved his hand then placed it back on the wheel. "These last few months we've gotten a lot closer since I've come back, and honestly, I uhm," he began to stumble over his words like he was unsure or didn't know quit how to put the words together, "I even think that I- I'm falling in love with you."

He glanced over at me and I began shaking my head in disagreement. "No Amir you can't do that," I tried to plead with him like falling in love was a bad thing. I mean its not, but it's just that right now I'm not ready for that kind of commitment, "you can't fall in love with me, I mean uhm, just not right now is what I mean."

"Why not Summer?" Amir said softly as if he had lost his best friend, "I uh, I thought that you were feeling the same way too?"

"I honestly don't know what I'm feeling right now," I said looking out the window noticing that we were getting closer to my mom's house, thank God. That means this conversation would soon be over. "Amir please don't get me wrong, I do like you a *whole* lot, but I'm still healing from Damon," I said as he turned into the driveway of my parents house, "I mean I'm still trying to get over all of that."

"I uhm I understand," he put the car in park then put his hands together like he was about to pray, "I just thought that maybe you were starting to have the same feelings that I was having for you, I mean we kiss and flirt all the time."

"I know, I uhm," I looked down then began to take my seatbelt off, "look can we just go into the house so we can eat and party, then later I promise we can finish talking, Amir I promise we will finish talking about this okay?"

He didn't say anything put opened his door and climbed out of the car, for the first time I was stunned by his actions. I put my hand on the door about to open it, when Amir appeared and held it open for me, "Summer this conversation isn't over."

"I know," I said looking into his eyes that were just glistening with excitement about fifteen minutes ago, but were now overcome with hurt, something I never wanted to do especially to someone like Amir. I just knew that now the conversation later would be a lot more heartfelt than it was going to be before. Now I would have to completely open up to him, something I was trying to avoid, but in order for him to understand my reasoning he was going to have to hear the truth. The whole truth and nothing but the truth, Damon still has a strong hold on my life even though I let parts of him go in that emergency room.

I opened the door to Mama's house, "whoa!!" Everyone began to clap and cheer as I walked through the foyer with Amir in tow. "Good, I'm glad you are finally here," Malachi said already having his paper plates in his hand, "cause now its time to eat, and I am *too* ready for this meal," he looked at the table filled with fried chicken, my favorite collard greens, Daddy's famous rib tips, baked beans, potato salad, macaroni and cheese, topped off with Grandmother's famous cornbread. "God sure is good, look at all this," he began shaking his head like he was going to cry.

"Boy stop playing," I playfully hit my brother laughing, "Gabbie I bet you didn't know just how crazy this boy was uh?"

She laughed, "I kind of guessed that Kai had a crazy side."

I smiled at my brother, "Kai after the food is blessed you just better let your sister go first to get some food," Mama said giving out instructions, "then after your sister you let Gabbie get hers next since she is a guest." She then nodded at Daddy, "go on Charles so your greedy son can fix his plates." Mama chuckled as Daddy started his very short blessing, my guess was that was for Kai's benefit, "now everybody let's eat!"

"Amen," everyone sang again as plates were being passed around. Clinking glasses and dishes of people fixing plates faded into total silence while we began to eat. Even Aunt Regina's six year old chatterbox son, Jacob Jr. was quiet at the kids table. It seemed nothing could ever stop that boy from running his mouth, but today fried chicken seemed to be the cure.

"Mrs. Parker I must say that this food is delicious," Amir said breaking the silence.

"Oh thank you baby," Mama said about to put a fork full of greens into her mouth, then Aunt Karen started coughing, "but Karen's world famous fried chicken is just absolutely wonderful as well."

"Oh I'm sorry Ms. Karen," Amir covered his mouth as chuckles were spreading around the table, "let me just say it like this then, *everybody everything* is delicious. I hope that now I've covered all the cooks," he laughed as the rest of us laughed at him too. Amir then excused himself from the table to throw his plate away, as I followed him into the kitchen.

"Hey can I just explain something to you first," I started as he turned around slowly. I grabbed his hand, "come on follow me," I led him to my childhood room which was mostly in tact. It looked pretty much the same as it did when I left for college pink and white all over the place.

"So what's up?" Amir asked closing the door behind him.

"Look," I sat at the edge of my old daybed as he took a seat in the desk chair, "let me start by saying that I *am* falling in love with you too, but I don't want a relationship just yet," I closed my eyes and exhaled slowly then looked at Amir who was very attentive. "There's so much more that you don't know about that I went through with Damon. And a lot of those things, I just haven't got over yet because some of those things cut so deep."

Amir blew into his hands, "but Summer its been a little over four months since ya'll broke up," he tried to plead his case.

"Exactly *only* four months," I looked at him with tears forming in my eyes, "four months of freedom compared to six years of imprisonment. Six years of feeling like I'm worthless, six years of feeling lowdown and feeling like scum. Six years of getting beat up by a man who turns out to be married, then he lies to his wife and tells her that I'm his freaking sister." My voice cracked as tears began to flow down my face, "do you know how many times that I've tried to hide bruises, or try to cover up hair that I lost because I was so stressed out that my hair began to fall out? Plus how many—" I started sobbing biting my bottom lip about to confess to Amir something I never even told my cousins or anybody else for that matter about countless miscarriages that I've had over the last six years which totaled out to be three including this last one at the beginning of the year. Two of the miscarriages were the result of heavy stress including the latest, but the other was the result of being kicked multiple times in the stomach after telling him that I *might* be pregnant. Yeah Damon was that nasty and cruel, but he mostly did that because the baby wasn't going to be his, but it was Lamar's baby.

"Come here," Amir stood up and pulled me into his arms holding me tight, "I am so sorry, I know he put you through a lot," he kissed my forehead.

"That's not even the half of it," I pulled back and started to wipe one side of my face as Amir helped me wipe the other side, "there's still so much more that I haven't even got to tell you yet."

"Shhhh," he said barely over a whisper still holding me, "I can't bear hearing anything else he did to you right now," the room fell silent as Amir continued to make me feel so safe as my tears started to dry up. Even though we weren't talking, his actions and the way he held on to me spoke louder than any words. With his simple touch it let me know that he wasn't going to let anything like that ever happen to me again. My response by holding tightly to him was saying that I trust that you won't hurt me.

A knock at the door interrupted our silent conversation, "hey it's time for the gifts," Brandi said as she opened the door, "oh my bad, am I interrupting something?"

"Naw girl," I smiled hoping she didn't notice the dried up tears, "we were just talking that's all," I released the tight grip I had on Amir.

"Uh-uh," she smirked as if she didn't believe that was the only thing going on, "your mother said come on back in here to get your presents."

"Thank you B," I said to Brandi as she walked out the door, "we'll talk later ok?" I said to Amir.

"Summer," Amir pulled me back into him then looked into my eyes, "it doesn't even matter the other thing you were going to tell me. Just know this, I'm not going anywhere."

I smiled at Amir then grabbed his hand and began walking back into the dining room without another word. When we got back into the room there were two big gift bags on the table next to a small box.

"Thank you all so much," I sat at the table in front of the gifts. The first one was a frame so that I could place my degree inside. The next gift was a big graduation teddy with a cap and gown. My family really knew me, because I still love teddy bears and stuffed animals to this day. When I finally opened the small box it contained keys that looked like it belonged to a car. "Okay now whose keys?" I asked holding them in the air smiling, "ha ha good joke."

"That's no joke little sis," Malachi said reaching for my hand, "come follow me," he pulled me up.

"Please don't play Kai," I said following him into the kitchen where the door was that leads to the garage.

"You ready?" He asked as most of our family stood behind us as he started to open the door. Once Malachi opened it all the way there set a brand new silver 2008 Range Rover Sport with a red bow, "it's all yours."

"Oh my God!" I clasped my hands together over my mouth, "its mine? You're not playing with me?"

"Congratulations little sister," Malachi dangled the keys in my smiling face. I grabbed them and ran to my new truck.

*   *   *

"And I say so long farewell, my life's moving forward, my ship has sailed," I sang quietly along with Ciara as she blared through the speakers of my new car while I drove down the street with my cousins, "and I'm so glad *it's over, my heart is well. After all that I've been through,* **I found myself***!"* Although I was singing softly, I sung *I Found Myself* boldly. I bought Ciara's CD a couple of months after the emergency room thing with Damon. I remember the first time hearing this song and I just started crying because the words of that song meant so much to me. It was like she was singing everything I wanted to say to everybody, I found myself, and I'm glad that I finally did.

"Summer this truck is so dope," Brandi said from the passenger seat, "your brother really spoils you."

I shrugged my shoulders smiling, "I guess that's what happens when you're the apple of your big brother's eye," I laughed, "and the fact that I'm his only sister helps too."

"Girl," that was Ken from the backseat, "you know it's been so long since we've *cruised* around on a Sunday night."

"Oh God it's been *way* too long," Bri said also in the backseat, "man it has to have been about five or six years ago at least."

"Yeah the last time I remember was when Ken got her brand new Mercedes from her brand new hubby," I said cruising down the streets, "and before you heifers started having babies and stuff."

"Oh miss thang," Brandi said pointing her finger at me, "you gonna be next after Bri."

"Excuse me?" I said caught off guard by her comment, "what does that suppose to mean?" I asked nervously laughing, *man if they only knew, Bri and I could have been having our babies around the same time*, I thought.

"Whatever Summer, you know what or *who* I'm talking about," Brandi said as I glanced at the smirk she wore proudly, "I saw you and Amir all hugged up in your old room today," she announced.

Kennede and Brianna stopped their private conversation to join ours, "what?!" Ken exclaimed, "So what was going in that room Ms. Summer?"

"Nothing you guys," I said blushing now turning the corner heading back to Mama's house so these heifers could get their kids and their cars, "Amir and I were just talking, the conversation got a little emotional for me and he was comforting me that's all."

"Uhm," they said in unison as if they didn't believe what I was saying, "so girl are ya'll together or what?"

"Well," I exhaled, "he wants a relationship, but ya'll know that things with Damon ended only four months ago. I'm learning to love myself and I'm comfortable by myself right now. Plus I'm still healing over everything that Damon put me through," I continued to plead my case, "six years of hurt, beating, and other stuff, I can't get over all of that in just four months. Amir seems to understand though; he says he'll wait for me."

"Yeah he may wait, but for how long?" I heard Bri say behind me, "I mean he says he'll wait and that sounds nice, but how long is he actually going to wait Summer? I mean most men aren't going to keep waiting for a woman especially in your predicament."

"What does that mean Bri?" I asked beginning to get an attitude, "what do you mean *my predicament?*"

"Well," she shrugged her shoulders, "you just got out of an abusive relationship so you have a lot of baggage," I rolled my eyes at her statement even though what she was saying was true. "If he waits any longer he'll began to get tired, then he may realize that he doesn't want somebody with all the emotional baggage that comes with what you've been through."

"Now I disagree with you on that Brianna," Kennede stepped in for my defense before I could respond, "if he's a *real* saved man, then he will wait and he'll do what he can to help her through the emotional baggage. Plus he'll help her without trying to sleep with her or interfere with what God is trying to do with her."

I had came to a stoplight and I was able to look back at Kennede, "thanks Ken," I winked at her and she nodded.

Brianna rolled her eyes, "here you go," she started to say with much attitude, "Kennede you always acting like you are *'holier than thou'* just because you go to church two more Sunday's than the rest of us."

"I never said that I was trying to be all holy and stuff," Kennede spoke up, "I have my struggles and my sins too, but I'm just telling my cousin who is more like a sister to me to consult with the Lord before she makes any life changing decisions."

"Before this gets too heated I do want to say something too," Brandi finally spoke up next me, "all I want to say to you Summer is, anything that's apart of your destiny you can't afford to lose, but anything that's not you can't afford to keep."

"Wow," was all I could say as I glanced over at Brandi who looked like she was speaking to herself as well, "that's pretty deep B."

"Girl you just do you until you're ready for a relationship again," Brandi began to say, "and if he's still there in the end, then he's the one, if not keep on moving forward because God has it all worked out either way."

"True," was all I could think to say as I pulled into Mama's driveway pondering the words that Brandi just shared. "Well ladies it's been a wonderful evening, but its time for me to say holla."

"Yes it's been an *interesting* evening," Kennede said opening the door as the rest of them did, "bye girl be careful," she said and the others followed suit by saying their goodbyes as well.

While they were walking up to the door Amir opened it, almost as if he knew the girls were on their way up to it, "hey are you leaving?" He leaned into my car.

"Yeah I need to go, there is so much I need to just sit back and think about," I said to him referring to the conversation I just had about him with my cousins, "do you wanna follow me home to make sure I get there safely?" I asked mostly because I did want his company plus I wanted to finish our unfinished talk, I was ready to be completely honest with him about the miscarriages and everything.

"Sure," he smiled, "don't be driving to fast either, Ms. Thang."

"Whatever boy," I waved my hand at him, "you just try to keep up," I said then took off going 45 mph after hitting the street. I made it home in ten minutes when it normally took me about twenty-five minutes. "So what took you so long?" I asked Amir as he walked up next to me while I was walking to my apartment door.

"Oh girl please," he said, "I was right behind you the whole time," he moved closer to me and I could feel his body pressing up against my back. "Like I said, I was behind you the whole time," he whispered in my ear.

I closed my eyes and butterflies hit my stomach as I was trying to unlock the door. "Boy you better back it on up," I said nervously lying. I really didn't want him to stop talking in my ear regardless to what he was saying, "But I was totally shocked by my brother's gift." I said trying to take the focus off this moment that could end in a way that I wasn't quite ready for yet.

"I know," he said as we walked into the living room and put my other gifts on the couch, "uh Summer this was on the floor I think you dropped it walking in," he handed me a pink envelope.

I looked at the back of the card then turned it to the front where it had my first and last name. "No I don't think I dropped it," I proceeded to open the card. It was very pretty a light pink card that simply spelled out the words Congratulations with multi colored balloons. I opened the card, "oh my God."

"What's wrong?" Amir asked, but I couldn't answer because of the shock, "Summer who is the card from?"

I looked up at him with confusion and fear then simply said, "Damon."

13
Brandi

"What?!" I said in total shock as I was talking to Summer. She called me to tell me that Damon's crazy ass left a card at her house, which hit home with me. After the whole rape thing, that nigga would show up at random places trying to give me things too. That lasted for about a month or two, right before I moved in with Jayson. I tried really hard to keep that on the low, and so far it's worked, but recently I swear it's like it's happening all over again making me totally paranoid in front of Jay. Something I didn't want to do, let him know what happen before he gets locked up for killing that man because that's exactly what would happen if I told Jayson Hill. But I think my shouting startled Jayson because he flinched when I started screaming.

"What's going on babe?" He asked but I held up my hand because I was still trying to listen to Summer too, "well excuse me," he said mocking my voice.

"B, I'm so scared," Summer said frantically, "I mean, Amir is still here with me. Ken and Bri are on their way over here after Raymond gets over Ken's to watch RaeLynn."

"Well I'm on my way too," I said looking over at Jay, "baby turn around and head toward Summer's to drop me off, please?"

"Thanks B," she sounded relieved, "I think that's them at the door now, I'll just see you in a few minutes."

"Okay girl," I closed my cell phone, "I can't believe this crazy nigga."

"What's up baby?" Jayson said totally clueless to why I was making him take me over my cousin's house when we were only three blocks away from our home. "And who's crazy?"

"Damon," I said with disgust, but Jayson glanced at me puzzled, "I know right," I stated as if I already knew what he was thinking, hell what we *all* thought.

"Yeah, I thought he died," Jayson said just as surprised as I was.

"We did too," I said shaking my head, "well, I guess he didn't and now this crazy Negro is leaving stuff at her door."

"So did you want me to just drop you off?" He questioned.

"Yeah," I simply replied, "because Jordan doesn't need to be around all of this. Plus Kennede isn't even bringing RaeLynn over either, so you can drop me off and I'll have Bri or somebody bring me home."

"Okay that's cool," Jayson said as we pulled into Summer's apartment complex, "babe if you need me though, I'm only a call away and I can drop Jordan off with my mom's."

"Thanks," I responded to his offer, "hopefully it won't get to that point, plus Amir's with her now."

"Okay," he chuckled, "pretty boy, what's he going do?"

I twisted my face up and looked over at him, "what's that suppose to mean? That just because he could be a male model he can't protect her?" I questioned.

"Naw man," he smiled and pulled in front of Summer's building, "go on and be with your cousin alright?"

"We gonna finish this," I said taking off my seat belt, "and for your info, Amir is a second degree black belt and he's registered to carry a gun. So he can kick butt and he's packing," Jayson continued to laugh and waved his hand at me, "so just because he has a pretty face, no excuse me, a fine face and the body of a God," he cleared his throat to remind me he was still sitting there, I just waved my hand back at him. "Anyway, just because of all that doesn't make him unable to handle his business. Some people could say or *think* something of you, a hard core hustler with a tongue ring and braids," I snapped my fingers and then quickly got out of the car laughing.

I slammed the door, but Jay rolled down the window, "ha ha funny B," he pointed his finger at me no longer smiling. "You gonna pay for that when your but gets home."

I blew a kiss at him, "I still love you Jayson," I said still laughing, "Trust me I know what that tongue ring is for," I raised my eyebrow.

"Bye Mommy!" Jordan said hitting the back window. For a minute I almost forgot that he was back there. Let me stop, I did forget that boy was back there, otherwise I wouldn't have said my last comment to Jayson.

"Mommy will be home a little later okay?" I opened the back door and kissed Jordan on the forehead, "I love you."

"Love you too," he smiled as I waved at him closing the door.

"And I love you too," I said now speaking to Jay, "we *are* gonna finish when I get home."

"Yeah you right," he smiled, "because there's something that I need to explain to you."

"I can't wait for your *explanation*," I smiled, "because you just *explain* things *so* well."

"You are too much," he waved me off laughing, "hurry up and get in there so I can pull off please."

I walked up to Summer's door, "hey girl its me Brandi," I said so they wouldn't pull the guns out at me when they opened the door. Ken answered it and I waved at Jay, "hey girl, so now what's going on?"

"Girl this," Ken reached over to Summer's coffee table and handed me what seemed to a birthday card, "girl I can't believe this," she said as I was looking the card over.

"What I can't believe is that he's still alive," I said sitting down on the couch next to Summer, but before getting comfortable I hugged her. I thru up the peace sign to my sister who was sitting in the living room chair. "What did he do, did he get *raised* from the dead?"

Summer shook her head then put her hand on it as if she was getting a headache, "I don't even know. I was sure that he was going to die after the injuries that he sustained that's the reason that I never pressed charges I was just sure that he would die that day." she stated looking over at me and I could see that she had been crying, " But Amir is in Chyna's old bedroom trying to get in touch with him to find out what happen."

"Amir is gonna call Damon?" Brianna questioned, "are you sure that's safe?"

"Well, he's calling Damon's house," Summer said running her fingers through her hair, which she recently cut again into a cheek length bob, "but hopefully Amir can just talk to his wife to find out what happen with him."

"Who's wife?" We, Kennede, Brianna, and I asked at the same time.

"Damon's wife," Summer said as a tear rolled down her face, I put my arm around her, "I found out that night I had to go the hospital that he was married."

"Hold up," Kennede said standing in the space that was near Summer's dining room table, "back it up, now I know that you went to the hospital because Damon beat you down, but huh you left out the part where you found out he had a wife."

"I didn't tell any of you because I was," she paused and exhaled, "I don't why I left that out. I guess I was just feeling a little bit of deliverance because I thought I was finally gonna be free from him forever. I thought God had taken him out of my life and I was *finally* free from that demon, but now here he is again," she looked over at the card with tears in her eyes, "why won't he just leave me alone?"

"Don't let him win Summer," Kennede came over and sat on the other side then she wrapped her arm around Summer, "this is just satan trying to get the best of you, don't let him win girl. As long as we are here and God is watching over you, God's not going to let the devil get the best of you. Baby the devil is a liar, and he's defeated," she held onto Summer.

"I know God is keeping me," she began to sob, "but I'm just scared you all," she wiped her tears, "ya'll know better than anyone that Damon's crazy and he's beat the hell out of me before. I'm afraid that he'll do something like that again."

"Don't fear him because God is with you," I said this time as we all gathered around Summer, "Lord please just protect her Jesus name," I said a small prayer as we all cried.

"Well, I was able to talk to Linda because Damon wasn't home yet." Amir said coming from Chyna's room standing in the hallway entrance.

"Who the hell is Linda?" Brianna asked before any of us could say anything, "by the way, I'm starving can I go meddle in your kitchen?" She asked Summer.

"Go ahead," Summer waved her hand toward the kitchen, "but Linda is Damon's wife, so now what did she say?"

"Can I sit here first?" Amir asked if he could sit in the seat that Brianna left available to rummage through Summer's refrigerator. "Okay, so he obviously survived the ordeal at the hospital, I didn't get to talk much to Linda because I didn't want to seem suspicious or anything. So she just briefly told me that he's been out of the hospital for about three weeks, but he's not able to walk yet."

"But he's able to move around in some kind of way," Summer said, "that nigga must be doing well enough to bring his crazy self over here."

"Well maybe not," Amir started, "Linda said that he was out with his brother because he can't drive or anything either so his brother's been taking him places when Linda isn't able to, she said he was gone when she came back home from work."

"Okay I know he had an accident but what happened to him that he can't walk?" Brianna asked smacking her lips as she came from the kitchen and sat on Summer's ottoman, "oh yeah, thanks for the food too Summer."

"No problem," she looked over at Brianna who had a paper plate full of Cool Ranch Doritos, some type of sandwich, and a Nutty Bar with a cup of some kind of red drink, "but you know you owe me some more Hawaiian Punch now?" She gave a smirk.

"Okay people," I said to my sister and Summer because I wanted to hear the rest of the story from Amir, "Amir baby, can you please finish what you were saying please?"

"Okay," he chuckled at us, "to answer your question Brianna somehow he injured his spine during the accident which now makes him unable to walk," he paused to take a drink of bottled water, "but she didn't get to talk to me for a long time, she said that she would have him call me whenever he gets back in the house, maybe then I will find out the rest from him."

"Oh my God," Summer leaned forward and blew into her hands, "so with him not being home yet, there's a possibility that he could be still circling around here. Do you think he'd do that?" She asked looking over at Amir.

"My car is outside and he knows my car," Amir answered, "so he may not try anything knowing that I'm probably here, well at least he better not try to do anything," Amir came over as I moved to the side so he could sit next to Summer, he put his arm around her, "don't worry baby girl, we won't let anything happen to you."

"Yeah Summer," I said, "that negro is not going to get close to you, and if he tries to he has to go through *us* first."

"That's right," Brianna said loudly now munching on the Nutty Bar, "I maybe pregnant but I'll hit him with my big stomach then he won't be able to go anywhere," she laughed and we joined in with her laughter.

"Bri you are crazy," Kennede laughed, "but on a serious note, Summer I don't think that it's safe for you to stay here by yourself. Maybe you can stay with one of us or one of us can stay here with you, but I don't think that you should be alone."

"I know I shouldn't be alone, but I'm not trying to put anybody out of their houses," Summer said looking straight, "plus if I just stay there for one night, what about the night after and the night after that. I mean that's really nice of ya'll to offer, but I...uhm—"

"Summer I can stay with you," Amir cut her off, "I mean if you want me to, but that's a good idea because you don't need to be alone. And it would probably be better if I stay here with you because I think Damon knows where I live and he'll probably figure it out that you'd stay with me if you're not here."

I looked over at them with my eyebrows raised then I looked over at Kennede and Brianna who also had the same reaction that I did, "but Amir is right," I said, "you just don't need to be by yourself and maybe you should even consider moving or something."

"Actually Brandi I've been thinking about moving even before all of this, ever since Chyna moved out I felt there's no point in me having a two bedroom apartment when it's just me. So I've seriously been thinking about that." Summer said.

"Hold on Summer," Amir kind of perked up, "Damon knows where I *use* to live, he hasn't been to my new house the one I just bought. He only came to my apartment before I moved, so if you want to you can stay at *my* house I have plenty of room because it's four bedrooms and I can only sleep in one bedroom at a time."

"I mean that's fine with me if you really want me to," Summer's face brighten, "but can we just make sure that he's not gonna try to follow you or something."

"Right," Kennede said, "we can even follow you to make sure that he's not going to try anything."

"Remember though," Amir paused as if he were thinking, "I asked Linda to tell him to call me when he gets home. So as soon as he calls and we know that he's in for the rest of the night then we can go on and make the move to my house and-" Amir was cut off by his cell phone ringing, "here's Damon calling me now," he looked at the caller id, "I'll be right back, Summer you go pack you something for a couple of days okay?" he said looking at her.

"Okay," she said raising quickly from the couch, "I thank you guys so much for being here with me," she leaned down and gave me a hug first then the rest of the girls.

"Girl we are family, we'll always be here," I said to her, "and since we are all family and there for one another, I need a ride home from my *family*, so anybody going my way?"

"I got you sis," Brianna spoke up, "I have to pass that way anyway."

"Thank ya girl," I smiled and blew a kiss at her, "and when my niece is born, I'm ready for babysitting duty."

"Alright I'm gonna remember that," Brianna pointed to me.

"Okay, Damon is at home for the night," Amir said as he walked back into the room, "so we better get going Summer, are you gonna ride with me or are you driving?"

Summer walked back in the room with a small roll away suitcase and duffel bag, "yeah I'm driving," she stated, "I just got one of my dream cars so yes I'll drive it to your house."

"Alright girl lets go," Amir smiled taking the bags from her and heading toward the door, "you guys are so much more than cousins to her, ya'll have got to be the closest cousins I've ever seen. But thanks for being there for Summer."

"That's our girl," Brianna said, "like you said that's family, and nothing I mean *nothing* can break that up."

"Or nobody either," Summer spoke up heading to the door as we all followed, "again thanks so much guys you have no idea how much you mean to me."

"Thanks again Bri for bringing me home," I said as Brianna pulled up to my driveway.

"You know its no big deal," she said to me, "I'll see you later."

"Okay girl," I said getting out of the car. I walked up to the door, "dang boy was you sitting by the door waiting for me?" I asked because just as I was about to put the key into the door Jay opened it swiftly

"I wasn't waiting for you, but I heard the car door so I glanced out the window and saw my beautiful fiancée," he said hugging me then kissing me on the lips, "and yeah I still got something that I need to *explain* to you from earlier," he looked down at me with this sexy face.

"Is Jordan already asleep?" I held on to him, "because I *do* want to know what you have to *explain* to me."

"Yep he's sleep," he bent down and started to kiss me again, this time giving me more tongue action, "but I've gotta to make a quick run."

Oh hell here we go again, I thought as I frowned and backed away from him then started to head toward the steps. "Okay Jayson, I'll just see you later." I through my hands up in the air.

He grabbed my arm and pulled me back closer to him, "see you getting all upset and it ain't even like that, I told you I'm done with all of that baby and I meant it." he looked into my eyes.

"So baby where do you have to run to huh?" I looked at him as if I was pleading with him.

"Baby one of my boys is downstairs in the basement, his girl dropped him off and I told him that I'd take him home as soon as you got back," he pulled me into him then kissed my forehead. "Brandi I love you, and I promised you I wasn't going to do that anymore and I meant it."

"Alright Jay," I softly said still looking into his eyes as well, "please hurry back I'm gonna go on and go upstairs to wait for you to come back to me," I pulled away from him again and headed toward the steps, "oh by the way who is the friend?"

"Oh you remember the dude I told you I was working with on the mini mall thing?" He asked and I shook my head, "it's him, let me get him so you can meet him," Jay walked to the basement door as I stood on the bottom step, "ah LB, my girl is back so I can take you now if you ready."

Jay came to the step in front of me and kissed me again, "I love you Jay," I said with sincerity.

"I love you too," he replied.

"Alright Jay here I come," I heard a voice say in the distant as I also heard footsteps. Jay turned around and I put my arms around his neck then started to kiss him.

"Girl you better stop before you start something," he said and I smiled still playing with him.

"Damn man you sure gotta lot of steps from your basement," the voice said clearly this time and I stopped kissing Jay's neck because this voice sounded so familiar, "man that damn, oh my bad, how you doing Miss?" The voice said again this time I cringed.

I looked up and I was face to face again with Lester Black and I froze. "Baby this is my partner LB or Black whatever you wanna call him." I was so stunned with a touch of fear that it caused me not to even be able to allow my eyes to grow big like someone in my situation would probably have done.

"Hey how you doing?" He smiled and extended his hand for me to grab, I just looked at it then back up at him.

"Babe, are you okay?" Jayson turned around and looked at me, "babe the man is trying to be nice."

No he's not, I thought, *that man raped me, he beat me and left me for dead there's nothing nice about him!* I wanted to scream. I wanted to say anything but no words came out at first. "I uhm I'm sorry," I apologized but definitely not to Black but to Jay, "babe I'm really not feeling to well now, uhm I'm going upstairs I'll just see you when you get back," I turned around about to walk up the steps, "uh see ya'll later."

"Wait a minute," Black said, "do I know you, cause you look really familiar?" My heart was now in my stomach as I stopped walking up the steps and began to turn around slowly, *I know he's not about to say he knows me from the club*, I thought.

"She works at Mercy Hospital," Jayson said and I turned back to look at Black again, he wore this sick looking smile because he already knew who I was, and it made me want to throw up. I rolled my eyes then started to think, *did this bastard do this on purpose? Did he become friends with Jay to get to me so he could try to hurt me further?*

"Yeah that's probably where I've seen you," Black said with a sly grin. *No you idiot! You raped me; you hurt me and got me pregnant, damn you!* I continued to think and tears were trying to escape from my eyes, but I couldn't let them fall in front of them. "Yeah I'm sure that's where I've seen you, my mom's was just in there for a couple of days."

"You probably saw her then," Jayson said as if he were talking for me, "well babe I'll be right back."

"Okay," I quickly said and got out of sight up the steps, *what the hell is that bastard up to?* I thought. *Oh my God he's been in my house for God knows how long and he probably has the layout already memorized and just waiting on a chance to catch me alone.*

"It was nice to meet you," I heard Black say but I didn't say a word.

"I'm out babe," Jayson said and I heard the front door open and close, that's when the tears began to flow.

"Oh my God!" I cried out softly because I didn't want to wake Jordan. "I can't let this happen again what am I going to do?" I asked and my body was shaking just as much as it was the night he raped and beat the hell out of me. Even in my shaken state I managed to grab my cordless phone and dial Kennede's number. She was the only one that knew about that dreadful night and the nightmare that continued to happen even until now.

"Hello?" Kennede answered and all I could do was sob, "Brandi is that you?"

"Yeah it's me," I said palpitating, "he…was… in… my…house…Ken… he…was here."

"Who was there B?" She asked, "Brandi please just take a deep breathe baby and calm down so you can tell me what's going on."

I took a deep breathe as she suggested, "Lester Black was here, he was in my house," I managed to say before busting into more tears.

"Oh my Lord, how did he get in there? Do you need me to come over?" she asked very concerned.

"No, no," I calmed down a little bit, but still shaking, "he was here with Jay."

"Oh my God," I heard her exhale, "and Jay still doesn't know about what happen?"

"I can't tell him about that Ken," I protested, "Jay would lose it, then if he finds out its him he'd kill him for real," I got up from the bed and went to the bathroom to wipe my face before Jayson got home and started to ask a lot of questions.

"Brandi what are you going to do then?" Kennede asked as if she were fed up with me and this situation.

"I don't know," I simply said looking at myself in the bathroom mirror, "this was the first time I've seen him face to face since that night Ken, but I know that bastard has been following me or stalking me since then, but it's been almost five or six years ago. I thought I uhm, I've tried to put it out of my mind."

"B, that's because you've just tried to hide it instead of dealing with it," she started. "I mean girl you went through a lot that night and days following. Brandi you were pregnant as a result of a rape, then you had an abortion because of it, girl you never dealt with it. Then on top of all of that, you say he's been stalking you and that's a lot to handle by yourself. Then actually seeing him like that tonight has caused you to have a near breakdown, its time to tell Jay and start working through this. Honey you two are about to get married next month and he needs to know."

"Kennede I know all that, but I can't tell him," I said still looking in the mirror then beginning to cry again, "how am I going to tell him that I was raped while I was stripping. Then as a result of that I ended up pregnant and because I didn't want to bring a baby into this world under that kind of condition that I had an abortion? Huh Ken, how am I going to tell Jay all of that?"

"You don't have to worry about telling me," my heart was headed toward my stomach again, I turned around and saw Jay standing in our bedroom doorway, my mouth flew open.

"Uh Ken," I said almost forgetting that she was on the phone, "I have to go."

"Is that Jayson I just heard?" she questioned.

"Uhm yeah," I clicked the off button before she could say anything else, now it seemed I was shaking more than I was before. "Jayson baby I didn't hear you come in."

"Brandi," he said with a blank look, "what were just saying to Ken? I hope I didn't hear you right, rape, pregnant, abortion?"

I shook my head crying even harder walking toward him, "baby-I-uhm," I exhaled, "I just didn't know how to tell you something like that."

He didn't say anything and walked closer to me then pulled me into him and held me tight, "Brandi, I love you so much," he said continuing to hold me tight as I sobbed even more, "baby you could have told me," he walked me over to the bed then he brought my vanity chair in front of where I was sitting, "tell me everything baby, please."

"Jay, I just don't, I mean I can't uhm-"

"Baby yes you can tell me," he rose his voice, but he paused then closed his eyes before saying, "look I'm sorry, but baby please, please tell me what happen."

"Jay," I exhaled hard, "okay it was the last night that I was working at the club and I was on my way home," I paused to swallow the huge lump in my throat. "While I was walking down the hallway I was forced into a closet by somebody that was behind me. Once he forced me into the closet-" I said as tears fell like raindrops on a stormy night, "He just, he—"

"Who is he?" Jayson asked cutting me off. I looked up and I could see the anger in his eyes.

"Please let me finish," I said looking into his glossy eyes, "so once I was in the closet, he starting slapping me and ripping my clothes off and—"

"Who is he Brandi?" Jayson asked again with more anger in his voice. I looked down and saw his fist balled up, "Brandi do you remember who he was?"

I barely shook my head, "I remember the pain from him punching me," I started to say with tears continuing to fall as I tried to wipe them away, "I remember the pain from the rape, I remember finding out I was pregnant—"

"Pregnant?" Jay whispered cutting me off yet again. I looked back up and saw tears on the brim of his eyes like they were waiting to escape.

"I-I knew it wasn't yours because we weren't even back together yet," he grabbed my hands, "I remember going into that clinic with Kennede by my side, I remember the pain from that abortion," I sobbed again as Jayson pulled me into him.

"Thank you," he kissed my forehead, "thank you baby for telling me," he sniffed and I felt a tear drop my shoulder. "Baby I swear if I *ever* found out who did that to you, I swear I'd kill him," he said very seriously, then pushed back and began to look at me with this strange face, "did that dude LB have something to do with this?"

My heart dropped again, "huh?" was all that came out of my mouth at first, "babe why would you say that?

"B, you started to act kind of uncomfortable around him," he said and my mind went blank. I didn't think that Jay had noticed my actions, "So was it him?"

"Uhm," I said trying to make a quick decision, whether I should tell him the truth and get everything out in the open or just continue this lie, "no baby, but his voice sounded a lot like the guy that did it," I opted for the lie. We had about a month before we were supposed to be married, and right now I didn't want to be alone. If I had said yes, Jay would have taken every gun he owns out of this house so he could kill Black. As much as I didn't want to worry about him stalking me again, I couldn't bear being without Jay because he would get locked up for life and right now my heart wouldn't know how to handle that. "But it was just the voice thing that got to me, because if I can try to remember I think the guy was a lot lighter," I closed my eyes tight, but tears still managed to escape, "I only saw part of his arm, I never saw his face," I now sobbed, I felt Jay pull me into his arms and he held onto me firmly.

"Brandi baby please don't ever feel that you can't tell me anything," he squeezed tighter, "but like I said before, I swear if I *ever* found out who did it, I'm gonna kill him."

"Jay don't even think about that because I don't want you going to jail over it, I need you here with me baby," I sighed still sobbing in his arms, "I love you babe."

"Brandi I love you too," he said with a cracked voice, then he squeezed me tighter, "God please keep us, please."

14
Brianna

"Knock, knock," I said as I opened the door to Grandmother's house.

"Hey baby," Grandmother said coming around the corner meeting me in the living room, "I'm surprised to see you today; you don't normally come over on days you've worked."

"I came over because Mama said she had something for the baby's room or something like that," Mama lived with Grandmother. She moved in right after Granddaddy died so Grandmother wouldn't have to be alone in this big house.

"Oh yeah," she sat on the couch and I sat next to her, "she had something for you, but I done forgot what she said it was now, although I am making the baby an afghan."

"Thank you so much," I said smiling as I began to remember when we were younger how she always made them for me and Brandi in our favorite colors, "I still have the one you made me when I was twelve years old."

"I'm glad that you still have it," she said then her face became serious, "Brianna baby, I have a question for you."

"Okay," I said hesitant assuming that her question had something to do with my pregnancy, "what do you want to know?" I asked softly.

She patted her lap, "come on lay your head on my lap," she said then I laid my head across Grandmother's lap like I was three years old instead of a grown woman.

"Grand-Mama can you scratch my scalp while I lay here?" I asked thinking back to my childhood and how she would do this when Brandi and I would spend the night when we were a lot younger.

She grabbed a comb from the coffee table and began to comb my hair, "so sweetheart," she began to say then exhaled hard, "now I maybe old but I'm not stupid. I know you didn't get pregnant on your own, so I want to know who this young man is, do I know him?"

"Well uhm," I hesitated again. I didn't want to lie to my grandmother, but I couldn't tell her that the baby's father is a married man who is older than her youngest daughter. "You might remember who he is, I grew up with him in Fort Knox." I started to lie.

She put two fingers to her chin like she was trying to think, "oh I think I remember who you're talking about, that big brown boy."

I chuckled, "Brian is his name," I said still laughing at her description of Brian, "Grand-Mama you are a mess."

"Well he is a *big brown boy*," she smiled, "so is he going to marry you before this baby comes or what?"

My smile faded, "uh no ma'am we're not going to get married," I looked up at her as she was still combing my hair, "it's not like that between us for us to get married."

"Excuse me?" She stopped combing, "what do you mean it's not like that between you two? It had to be something in order for you to end up pregnant by this young man."

"Trust me Grand-Mama it was nothing but what it was," I said hating the fact I couldn't tell my grandmother the truth. My unborn child's father is Doctor Lance Hamilton, a forty year old man who is fine as hell that I am *so* in love with him. Oh yeah by the way he's currently married with two other kids, but he said that he's leaving his wife for me. *Lord what have I started by telling her this lie?*

"So what was it?" Grandmother asked with an attitude, "just sex? Is that all it was, unprotected sex that wasn't suppose to end up like this?" She asked and my eyebrows rose.

"Grand-Mama," I said shocked by her obvious rhetorical question. I set up then began to look at her, "I mean this is kind of uncomfortable to talk to you about."

"Baby I'm almost seventy years old and I've been pregnant eight times and as I recall none of them were *immaculate conceptions* either," she stated boldly as I looked at her puzzled, "what is it?" she asked.

"Grand-Mama you just said that you were pregnant eight times," I looked down at my hands and began counting the kids she has in the apparent order she had them, "ok there's Uncle Bill that's one, Aunt Julie, then it was Uncle Marvin," I held up three fingers as I continued to count. "Alright then there's my mama, Aunt Karen then the last one was Aunt Regina," I held up six fingers then looked at Grandmother as she closed her eyes then nodded, "uhm Grand-Mama that's only six kids, but you just said *eight* pregnancies."

"Exactly eight pregnancies but I have six children," she touched my chin with her palm, "baby you're a smart girl so do the math."

I sat there working the math equation that Grandmother had given me. "Oh you were pregnant eight times, but only had six children," I said with wide eyes, "so you had two miscarriages or something?" I asked and she shook her head in disagreement, "okay now Grand-Mama I'm confused again," I said with my arms folded.

She chuckled, "I'll tell you this much, I did have a miscarriage when I was thirty-one years old. That was a few years after I had Karen and three years before I had Regina," she paused then looked down at her hands that were now clasped together as her smile faded. "Well the other pregnancy," she sighed, "let's just say I was young and dumb once too, before I got saved though."

I sat waiting to hear more of the story but she got quiet, "so what happen?" I broke the silence, "and how old were you? Didn't you and Granddaddy get married when you were like eighteen or something like that?" I quizzed.

"Yes baby I was nineteen when I married your Grandfather," she looked up at the black and white wedding picture of the young couple, Granddaddy wearing a regular suit with a tie, and Grandmother wearing a cream colored suit. Everyone that saw the picture thought it was just a regular picture rather than their wedding photo because Grandmother and Granddaddy couldn't afford a wedding so they married at the courthouse. I looked at the photo also, then drifted my eyes to a family picture of her, Granddaddy, and their young teenaged kids that sat right next to the wedding photo. "But I was a lot younger when I was pregnant for the first time. That's why I'm so concerned about you girls when ya'll are having these babies without having a husband, because I've been there although I have never mention that."

My eyes grew big then I became concerned, "did someone hurt you?"

"I wasn't hurt by anyone," she shook her head, "like I said it was me being young and dumb."

"So when you say that you were young and you weren't hurt," I paused, "so how young were you the first time you got pregnant?"

"You're a nosy little thing," she said in response to my question, "your aunts and uncles didn't even ask all these questions, but then again they don't know about the pregnancy I had when I was a lot younger," she paused, "to answer your question though, I was only fifteen years old the first time I was pregnant and—"

"Fifteen years old?!" I questioned in surprise cutting Grandmother off. "So what was going on that you were—"

"Hey what are you doing over here?" Mama asked walking through the front door cutting the conversation I was having with Grandmother short.

"I uhm, I came by because you said you had something for me," I stumbled for words because I was still astounded over the conversation I was just having, "so what was it that you had for me again?"

"Oh yeah," Mama sat her purse down on the couch, "last week when Mama and I was at the store I saw the cutest little pink jumper and some other stuff I couldn't pass up."

"That's right," Grandmother said snapping her fingers as she remembered, "we sure was at the Wal-Mart I remember now. I told Bri when she first got here I forgot what it was you had for her."

"Yeah, well let me go get it for you." Mama walked out of the room toward her bedroom.

"So are you going to finish telling me the story?" I whispered to Grandmother when Mama was out of sight.

"Maybe some other time," she waved her hand at me like she was about to hit me or something, "there's a lot more I would have to explain and I just don't feel like going into all of that right now, maybe another time."

"Uh," I frowned like a child that didn't get their way, "Grand-Mama you can't just leave me hanging like that," I whined.

"Okay here it is," Mama came back in the room with two Wal-Mart bags, "I hope you like it, I just thought this was so cute so did your grandmother."

"Oh Mama I love it," I smiled at the pink and white jumper she held in front of me, "oh you got the shoes and socks to match too."

"Of course this is my first *real* grandbaby so yes she's about to get spoiled," I looked at Mama because I knew she was referring to Jordan not being her biology grandchild. "What? I'm just telling the truth, that little boy isn't Brandi's child and everybody knows it too."

"Mama you know you ain't right though," I said and she shrugged her shoulders, "but thank you anyways for the stuff. I wish you guys would stop doing all of this before the baby shower, ya'll gonna run out of stuff to get when that time comes."

"Oh no we will not," Grandmother said standing up, "well Bri your old Grandmother is getting tired and I'm going to go lay my old bones down," she said blowing me a kiss.

"Goodnight Grandmother," I said blowing a kiss back to her, "I enjoyed *talking* to you today," I smirked.

"Me too baby," Grandmother squinted her eyes as if she was sending me a message to not repeat anything that we had talked about before my mom walked in the door. Once she was out of Mama's view she turned around then looked at me, she put her index finger over her mouth as to tell me to be quiet.

I nodded my head and she sauntered to her room. I folded my arms and began to think, *I see that I'm not the only one in this family with some serious secrets.*

* * *

"So how's life in the big ATL?" I asked my older brother.

"Well you know," I heard the smile in his voice, "when you're a handsome successful young black man in Atlanta things are great," he laughed.

"Yeah I bet things are great, big time," I said referring to Donte's occupation as a sports agent. One of his *many* clients recently signed a thirty-five million dollar NFL contract with the Arizona Cardinals, so that meant 9.5 percent for Donte.

"Anyway, how are you doing Ms. Soon-to-be-mama?" he asked as I heard a car horn on his end, "Kai told me when he was up there for Summer's graduation that you were getting big."

"Yeah I am," I laid back on my couch rubbing my big belly, "well I'm going into my sixth month and your *niece* will or should be here on September 19th."

"Oh you're having a girl," he sounded excited, "so who's the nigga?" He asked with his voice now in a stern tone sounding like Granddaddy.

"You know who you sound like?" I asked laughing.

"Ha ha Bri," he said sarcastically, "I know who I sound like, but I am for real who's this nigga?" he asked again as I heard the music from his end stop and a car door shut.

"Oh so you were serious?" I asked thinking he was just trying to be funny.

"Uh yeah Bri I am serious," he replied.

"Well," I bit my bottom lip trying to quickly decide whether or not to tell my older brother what I told our grandmother or just tell him the truth, "how much time do you have?"

"I just walked in the house, I don't have anywhere to go until about eleven-thirty tonight," he paused and I guessed he was probably looking down at his watch or looking at a clock that revealed that it was only eight forty-five. "So go on, I'm sitting on my couch waiting."

"Okay," I said and exhaled hard, "well, I-uhm, I work with the baby's father, he's a doctor," I started to tell Donte. I chose to tell him the truth since he'd be here in town in a couple of weeks for Brandi's wedding. More than likely the lie I told Grandmother about Brian being the father could blow up in my face since he and Donte may come in contact with each other during my brother's visit home. Donte still kept in contact with Brian's sisters Janie and Samantha, but more than likely he would be seeing Sam as we called her because those two have had an on and off again relationship for years. But the Samantha and Donte saga is whole other story.

"So you done caught yourself a doctor," his voice changed back to the way it was when we first got on the phone, "what's his name? Do I know him?" he asked.

"I don't think you know him," I said, *well I hope you don't know him*, I thought, "but his name is Lance."

"How you know I don't know him?" he asked then I heard a phone ring in the background. *Thank God, saved by the bell,* I thought. "Hold on a minute, hello?" He said answering his other phone, "yeah but I thought we- okay, I'll be there as soon as I can. Damn!" I heard something slam, "hey Bri I'm so sorry for that, but I've gotta get out of here like right now."

"Okay that's cool," I said relieved that our conversation about Lance wasn't going any farther, "I'll talk to you later."

"Yeah I love you," he said.

"Me too," I said hanging up the phone. I sat there a minute just starring at a blank television screen before I decided to go to the kitchen for a bite to eat. Just as I was about to get up, I saw my cell phone light up then it started beeping letting me know I had a text message. I slid my phone open.

1 New Message from Lance: Hey Beautiful I miss you.

I smiled and typed back; **I miss you too, let's do something about it☺**.

He replied; **Come over please?**

I got up from the couch; **I'm on my way**; I typed back to him. *I'll just stop at McDonald's before I get to his place*, I thought.

Well Lance did what he said he would do, he left his wife and moved into his own apartment about two weeks ago. Of course you know I've been there almost every other day I could be. I was falling even harder for this man and I loved every minute of it. "Dang girl, anything for me in that bag?" Lance asked as I was walking thru his apartment door.

"I mean you can have some," I said putting the bag on the coffee table, "but I was so hungry I think I ordered everything on the menu, so there's probably a burger or something in there I could give you."

"I'm just kidding baby, but come here though," he grabbed my hand, "the only thing I want right now *isn't* in that bag."

"Really?" I asked looking into his eyes as he bent down and kissed me. I closed my eyes for a brief moment, *God I love this man. I can't wait until his divorce is finalized then we can be with each other exclusively.* "As much as I love you, I am starving ten times more and so is your daughter." I rubbed my stomach and he kneeled down to kiss it.

"I can't wait for you to get here," he said speaking to my stomach. I smiled so hard that my cheeks started to hurt, then he looked up at me, "I bet she's gonna look just like you, I hope she does look like you. It doesn't matter though because either way she's going to be so beautiful."

"She's gonna have some of you in her too you know," I said sitting down about to eat my food, but Lance grabbed my hand, "what's wrong babe?" I looked down at him.

"Do you understand how much I love you?" he raised up from the floor as I took a seat on his couch. I smiled then took a bite of my burger. "Bri, I'm trying to talk to you and you just gonna sit there eating?" He smiled at me with those damn dimples leading into that beautiful smile.

"Baby I understand all that," I said covering my mouth because it was filled with food, "but your child is kicking out of hunger, so I'ma eat while you go on and talk."

He chuckled, "you are too much," he kissed me on the forehead then walked toward his bedroom, "but that's what I love about to you," he yelled from the room. Lance's apartment was a simple two bedroom layout, both bedrooms having its own separate bathrooms. One of the rooms he used almost like another office, it had his computer, a bookcase filled with tons of medical books, and a futon on the opposite side.

"I love you too," I yelled back to him but was interrupted by my cell phone ringing, I looked at the caller id and answered, "hey big bro, is everything cool?"

"Well yes and no," he exhaled hard, "that call I got when we were on the phone earlier it was to let me know that one of my clients got injured. So the plans that I had made here I'm going to have to cancel so I can hop on a plane to New York to survey the damages," he said sounding disappointed.

"I'm sorry to hear that," I said sipping on my Hi-C, "it wasn't the client that just signed that big deal was it?"

"Man, oh naw," Donte busted out of his professional talk to go straight hood! "I thank God it wasn't him, but hell this one is just as bad. I hate to see any of my clients in this position."

"Yeah I guess that is true," I said as Lance walked back into the living room wearing only boxers and I started coughing.

"You alright sis?" Donte asked losing his "hood" talk.

"Yeah, I'm good," I put my hand over my chest as my eyes traveled up and down Lance's almost perfect butter scotch colored body, "uhm, I'm going to be honest, I'm with my baby daddy and he caught me off guard."

"Uh uhm," Donte simply sighed then began sucking his teeth, "ya'll better be glad I don't have time to talk to him, but I do plan to grill that nigga when I get there."

"My brother says hi," I partially covered the phone this time talking to Lance.

"That ain't what I said," Donte spoke louder as if he wanted Lance to hear him, "naw you tell that nigga to get ready to be grilled."

"Tell him I said hello," Lance said to me.

"Donte, he says hello back," I said acting like Donte wasn't making threats on the other end.

"Uh uhm," he said again, "you better be glad I've got to head out of here, I love you little sister and be careful."

"I love you too Donte," I said smiling at the thought of my brother playing the dual role of big brother and father. Either way I know he's trying to protect me, "and you be careful too."

"Always sis, always," he replied, "one," he hung up as I did too.

"Are you done eating yet?" Lance sat on the opposite side of the couch and grabbed the leg I had on the couch.

"Yes I—" I began to say but was cut off by my phone beeping, "who is text messaging me this late?" I asked aloud but was really talking to myself.

"That's what I'd like to know too," Lance said with an eyebrow lifted as he began to massage my swollen feet. I opened my phone and saw it was from Brian and I rolled my eyes, "so who is it?" Lance asked.

I looked up without saying a word but thinking millions, "uhm it's just a friend of mine," I lied, well in a way.

Brian was a friend, but he's a friend that has been *really friendly*; *I* just tried to call but it went straight to voicemail, I need to talk to you.

But I don't want to talk to you, I thought as I kept starring at the message trying to decide whether or not to reply, "ouch," I yelled out as Lance pinched my toe.

"Earth to Bri," he lifted one of his hands to wave at me, "you zoned out for a minute there." I looked at him looking gorgeous then back at my phone picturing Brian. Compared to Lance, Brian was, wait there is no comparison when it came to the two.

I closed my phone, "I'm so sorry about that baby," I said then lightly pitched my phone on the recliner after turning it off completely. "Okay baby you have my undivided attention."

He nodded his head without a word then went back to massaging my feet using his fingers to slowly creep up my leg. I let out a huge sigh then let my head fall back on the arm rest thinking, *forget Brian because I was already with the man that's the father of my child, the man of my dreams, and the man that is the love of my life.*

15
Summer

I sat on the couch, well to be politically correct the sectional in the living room watching the rain fall up against the window. Hearing mild drip drops as Raheem DeVaughn and Floetry crooned in the background about a *Marathon*. Ever since I moved in with Amir he has turned me on to a whole new style of music known as Neo-Soul, and since that union Raheem, Floetry, Jill Scott, with some Musiq Soulchild, India.Arie, Tweet, Maxwell and John Legend now lived in the CD changer and on my iPOD. And of course Common and The Roots with some Erykah Badu thrown into the mix for the touch of hip-hop/soul now invaded the speakers inside my Range Rover. I closed my eyes bopping my head to the music thinking that being here with Amir has been the happiest I've been in a long time.

After the night of the *graduation scare*, I haven't seen or heard from Damon and he hasn't tried to contact me and I am so relieved. I think one of the main reasons he hasn't tried to contact me is because he moved to St. Louis. Amir talks to him every now and then, the last time they talked Damon told Amir that he was moving away so that his wife could be close to her sick mother. Although I really didn't care why, but for whatever the reason he left this city, I was so glad to hear that news last week. The strange thing though is that I've gotten *very* comfortable in this short time staying with Amir. He doesn't seem to mind me staying here either, so the conversation hasn't come up yet about me moving out since the main reason

I moved in here in the first place has moved out of the city. Also since I moved in here a lot of other things have changed in my life as well.

One of the major changes is that I stopped working for Daddy at his law firm since I wasn't feeling the law thing anymore, but it's not like I'm just been sitting around on my butt doing nothing. I've started volunteering at this center that works with the Women's Ministry at church; the center is for abused women, ex drug abusers, and women who have been recently released from jail and stuff like that. Because I don't have my doctrine in Psychology, I'm unable to clinically counsel the women, but I am able to lead some of the group discussions especially the ones that deal with abused and battered women. I know for some people hearing these sad stories day in and day out, especially without any pay could be overwhelming. For me though, I'm glad I'm able to help some sister whose been where I've been, or any other sister that maybe headed in the direction one of my cousins may have experienced or even what I've been through. I think I've found my calling helping these women and giving some of them hope. I've even thought about going back to school so I could get my master's or doctrine so I can be a clinical psychologist. And staying here with Amir would help me out if I did decide to go back to school as far as money is concerned.

Okay let me quit acting like I don't have any money at all; I do have money in the bank, twelve thousand seven hundred-twenty-four dollars and ninety-eight cents, is in my checking to be exact; and I have two hundred thousand dollars in my savings account. So as far as money is concerned I'm good thanks to my brother as well as working for Daddy for the last few years. I know it's probably plenty of money to go out and buy my own house, but I'd rather finish school since I've changed my career again. Staying here would allow me to continue to save up until I'm ready to start life on my own.

I heard the garage door opening, which meant Amir was home. I looked down at my watch that read *8:15 p.m.* He had been working some serious overtime and was coming home a lot later than his five-thirty usual. Not only was he working overtime, but he began to talk to this girl from his job. I mean I know we agreed to just be friends and stuff, but I must admit every time she calls his phone or he mentions her name which is Asia, it makes me roll my eyes with jealously. That's when Amir conveniently reminds me that it was *my* decision to just be friends, and I conveniently roll my eyes again at him. Being '*just friends*' was a lot easier when I didn't have to look at his gorgeous face and beautifully sculpted body everyday. Trust me, I'm not complaining at all about what I get to see, but I tell you it makes it hard to say that's just my friend to someone who is as *fine* as he is.

The thing that has had me shook up was what happened last week. Here's what went down; I had got home a little later than I usually do, I normally get home about five in the evening, but on this day it was a little after seven when I finally made it home. Most times when I come home late or if either one of us gets home after the other, we'll let one another know that we've made it in safely. Well, this particular day Amir must have forgot that I lived there. Apparently after work he took a long shower because the scent of Dial Soap for men hit me as soon as I came through the door. I crept slowly down the hall to his bedroom to let him know I was home. Once I reached his cracked bedroom door I stopped and began to announce my arrival. I was quickly caught off guard by Amir appearing in the bathroom doorway wearing nothing but a towel with water still running down his chiseled chest and down to his legs. I know this because my eyes traveled up and down his six foot two frame thousands of times within ten seconds. The lump in my throat wouldn't allow me to talk, and I think Amir knew I was speechless because he began to laugh showing off that beautiful smile which made things even worse. The palms of my hands began to sweat and I kept trying to tell my new sea legs to move so I could leave his room, but I it seemed I wasn't going anywhere. Once I got the courage and *strength* to move after about thirty seconds, I backed up and ran to my room. After that day I haven't been right since.

"Hey Summer," I heard him say then I heard the door close. I walked into the kitchen where the door that leads to the garage was, "it smells too good in here, so what did you cook?" he asked putting his briefcase on the kitchen table and adjusting his tie as if he was about to take it off, which is exactly what he did.

"Oh thank you, I left some on the stove for you if you want it," I said turning toward the stove so I wouldn't have to watch him pretty much stripping in front of my face. "But I cooked some baked chicken breast with steamed broccoli and brown rice," I said with my back still turned away from him.

"That sounds good and I know you can cook because, well look at your family," he said and I heard him open the refrigerator. "Oh snap did you make some *Blue Ice Kool-Aid* too?"

"Oh damn," I said as I turned around to see Amir standing in front of the fridge with just his wife beater on. Most of the blood rushed from my head because I was left dumbfounded.

"Is everything okay?" Amir looked over the refrigerator door to look at me.

"Uh yeah," I said trying to find words to say while I stared at this beautiful man that stood in front of me. "I had just remembered I needed to tell my cousin something," I lied quickly because I didn't want him to know that I said *'oh damn'* because he was standing there showing off those muscular arms. "Did you want me to fix your plate?" I asked.

"Naw girl I can do it, but thanks anyway," he closed the refrigerator door with the pitcher of Kool-Aid in his hand, "I mean its not like we're *married* or anything. Even though it kinda feels like it sometimes," he began to say. "I mean I come home to a fine woman everyday then you cook most of the times and clean up, Summer you know you don't have to do all of that," he said going into to the cabinet to get a cup.

"Well you won't let me pay any rent so I have to earn my way around here somehow," I turned back toward the stove then started to remove the tops from the Tupperware. "So until you let me pay you for staying here, I'm going to continue to cook, clean, and buy food occasionally," I turned around about to sit down at the kitchen table, but was greeted by Amir's chest outlined in the white wife beater. I looked up into his eyes and saw something different this time. This time it was like he was searching for something, "uhm, is there something you need to say to me?" my voice grew soft as more blood began leave my head. He didn't respond, but he blinked his eyes slowly making him look even more sexy, "so are you—" I was cut off by a kiss, and not a peck either.

After the shock wore off to some extent, I noticed that his hands were gripping the back of my head. I closed my eyes and started to return the passionate kiss that he started; I wrapped my arms around his neck as we continued to kiss like he was just released from prison after serving a ten year sentence. Amir released his hands from me, then he went back to staring into my eyes, but this time his eyes weren't searching. His beautiful green eyes sparkled in satisfaction as if he received an answer to his once questioning eyes.

"So is that the way you want me to earn my way around here?" I asked then his arms dropped in disappointment and he sighed like he was annoyed.

"Summer its not even like that," he walked away, but I grabbed his arm, "what?" He sighed like he was irritated.

"Look Amir I'm sorry, I uhm," I started to say but grew speechless, "I just thought because we were talking about me earning my way around here then you did that, I just assumed *that's* the way you wanted me to earn it," I held onto his arm and he turned back to face me.

"No no, no Summer," he shook his head, "I didn't mean it that way at all. What I was trying to express to you was how much I love you."

Shock began to take over my body and legs started to grow weak, "you... you love me?" I questioned using my arm to hold myself up as I leaned on the counter. Amir stepped closer in front of me and we began the staring contest again, "did you say—"

"Yes I said that *I love you* Summer Parker," he said then wrapped his arm around me and pulled me into him as if he was going to hug me. "I've always loved you, but ever since you've moved in here and we've been spending all of this time together, I've just *completely* fallen in love with you," he spoke like he was being completely truthful. All I could do was continue to look in his eyes since I was being held up by his arms, "I'm sorry to catch you off guard by all of this, but I couldn't keep walking around here pretending that I don't have any feelings for you or that I'm not in love with you. I'm tired of it so I just had to let you know how I *really* feel."

"So I mean," I simply stated while I was trying to collect my thoughts, "so what about Asia?" I asked and he loosed his grip while rolling his eyes.

"What about her?" he asked sounding aggravated, "Summer I'm telling *you* that *I love you*, Asia was," he paused before he blew hard like he was blowing out candle, at that moment backed away from me again, "I hate to admit this, but I was using Asia to make you jealous."

"What?" I asked with my arms folded wearing a confused look on my face, "Amir why would you do that?"

"I know it was a little immature on my part," he looked down, "but Summer I was getting tired of waiting on you. I mean it's not like that I wouldn't wait, honestly I'd wait *forever* for you, but I guess I was trying to speed things up. I know I just need to wait on God to finish what He's doing in your life. I guess I was being a little selfish."

"I love you too," I said softly and Amir looked me in the eyes. I reached up and touched the side of his face, "I can't lie to you anymore either, I've been feeling exactly the same way I've fallen in love with you too." This time I pulled him closer to me to kiss him, not holding back anymore.

"Wow," he said opening his eyes then smiling, "so uh, was you serious when you said that you loved me too?"

I shook my head, "yeah I guess I was too scared to tell you the truth too," I looked down briefly then looked back at him. "I was finally getting over this whole thing with Damon and I was too scared to fall for anyone especially while I was still healing. But I just can't help feeling the way I do about you Amir, I *really* do love you."

Amir had the biggest smile on his face, "I'm so glad to finally hear that you love me," he chuckled and I smiled, "and I love you too Summer. Trust me this time its real and its going to last."

"I know," I said believing everything he was saying. I knew Amir was a good man because even while we were growing up he was always a good person. The most important thing is that he is a saved man, meaning that the true relationship that he has with the Lord will make it easier for him to have good relationships with others. Allowing him to be true to that person, faithful, honest, and not trying to deliberately hurt the person he's in a relationship with. "So what do we do now?" I asked as far as our relationship was concerned. Would we continue to be '*friends*' or just be real with ourselves and become the couple everybody already thinks we already are?

"What do you mean 'what do we do now' Summer?" he asked with his eyebrows raised. "What do you think we should do?" he quizzed even though I knew he didn't mean anything sexual. Amir was celibate and he always makes it known that since he's been saved, he's made a vow to God that the next woman he slept with would be his wife.

"What I mean is do we put a title on this?" I asked smiling, "and if we do put a title to it, what would that title be?"

"Oh okay," he shook his head then grabbed me again, "Summer Jade Parker, will you be my girlfriend or rather would you be my woman?"

I smiled and continued to look into his beautiful eyes. I put my hand on the back of his head and pulled him in for yet another sensual confirmation kiss, "I'd *love* to be your girlfriend or woman," we laughed before we started kissing again.

Three Days Later:

"Summer, girl what is on *your mind*?" Brianna set down next to me on the couch, "girl what or *whoever* it is has got you smiling like a kid in a candy store," she continued to say while sipping on a virgin strawberry kiwi daiquiri. We were at Brandi's house for her last night as a 'single woman.' That's right her and Jayson were finally tying the knot tomorrow.

"Well," I sang continuing to smile, "I was just thinking about something that happened earlier this week."

"Uhm," Brianna sighed smiling, "so what's going on?"

"Alright here it is, the *real* strawberry kiwi daiquiri," Kennede announced walking into the living room before I could respond to Brianna's question, "now Ms. Soon-to-be-Mrs.-Thang made them and she acted like the Bacardi was water instead of rum."

"Whatever Ken," Brandi said walking behind Kennede with oversized wine glasses, "it's really good with the extra rum in it, don't hate because you can't hold your liquor."

"Well I hate it because I can't drink right now," Brianna said with her mouth poked out before she started sipping her drink. "But anyway before ya'll walked in here interrupting our conversation, Summer was about to tell us about this constant smile that she's wearing now."

"Oh," Kennede and Brandi said in unison, "so what's going on girl?" Brandi smirked, "does it have something with you and Amir?" she questioned.

"Dang Bri," I said joking. I had all intentions of telling my cousins that I've let go of my fears and fallen in love. And this time it was real because this time it is true love.

"Oh girl you already know we would have found out anyway," Ken said, "you know you can't keep or hide something "major" especially in *this* family. That's just like a couple of weeks ago when ya'll found out that Raymond and I were dating again, thanks to your big mouth brother Summer," she laughed then we all joined in.

"That's what you get, trying to sneak around hiding stuff from us and that's why you were cold busted," I said to Kennede as I continued to chuckle. Here's how we found out about Kennede and Raymond, it was a couple of days after my graduation and those two went out on a date when they ran into Malachi and Gabbie at the movies. Well Raymond slipped up by mentioning that he and Ken were dating again. So Kai being the nosy person he is called his best friend and manager our cousin Donte to find out the scoop between Ken and Ray. After calling Donte and not finding any additional info, Kai calls me while Donte called Brandi, who then called me and we called Brianna on three-way; then while I was on three-way with the twins, Brandi calls Kennede to find out the truth with all of us still on the line.

Kennede waved her hand toward us, "I still don't understand how both of those nosy Negros can live in Atlanta, Georgia but continue to meddle with what's going on here in Louisville, Kentucky," she chuckled as she talked about Donte and Kai. "But it's all good though, I wouldn't know how to love either one of them any other way, with their nosy selves."

"Okay back to Summer's new look," Brandi said, "so what's up?"

"Alright since ya'll wanna know so bad," I rolled my eyes before I produced this huge smile on my face, "Amir and I finally made it official we're a couple now."

"Ahhh," they all sighed with smiles on everyone's faces. "Summer that's great and it's about dang time," Kennede took a long sip, "so when did this happen?"

"A couple of days ago," I took a sip of my drink as well, "matter of fact it was this past Tuesday on the tenth."

"I'm so happy for you Summer," Brandi stated with this gigantic grin. "Amir is a good man and you deserve all the happiness in world," she lifted her glass in my direction before taking a drink.

"Thanks B," I said as tears started to fill the brims, but I was determined not to let them fall, "the thing that I'm most happy about is like you said I deserve this. Now I know I deserve to be loved the way Amir has been trying to love me, but first I had to learn to love myself." I paused for a second before I continued to tell my confession, "I just thank God because if it wasn't for Him, I wouldn't be in this position that I am in now. I am able to help women who have been or they're on the same road I just got off of, and I'm able to give them hope plus a little Jesus to go along with it, because He is the only way."

"That's right," Kennede nodded her head smiling, "wow Summer, if I didn't know God for myself I would find it hard to believe how much you've changed for the best just in six months."

"That's God for you," I said, "and you know how Pastor Williams has been preaching about this being 2008, the number eight meaning 'New Beginnings' in our lives?"

"Yeah," they all answered at the same time.

"I just really have a good feeling about that whole "New Beginnings" that I'm on the way to it, and I have already started and completed some of the journey. I think all of us are walking in this "New Beginnings", because of that I say that we toast to it." I lifted my glass, "I mean tomorrow our girl is going to be Mrs. Brandi Hill *finally*," Brandi smiled then lifted her glass in my direction. "In less than three and a half months Brianna will be somebody's mama, also Ken and Ray are doing their thing again," I said tearing up, "and I am in love for real, so let's do it, a toast to New Beginnings," we all lifted our glasses in the air.

"Yes let's do it ladies," Brandi spoke up while lifting her glass and the rest of them followed suit.

"Okay," I sat silent for a few seconds to gather my thoughts and also trying to control the upcoming waterworks, "may God bless all of us on our journeys through these New Beginnings."

With our glasses already lifted to the sky we said in unison, "to New Beginnings!"

Kennede

"*Can I just see you every morning when I open my eyes...*" Tamia finished singing *Spend My Life with You* along with Eric Benet while Brandi and Jayson finished dancing to their first song. After the last note of the song was played everyone began clapping and cheering for the couple.

"Alright everybody it's now time to party," the D.J. announced before he started to play Chris Brown's song *Wall to Wall*, "okay everybody let's pack the dance floor."

"Oh Mama that's Chris Brown," RaeLynn said jumping up from the wedding party table. "Come on Mama, let's go out there to dance," she grabbed my hand then started to pull on me.

"Alright girl," I rose from my seat and headed to the dance floor like the other guest. The ceremony was absolutely beautiful along with the best looking wedding party in history. Brandi and Jayson's wedding colors were ivory, pink pearl, and platinum. The bridesmaid's dresses were beautiful, it was a pink pearl satin trumpet dress with spaghetti straps and we wore platinum or silver jewelry to top off our elegant look. The groomsmen wore black tuxedos with a matching pink pearl vest that had platinum designs woven in them. Of course you know that Jordan was the ring bearer and his tux was exactly like the groomsmen, and of course my baby RaeLynn was the flower girl. Her dress was a white satin princess A-line gown with a pink pearl sash; she also had the same color ribbons placed in her spiral curled ponytail. But Brandi and Jayson looked so amazing as the bride and groom.

Brandi wore a strapless satin A-line gown with platinum embroidery along with a chapel train, and Jayson had a white tux with a pink pearl vest and tie. And you already know that I hooked up everybody's hair for the wedding, but instead of wearing an up do for her wedding day, Brandi wanted to wear her hair down in loose curls to show off her long mane. The shock of the day was Jayson who decided to loose the braids for their wedding day; he had what Destiny's Child described as the *'low cut Caesar with the deep waves'*. Personally I thought that him cutting those braids was a wise decision because the haircut made him look so much better and not only for the wedding either.

RaeLynn and I continued to dance to her favorite song or rather her favorite singer when I saw Raymond walking in our direction, "look at my two favorite women." he said walking up behind me. "Go RaeLynn, get it girl," he chuckled while encouraging our daughter's dancing.

"Ya'll are too crazy," I stated while I continued dancing even though I was laughing at Raymond and RaeLynn who were now dancing together as *Wall to Wall* came to an end. It was the cutest sight to see the two of them dancing together, but anything that has something to do with Ray was cute to me. Plus he looked so handsome today; even though he wasn't in the wedding party he wore a black suit with a pink and white tie.

"Hey RaeLynn come on," Jordan ran up to her after he was just dancing with Brandi and Jayson, "come on cause I wanna show you something."

"Can I go with him Mommy?" she asked me. My guess was what Jordan had to show RaeLynn had something to do with the big chocolate fountain on the desert table, or it was doing something else other than dancing since the D.J. changed the song to something they probably couldn't get with. He changed the song to Erykah Badu's 'Honey.'

"Go on girl," I waved at her as I lightly bopped to the music, "you two be careful and be good."

"Okay we will," they said in unison and ran off.

"Come on now," Raymond grabbed my hand and pulled me closer. "Don't leave me hanging out here on the dance floor by myself," he said as we began to move in sync with the music.

"Oh naw baby, I ain't leaving you out here by yourself," I said moving closer to him and looking him in his eyes, "do you see all these other females around here? And you think I'm about to let you out of *my* sight looking as good as you do?" I asked referring to the great number of women on the dance floor. Most of them had to be either co-workers of Brandi's or either some of Jayson's family too.

"Baby you don't have to worry I ain't going nowhere," he gave me this sexy look as he keep on gazing into my eyes. "But do you think I'm gonna leave you out here alone?" he put his arm around my waist then pulled me closer to him, "I saw how homeboy that you were paired with during the wedding was checking you out in church earlier." He said which made me wear a half smile before he bent down and kissed my lips softly, "naw there ain't no way," he shook his head from side to side. "Now I know I'm not letting you go anywhere," he laughed while squeezing me tighter.

"You are a mess," I laughed along with him then hitting him gently.

"I'm serious Kennede," he said with a smile on his face. "But on the real you looked amazing up there," he bent down to whisper in my ear and I closed my eyes.

I had to compose myself because there were more than one hundred people around here including children, and I couldn't do what I really wanted to do to Ray after he did that. I had a feeling that he whispered in my ear on purpose because he knows what that does to me, and he knows after that I can't control myself.

"Thank you," I simply replied to his comment, "and if I must say you're not looking too bad yourself." I said smiling then he raised one of his eyebrows, "what?" I questioned.

"You are *too* beautiful," he said continuing to stare at me even though we were still dancing. "I can't tell you how happy I am that we are back together. Throughout the entire ceremony and even now I've thinking about how much I wished it was *us* up there getting married again."

"What?" I stopped dancing to look up at him with shock on my face, "so what do you mean by that Ray?" I asked out of curiosity.

"Kennede you just don't understand how much I," he paused then looked at me with the sexiest expression and at the same time licking his lips, "how much I want to be with you in *other* ways." I then nodded my head because I pretty much knew what he meant by those *other* ways, "but I know that you said you weren't trying to do that anymore since you've gotten saved and trying to stay close to God."

"Yeah," I said then began to slowly back away although I don't know why I was doing that, "so what are you saying?"

"Baby it's nothing bad," he pulled me back into him. "All I'm saying is that with you looking the way you do now, you're just making it hard for me not to say no to you. To tell you the truth, I really want to take you out of here and just make some mad passionate love to you," he whispered in my ear again, this time I closed my eyes and started feeling exactly what he felt about us making love. "But I respect your decision to stay celibate and because of that I won't try anything. Also now I am working on my own relationship with God, so I'll wait as long as it takes for you."

I looked at him with surprise, "really? So you are willing to wait for me again?" I questioned.

"Yes Kennede and that's what I'm saying that I'm going to wait for you *again*." He kissed my forehead, "but just know that it's *not* going to be easy for me at all."

"I know it's not going to be easy for me either," I exclaimed, "it looks like we are going to have to stay prayed up for real," I said with all seriousness. Like I just told him it was going to be really hard for me as well because Raymond is just too fine and too sexy which turns me on so bad that I lose control of my body. That's the reason that we keep having these frequent "*slip ups*" due to the lack of control over our bodies.

Even though we know it's wrong because we're not married anymore, it just feels right and it feels so darn good when we do it. Our most recent "*slip-up*" was about two and a half months ago on the night of R.J.'s prom. It was the perfect scenario; both Ray and I were at my parents to see R.J. off that night, once he left, we were about to leave too but RaeLynn wanted to stay all night with my parents. That's all my parents needed to hear that their only granddaughter wanted to spend the night to be spoiled more than she already was by them. To make a long story short, Ray and I went back to my house *alone*, then one kiss lead to another and those kisses lead to our clothes falling off as we ended up in bed making yet another *slip-up*.

"Ken uhm, could you come over to my place later?" Raymond asked as we walked off the dance floor.

"Okay," I said slowly, "but you know your daughter doesn't need to be out real late."

He chuckled, "no baby I need to have a private conversation with you," he said appearing sexier than ever to me. "I've already made arrangements with your parents so RaeLynn can spend the night with them."

"Ray," I sat down with some disappointment, "baby I thought we just had a conversation about waiting on the sex thing?"

"Who said anything about us having sex?" he asked and I looked at him wearing an expression that said *yeah right*.

"Come on now Raymond give me some credit," I started to explain, but Ray had a blank look on his face, "you've arranged for RaeLynn to spend the night with my parents so that we can have a *private conversation*."

"Okay," he simply said folding his arms and pressing his lips tightly together.

"Okay," I repeated, "by you doing all of that just for a conversation to me seems like you are up to something. Hello all of that right there screams 'I want to bump-n-grind!' Well at least to me it does to me."

"Don't get me wrong I want to have you screaming because of that," he chuckled as I stood speechless at his comment. "But I'm not going to do that though, honestly Ken I really do just want to talk to you because I feel it's time to start discussing our future."

"Excuse me?" I looked up at him with confusion because I was caught off guard by what he just said, "You want to talk about our future, are you saying—"

"What I'm saying is be at my place at nine-thirty tonight," he said interrupting my statement, he bent down to give me an adoring and heartfelt kiss. "And at nine-thirty you will find out what I am saying, okay?"

"Okay baby," I softly sang in my sweet innocent voice.

"I'm going to go ahead and leave now so that I can get ready for your visit later," he said before looking down at his watch, "I will see you in exactly two hours."

*   *   *

"Oh my God Raymond's going to kill me," I said aloud looking at the clock that read 9:25 p.m. I know that he said to be at his place at nine-thirty, but he should know by now that I am on CP time to the fullest. I stood in the mirror giving myself the last once over approval. Once I came home from the reception I took a quick shower then decided to change my clothes and smell before I went to meet Ray. At the wedding I was wearing the perfume by *Ralph Lauren Romance*, but I came home and showered with *Sensual Amber* body wash that I got from Bath & Body Works.

"Oh Lord it's already nine-thirty," I panicked while spraying *Sensual Amber* body spray on my skin and across the sun dress I was wearing. I grabbed my keys and purse then rushed to the door, "what?" I stopped on my front steps after I had locked the front door. I had turned around to see Raymond leaning up against his brand new light blue *2009 CLK 63 AMG Mercedes*. "Am I that late that you had to come and get me?" I asked.

"Naw baby I had planned to come get you anyway," he shook his head smiling looking as good as always. It looked like he had changed his clothes from the wedding too. He had ditched the suit for a white collar shirt and some khaki slacks while wearing a tan Kangol cap. "I mean even though you just now walking out of the house and its way pass nine-thirty," he chuckled.

"*Summer nights on the beach, underneath the raindrops, wind blowing through your hair, this is what it feels like...*" Day 26 was playing softly from Raymond's car as I walked closer to him. He had the top down on his convertible which is the reason I was able to hear the song playing as I approached the car.

"Well you know me," I stepped in front of his face and he smirked, "you know beauty takes time." He chuckled again with his head tilted to the side. He didn't respond with words but he grabbed my arm then softly pulled me in between his legs as he wrapped his arms around me and we began to kiss. With each expression from our tongues I could feel Ray using his fingers to glide down my back, taking advantage of my backless halter dress.

"You aren't going to make this '*no sex policy*' easy," I said as I shuddered from Raymond barely touching the small of my back then placing his hand on my waist before he started kissing me yet again. "See what I'm saying, you're playing Day 26 and holding me like this—" he kissed me again before I could finish my statement. "Woo and kissing me like that, whoa *Heavenly Father* help me please Jesus!" I said tossing my head back.

He chuckled again still holding me while he continued to lean against the car, "come on I want you to go with me somewhere." He said moving me to the side as he started walking to the passenger side while I held onto his hand; he opened up the passenger's door for me then said, "I have something for you."

"You have a surprise for me?" I questioned getting comfortable in the leather seats, "Ray you know I love surprises."

He shut my door, but continued to stare at me with a smile, "I know you love surprises and I love giving them to you because I love you."

"I love you too baby," I smiled feeling a combination of butterflies and excitement. "You know what Ray, I feel so...uhm. I don't even know how to explain the way I feel being with you again," I laid my head on his shoulder when he positioned himself in the driver's seat. "I just never want to lose this feeling that I have for you."

Raymond grabbed my hand and locked his fingers with mine, "I'm going to do everything in my power to make sure that this time it's going to last." He paused to raise our intertwined hands to his mouth kissing the back of my hand, "I promise baby."

I moved my head from his shoulder so he could back out of the driveway, "so can I get a hint to where you're taking me?"

"Well...uhm nope," he pulled out of my subdivision laughing and I squinted my eyes, "but trust me you won't be disappointed, so don't worry yourself about what it is. Just sit your fine self over there and listen to the smooth sounds of *Day 26* singing *Co-Star*," he said sounding like a late night radio D.J.

"Raymond you are a mess," I laughed and he joined in with my laughter. I now laid my head on the headrest and began to take in the words of the song that was playing; *"I'm in the right place at the right time."* I closed my eyes as the breeze from the top being down was going through my curly hair, but not knocking any curl out of place. I guess it was probably eighty degrees, actually that's what Raymond's thermometer on the dashboard said before I closed my eyes. With the weather feeling the way it was, the music being so soothing, for the first time my mind was completely clear. I took advantage of moment by having a quick silent conversation with God. *Thank you Lord for this moment*; I began to think and quietly pray; *I thank you for my beautiful daughter, for Raymond, and Lord I pray that things will be right with us this time, it feels so right though this time, thank Lord.*

"Hey you," Raymond said touching my hand and I opened my eyes slowly then looked over at him, I was greeted by his half smile, "are you asleep over there?"

"No I'm just enjoying the ride, doing a little praying," I said as I began to look around the familiar neighborhood, "we're not going to pick up RaeLynn are we?" I asked that question because we were approaching my parent's neighborhood.

"Didn't I tell you earlier she's spending the night with your parent's?" he asked and I simply nodded, "our daughter is safe and sound at your parent's and that is where she's gonna stay."

"Okay Raymond."

"Now you just said you were praying, so do you mind if I ask what it is you were praying about?" he glanced over at me.

"Us," I said placing my head on top of his hand that wasn't on the steering wheel.

"Us," he repeated, "that's funny because my surprise involves *us* too."

"Ray what is it that you are up to? Can you give me a hint please?" I asked and he put his finger over his mouth telling me to be quiet.

He never answered my question, but he continued to drive about six blocks away from my parent's subdivision. He turned into this neighborhood that welcomed us with big beautiful homes that could almost be mistaken for mansions. We drove about four houses down before we turned into the driveway of this two story house that had light colored bricks. The house looked as if it was just built and it was absolutely beautiful.

"Raymond what is this?" I asked as he continued to give me the silent treatment again, but he opens his door and walked over to open my door.

"Come and see," he held out his hand and I grabbed it. I was shaking out of excitement because I just didn't know what to expect. We approached the double doors and Raymond pulled out a key to unlock the door, "are you nervous?" he asked chuckling and he acted hesitate to open the door.

"Yeah a little," I said nervously smiling. Once the door was opened I was greeted by a double winding staircase something I always wanted in my house. "Oh my God, this is beautiful," I said mainly about the staircase because the rest of the house from what I could see was empty except this gorgeous chandler that hung in between the staircase.

"Surprise," Raymond said mildly and I looked over at him with confusion, "yes this is all yours, if you want it."

"What?" I simply asked because I was speechless with my hand covering my mouth as I walked in front of him releasing his hand. "Ray I…uhm… Ray are you serious? This is mine?" I asked with my back toward Raymond, "oh my God!" I said when I turned around and saw Raymond on one knee with a ring box in his hand.

"Kennede, when I said I never stopped loving you I meant it," he said and I walked closer to him with both hands now over my mouth. "I feel like this is our new start and this time I want it to be right. This time, a new home of our own, but only if you answer this question, Kennede Marie Johnson will you marry me again?"

Tears began to fall down my face which I already knew was probably red, "yes!" he stood up and I jumped in his arms, "Raymond I love you, so very much." I said kissing him.

"I love you too," he said holding onto me, "baby you haven't even seen the ring yet."

"Baby it doesn't matter," he backed away a little so he could open the ring box which revealed a four carat princess cut diamond with diamonds going around the band, a much bigger engagement ring than the one I had years ago. "Raymond this is beautiful but honestly if it were a Cracker Jack box ring, I'd wear it because I'm just happy to be back with you."

"Well you know I can go take this back and pick up a Cracker Jack box," he said laughing and walking toward the door.

"Uh uh, I'll just take the one that you already have," I said laughing pulling his arm and we kissed again, "it's a beautiful ring though."

"It is all platinum baby," he said taking the ring out of the box and placing it on my ring finger with a perfect fit. "But then again you do deserve the best."

"Thank you," I said looking at how the ring was blinging on my finger, "oh so are you gonna give me a tour of *our* house?"

"There's really nothing too see," he said grabbing my hand as we walked through the bare house. "I'm waiting on you to add everything from the kitchen counter tops to the tile or marble in the bathrooms, and down to what type of pool you want out back," he said spreading his arm out.

"Are you serious?" I asked in shock.

"Yes Ken," he pulled me close to kiss my forehead, "this five bedroom house is empty like it is for a reason. The reason is so we can fill it with all new things since this is our new start." He pulled me into hug formation and started so stare in my eyes, "and once we're married again and finally move in, we're gonna fill up the rest of those bedrooms with some siblings for RaeLynn," he said with a smirk on his face.

"Oh most definitely," I smiled kissing his lips, "Raymond I can't wait to start on that project, it's gonna be *so* much fun."

"Yeah me too," he raised his eyebrows laughing, "well let's just concentrate on one project at a time, so let's finish doing this house first." A kiss to my forehead, "then our next project getting married," a kiss on my nose, "then project *Collins Family extension* will begin."

"That sounds like a plan to me," he kissed my lips this time, "alright so let's get project number one and two out of the way so we can do some *serious* concentration on the *Collins Family extension.*"

"I love you Ken," Raymond said staring in my eyes. *Thank you God for that prayer being answered,* was all I could think of because I was so excited about everything that was to come in my future.

17
Brianna

(4th of July / Grandmother Spencer's Birthday Party)

"Bri I would love it if you could come up to Indy with me to help me open my clinic for Sickle-Cell Patients." Aunt Regina said as I was sucking up the cool air inside the church. The other family members were setting up for Grandmother's Birthday party and 4th of July celebration at the little park next door that was owned by Grandmother's church. "I'm saying that because I always knew you were the one who said you didn't want to stay stuck in Louisville forever, plus didn't you say that you enjoyed Indianapolis when you came up to visit?"

"Yeah I really did enjoy myself when I was up there," I said. I had spent sometime there last summer around the time of the Black Expo. Because Aunt Regina lived there I didn't have to pay for hotel cost, so I stayed with her and her husband Jacob Andrews who is a big time defensive end football player for the *Indianapolis Colts*. So during my stay and during some of the events at the Black Expo I was treated like a rock star because I was rolling with them. As a matter of fact, I met a few players that played on the team with Jacob who tried to throw some game my way, but I was too caught up in Dr. Hamilton's world to even give any of them a second thought. Don't get me wrong, if I wasn't so into Lance I would have given one of them some play because most of them were way too fine. "But I don't know how I'd be able to do that now with me about to have this baby and all."

"Girl," she waved her hand at me, making this face that made her look even more like the actress Sanaa Lathan. "I have three kids and my youngest isn't even a year old yet."

"Yeah, but Aunt Gina you have a husband and I don't" I said rubbing my stomach, "it'd just be me and the baby if I moved there."

"And us, we are family Bri and you know you could count on me and Jacob," she said like she was almost pleading with me. "Besides I'm not opening my clinic until March of 2009, that's plenty of time to make a move like that. Speaking of the baby's father, what is up with you two anyway?" she asked nodding toward my stomach.

"Well," I sighed, here I was once again contemplating whether or not to tell the truth or the same lie I told my grandmother, "it's kinda complicated."

"Complicated?" she questioned now folding her arms, "what's so complicated about it? Either you all are together or it was just a one night stand, so which one is it?"

I rolled my eyes, "we're just not together," I chose to give her the same story I gave Grandmother because Aunt Regina lived almost two hours away and I'm pretty sure she had no ties to Brian. "Let's just say it was a one night stand that continued to happen until boom," I pointed to my stomach, "I ended up pregnant."

"Okay," she shook her head like she understood my story, "so I'm saying, is he gonna—"

"Uh-uh Gina you need to come help us with something," Aunt Karen said coming from the church's kitchen with her *'God Bless the Cook'* apron around her white Capri pants with her red and blue sleeveless blouse,. "I understand why Bri is sitting in here, but you can do *something* too."

"Uh-uh *Ms. Bossy*," Aunt Regina stood up putting a plain blue apron around her blue jean gauchos and sleeveless red collared shirt. "I was taking a breather because *I* was transporting the ribs from the grill to back into the kitchen to stay warm in the oven. I'm up now so what do you need me to do big sis?"

"Can you please check to see if either Bill, my husband or Charles have any more ribs ready." She said referring to the three "grill masters" outside. We were expecting such a large crowd that we needed three grills to handle all of the ribs, hamburgers, and hotdogs (which was mainly for the kids). On top of all six of Grandmother's kids that were already here to help set up, there was all seventeen of her grandkids and some friends from the church, plus people's spouses were here. In all we were expecting a total of one hundred-fifty to two hundred people adults and children, and that number was at the least. Most of the people had already showed up to drop off their dishes in the kitchen then returned outside to sit under the shelter to either play some dominoes or spades. But Grandmother and a couple of church ladies were playing a serious game of bid whist.

"Okay Karen," Aunt Gina walked over to Aunt Karen to retrieve a huge aluminum pan from her.

"Aunt Karen do you need me to do anything?" I asked getting up waddling toward in her direction.

"Baby *you* don't need to do nothing," she said going through a grocery bag on the serving table, "but if you feel you just need to do something, you can take these bags of hotdogs to one of the grillers because we're almost finished with everything else in the kitchen." She said talking about herself, Mama, and Aunt Julie cooking up some side dishes and probably doctoring up the other ones that people outside our family *tried* to donate.

"Okay," I grabbed two grocery bags that were filled with hotdogs and I saw a few packages of smoked grillers smoked sausages in the bags as well. As I approached the door to go outside a petite but thick in the hips woman walked through the door with some grocery bags in her hand and a tall teenaged boy behind her carrying two big bags of ice. "Hello, how are you?" I asked the woman amazed at her beauty. She reminded me of the actress who played in *A Low Down Dirty Shame* and *Antwone Fisher*, Salli Richardson-Whitfield, but this woman had a shorter hair cut.

She smiled at me with beautiful straight white teeth, "Hi sweetie, my name is—"

"Carla!" Aunt Karen shouted from behind me. Her screaming startled me as she ran up next to me to embrace this woman, "oh my God Carla it's so good to see you, oh here baby take these bags into the kitchen," Aunt Karen said to Kayla as she took the bags from the woman's hands.

"Okay Mama," Kayla replied looking like a seventeen year old *taller* version of her older sister Kennede.

"Marcus follow her and take that ice into the kitchen," the woman said to the teenaged boy that was behind her.

"Yes ma'am," he replied smiling as if he didn't mind following my little cousin into the kitchen.

"Oh my God, where is my manners," Aunt Karen said with one arm still around the woman. "Bri this is my best friend from well, here at the church, we met here when we were both ten years old." She laughed and the woman joined in, "but this is Carla, and Carla this is one of Lisa's twins, Brianna."

"Hello," I said smiling, "I would shake your hand or hug you but my hands are full," I raised the bags that were in my hands.

"Oh honey," Carla leaned over and hugged me with one arm then kissed my cheek. "I can't believe this is one of Lisa's twins. Honey the last time I saw you it was when *you* were in diapers and how old are you now?" she asked.

"I'm twenty-three, but I'll be twenty-four real soon," I said about to exit the room, "I don't mean to be rude, but let me hurry and get these hotdogs and stuff over to the *master grillers* so we can eat."

"Okay," they said in unison, "but Carla how old is your son now? That boy has gotten so big and tall since the last time I saw him."

"Girl he's sixteen now, can you believe it?" Carla's voice began to fade as I approached the *"Three Grill Stooges"* who had the stereo blasting with some *Maze featuring Frankie Beverly*.

"Here goes the hotdogs!" I shouted to the *"Three Grill Stooges."*

"Okay," they all shouted back raising their forks, "girl you betta get back in that cool fellowship hall before you give birth out here due to all this heat," Uncle Charles said smiling at me.

"Yes sir," I waved my hand at him in agreement. I wasn't about to sit out here in this ninety degree weather and risk having an asthma attack even though I had my inhaler very close to me. Although this day lacked the usual Ohio Valley humidity, it was still too hot for someone in my condition, or at least while the sun was still up, but I am going to come out here when it's time for the fireworks. Donte and Malachi had bought fireworks and firecrackers galore. They had planned to have their own little firework show which they have named 'Thunder over First Baptist' mocking the firework show we have here in the city for Derby called 'Thunder over Louisville.' When I went outside I saw the two of them running through the park sprinklers with some of the younger kids along with Kennede and Raymond running around in them too. While Ken and Ray was acting like two big kids playing in the water, Brandi and her new husband were swinging on the swing set like some kids with Summer and Amir swinging right next to them. I smirked, but seeing all of them coupled together made me wish that Lance could be here with me.

"So how are your parents' doing?" I heard Aunt Karen ask Carla as I walked back into the church's fellowship hall.

"Oh girl they're good, living the retired life down in Florida," she said, "I just got back this afternoon from being down there since about the end of May when the kids got out of school for the summer, hence the tan I have."

"Yeah girl, I see that you are a shade or two darker," I sat down next to Aunt Karen as she continued to talk, "speaking of your kids, where is the other three?"

"Other three?" I butted in their conversation in shock. This woman didn't even look like she had that big teenager she claimed when they first got here, let alone to have three other kids, "so you mean to tell me you have a total of four kids? I mean how old are you, if you don't mind me asking?"

"Brianna Wright," Aunt Karen said waving her hand toward me, "that is so rude of you to ask a woman all these questions."

"Oh Karen it's okay because I'm proud of my age and my kids," she continued to smile, "yes baby to answer your first question I do have four kids," her smile then faded and she kind of hung her head. "I probably would have just given birth to my fifth child a couple of weeks ago, but I lost the baby back in February."

"I am so sorry to hear that," I started to reach for my stomach, but I soon stopped.

"Me too Carla," my aunt grabbed her hand, "I wish I would have known a lot sooner, I sure would have taken care of you or something."

"Karen that's okay because God has blessed me to have a loving caring husband who was by my side the entire time, along with my loving children who made me feel better about the whole thing," I could see Aunt Karen squeeze her hand tighter as she used the other hand to wipe the corner of her eyes. "But anyway Brianna, to let you know about my kids, the oldest is nineteen years old and he's pre-med at University of Louisville, but right now he's down in Florida with my parents for his break. Then my other two rug rats are out there somewhere playing with the other kids. Now those two are a couple of years from being teenagers and both of their birthdays are in November. Elliott will be twelve and Lailah will be ten years old. Then of course you saw my sixteen year old son Marcus."

"Wow, I still can't believe it," I said shaking my head, "there's no way you have kids that age when you don't look a day over twenty-five years old your self."

"'Thank you honey," she started to smile again, "but to answer your other question about my age, I'm the same age as Karen, forty-three years young."

"Hey, hey now," my aunt twisted her mouth with a smirk, "didn't nobody need you telling my age just because you the one secure in your old age," she laughed.

Carla started laughing as well, "Karen you should be proud of your age because girl you look good too," Carla stated, "I know I'm blessed to be forty-three and looking like this especially after four kids. There are some women our age who look like they're older than your mom who by the way doesn't even look one bit of seventy years young."

"Yeah that is true," Aunt Karen nodded.

"But I'm so blessed to have my four babies and my old rock head husband of twenty years."

"Oh my God, you've been married for twenty years too?" I asked with wide eyes as she nodded.

"Well Bri, Robert and I have been married for twenty-five years already," I shook my head in amazement, "matter of fact it'll be twenty-six years on November 1st."

"That's amazing you guys," I said, "wow I just hope that I can say something like that in twenty years."

"I see that you have a little one on the way," Carla half smiled looking down at my round belly, "so are you married? I know I don't see a ring, but I understand how your hands can swell along with everything else when you're pregnant."

"Well," I started to smile very hard thinking about Lance, "I'm not married yet, even though he did propose this morning." I said recalling the proposal Lance gave me while I laid in his bed after a round of early morning love making.

"I can see in your eyes that you must really be in love with this young man," Carla said and I thought, *if you only knew he's just a couple of years younger than the two of you.*

"Yeah I am so in love with him," I said and without looking in a mirror I could tell my eyes were probably sparkling. I went back to thinking about Lance and our *wonderful* morning. After we finished round one of making love and right before he got up to cook me breakfast, he asked me to marry him and you already know what my answer was, a resounding YES!

"Oh Bri, so Brian finally proposed uh?" Aunt Karen asked and I snapped back into partial reality. My aunts, Mama, and Grandmother did think Brian is the father of my unborn child based off my conversation with Grandmother.

"Uh yeah," I staggered for words, "uh yeah Brian did," I simply lied to them, "uhm excuse me a minute, I need to go to the bathroom."

"Okay baby," Aunt Karen said, "by the time you come out it should be time to eat," she stood up like she was headed back into the kitchen. "I'm about to go round up everybody to come clean up so we can eat dinner."

"Karen I can do that," Carla stood as well, "you can go and finish up back there with your sisters so ya'll can bring the food out and I'll be back to help afterwards."

"Thanks girl, but honey you have a soft voice and my family don't understand that." Aunt Karen said walking toward the opened door that lead to the park, "but you can go on back into the kitchen and start helping them and I'll be on my way back in the kitchen after I do round-ups."

"Okay," I heard Carla say as I turned the corner walking to the other side of the church where there was just a single bathroom. I didn't want to get caught up in the crowd of people that was about to flood the restrooms and ladies lounge to clean up before eating.

"Lord please forgive me for telling that lie to them about Brian," I said whispering to the Lord as I walked in front of the sink to wash my hands. I looked up into the mirror and began to stare at my reflection, but this weird feeling came over me. "Lord please be with me, I don't know what this strange feeling is that I'm having." I said still looking at myself in the mirror, I touched my hair which was in cornrows before I put my hand on the denim dress I was wearing that seemed to show off my big pregnant stomach even more.

I dried my hands then headed toward the door to return to the fellowship hall, "Lance?" I questioned with squinted eyes as I saw a silhouette that resembled Lance passing the bathroom when I opened the door.

He turned around to face me and his face looked as if he was extremely shocked, he looked as if he just saw a ghost, "uhm Brianna?" he stumbled over his words, "uhm what's up? What are you doing here?" he whispered.

"Uhm well, this party is for my Grandmother," I said and he held his head down then began shaking it.

"Wait a minute, are you saying that Sister Spencer is your grandmother?" he asked raising his head to look back at me.

"Yeah," I answered his question, "but my question is what are you doing here?" I walked closer to Lance so I could embrace him. "Baby what's wrong?" I asked, but when I tried to kiss and hug him he quickly grabbed my wrist slightly pushing me away from him.

"Brianna first off, this is my church where I am a deacon and it is not the place for all of that," he said coldly plus the fact that he called my full name let me know that he was either mad about something or the situation was just that serious. "Look Brianna the second thing is that my wife is out there and I don't need her seeing us together like this." He continued to whisper with a cold tone while wearing this solemn face as he turned his back to me and began to walk toward the dining area of the fellowship hall.

"What?" I asked with a confused look on my face. I reached out to the wall to help hold me up since I started to feel very weak, and it felt as if my legs were about to give out. "Your... uh... your wife?" I questioned and tears began to swell up in my eyes.

He stopped walking then turned around to look at me, "I'm sorry Bri," he whispered and quickly turned back around.

I grabbed my stomach and bent down slightly, "I don't understand," I said with a faint voice wanting to cry, *needing* to cry, but I had to try to compose myself. "How could—" I bent down because I was starting to have pain, plus I was cut off by Carla walking around the corner.

"Hey baby," she said as I looked up to see her greet Lance with a hug and a long kiss, the way I wanted to greet him. Seeing this made me feel nauseated, so I bent down again feeling more pain from my heart breaking rather than my stomach that I was holding onto. So Carla is his wife, a drop dead gorgeous woman that could pass for a petite model, and on top of everything else she looked like she could be my age even though she was over the age of forty. This was the woman who was just bragging about her loving, caring husband of twenty years. "Oh my God Brianna, are you okay?" Carla asked as she rushed passed a startled Lance to come to my side.

"Uhm, I...just...need...to," I said gasping for air. *Oh God please help me*, I thought while I was struggling to breath. Carla grabbed my arm and placed it around her neck so that I could lean on her, "I have asthma and I need to lie down for a minute," I gasped.

"Okay baby doll," Carla said walking toward the nurses room of the church. "Just take some deep breaths," she coached me before turning around to look at a stagnant Lance. He was probably in so much shock it paralyzed him at the sight of his wife holding up and helping his pregnant mistress. "Lance baby don't just stand there looking silly, baby come help me help this poor child to the nurses room."

"Oh okay," I heard him stutter.

I stopped walking and tried to catch my breath, "I'll be okay Carla," I struggled to say reaching in my pocket to get my inhaler and I took a puff, "really I should be fine." I said in a more calm voice after using the inhaler.

"Uh-uh sweetie we're going to get you to this nurse's room and Lance can take a listen to you," Carla shook her head. "Oh I'm sorry, I'm acting as if you two already know each other, this is my husband Lance, excuse me Doctor Hamilton," she said opening the door to the nurse's room and all I could think about after that statement was, *honey if you only knew how well we really do know each other.* "That's why I said he can take a listen to you," she said helping me to sit on the exam table while Lance was slowly creeping behind her.

"Oh alright," I said still having some difficulty breathing, but feeling better than I was before.

"Nice to meet you," Lance held out his hands for me to shake it as if we were *really* strangers, and as if he didn't just see me butt naked less than twelve hours ago. I reluctantly grabbed his hand, but instead of the usual sparks I would get from Lance's touch, this time I felt pure disgust. "Uh baby I need my bag so I can have my stethoscope to listen to her. I'm going to run to the car real quick so I can get it."

"No baby," Carla shook her head bending down to the mini fridge to retrieve a mini bottle of water. "Just tell me where it is and I'll go get it, she doesn't need to be alone in here with me when you're the doctor. And just in case something happens to her between the trip to the car and back at least she would have a doctor to help her. So you just stay in here and I'll go get your bag plus one of her family members to be back in here with her, "Carla stated after handing me the little bottle of water.

"Okay baby," Lance said sitting across the room in the doctor's chair, then he began slowly to ease toward the bed, "my bag is in the trunk in the left corner."

"Alright, we're gonna get you together so we won't have any problems with that baby."

"Thank you so much Carla," I said taking a sip of my water, while I was still lightly wheezing. Carla walked swiftly out of the room and I could tell Lance was about to speak, "don't even, please just don't even try it," I held up my hand, not even looking in his direction.

"So you're not going to let me even try to explain yourself?" he moved the chair closer to me, so he could be in a position where I'd be able to see his face.

"What could you say uh?" I glanced at him, "tell me what in the—" I stopped myself from cussing because we were still in church although we weren't in the sanctuary. "You know what, just drop this whole thing and drop it like I should have dropped you at the beginning of the year like I started to do."

"Come on now Bri," Lance tried to plead with me as he held up his left hand to his head.

"Oh God nice ring," I said sarcastically as I chuckled at the sight of his gold wedding band on his ring finger, that was something that I never saw before. As a matter of fact it was the first time in almost two years that I've ever seen that. "You know what, you should wear that more often and maybe stuff like this wouldn't have to happen." I said pointing toward my stomach before placing my hand on it and rubbing it.

"Brianna please," Lance began to speak.

"Bri, girl what is going— Lance?" Brandi rushed through the door first with Kennede and Summer in tow, she had started to ask a question but was caught off guard by Lance's presence in the room. "So Bri what's up with you?" she asked in a very slow speaking voice.

"Girl it was an asthma attack that kind of *snuck up* on me," I said taking another drink of water, "but if it wasn't for *Doctor Hamilton* here and of course if it weren't for his *lovely* wife Carla, I probably would have died. Even though it was because of *dear* Doctor Hamilton, that I had an attack anyway."

"Hold up, did you just say wife?" Brandi asked softly with her eyes wide along with Kennede and Summer's eyes. "Your wife is here?" she asked sitting next to me as she was rolling her eyes and neck at Lance.

"Wait a minute," Kennede now said holding up her hand, "did you just say 'lovely wife Carla,' or was I just hearing things?" I nodded at her, "oh my God Ms. Carla is your wife?" she asked looking in Lance's direction.

"Now you all have to let me—"

"No there is nothing to say," Brandi spoke up cutting Lance off from finishing his comment, but before Brandi could say anything else Carla showed up in the doorway with Lance's black bag.

"Hey Kennede," Carla said breezing pass Kennede and touching her shoulder as she stood by the doorway.

"Hi Ms. Carla," Kennede said glancing over at me with an I-can't-believe-what-I-am-seeing-look while Carla handed Lance's bag to him.

"Here you go babe," Carla said to Lance and I looked at the expressions on the faces of my sister and cousins, they all had wide eyes plus shock was written all over them. "Maybe I should just go back in here with everyone else or everyone my age," Carla chuckled as she patted the back of my hand.

"No Ms. Carla please don't leave go," I held onto her hand as Lance wore a disturbed look on his face, "could you please stay in here with me and my cousins until your husband finishes looking me over." I said sounding like I was a little girl, which put smirks on Brandi, Kennede, and Summer's faces.

"Okay baby doll," she put one arm around me and squeezed me tight, "I'll stay right here with you as long as you want me to sugar."

"Thank you so much Mrs. Carla," I said with a smirk while I was looking in Lance's direction. Once he finally looked over at me I laid my head on Carla's shoulder, and all he could do was wear this weird blank expression. I squinted my eyes toward him as I was thinking, *you lying cheating bastard.*

* * *

As the single tear rolled down my cheek and I stared at the wall, my breathing ceased; holding back the tears that fought their way to the surface, but now the right side of my face matched the trail left by the tear that started this emotional episode. Suddenly I realized it was over;
No more you; never to return again;
As my heart was ripped out, crushed, and quickly put back so I could feel every pain and I could do nothing; Feel nothing; nothing but pain.
As the torment of your falsehoods ripped my soul,
I felt sick to my stomach, which at the moment had nothing to do with your legacy I carried in my womb;
As your obvious mistruth of having no connection with her presented themselves as reality; I suddenly questioned everything you've ever said, which only made me question who I am and how I could have allowed myself to fall victim to you; Now after many nights of roll call, you walk pass me and have the audacity to pretend you don't know my name. With a sly grin that say's Victoria's Secret has nothing on what I could reveal, but to make that proclamation I'd be putting my own peace in jeopardy;

So I say nothing, but I take my broken heart and leave the awkward situation.

As the tears dry and I realize maybe this is exactly what I need to finally rid myself of something a pain only this massive would help me get rid of;

I almost for a second feel free, and like the straw that broke the camels back, this is it for me.

So I'll collect the broken pieces of my heart, put them in my pocket and move on; Not leaving much time to mourn;

Because now, I've become a bigger woman than what I expected. ~July 2008

I placed my notebook down after writing my thoughts/poetry about today's unbelievable events. I now felt a combination of emotions, sadness mixed with hurt, rage, disappointment, and most of all embarrassment. Even though I personally didn't feel embarrassed, I felt that for Lance's wife who I know now as Carla. She's nothing like I ever imagined her to be. I thought she would be this unattractive woman that maybe looked a lot older and possibly on the chunky side or either super duper "*crack head*" skinny, but that wasn't the case at all. The woman that I met today wasn't any of those things; as a matter of fact Carla is absolutely beautiful with the body of a woman who hasn't had four kids. That's another thing that he lied about too, telling me that he only had two kids that were very young. The reality of the situation is that they have four kids and it would have been five, but she just miscarried the most recent child.

"That lying bastard," I said aloud looking at floor thinking about my last thought, *she had a miscarriage recently*. So if she had a miscarriage sometime this year, that means what he told me about them not sleeping together in however long, was total lie too. Hell him telling me he wasn't "getting none" at home was the reason that *I* was sexing him like crazy. *He was such a liar*, I thought as my phone began to ring and I rolled my eyes, "it better not be him," I said aloud to myself before looking down at the Caller I.D. "Hello?"

"Hey Bri," Brandi said on the other end, "How are you feeling sweetie?"

"Health wise I'm feeling okay," I sniffed then I started to wipe away the newly fallen tears, "but emotionally and mentally, I uhm—" I paused before I began to sob.

"Bri please don't, Bri," my sister whined, "do you want me to come over there?" she asked.

I shook my head before saying, "no I'll be alright." I took a deep breath before I spoke again, "I just…I just feel like a big fool to believe anything that he said to me, do you know how many *lies* that he's told me that I found out today weren't *even* true, or the things that he didn't even tell me?" I asked.

"I can only imagine," Brandi said when I paused.

"B, you just don't understand," more tears started to fall, "girl I trusted him, I believed those lies, *all* of those lies because I *thought* he loved me, and I loved him. I mean I really, *really* was in love with him."

"I know you were Bri," she stated, then she let out a sigh, as if she was reluctant to go on with what she was about to say. "I know you loved him, but you knew he was married though. It wasn't like you walked into the situation not knowing about his wife."

"Yeah I know that but you," I paused then wiped face again, "but what you don't know is just this morning while still laying in *his* damn bed he proposes to me."

"What?!" Brandi shouted then she began to cough, "how in the hell, did I just hear you right?" she asked.

"Yes B you heard me right," I replied to her question, "this *lying* bastard asked me to marry him this morning. Then less than twenty-four, hell less than twelve hours later he shows up to Grandmother's Birthday party with his wife and three out of their four kids. He has *four kids* Brandi!" I continued to ramble on, letting out my feelings, "B do you know he told me about only two of his kids? He told me about the ten year old and the eight year old, but he forgot to mention the other two that are nineteen and sixteen years old. Do you know that's only four and eight years younger than us?"

"Are you serious?" Brandi managed to ask in between my rambling, "he has kids that old?"

"Yes girl," I answered, "Carla was talking about their nineteen year old son who is pre-med and I think you may have seen their sixteen year old son, the boy who following Kayla around and flirting with her and stuff."

"Oh yeah I saw him, so that was one of their kids too?" she questioned.

"Yep, that's one of theirs kids too," I replied by repeating my sister's question, "girl I'm just *too* over and done with him and just everything, especially this damn city."

"Girl I don't know exactly what you're going through, but I do understand wanting to escape from someone or something," Brandi said.

"Yeah," I sighed looking down at my stomach then I began to rub it, "look sis, I'm going to get off of here and try to get some sleep."

"Okay sweetie," she said, "are you sure you will be alright?"

"Yeah girl I'ma be okay," I waved my hand as if she could see me, "I'll just talk to you later."

"Alright later, and I love you," she said.

"I love you too," I said before ending the call. I closed my cell phone, but continued to look at it. "Before I try to get some sleep I have one more call to make," I said aloud as I reopened my phone then began to dial the numbers. "Hey are you busy?"

"No Bri, what's up?" Aunt Regina asked.

"Well, I uhm, I want to talk to you about our conversation earlier," I said looking at my swollen stomach, "when are you going back home to Indy?"

"Oh, are you thinking about rolling with me?" she asked and I closed my eyes.

"Yeah," I said in a sigh as a single tear fell from my left eye, "I just need to get away from here for a minute."

"Okay baby I can understand that," Aunt Regina stated, "but going to leave here Monday morning."

"Oh okay," I sighed while closing my eyes again, but this time I was hoping to block more tears from falling. "Uhm, do you mind if I tag along to Indianapolis with you?" I asked.

"Of course you can come with me suga," she replied, "You already know it's not a problem and that you are more than welcomed to come home with me."

"Thank you so much Aunt Gina," I said feeling a sense of relief, "just call to let me know when you want me to be ready."

"Okay suga I will do that," she paused then said, "well my husband's calling and I'll just talk to you later."

"Okay Aunt Gina," she hung up with me to answer her husband's call, I hung up feeling more relief. "Okay Step one into my new life, move out of Louisville." I rubbed my stomach and tears fell, "I'm sorry baby," I spoke to my big round belly, "I mean *our* new life."

18
Brandi

"It smells good in here if I may say so myself," I said aloud, but speaking to myself as I took the garlic bread out of the oven. Since Monday's are one of my days off I decided I'd cook dinner for my husband for our first night we were about to spend alone since our honeymoon, which was almost a month ago. Jordan was on his way down to South Carolina with Jayson's older sister Jena, her husband Paul, and their three kids. Jena and Paul were just here in town over the 4th of July weekend and they asked us if Jordan could spend a few weeks at their home in South Carolina with their kids while all of them were out of school for the summer. Well you already know with Jay and I being "newlyweds" and all, we jumped on that opportunity to be alone to do those newlywed type things. They left early this morning because according to Jena and Paul it's about a ten and a half hour drive from here to Myrtle Beach, and my guess is they are probably still on the road since neither of them has called to say otherwise. Then again if they have already made it there they could've called Jayson at work and I wouldn't know until he gets home.

That's right I said work! Jayson finished his realtor license a few months ago and went straight to work. Well actually he and his little brother bought this mini strip mall type of property that had about three or four vacant spaces, they purchased it a discount rate and now have filled two of those vacant spaces. One of the spaces is occupied by Jayson's mother Mrs. Janet Hill who is a caterer; she now has her own shop inside of the mini mall as well. Her business is called **Ms. Janet's Delights**, the business has improved a whole lot from its start in her kitchen, but now she's in her very own shop. Coming from a family of "great cooks" I can say that her food is very good, so good that her company took care of the food that was served at my reception, even though Ms. Janet wasn't physically in kitchen that day her recipes were the ones that we stuffed our faces with. Another one of the spaces is used for Jayson's little brother Jerrod who is a barber, so Jay decided to help him open his own barbershop. *The Brother's Barbershop'* is actually ran by Jayson even though he doesn't cut hair he has his own office and is pretty much the boss, but the barbers are Jerrod and three of his friends that graduated from barber school with him about two years ago. Also Jayson and Jerrod's cousin Donna is now working at the shop too; she's a barber and hair-braider for the brothers that want to have the long hair and stuff. I must say the girl is good at both her jobs, matter of fact she was the one who used to braid Jayson's hair before he got it cut off the morning that we got married.

Jay is looking at some other business to fill the last few spaces, but he told me that one space will be totally saved for me to become a dance studio. He tells me all the time I need to use the gift of dancing that I have to help teach some little girls who may not have the money to learn the stuff that I was blessed to attend school for while I was in high school. I know I've shared it before how I loved to dance and how I was blessed to go to New York one summer to study it with the professionals. But after I graduated high school I decided to take the safe road especially after the whole "stripping ordeal" and went to nursing school. I put my gift of dance on the back burner so that I could make some real money, but Jayson tells me all the time how its time to put that gift God has given me to use.

Honestly I've already started to do that in a way, since I've been back into to church one of the ministries that I signed up with one the dance ministry. We dance for special services that are held at the church, our group has gotten so good that sometimes we are asked to perform outside of our church but for other functions that happen throughout the city. And I must say that each time that I am able to get out there to dance for Lord and for the audience I get a rush that makes me feel so fulfilled, like this is what I am suppose to be doing with my life. Jay and I talk about those feelings I have all the time, that's part of the reason why he says that he is saving a space for my dance studio, he says that he believes in my gift every time he is able to watch me perform. He says that is why nobody will ever get that space which is located on the right side of his barbershop; he says his right hand woman should be on his right side pursuing her purpose in life. I swear that I love that man, and I don't know too many men that support their wives dreams that haven't even come true yet like he does. Shoot if it wasn't for him constantly telling me how much he believes that dancing is my purpose rather than staying in a hospital being nurse, I wouldn't even be giving actually going back to study dance a second thought if it weren't for Mr. Jayson Hill. I began smiling while I finished up cooking at thought of all he does for me. Another thing that Jay has done that he doesn't even know I really appreciate is not communicating with that ole' Lester Black anymore.

I was so happy that day Jay told me that he no longer fooled with that fool, although he never went into the details of his decision other than saying that Black was shady and something wasn't right about him, and now that Jay was back on track with his life, he didn't need anybody negative like Black lurking around his life. When Jay said that it was like music to my ears, because I would no longer have to see this fool in my house anymore, plus I thank God that I haven't seen him anymore since the day that he was up in here. I had to give my fears about him following me over to Jesus, and since I've done that I haven't had those feelings that Black was following me like I use to feel all the time. Anyway I am also happy that Jay hasn't brought up or asked me anymore questions about the whole "rape" thing again. I think that he bought my story I told about being unsure who the person was and that it was so dark that I couldn't see the persons face. Whatever the reason he wasn't asking anymore, I was just happy that I didn't have to relive that time plus have to lie about some of the things just so I could save my husband's life. As I said before, Jayson Darnell Hill would kill Lester Black if he knew the truth and he knew that he was the one that raped me.

"Baaaaaby!" Jayson yelled as he entered the front door, "Dang baby it smells too good in here."

"Hey baby," I turned from the stove as he walked from the living room into the kitchen doorway. *My God if I didn't have the finest husband in the world*, I began to think to myself. Even without his braids in anymore he looked so good, and now he was wearing this light blue buttoned down polo shirt that was hanging outside of his long length khaki shorts. "Damn baby if I must say, you are looking too good today," I said to him looking all sexy.

I walked up to him then stood on my toes to kiss my fine sexy husband, "baby uhm," he licked his lips, "as hungry as I am now, and as good as the food smells, I'd rather just take you on upstairs first." He bent down and kissed me again, this time kissing on my neck and that's when my eyes went in the back of head making his suggestion of skipping dinner sound real good. "Come on babe, I know I got you ready to go now, we can eat later."

"No nope," I tried to contain myself before I wrapped my arms around his waist and began looking into his eyes. "I have something *extra* special for later," I kissed his lips slowly, trying to remind myself of what I planned for our night of uninterrupted of love making. Since Jordan was gone there was no need in us being interrupted by anything, that's why I wanted to get dinner out of the way just in case our son tried to call before his bedtime so he could at least talk to us. "So this is what we're going to do, we're going to eat this dinner I prepared for us first, then we can have desert wherever you want it all night long, I promise."

He smiled and nodded in approval, "yes ma'am Mrs. Hill," he said while saluting me like he was in the army.

"Oh I can't tell you how much I love hearing you say that, Mrs. Hill," I smiled then went back over to the stove to take out the baked spaghetti. "Okay baby, its time to eat, so go on in there and wash your hands please."

"Yes ma'am," he saluted me again before he walked to the half bathroom that we had on the first floor of our house. While he was doing that, I sat some oven holders on the table so I could sit the hot dish on it. I then went to the refrigerator to take out the salad and lemonade that I had made while the other food cooked. "B everything looks too good too, and I am too hungry," Jay said as he was taking his seat at the table.

"Well I hope it all taste good," I said now taking my seat as well.

"Don't play girl, you come from a family of cooks," he said grabbing my hand as he then began to bless the food.

"So baby, how was your day today?" I asked smiling with my mouth closed but full of food. I was so happy that I could ask him a normal question like how was work since most of the time we were together he was doing the illegal thing.

"Oh it was pretty good today," he said smacking his lips, "you know the shop is closed to customers on Monday's, but we did have a little meeting with all of the barbers today. I finished with that about three o'clock, then I went next door to Mama's restaurant to talk to her, but she was so busy that I ended up helping her out for a little while," he chuckled and I did as well. "But get this when I got there she was doing some interviews for extra help, so I tried to help by answering the phones and little stuff like that." He pause to take a drink, "I love my moms and all, but trust me when I say I'll be glad when she finds her help because doing that stuff all day is not for me."

"Oh trust me I know about that too," we both laughed again, "shoot why do you think I never worked in a place like that," as soon as those words finished leaving my lips my smile faded as I started to think of *'The Black Foxx Gentlemen's Club.'*

My guess was that Jay could tell by my new quietness along with my facial expression what I was thinking, "baby I must say this dinner is off the hook," he said changing the subject, and I didn't even look up at him. "Brandi, baby look at me please," he said reaching over to grab my hand and he laid our hands on the table then I looked up at him, "I know that you are probably thinking about that damn club and what happened there, aren't you?" he asked.

I gave him a half smile and rolled my eyes, "yes baby, but I—"

"Baby just let it go," he said cutting me off, "I know that what happened there hurt you, but baby you have to let it go because you are going to let it drive you crazy." He squeezed my hand tighter as I thought; *shoot it has already driven close to crazy if he only knew.* I simply nodded my head before he said, "we're not about to let that ruin our possible beautiful night, okay?" he squeezed a little bit more, not hurting me at all but making me feel like I was protected.

"Okay baby," I closed my eyes briefly then placed a full smile on face. Nobody wanted to get over what happened at that club that night more than I did because I was the one that suffered, even though I understood Jay's reason for doing what he just did and saying that I needed to let it go because that's exactly what I needed to do. *Lord just please help me to let it go,* I thought while I closed my eyes again for just a second.

"I can't wait to see what you have planned for later," he said with a sneaky grin now on his face which made me smile too, "yeah that's what I love to see on you," he said as he took the back of his hand and rubbed it down the side of my face.

I closed my eyes and tilted my head to the side as he rested his hand on my neck, him doing all of that brought me back to the moment. "Oh you're just going to have to wait to see what I am going to do to you, Mr. Hill," I said pushing my plate back then standing to my feet. "As a matter of fact, you stay down here while I go upstairs and get things prepared for you," I smiled the sexiest that I could, and he smiled back.

"Okay," he said and I started kissing on his neck as he began to moan softly, "uhm I can't wait to see what you are about to do."

"I want you to do me a favor though while I'm upstairs," he moved his chair back and I then sat on his lap straddling him as I started to kiss his lips, "what I need you to do is call your sister to make sure that they have made it home safely with our baby."

He wrapped his arms around my waist and began kissing me again, "oh that's already taken care of baby," he grabbed the back of my neck to bring me closer into him for another kiss, "they called me on my way home and said they had just made it in and Jordan told me he was gonna call you tomorrow so he could play with cousins all night." He said then immediately started in on my neck; I closed my eyes and began to get as excited as I could feel Jay was while I was still on his lap.

"Okay that's good that you already talked to him so he won't have to interrupt what I have planned," I said kissing him while I was trying to ease off of him, "because what I plan on doing we're going to need total concentration and means while I'm upstairs I need you to turn off our cell phones, and take the house phones off the hook, so I'm about to go get ready." I said now standing in front of Jay.

"Oh come on baby, you already got me ready," he said using one hand to try to pull me back on him while he used the other hand to point toward his crotch, but I used all of my strength to breakaway completely.

"Jayson baby, I promise it will be worth the wait, okay?" I said bending back down to kiss the back of his neck, "please just wait one minute for me and be a good patient boy, I promise you will get rewarded very *very* well, okay?" I said in the sexiest voice that I could with my lips grazing his ear while I spoke.

"Uhm o-oh okay," he managed to say while I was licking on his earlobes, "okay baby, please hurry up please."

I started to giggle at how turned on I had made my husband, "okay babe, I'm going to call for you when I'm ready okay?" I said walking toward the steps, all he did was nod his head with his eyes closed. I ran up the stairs then straight into our bedroom and right into my closet to get this pink lacy sheer halter camisole and boy short set with the matching silk pink short-kimono style robe that I recently bought from the *Frederick's of Hollywood* catalog. I placed the lingerie on my vanity while I grabbed the bag of rose petals that I hid in the closet the other day and started to scatter them across our bed, I then used the petals to also make a trail from the hallway that ended at the foot of the bed.

After that I started to light all of the candles that we already had throughout our bedroom because we both loved to have candles for decoration and for relaxation as well. I also think that candles give any room that extra romantic feel especially if you're about to do what I am to do, there's nothing sexier than having a sexy man with a beautifully sculpted body like my husband and making love to him by candle lit, whoa. Thinking about it made me wanna hurry up and finish everything else I needed to do to set up for our romantic evening so I could go on and get to candle lit lovemaking. I ran back into my closet to take off the clothes I had on so I could take a quick shower and be *very* fresh for my man. That's one thing that I believed in being "squeaky clean" before doing the do, I believe a woman should be *extra* fresh and clean before getting down and dirty. You never want your man walking away thinking, "damn my woman needs to *squash, squash* before I go down there again!" Ladies please make sure that you are super *duper* fresh especially if you already know something is about to go down, or if its spontaneous sex and you know you aren't smelling so fresh, its okay to tell the brotha to put it on pause for a minute so you can run and take care of "Miss Kitty." Trust me the brotha will appreciate it plus if you want that man to continue to make frequent visits if he's not already your husband, then it will keep the brotha coming back to visit "Miss Kitty" on a regular basis knowing that she keeps a "clean house," if you know what I mean.

    I took everything I was going to put on into the bathroom, which included my deodorant and lavender baby oil gel just in case Jay tried to come up here before I called him. At least if he did try to sneak up to the bedroom before I was finished with my shower, I'd be ready when I came out of the bathroom. Before I actually stepped in the shower I started to take the rubber bands off of the ends of my long cornrows, so when I took the braids down after my shower I would have that wet wavy look. Yes I was planning to look extra super sexy for my husband, because he deserves it after working so hard. I had to show him in at least one way how much he was appreciated and loved around here.

    "Jayson," I called out his name in the sexiest voice that I could, "baby can you please come here?" I asked now standing at the top of the steps, I was surprised that he didn't try to come up to the bedroom before I finished my shower.

    "Okay babe here I come," I heard him running up the steps as I ran back into the room so I could lay on the bed of roses waiting for him to hit the door. "Oh my damn, baby you look amazing," he said standing in the doorway. It looked like while he was waiting for me downstairs that he had ditched his shirts because he was standing there with his six pack showing.

    "You look good too," I said referring to how the candlelight flickering on his bare chest made the mood even sexier and made my husband look even better. On top of everything else I had put on what I liked to call my "*Bump-n-Grind Mix*" that I put together for times like this that set the mood off even more. When I got out of the shower I made sure that I started that CD and put it on repeat because I was hoping for a very long night. Even though what we were about to do by making love doesn't seem special from any other night, being that we were now a married couple and us doing it was something that didn't be as special as I was making tonight. But what made tonight different from any regular night was the fact that I was *finally* going to "return the favor," meaning I was finally going to go down on my husband for the first time. And it's not like its going to be the first time I'm doing this with Jay as my husband, but this was the first time ever. I had always thought that the idea of "going down on a man" was a little on the nasty side, but after talking to Kennede of all people, about what I could do to change things up in the bedroom, she suggested that and gave me a few tips that will make men go wild. So tonight was going to be the night that I tried something new on my new husband, I just hope that he likes it because I know that I love when takes frequent trips downtown.

I motioned for him to come to me with my index finger, "Brandi you look so sexy," he said now standing in front of me, I then uncrossed my legs and stood up so we were now looking into each others eyes. He gave me a serious look, "I swear that I love you so much baby," he kissed my lips while holding onto m body. Any nerves that I had about what I was going to do now went out the window.

"I love you too Jay," I finally said once I was able to catch my breathe, "come here baby, I have something for you," I grabbed his hand and led him the spot on the bed that I was just sitting at, which was at the end of the bed.

"Brandi what are you up to?" Jay asked before I slightly pushed him down on the bed and stood right in front of him as I began to untie the belt on my robe.

"Shhh," I put my finger over my mouth as I finished untying my belt, "you just sit right there and let me do *my* thing."

"Yes ma'am, oh my God," Jay said after I had opened the robe all of the way to reveal one of my many surprises of the evening. "Baby you are oh my…thank God for my beautiful wife," he said looking toward the ceiling as I continued to model my lingerie for him.

I laughed, "So do you like this?" I turned around slowly after throwing the robe on the floor. He shook his head in agreement and grabbed my arm pulling me on top of him so he could let our tongues meet. "Baby you are gonna mess my other surprise up, I told you that I've got this," I said rising up, but I was still straddling him.

"Go on baby and do your thing," Jay said and I could feel him "responding" to our heavy kisses.

"Thank you," I simply said then kissed him on the lips once more before I started sucking on his earlobes before making my way down to his neck. His moans told me he was enjoying me being in control, so I took it further, moving down to his chest trying to make hickeys on it, before moving down to his navel.

"Brandi baby," Jay moaned as I started to lick below his navel. I sat up trying to unzip his pants so I could remove them, "baby are you gonna—"

"Shhh," I said taking his pants off then removing his boxers that now showed him in his full stiffness. I kneeled down and started to "take care" of my husband in a new way.

"Oh my…Brandi," Jay yelled out in satisfaction, I then became confident that I was doing it right, "baby you…uhm…damn baby that is…uhm." He tried to speak in between the moans. I could feel him trying to remove the halter camisole while I was still on my knees, because he couldn't concentrate on trying to take it off, I used the other free hand I had to help him take it off.

"I told you that I had a surprise for you," I said after I had licked a trail back up to his face that now wore this huge smile.

"B, I…I don't know what to say," he had a blank expression on his face now, "I just love you so much."

I smiled then kissed his lips, "I love you too," we kissed again, this time longer and more passionate. We stopped for a split second so he could grab my shoulders to turn me around so that he was now on top of me. He removed my boy shorts and threw them on the floor. Jay then licked me from the top of my foot, up to my thighs and continued to move up my stomach all the way up until he reached my neck. As he was kissing on my neck he also entered inside of me at the same time, "baaabyy," I closed my eyes and moaned at the exact time Jay was moaning too. For about two and half hours we played this game to see whose yell was the loudest while we made love. This was a "game" that I loved to play with my husband, a man who knew just how to make yell his name. But not only yell his name, he made it so good that I had to spell it and vice versa.

*   *   *

I was walking toward the garage after leaving Dr. Grant's office complex with a smile on my face. I was happy that there were no signs of blood clots because my blood was thin enough by now. It seems kind of crazy for someone so young to have blood clots, but I did have them a few years ago because I was taking birth control pills. But the reason that I started taking the birth control pills wasn't because of Jayson; I started taking the pills after the incident that happen at the club. After I had the abortion I decided I had to be safe especially with that fool still stalking me after the rape, just in case somehow he was able to rape me again I wouldn't get pregnant this time if it were to happen. Even though I started to take the pill at the age of eighteen, it was last year at the age of twenty-two that I had two blood clots that formed in my right leg. It scared my family really bad when I was hospitalized for it, but Jayson seemed to hurt the worst. He was so scared that I was going to die that he never left my bedside when I was in the hospital for those four days and three nights. I think it scared him more than anyone that was in my family, quiet as it was kept, I was just as scared as Jayson was too.

Well anyway, Dr. Grant did say that because my blood was now thin enough, I could stop taking the blood thinners for about six months just as a trial. After the trial period is over and if there is no signs of blood clots, then I can stay off of the blood thinners for good, just as long as I don't take the birth control again. But now that I'm married and not too worried about Black trying anything anymore, I wasn't scared of becoming pregnant just as long as it was my husband's baby. My cell phone began to ring as I was standing at the elevators waiting for one to take me to the sixth level of the garage where my car was. The doctor's office complex was also adjacent to one of the hospitals so parking even in the garage was a headache, and that's the reason that I ended up on the sixth out of seven levels in the garage.

I rummaged through my purse trying to find my cell phone that I had shoved in there, "hello?" I finally answered quickly before the last ring.

"Hey girl, are you busy?" Kennede asked when I answered.

"Oh no girl," I said trying to catch my breath, "I'm just now leaving the doctor's office and now I'm just waiting for the elevator to take me up all the way to the sixth level to get my truck."

"Oh God the sixth level, woo girl," Ken said, "Are you going to be busy after you leave there?"

"Well I need to go to the post office," then the bell dinged as the elevator doors opened, "hey Ken I'm about to get on this elevator so I might lose reception."

"Okay girl, just call me back when you get out of that garage," Ken said then she started to break up after the doors closed. "I…you…come…shop," was all I heard.

"Ken if you can hear me, you're already starting to break up, I'll call you when I get out." I said not waiting for a response from her so I just closed my phone, even though I held it in my hand along with my keys.

"Sixth level," the elevator announced and the bell dinged again. I began to walk toward my 2006 *Chevy Trailblazer*, once I got into my S.U.V.; I noticed something was in between my windshield and the wipers. I hopped back out of the truck and grabbed the white envelope. I got back in truck then looked at the front which was blank.

"What in the world is this?" I asked aloud before opening it, "Oh my God!" I said loudly as I began to shake in fear because of what I was holding in my hand. There was a picture that was of me dancing on the pole at the Black Foxx, "who in the world would do this?" I asked myself as tears began to fall. I turned the picture around and there was a sticky note that said:

'Cocoa I remember you now! ☺'

Although it wasn't signed, I already knew who it was from. There's only one sick bastard who would do something like this, Lester Black. Out of fear I turned around to look in my backseat just to make sure he hadn't tried to hide out in it or something.

I turned back around and laid my head on the headrest trying to hold back the tears, so I closed my eyes. *But how did he know where I was*, I thought, *that fool had to have followed me or something*. I looked around outside of my car, there were no signs of people lurking, so I hurried to start my car and get my butt up out of this parking garage before this crazy fool could try something else. *I know one thing, I'm not about to go home alone*, I thought. I decided to go straight to the barbershop to be with Jay. Hopefully Black wouldn't be crazy enough to follow me over there knowing my heat packing husband would be around. Even though Jay wasn't in "the streets" anymore he still carried his gun just in case someone tried him for any reason.

"Hey what's going on?" I said walking into the barbershop speaking to all the barbers.

"What's up B?" they all said back to me, "your husband is back in his office," Jay's little brother Jerrod said to me as he sat in his vacant barber chair. The shop wasn't crowded at all, Donna was braiding this guy's hair while another barber was cutting a little kid.

"Thanks a lot," I said walking up to the office then knocking lightly on the door, "baby it's me," I said softly before walking in. Jay was leaning forward reading over some papers while he also on the phone. "Sorry," I whispered as I sat on the couch that was across from his desk and up against the wall.

He shook his head and mouthed, "You're good, don't worry about it beautiful," he gave thumbs up. I smiled then crossed my long legs which must have through off Jay's concentration because he started staggering for words while talking to whoever was on the phone. "Uhm…yeah, actually… uhm," he said staring at my smooth hairless legs in this white skirt that was just above my knees, well when I'm standing. I also had on a black and white striped V-neck halter top with a built in bra. With the heat index of one hundred and five degrees outside I wanted to wear as less as possible without looking like a slut that is, but I sure didn't want to die of a heat stroke because I was wearing *too* many clothes.

"Okay I'll see you next Monday, that will be the best time for an interview," he licked his lips before mouthing to me again, "I want you." Then he went back to his phone conversation, "okay I will see you then, bye," he hung the phone up so quickly I don't even think that he actually said bye into the phone. "Damn baby you are looking too good in that skirt," he said jumping up from his desk chair and walking over to the couch were I was sitting then bent down in front of me so we could kiss.

"Uhm," I moaned, "so are you going to finish—"

"Knock, knock," Mrs. Janet said before she busted into the office with a grocery bag that had two Styrofoam food boxes in them. "Oh I'm sorry to interrupt ya'll, but Jayson I told you I was bringing you and the guys some food for lunch since I was going to have so many leftovers from the big order I had today."

Jay stood up straight, then walked toward his mother, "oh yeah thanks Ma," he took the bag from her hand, "this isn't all of the food is it?"

"No boy, your dad is bringing in the other food for the guys," she said waving her hands at him as she made her way to the couch where I was still sitting. "So how is my favorite daughter-in-law doing today?" she asked as I stood then she gave me a hug, "ooohh Brandi you hair so cute like that with the wavy ponytail going on."

"Thank you," I said smiling, "but to answer your first question, I'm doing okay other than all of this heat that we have."

"Child I know," she said putting her hand on her hip and using the other hand to fan herself, "honey that's why I'm wearing this little sundress today so I can make my deliveries in this heat to some company downtown that is having some kind of function in their office, but I'm glad your dad isn't working anymore so he can help me because it's a pretty big order," she said looking over in Jay's direction. I must say that Mrs. Janet looked good for a woman who was less than two years away from turning fifty years young. She reminds me of Ken because they have the same complexion with almost the same short curly hair, if Ken keeps her hair short when she gets that age Ken would look just like Mrs. Janet. But instead of being mixed with black and white like Ken, Mrs. Janet's mother was mixed with black and white and her father was from Cuba.

"So where's Dad at anyway?" Jay asked sitting back at his desk opening up one of the boxes and began to eat some food he picked up with his hands.

"Hey, hey," Mr. Hill said as he walked through the door, "what's going on there son?" he nodded his head toward Jay.

"Nothing Pops," Jay said smacking his lips, "it's all good for me, how about you?"

"I can't complain," he replied then walked over to me and gave me a hug, "and how are you doing today the new *Mrs. Hill?*" he ask with a chuckle.

I laughed too, "I'm doing fine today Mr. Hill," I said looking up at him after letting go from our hug. Mr. Hill is a very tall man, he had to be about six foot three with a medium build, and if you looked at him and Jay together you would see where Jay gets his statue from.

"I came in here to hurry your mother along," he grabbed Mrs. Janet by her waist, "baby we've got to get a move on so we can be at this place before one-thirty to set everything up."

"Alright, alright Jackson Hill," Mrs. Janet said giving me a goodbye hug, "I'll see you all later," she said to us, "but sweetheart I had to make sure my babies had something to eat before we made our deliveries," she said now talking to Mr. Hill who had one eye brow raised.

"Babies?" Mr. Hill chuckled, "Janet these kids are far from babies they are grown, but come on now so we can get back to the shop before something happens with us leaving it unoccupied."

"Are you serious, nobody is watching the shop while ya'll are gone?" Jay asked.

"Yes there is somebody there at the shop," Mrs. Janet said and Mr. Hill rolled his eyes, "stop that Jackson, Janea is capable of watching the shop for a little while," she said hitting his arm lightly.

"Yeah alright," he said with his hand on the door knob about to open the door, "God knows I love my child, but that girl can be a little ditsy some times, you all know it."

Jay shrugged his shoulders, "well Ma, I have to agree with Pops on this one," he said talking about his twenty-one year old baby sister. Although she is only two and a half years younger than Jay, the girl could be a little scatterbrained. "Ma you know that Janea can act a little *blondish* at times."

Mrs. Janet scrunched her face as Mr. Hill, Jay and I laughed, "ya'll aren't right at all for talking about my baby like that," she said this time opening the door all the way and Mr. Hill grabbed it so he could hold the door open for her to walk out first. "Come on here Jackson let's go then, I'll see ya'll later babies."

"Bye," Jay and I said in unison as I walked toward the door behind them. Once they closed the door I then locked it, "finally alone at last," I said turning around and leaning up against the door, then Jay leaned back in his chair with his cell phone in his hand. "Babe what are you doing?" I asked.

"Hold on a minute, let me just send this real quick," he said without looking up at me.

"Jay what are you up to?" I asked while walking slowly in front of is desk then I leaned forward, "babe what's up?"

"I'm just about finished," he hit one more button on his phone before sitting it on the desk. After he put the phone down, he then looked up at me with his sexy bedroom eyes. "I had to send out a text to everybody out there to tell them that I was going on a very long extended lunch and they should do the same." He said as he stood from his chair and I straighten my posture as he walked closer to me. Jay grabbed my hand and turned me so that I could face him. "I told them if they wanted to they didn't even have to come back to the shop for the rest of the day," he paused so he could start kissing me, first on my nose then on my lips. "I also told them to lock up the shop on their way out," he continued to kiss my lips softly while he wrapped his arm around my waist still maintaining to passionately kiss with his fingertips grazing my back that wasn't covered by my halter top.

I closed my eyes and sighed with pleasure, "so are you telling me—"

"Alright Jay, we're out man," Jerrod said from the other side of the door, "See ya'll tomorrow braugh."

"See tomorrow Jerrod," Jay said loudly but staring at me like he was ready to do some damage to me, but in a good way, "oh could you please don't forget to lock up when you walk out okay?"

"I know I got you," he replied, "later Jay, later Mrs. B."

"Bye Jerrod," I yelled to him, then I heard him walking away from the door. "Mr. Hill did you get rid of them so you could get some?" I asked with a smirk on my face.

He began to smirk as well before his hands began to travel down to my lower back, "uhm that was the idea," he replied as his fingers were going down the back of my thighs before he started gripping backside.

"Uhm…baby," I moaned while we continued to kiss, "you… are… so… bad," I said in between our lip locking. "But that's what I love the most about you, being a bad boy."

"Well, I'm about to be the worst bad boy ever," his said moving his hands from my backside then he went under my skirt and began to remove my panties. "Come on over here," he said taking my hand then walking me over to the couch. Jay sat down as I remained standing waiting on him to finish unzipping his jeans, "come here," he said patting his lap as if he wanted me to sit there.

"Okay," I sat on his lap and we began kissing so hot and heavy that we ended up making love right there in his office on the couch.

Later that Evening:

"Babe I thought you were following me home?" I questioned Jay. I had pulled into our driveway and noticed that he was not longer behind me. Immediately I started to panic that's why I ended up calling his phone.

"B you remember before we left the shop you said that you wanted some Chinese food," he began to explain, "so I just stopped by the restaurant up the street so you wouldn't have to cook, are you alright?"

"Yeah, yeah," I said as I looked around making sure I didn't see any signs of Black. I guess I had got so caught up into my husband that I temporarily forgot about Black's crazy ass, but now reality has set in big time. "I mean, I'm just glad that the sun hasn't gone down all the way so it's not completely dark yet," I said aloud but I was really trying to convince myself that nothing was wrong.

"Baby when did you start being afraid of the dark?" Jay asked laughing.

"I…I'm not, but I was just saying," I said stepping out of my truck. I was praying that this fool wouldn't try to do anything to me while I was on the phone, so I dashed to the front door with my cell phone still to my ear. "Well, alright babe I'll just see you when you get here," I said after I closed the door behind me with a sense of relief, hopefully that little thing Black pulled at the doctor's office was over.

"Alright B, I'll see you in a minute," Jay said before hanging up the phone.

I hope I didn't worry him with my paranoid concerns. I tried to play it off as much as I could over the phone, but I just felt relieved that nothing happened while I was outside. I went into the living room trying to kill some time, and to calm down a little more before Jay came home, so I sat on the couch to watch some television. After flipping through the channels about a million times I finally decided to watch MTV to possible catch a video, but the only thing that was on that station was *The Real World*.

"I wonder how my Bri is doing." I said aloud to myself after watching the show and one of the girls on there shared my sister's name. I hadn't talked to her since the whole fiasco that happened on the 4th of July. I knew she was going to Indy to visit although she was catching a ride with Aunt Regina, but I hadn't heard from either of them since she left.

I picked up my cell that was sitting on the couch next to me and began to type: `Hey sis, how are you doing? And how's Naptown treating you?` Then I sent the message to her.

While I was waiting for Brianna to respond I heard what sounded like the wind blowing the trees very hard. I sat up from my relaxed position and was about to look out the window until my phone chirped letting me know I had a message. It was Bri texting me back; `Nap is GREAT!!! I love it up here; I don't want to come back to Louisville at all`☹.

I typed back to her; `Do your thang girl! You just do you.` I sent the message then I started to hear a faint tapping on my window, but I thought nothing of it because I just assumed it was a branch that grazed it.

Just to make sure I got up then walked to the window and pulled the vertical blinds to see Black walking through my bushes up to the front door which made my heat drop. "***BANG, BANG, BANG!***" he knocked on the door and I damn near jumped out of my skin. I quickly closed the blinds even though I was shaking like a leaf.

"Who…who is it?" I yelled to the other side of the door. I was not about to open the door for this fool, I wasn't that crazy because I knew he would do something if I did open it.

"It's Black," he said with his scratchy voice, "can you please open the door."

"Uhm Jay...uh isn't here right now, I'll tell him to call you," I said without thinking first because I was so terrified. *Oh damn why did I say that about Jay not being here*, I thought, *Lord please protect me, and please Lord don't let him do anything to me anymore.* "Look I'm sure he already has your number. I...I'll tell him to call you, he's on his way home soon."

"*BANG, BANG!*" I jumped again, "I'm not here for him *Cocoa*," he yelled and my heart was now in my throat as a chill went down my spine. Nobody has ever called me that name since the night he raped me, that was the last time I heard it and it was from him. "Yeah that's right, I remember you now," my eyes began to swell, "but if you don't want to talk now that's cool, but we will talk trust me, and very soon."

"Look you better leave before *my husband* gets here," I said with a shaky voice, "if he knows what..."

"Well you better make sure that he doesn't," he cut me off before he paused, "look I'll just see you around, believe that." I heard a car door close then the sound of screeching tires.

I closed my eyes and sighed as tears started fall, that's when I began to panic again. *Jay can't see me like this or he'll know something is up for real.* I ran upstairs as quickly as I could before snatching my clothes off and hopping into the shower. As the water hit my face it started to mix with the tears that had fallen, I looked up to the ceiling, "Lord please, please, please protect me. God don't let that fool hurt me again please Jesus." I sobbed briefly before I heard Jay hollering that the food was here. "*And God when the time is right, help me to tell my husband what really happened without him going crazy.*

19
Summer

"Wooo," I sat down in the chair at the desk in my office. Even though I had only been working at the center since June they offered me my own office two months later which was about two weeks ago. I pulled out my cell phone to see if Amir had text me back from earlier, but when I opened the phone I saw that he still hadn't text or called me. Things have been going really good for Amir and I since we've decided to become a couple, even though this week he's been acting very strange. I mean he hasn't been acting rude or nasty toward me, he's normally a touchy feely romantic type but this week he hasn't been himself. I had text him about nine o'clock this morning to make sure everything was okay because he had left the house earlier this morning in such a hurry that he didn't give my normal wake up call with kisses. That's just not like Amir to act like that without a reason and we haven't had any type of argument or anything to cause him to act distant, that's why I'm so concerned and I pray that nothing bad is going on with him.

"Hey Summer," the director of the center Ms. Deborah knocked on my door before entering, "do you have a minute so I can talk to you?" she asked peeking her head around the door.

"Sure come on in," I sat my phone down and extended my arm to let her know that she could sit in the chairs in front of my desk.

"Thanks for giving me a minute because there is something very important that I want to talk to you about," she sat down in the chair trying to get comfortable. "Well first I want to say that you are doing such an amazing job with the abused women's group."

"Thank you Ms. Deborah," I said smiling and she began to smile as well, "I think that my own personal experience has helped me to relate with the women a little more."

She nodded her head in agreement, "what I want to talk to you about is making you a full time counselor," she paused for a moment and I was about to speak but she held her hand up as her chocolate colored face lost its smile. "I know the counselors' position requires that you have a bachelor's degree in psychology, but because you already have a bachelor's degree the only thing we would require that you do is take a few classes that could make you become a certified psychologist."

"Wow," I said as I leaned back in my chair, "I've never thought about doing counseling like that before even though I do love what I do now. I mean… wow; this is something that I would really have to pray about, seriously."

"That's very understandable, but just know that we are really interested in making you a full time worker because of your work ethics among other reasons," she said before she stood up, "now keep in mind there is no time limit on this, so take as much time as you need. Trust me I understand about praying for such a decision like this one because if you decide to take the job, that means you would have to go back to school and I know with you just graduating a few months ago going back is the last thing on your mind."

I nodded in agreement, "but then on the other side there is a salary increase right?" I questioned.

"Oh of course, I wouldn't want you to waste your time going back to school for how ever long and not increase your pay. As a matter of fact, if you do decide to take the job, we will even pay for your classes, books, and for whatever else that you would need in order to become a certified psychologist." I sat silent for a minute because I couldn't believe what I was hearing, it sounded like a wonderful thing especially when she said that my school expenses would be taken care of because college is very costly. "Sweetie I hope that you will agree to do this, but again please take as much time as you need to talk it over with God. Honey I will be praying on my end as well, I will see you later."

"Okay, thank you again Ms. Deborah," I said now standing so I could shake her hand before she exited my office. "Wow," was all I could say as I sat back down in my chair because this was something serious to think about. I mean I would love to do something like that where I am helping these women and getting paid for doing something that I've grown to love.

Even though now I am getting a little check for the work I do in the group sessions which are only three times in a week I could make even more by doing private counseling sessions, but I wonder if I decide to become certified will I be able to keep my group sessions along with doing private ones? Like I told Ms. Deborah it's just something I would really have to pray about. As I sat there thinking over the offer that was just presented to me, my phone began to ring and I quickly grabbed it hoping it was Amir, but it wasn't him, "hello?" I answered.

"Hey Ms. Thang," Chyna said on the other end, "What is going on girl?"

"Chyna is that you?" I questioned even though I knew it was her.

"Yes ma'am," she said and I could hear the smile in her voice, "I've missed my friend."

"Well you did move across town leaving me to go crazy," I laughed as I talked, "so how's your *man* doing anyway?"

"Chad is doing just fine," she cleared her throat, "but forget about me and my boring life, so what's up with you and Amir?"

A half smile came across my face, "we're doing good," I said thinking about how much different this relationship was compared to being in one with Damon. "I am in love and it's really real, he doesn't disrespect me, he doesn't hurt me at all in any kind of way, I just…I don't know how to explain how happy I feel now."

"Oh Summer, I am so happy for you because you deserve it, so how's *other* things besides you man?" she said.

"Girl that is too funny that you should ask that," I chuckled, "the director of the center just left my office after offering me a full time counselors' position."

"For real?" she questioned, "Summer girl you better go on then."

"Yeah it sounds nice," I said as my smile started to fade, "the only thing is that the position requires that I become a certified psychologist, which means I would have to go back to school. I just graduated a couple of months ago and right now I'm just not ready to go through that again, well at least not yet."

"Summer, you are only twenty-three years old and you are still young, I'm pretty sure you don't have make that decision today," she started, "girl live a little bit, if you want to stay there for a couple of years before you go back to school, then do it, but if you choose not to then that's cool too. You just do you, and what I mean by that is you just do whatever *Summer* wants to do, not what anybody else wants you to do."

"True," was all I could think to say at first, "I guess I've spent most of my life trying to please people, I forgot about what I want and what *I* want to do."

"I know girl, it's time for you to live your life," she said, "you've already been grown for too long even when you were suppose to be living a carefree teenaged life, you were too busy being grown. But now its time to be your age and have fun doing it."

"You know you're right. I've been into too many "adult" situations when I should have been enjoying being young," I nodded my head, "you're right I was too young to be dealing with what I was dealing with especially when I was dealing with Damon, shoot that right there was going to kill me one way or the other."

"Right, but let's not go there right now," she said sounding annoyed by the mention of Damon, "I'm just glad that part of your life is over and now you have true love with Amir."

"Yeah me too," I said looking at my clock which said I needed to get my butt out of the office, "hey Chyna girl its time for me to get out of here so I'm going to have to let you go."

"Okay girl," she said, "we've got to get together for lunch or something."

"I know, maybe you and Chad could come over to the house," I said while I was trying to get my folders into my briefcase so I could work on some things at home. "I could cook up something and then you all can get your butts whipped in some dominoes or spades."

"That sounds good," she said with a smile in her voice, "but I want to warn you that Chad and I have been known to leave people crying in both games, so just let me know when you all want that butt whipping."

"Yeah okay," I laughed now standing putting my purse and briefcase over my shoulder, "I love you girl and I'll call you soon about that whipping."

She laughed and I began to laugh too, "Alright girl I love you too." We hung up and I waited a couple of seconds hoping to see either the voicemail sign show up or a message that said that I had a text message, but neither one showed up. Becoming upset I thru the phone in my purse and was about to walk out of my office, "baby what's going on with you?" I whispered to myself.

*   *   *

I pulled into the driveway not parking into the garage because I had planned to go back out to the store to pick up Brianna's baby shower gift. Yes I'm a last minute type of person that's why I was planning to do the shopping the day before the event. The only reason I do that is so that I don't end up getting the same that someone else has gotten. Honestly I could show up to the shower empty handed because I already know that she is going to have a lot of stuff because this is her mom's first real grandchild, but luckily I'm not going to be tacky and not bring her something, she's my girl and I wouldn't do that. Because we're expecting a huge crowd, the baby shower is going to be over Grandmother's house tomorrow since that's where Bri's mom lives and the fact that Aunt Lisa is planning the shower is another reason why it's going to be over there.

Before I got out of my Range (Rover that is) I checked my phone again, still there was nothing. I rolled my eyes then shoved my phone back in my purse; I grabbed my briefcase and slammed my door. *I can't believe him*, I thought, *why is he doing this to me, something has to be wrong; oh God I hope nothing is wrong with him.* I began to worry and hoping that nothing had actually happened to him because my heart couldn't take that now. I quickly ran to the door and opened it with plans to go through the house to see if there were any signs of Amir being home, there wasn't any. I went to my room and changed out of the black gauchos and a coral collared shirt that I wore to work and changed into some chopped blue jeans and a white wife beater.

When I sat on the bed I bowed my head and began to pray, "Lord, I'm coming to you praying that Amir is safe and everything is okay with him," I spoke to God, "but God if," I paused to exhale hard, "I don't even want to think like that, but just if woooo, please Lord just give me strength." I began to get misty eyed just thinking of the bad that could happen.

"Okay," I quickly stood up, "let me just get up and do something," I said putting on my slippers so I could go into the kitchen to possibly fix something to eat even though I really didn't have an appetite, but I had to do something to get my mind off Amir and something bad happening to him. As I walked passed Amir's room I heard something I didn't hear when I passed his room on the way to mine, but this time I heard voices. Immediately all kinds of thoughts entered my mind. *I know he's not in there with…naw there's no way; or what if it's a robber in his room because Amir does have some nice stuff.* I approached the cracked door and slowly eased my head in the door to survey the room. The TV was on and it looked like it was a home movie, then I noticed the man on the screen was Mr. Bryant, Amir's father. I looked over at Amir's bed and there he was propped up on the headboard with a half smile on his face as he kept his eyes on the TV.

I did a light tap on the door, that's when he looked in my direction then he began to wipe his face, "hey baby," he said plainly as I opened the door completely and he put the TV on mute.

"Baby, are you okay?" I asked as I approached the side of his bed, "I've been worried sick about you all day," I said, that's when I noticed he had been wiping tears away from his face.

"I'm so sorry baby," he reached out to grab my hand, "please baby sit down with me a minute."

"What's going on?" I asked facing him but still holding onto his hand, "because I've been trying to call you all day and I've been really concerned."

He lowered his head then gripped my hands tighter, "I am so sorry again Summer for not answering my phone, but I turned it off," he raised his head and his green eyes greeted me with tears. I moved closer into him so I could give him a hug, and hold him, and try to console him.

"Baby please tell me what's going on with you?" I asked again this time backing away from him so I could look into his eyes.

He pointed toward the TV, I turned around and saw his father's face and that's when it clicked, "it's been a year Summer," he started to say, "since you know, since he passed away."

"Oh my God that's right," I said now feeling guilty because of all the other thoughts I had earlier. Amir's dad, Saul Bryant passed away August 22, 2007 which was also his dad's birthday too. Amir and his dad were very close and when Mr. Bryant died he was crushed. I tried to be there as much as I could for him as a friend being that I was involved with a possessive maniac at the time.

"I knew this day would come," he began to say, "I just didn't know how I was going to take it. I've tried to be strong and pray and everything, but it hurts today just like it was just yesterday that it happened," he started to get choked up.

I crawled over next to him so I could hold him; he then laid his head on my chest. "I know it's hard to deal with losing him, but baby I'm here for you," I said and he raised his head before taking one of his arms and placing it around my waist, then he began to look into my eyes again, "I'm serious Amir, you don't have to go through anything like this alone. Just like you've been there for me through *all* of my tough times, I am here for you, okay?"

He pulled me into him more so that I was now lying on his chest as he lay back on the bed. He continued to stare at me with a serious, but sexy face, then with his fingers he touched my chin lifting my head toward him, "Summer, I am so in love with you," he said and my heart melted because I knew he was for real. We continued to gaze into each other's eyes, "you are the best thing that has happened to me," he paused to bend down and softly kiss me as I closed my eyes, "I promise I love you so much."

We kissed again, "Amir I love you too," he said giving me another peck on the lips, "and don't scare me like that again," I lightly hit his arm and we both laughed.

"Again I am sorry baby," he kissed my cheek this time; "I promise I won't do that you again."

"You better not," I said then I jumped up, "come on and go with me to *Babies-R-Us* so I can get something for Bri's baby shower tomorrow."

"Okay," he got out of the bed, "while we're out let's go grab some dinner too."

"That's the reason I said come with me," I walked out of his bedroom, "I really didn't feel like cooking tonight anyway, even though I was on my way to the kitchen to do something to get my mind off of not talking to you all day."

He walked over and kissed me on the forehead, "one more time I am sorry," he smiled and I turned around, that's when he grabbed my waist, "you deserve to be treated tonight after dealing me not talking to you today."

"Is that right?" I stopped walking and looked over my shoulder at him while he was still gripping my waist tightly, "so is dinner the only thing I can get tonight or can we…uhm—"

"Yeah dinner and maybe a massage or something," I turned completely around and looked at him with my mouth twisted, "Summer nope, I know what you are thinking and I told you I'm celibate, so I'm not doing that until marriage."

"Dang," I snapped my fingers then began smiling, "but you know you don't make it easy for me at all."

He started to laugh and I was just so relieved that he was now smiling and laughing again instead of being sad about his dad. "Come on girl," he turned me around and began to push on my back, pushing me toward the garage door, "let's go get something to eat."

"Alright, alright." I said walking then suddenly stopping, "I've got to run back to my room so I can change out of these slippers, after I come back I'll drive us to dinner."

"Okay," he said walking toward the kitchen table, "I'll wait for you but are you sure that you don't want me to drive?"

"It's no problem baby," I yelled from my room then running back into the kitchen. Amir stood and I stood in front of him, I gripped the back of his neck and he grabbed my waist then I started licking his lips before we started kissing. "Everything that you do for me let me do this small thing just once and let me drive us."

He kissed me again, "alright girl," he dropped his hands from my waist and grabbed my hand, "let's go."

20
Brianna

"Bri that's too cute," Brandi said as I held up another jumper this time from Grandmother. "So who is that from again?" she asked with a notebook and pen in her hand so she could write down all the gifts that way I could send out thank you cards in a few days.

"It's from Grandmother," I said putting it back in the pink gift bag, "so was that the last gift?" I asked hoping that it was because I was so ready to go home because I was too tired.

"Yeah that was it," Mama said sitting down on the couch after handing me all of the gifts.

"Well I would like to thank all of you for everything," I said to everyone in attendance. Because I didn't have a whole lot of friends it was mostly family that was there, all of my aunts, female cousins, and my co-worker Connie and her sister Chelsea.

"Girl you know we love you," Connie said now walking toward me, "you know I would love to stay a little while longer but I've got to get out of here," she said giving me a hug.

"Go on girl, I understand," I said about to stand but Connie wave d her hand at me as if she wanted me to stay seated, "I was going to walk you to the door."

"No sugar I know my way out," she said walking toward the door with her sister in tow, "besides you look like you're exhausted anyway."

"I'll walk you out," Ken said standing then walking Connie and Chelsea to the door.

"Bye everyone," they both said before they were out of my sight. I was sitting in the chair that didn't face the front door.

"Hey come on in," I heard Kennede say with hesitation in her voice, then seconds later I felt a tap on my shoulder and I looked up, "heads up," Ken whispered.

"Heads up on what?" I whispered back looking at her with my face twisted; Ken cocked her head to the side then thru it back.

"Hey Brianna," Carla came into my view and I tried to hide the surprise on my face, but my heart dropped so low it was in the womb with my baby. "Oh my goodness look at you, so when is it that you are due again?" she asked hugging me.

"Oh…uhm, I…uhm, I'm due in three and a half weeks," I said trying to loosen up a little, "uhm but the baby should be here on the nineteenth of September."

"Really?" she questioned with her face lighting up and her eyes widen, I simply shook my head, "you know that's my husband's birthday September nineteenth." *Yeah I already knew that*, I thought, but I managed to give a half assed smile. "That is too weird, but you do remember my husband Lance, the doctor?" she asked and I wanted to laugh, but I just kept the smile on my face while thinking, *I couldn't forget him even if I tried.*

"Yeah I remember the doctor," I said sitting up in my chair, "so how is he doing and your kids?"

"Oh everybody is doing great," she said then her smile faded, "I'm so sorry here," she walked toward front door then she returned quickly with this over sized gift bag, "I got this for you, actually it's from me and—"

"Carla," Aunt Karen yelled her name cutting off her statement to me, "hey girl I was wondering if you were still coming," Aunt Karen said coming from the kitchen into the living room to hug her, I just sat there with a confused look on my face as they greeted each other. I was puzzled because I was unaware of the invitation that was extended to Carla to *my* baby shower. Although my problem isn't with her personally but it's with her trifling husband, it's still *very* awkward being around her knowing what I know and especially with what *I've* done too.

"I'm sorry for being so late," she said touching the back of her tapered hair, "I was getting my hair done and it seems that time just ran away from me," she explained to Aunt Karen.

"Yeah Bri, she said after the 4th of July thing she has been worried sick about you and the baby," Aunt Karen explained to me while she had one arm around Carla, "she told me she wanted to do something for you so I told her about this baby shower."

Carla nodded, "like Karen said, honey you have been on my mind since then too," she said still holding on my Aunt, "I tell you I thank God that Lance was there," she put her hand in the air as if she was in church or something.

"Yeah thank God he was there," I said sarcastically with a half smile on my face. Truth be told if he hadn't been there I probably wouldn't even have had an asthma attack.

"So how is that *fine* husband of yours anyway?" Aunt Karen asked and Carla smiled so hard that her skin began to turn red.

"Girl he's doing good," she said proudly and I began to get nauseated, I stood up about to go into the kitchen because I knew that's where my girls were probably hiding out. "That's actually the reason I went to the hairdresser today because he's taking me out on a date tonight, its been so long since we've done something like this," Carla continued to talk and I couldn't take hearing this anymore.

"Ooh, so where's the kids?" Aunt Karen asked.

"There staying with my oldest son Carlos at his apartment," she began to explain.

"Excuse me," I said waddling past them on my way to the kitchen, "I need to get something to drink."

"Go ahead baby," Carla touched my shoulder, then continued to talk to my aunt, "but yeah girl we helped Carlos get his own apartment downtown on 3rd street so he could be closer to school," when I heard her say that I paused. *That was where Lance's apartment was*, I thought, *oh my God he lied about that too, and that was his son's apartment*. I moved as quickly as I could to get away from hearing anything else.

"Girl are you alright?" Summer rushed to my side as I entered the kitchen. I didn't want to say too much because Kayla was in there as well.

"Yeah I'm good," I said, "just feeling a little queasy that's all," Summer then gave me this look that said *I already know why*.

"Here girl, go sit in the dining room or something," Summer shooed me out of the kitchen. "I'll bring you some water and anything else you may need."

"Thanks Summer," I said and made my way to the dining room where my mom, Aunt Regina, Aunt Julie, and my uncle's wife Aunt Catherine were sitting at the table. "Hey people," I greeted everyone as I entered the room.

"Hey," they all said in unison, then going back to their conversation. Soon after I entered the room Carla walked into the room from the other entrance with Aunt Karen along side her, "hey Carla," everyone now said in unison again.

"Hey everybody," she waved her hand still smiling then standing behind one of the dining room chairs.

"Why don't you have a seat Carla?" Aunt Karen said taking a seat at the table as I took a seat next to Aunt Regina.

"Oh no," she shook her head, "I actually wanted to just run this gift over to Brianna," Carla said then looked down at her wrist, "oh my goodness, ladies I would love to stay but my husband is waiting for me and I've got to get home so we can start our evening."

"Ooohh," everyone cooed, I wanted to roll my eyes but I would be too obvious if I did that.

"Stop it you guys," Carla began to blush, but quickly stopped to walk toward me, "Brianna please let me know when that baby comes because I would love to see her."

"Okay," I said hesitating at first, "if you want me to, I can have Aunt Karen let you know when I go into the hospital."

"Oh that's great," she snapped her fingers, "you know what Bri; I might not be able to make it to the hospital if you are having the baby sometime in September. I'm going down to Florida with my parents for about two months because my dad is going to have a triple bypass on September eighth and I'm going to stay with them to help my mom out."

"Oh that's okay," I said sad to hear about her parents, but somewhat relieved that I wouldn't have to see her when I have the baby. "I understand family comes first, I'll be okay I have enough family anyway," I chuckled.

"Yeah I've gotta take care of my parents now because they have been good to me down through the years while I was growing up," she said with a smile on her face. "But let's see, I'm leaving the day before his surgery and I probably won't return to Louisville until close to the end of October, so maybe I could get in touch with you about the end of October or maybe November?"

"Ooohh," I twisted my mouth, "that might not be a good time."

Carla's face showed confusion, "is something wrong with that time?" she asked.

"Oh Karen didn't tell you?" Aunt Regina spoke up and Carla shook her head, "well Ms. Brianna is going to be moving out of town around that time, Bri when is your actually moving date again?" Aunt Regina looked in my direction.

"My moving date is November 1st," I said and Carla had somewhat of a sad face, "yeah I decided to move at that time that way my baby will have more than a month or two under her belt."

Carla chuckled as everyone else at the table did as well, "so where are you moving to?" she asked.

"She's moving to Indianapolis, Indiana with me," Aunt Regina said proudly. That was probably due to the fact that she was excited to have someone in her family moving closer to her.

"Dang Gina," Mama spoke up, "the girl can speak for herself, she is twenty-three soon to be twenty-four years old in two months, she's not three or four years old anymore, she's grown."

"I know how old she is Lisa," Aunt Regina said smirking but rolling her neck and eyes, "I'm just so happy that one of my family members will be up there with me."

"Well that's wonderful Brianna, I'm happy for you," Carla said now with keys in her hands that she had retrieved from the white cropped pants she wore. "So is it going to be you and your fiancé that's moving, what was his name again, Byron?"

The smile I was wearing now faded into a *hell to the naw* expression. I had almost forgot about the lie I told them last month telling them that I was pregnant by my fiancé Brian, "well no *Brian* will not be going with us, it'll just be me and Lil' B," I explained referring to my unborn child as Lil' B since I've decided to name her Bianca.

"Lil' B?" Carla questioned.

"I call her that because I've decided to name her Bianca," I began to explain, "so that's why I call her Lil' B," I said rubbing on my stomach.

"Oh okay," Carla said then jingled her keys again, "well guys, I would really love to sit and chat with you all, but I've got to get back to my husband."

"Okay Carla I'll walk you to the door," Aunt Karen said walking next to Carla.

"Thank you so much Carla for the gift," I said then remembering I never looked in the bag to see what it was. "Can someone bring me that bag because I never opened it."

"Oh I'll just tell you what it is," Carla turned back around toward me, "it's a specially designed diaper bag with a matching baby carrier and a matching purse for you too."

"Wow," I said, "thanks a lot Mrs. Carla, but you really didn't have to do that."

"Honey its no problem," she said coming back to the table to hug me, "well I'll see everyone later."

"Bye Carla," everyone sang like they used to when they were in the choir.

"Oh Mrs. Carla," I called out to her before she was out of my sight, "tell your husband that I said thanks as well." I said with a smirk and I felt a kick to my leg from next to me, I looked up at Brandi with a big smile.

"I sure will honey," she smiled then walked toward the front door. I sat back in the chair hiding the laughter that wanted to erupt inside of me. Based off me telling Carla to tell Lance hello, I'm pretty sure I would get a phone call from him real soon.

*   *   *

I was walking around Bianca's room trying to prepare things for our temporary stay here in this apartment. I didn't set up a full nursery with stuff on the walls because I didn't plan on being here permanently. The room only contained the crib, changing station, and a rocking chair. The wall decorations and stuff like that including the gift that Carla and Lance gave me was sitting in a corner of Bianca's room.

"Let me see what's in here," I pulled the gift bag over to the rocking chair, "oh my God," I said aloud as I pulled out this huge pink and white *Louis Vuitton* diaper bag then underneath that was the matching baby carrier and inside of that was a medium size matching *Louis Vuitton* purse. This gift had Lance's name all over it, which to me meant "guilt gift."

I began to open the insides of the diaper bag first, knowing Lance there was something inside, sure enough it was. The diaper bag was filled to capacity with newborn diapers; there were bottles in the bottle compartments, and formula in an extra compartment. I smiled halfway then put the diaper bag down and picked up the purse. It was empty except for an index card that simply read:

Congratulations from Carla & Lance.

"Yeah right," I chuckled sarcastically then noticed that the zipper was closed, unusual for a new purse, I opened it and saw an envelope. "OH MY GOD!" I said slowly as I opened the envelope that revealed several bills of money starting with hundreds and as I continued to look it was nothing but hundred dollar bills. "This is nothing but Lance," I said as I started to count the stack of bills.

"What in the world?" I questioned once I finished counting two-thousand five-hundred dollars, there was a paper in between the money. I sat the note aside for a minute so I could finish counting even though I was very interested in what that note had to say. Once I finished counting all of the money which was a total of five thousand dollars, I picked the note back up with shock because of the money.

> Dear Brianna,
>
> First off I want to say that I'm excited about the baby although I can't openly show it now and even though I was against the idea of her at first. I'm sending this money in hopes that you will not take me to child support at the time. I wouldn't know how to explain this to Carla now. I am not trying to buy your silence or pay in cash for our child. I do want to be there for her as much as I can and I figured I can start by sending some financial help. This will not be the last of the money that you'll see. I pray we can work out some kind of arrangement so I can see her; I want her to know who I am. I still love you even if you don't believe it and I love our daughter too.
>
> Love, Lance

"Are you serious?" I sat there in shock at the letter now instead of the money. I can't believe him; I can't believe that he'd do something like this. I stood up about to go get my phone, but a pain shot through my back, "oh!" I yelled out before sitting back down. "Okay just breathe," I said to myself trying to calm down for a minute.

After about a minute, I got back up then went to retrieve my cell phone. Before I began to dial Lance's number I checked the date, it was September 9, 2008, that meant Carla was gone. "Hello?" Lance answered on the second ring.

"Hi," I said softly feeling butterflies or it could have been Bianca, I couldn't tell at the moment, "it's me—"

"Brianna," he said cutting me off as he exhaled, "I've been waiting to hear from you, I was actually hoping to hear from you a couple of weeks ago."

"The baby shower gift," I simple said looking over at the cash in the envelope, "is the reason that I called," I paused, "I just opened the purse a few minutes ago."

"I know the way it might seem but," he paused this time, "look I was actually on my way over there if it's okay with you."

"What? Oh!" I said closing my eyes as I felt a kick along with the sharp pain in my back again. "Oh God I…I don't care," I said gasping for air.

"Brianna are you okay?" he asked with worry in his voice, "look like I said I'm on my way over to your place."

"Okay," I tried to calm down, "it was just I felt a pain in my back that's all."

"Do you need to go to the hospital?" he questioned, "do you think that you're going into labor?"

"Lance I don't know," I said becoming annoyed with his questions, "this is my first child I'm not the pro like you are."

"Bri come on now," he said then he went silent, "I'm turning into your apartment complex now."

"Alright the door will be opened for you," I said slowly easing out of my seat to go to the door. With the luck I've been having I probably am going into labor with Lance on his way over here. Now how in the world would I explain this one?

Tuesday September 11, 2008:

What did I tell you? Sure enough once Lance got to the apartment I went into labor. I guess you could say he was kind enough to take me to the hospital that was close to my place. Luckily for the both of us it wasn't the hospital that we work at and hopefully nobody would know who we are, at least not the people that worked at this hospital. The best news is that Bianca La'Rayne Spencer was born at two forty-five in the morning on September 11, 2008, weighing in at six pounds five ounces and eighteen inches. Most of my family was still here when she came into the world like Ken, Summer, and Donte who stayed in the waiting room while Mama and Brandi stayed in the room with me. You would've thought Brandi had just had the baby the way she was crying all over the place. Grandmother, Aunt Karen, and Aunt Julie left the hospital around ten or ten-thirty at night, because Grandmother said she was too tired to spend the night up there. Honestly after the epidural hit along with the other pain meds I really didn't care who stayed or who went home.

Right now it was just me and my beautiful daughter all alone for the first time, but she lay in her little crib asleep. I had actually just put her down before I lay in the bed and closed my eyes, and then there was a tap on the door. *Oh no, who is it now?* I thought, it was around noon and I knew it probably wouldn't be my family since they said they weren't coming back up here until much later.

"Come in," I said reluctantly, I looked over and saw this huge bouquet of white roses that covered the person's face. Because I could pick his body out of a line up even if his face was covered, I knew it was nobody but Lance.

"Hey Bri," he removed the flowers from his face; he was wearing the biggest smile I've ever seen him wear. "Is she sleeping?" he walked over to the crib after sitting the flowers down on the night stand next to me. "So how are you doing, I mean how are you feeling?" he asked coming to my bed and touching my arm all I could do was cringe.

"I'm doing alright," I said moving my arm away from him, "even though I'm very tired and I was trying to get a little rest before my family came back up here."

"Oh," he backed up and his smile faded into a look of worry, "when will they be back, anytime soon?"

"Don't worry," I said sarcastically while rolling my eyes, "they won't be back up here until much later, sometime after rush hour around six o'clock tonight or so."

"Oh okay," he sounded and looked like he was relieved as he walked over to the crib and stood over it, "do you mind if I pick her up?" he asked looking back at me.

I nodded, "she's yours too, go ahead," I said then he picked Bianca up into his arms and began cheesing very hard like he was proud or something, "she's beautiful isn't she?" I asked.

"Yes she is," he replied looking at me with such truth, but since everything he's ever said to me has turned out to be a lie even while saying it with a truthful face, I didn't believe him now. "She looks like you when you're sleeping, absolutely beautiful," he held her like he was a proud father.

I smiled for a brief moment wishing that I could believe he actually was a proud father. I wanted to believe that this precious new life, this child's life wasn't going to be hurt by him or that he wasn't going to break her heart like my father did mine so bad that I changed my last name last month because I gave up the fantasy that a *"real man"* would one day change my last name for me.

"Bri are you okay?" Lance asked putting Bianca back into her crib as I came out of my trance.

"Like I said earlier I'm just very tired," I said laying my head back and briefly closing my eyes.

"So what's her full name?" he asked and I opened my eyes back up to see him sitting on the edge of my bed, "I remember you saying that you wanted her first name to be Bianca."

"Yeah that's her first name," I said, "Her full name is Bianca La'Rayne Spencer."

"Spencer?" he questioned.

"I changed my last name last month," I began to explain; "well Spencer is my mom's maiden name."

"Why did you do that?" he asked and I could feel him touch my foot again.

I looked at him an expression that said *please stop touching me*, "well," I said, "I changed my last name when I woke up from my daydreams and fantasies then realized that I would *never* find a man to change it for me," I said looking into his eyes.

His eyes looked glossy, "Brianna please don't" he exhaled loud and hard, "I'm sorry I really wanted to be the one to do that." "Lance I'm over it," I said not wanting to get into anything like this with him right now, "I realize now that that will *never* happen and I'm actually cool with it."

"So are you saying that you are giving up on us?" he asked with a straight face while my face was showing so much confusion.

"You have got to be kidding me, are you serious?" I asked rhetorically, "Lance there *is* no *us*. We did what we had to do to get her here for some reason. You are *married* and according to Carla, *happily* married at that," I paused and looked down before looking back up at his face. "Since July things have changed for me, *our* situation has changed because first off, I'm on speaking terms with your wife, **YOUR WIFE**! I couldn't do that woman like that especially after I've met her and now I know the truth."

"But Brianna," he tried to speak.

"There are no buts anymore," I said sternly, "it's over okay? It's been over for me since July 4th 2008 and I'm okay with it, so I don't need to hear anymore of your lies. As far as being in Bianca's life, that's cool with me but you don't have to feed me any bull just to see your daughter. And also," I paused, reaching in the nightstand to pull out the envelope of money, "we don't need your *guilt* money."

"Now Bri that's not what this is for," he stood and waved his hands as if he were saying he didn't want it, "I gave that as a gift and to help you with Bianca financially. Kids aren't cheap and I know this so I'm just trying to do my part."

"Uhm your part," I chuckled sarcastically, "I've got enough from you, matter of fact your part is laying right over there." I pointed to Bianca's crib, "trust me we're going to be just fine without your money," I said or rather my pride spoke, because honestly an extra five thousand dollars wouldn't hurt anybody.

"I'm not taking it back," he said leaving the envelope on the bed next to my foot, "that's for *my* daughter."

"Like I said, we're going to be alright," I said chocked up, trying to hold back the tears. He moved closer to me then kissed my forehead.

"Like *I* said," he stated, "I'm not taking it back Brianna, and I do still love you, whether you want to believe it or not," he moved closer toward the door.

I rolled my eyes, "okay Lance," I said sarcastically.

"I am serious Brianna," he said with his hand on the doorknob, "I do *love* both of you," he walked out of room. As soon as the door clicked letting me it was closed all of the way, tears immediately started to flow down my face, and I really didn't know why. Maybe it was because I was actually letting pieces of Lance go, and it felt good. It was almost like part of this heavy burden was being lifted, even though I hated to let him go, it was something that I needed to do in order to move on with own life. Because the way things were looking Lance was never going to let his wife go no matter how much junk he talked, so because I was actually grasping the truth, I had to let him go. And this time I couldn't go back to him.

21
Kennede

"Well when would be a good time to meet with you?" I spoke to the cake designer that was working on the actual wedding cake and the groom's cake.

"I could meet with you and your fiancé today about five this evening." he paused, then I squinted my eyes while I was walking through my front door, "yeah five this evening, does that sound okay to you?"

"Uhm, no today isn't a good time," I said laying my purse down on the couch, "actually my fiancé is out of town today, how about Monday and I'm pretty sure he can make the time?" I suggested, "I'm a hairstylist so I'm off on Monday's too."

"Okay," he said and sounded like he was turning pages or something, "how about eleven in the morning on Monday September twenty-ninth, is that okay?"

"Yes sir that sounds great," I said marking the date in my new wedding/moving day/R.J.'s game calendar. "Okay I'm going to call my fiancé now to let him know."

"Okay Ms. Johnson, I will see you on Monday," he said sounding very chipper, "bye now."

"Bye," I closed my phone then leaned back on my couch and closed my eyes for a moment. Since the day Ray proposed I've been working non-stop on my wedding, not to mention trying to finish getting our new house together so we can be completely moved in before December 6th, which is our wedding date. Yes Raymond and I chose to have a winter wedding that we've always wanted but never had the chance to do the first time around. For this wedding both sets of parents are sparing no expense. As a matter of fact once they learned of our engagement my parents took Raymond's parents out to dinner to discuss the amount they would both put into the wedding so that Ray and I wouldn't have a repeat of my prom night.

So just to show you how much our parents are willing to spend *not* to see that happen again, I'm going to run down the list of what has already taken place. First off, the dress I've chose for the wedding is fifteen-hundred dollars, and it's a white A-neck line dress that has silver embroidery throughout to give the dress that wintery feel. Then our parents have decided to pay for every single bridesmaid dress and every groomsman tuxedos, and luckily I only have 4 bridesmaids, my little sister Kayla, Summer, Brandi, and Brianna. Also my father has put a huge down payment on one of the most exclusive country clubs in the city for my reception. The crazy thing about the club is that when my father called to ask for availability they said they were booked up through October of 2009, but when he told them who he was and the event was for his daughter who is marrying the son of Senator and Mr. Collins, December 6, 2008 suddenly became available with the right price of course. Then the reception is going to include a six course meal followed by a six tier wedding cake that is a half white and half chocolate cake, with a special made Mercedes cake for the groom which will be a strawberry cake, at least that's what we are hoping for when we go to the cake designers because strawberry is Raymond's favorite cake.

Now with all of that plus the fact that I'm still working and now packing for my upcoming move which we now have set a date of November 8th, a week after Brianna's big move to Indy. I was so excited about everything that was going on in my life, but it was stressful with the wedding and the move.

"Oh shoot," I opened my eyes quickly because I had almost forgotten to call Raymond. He and RaeLynn went with my parents to go to watch R.J.'s football game up in Columbus, Ohio; they went up there because it was the first game that R.J. was in the starting line up. "Hello?" I answered my cell phone when it began to ring as soon as I opened it.

"Hey beautiful," Raymond said on the other end, "how is your day going? How did that wedding party you worked on today go?"

"It went good but it whipped my butt though," I said. "But speaking of weddings, the cake designer called today and they wanted us to come in on Monday at 11 in the morning."

"Cool, cool," he simple said, "You know all you have to do is tell me when and where I will be there," he chuckled.

"Okay baby," I chuckled with him, "so how's the game going? I really wish I could have been there."

"I know I miss you, but you already know when R.J. got his chance with ball he did his thing," Raymond said explaining what was going on at the game. "And now Ohio State is up by ten points thanks to the touchdown that your brother just made."

I began smiling very hard, "oh that is good, I am so proud of him. So what is my little boo doing?" I asked Raymond about RaeLynn.

"She's over here getting even more spoiled by her grandparents." He laughed and I frowned.

"Oh I wish I could be there with you guys," I said then I was startled by the doorbell ringing.

"Baby are you at home?"

"Yeah," I went to the door and saw Brandi standing on the porch so I opened the door. "Hey girl," I said reaching out to her for a hug.

"Are you busy right now?" She asked looking like she was scared or something.

"I am never too busy for you," I said with concern now all over my face. "Hey babe, Brandi is over here and we've got some stuff to do so—"

"I know, I know," he said cutting off my last sentence. "You've got women stuff to do; I'll just see you later on tonight when we get back, see you later."

"Okay babe, I'll be waiting up for you," I closed my phone and shifted my attention back to Brandi. "So what's going girl?"

"Lester Black," she paused as tears started to fall down her face. "Ken I think that this crazy ass nigga is stalking me again. I mean this stuff is getting too crazy to deal with especially without Jay knowing what's going on."

"You know what I'm going to say, you need to tell Jay everything." Brandi rolled her eyes at me.

"Ken," she said before exhaling hard, "it's not that easy to tell my husband that the man who raped me many moons ago is now stalking me for the second time. That's not as easy as it may seem to you."

"Come here," I put my arm around her and she laid her head on my shoulder then began sobbing. "I'm sorry that I don't know how it feels to deal with something like this. But one thing I know a little something about is marriage. I know that a marriage doesn't work without communication and I found that out the hard way." I said rubbing her arm as she continued to lay on me.

"I know that Ken," she sniffed, "but you don't understand how hard it was trying to tell him about the rape alone." She swallowed hard, "and he still doesn't know the whole truth about that night either."

"Brandi," I said with disappointment because I thought she had told Jayson the whole truth, "what did you tell him?"

"I told him everything," she paused, "but I told him it was so dark in the club that I couldn't tell who the guy was that did those things to me."

"Dang B," I exhaled slowly, "it's going to be okay. If there's one thing that I do know, that is God is protecting you."

"Humph, you know what?" she started to chuckle, "if I weren't saved, I would have said that you are lying because the fact that Lester is stalking me, but God really is protecting me although that man is getting close to me, he has yet to lay a hand on me again."

"See that's what I mean," I said, "and in the name of Jesus, that no good dog is not going to touch you ever again." I spoke with authority and tears began to fill my eyes, "I do have one question though, are you packing?"

She picked up her purse, "girl ever since this whole thing started," she said laying her purse back down, "but every time he pops up somewhere, there's so many people around that I can't do anything to him. Besides, if I just shoot him out of the blue I could end up in jail, but if he tries to attack me again it's over for him."

I moved her head from my shoulders then stood up and grabbed her hand, "come on we are going down to Jay's shop so you can tell your husband."

She sat still on the couch shaking her head, "uh, uh Ken I can't tell Jay," she protested. "Jayson will kill that man."

"Well somebody needs to do something," I said pulling her arm. "Now let's go because this thing is ending tonight," I demanded.

"Okay," she gave in and stood from the couch. "Let's go on and end it."

"Good, but I'm driving," I said grabbing my keys.

"Oh my God," Brandi said as we approached the mini-mall that Jayson's barber shop was located. "Ken I don't have a good feeling about this," she said as police had the front of the barbershop blocked with yellow tape. It had to be about 6 police cars that were in the parking lot of the mini-mall.

"Let's just try to think positive thoughts," I said as an officer stood in front of my car holding up his hand, letting me know I couldn't drive any further. Brandi quickly jumped out of the passenger's side.

"Whoa ma'am," the officer held out his arm trying to stop Brandi and I from walking toward the shop after I had put my car in park and jumped out too. "Is there something I can help you ladies with?"

"Yes this is my husband's barbershop," Brandi said with her voice somewhere in between panic and calm. "I just need to know that my husband is okay."

"Alright ma'am what's your husband's name?"

"Jayson...uhm, Jayson Hill," she said. "He's the owner of this shop."

"Hold on a minute," he said to us then called it in on the walkie-talkie. "Is there a Jayson Hill inside the building?"

"Ken what if something happen to him?" Brandi turned to me and I embraced her.

"Look it's gonna be alright," I said holding onto her.

"Did you say Jayson Hill?" the officer on the other end repeated.

"Yeah that's what I said."

"Uh, no Jayson Hill isn't located inside the building," the dispatcher said and I felt partial relief. "But he's in a bus on his way to University Hospital with GSW to the torso and leg."

"Oh my Lord," Brandi began to collapse in my arms, "no, no please tell me he's not dead," she sobbed.

"When he left here 5 minutes ago he was still alive," the officer in front of us said. "I can give you ladies a ride to the hospital."

"That's okay, but could you please help me get her into the car?" I asked because my arms weren't able to carry Brandi faint body.

The officer grabbed Brandi and carried her to my car. "Hey Brandi," I heard someone yell her name as I was about to get into the car.

I looked up and saw Jayson's little brother Jerrod running toward us, "Jerrod," Brandi managed to say as she turned around and fell into his arms now. "What happened? Did you see who did this to him?" she asked still laying on his chest with tears streaming down her face.

"Yeah it was this tall black dude," he said with anger written all over his face. "Apparently Jay knew the dude because he came out of his office and was talking to this cat like he knew him. Then they went back into Jay's office then within about 5 minutes they were arguing." Jerrod paused like he was fighting back tears, "then soon after the arguing started we heard shots. And the door flew open and the dude still had the gun in his hand and ran out of the shop."

"Oh my God," Brandi said repeating the phrase over and over. "I'm on my way up to the hospital now, Ken's gonna drive me do you wanna ride with us?"

"No thanks," he backed away, "I have to finish up here at the shop with the cops. But I will be up there later or just as soon as they finish." He embraced Brandi again, "it's gonna be ok," he said trying to console his sister in-law.

"Thanks Jerrod, but can you help Brandi into the car since the police has already went back inside, please?" I asked

"No problem," he said opening the car door for a distraught Brandi. "I'll see ya'll later."

"Thank you again," I said jumping into the driver's seat. "Brandi it's gonna be ok, Jay is still alive," I tried to give her a little encouragement.

"I know that bastard did this to him Ken," she said sobbing, "I just know it was him."

"Him who?" I asked, but I quickly answered my own question after the words left my lips. "Do you think Lester did this?"

"I *think* he did this, I *know* the bastard did this," she said. "He's just trying to get to me; he's crazy like that Ken. I just know it was him because did you hear Jerrod describe that bastard to a tee?"

I reached over with my free hand, "Lord, please be with Jayson in Jesus' name." I said a small prayer.

We pulled into the emergency room bay, "look you go on in there to your husband while I go park this car, and I promise I will be right in there with you."

"Okay," she wiped her face, exhaled hard and opened the car door. "Thank you so much Ken for being with me."

"It's not a problem, now go on," she quickly exited the car and I went to search for a parking spot. "Lord please be with my cousin and her husband," I said aloud as I began to pray again. "Lord whatever *your* will is for this situation, please give us peace and strength in this time. Amen."

Once I walked into the E.R. waiting room the first person I see is Malik, "hey Ken." He walked up to me giving me a hug, "I saw Brandi, I am so sorry this is happening to her and her new husband."

"Oh no," I said covering my mouth expecting to hear the worse about Jayson's condition. "Please don't tell me he didn't…or he isn't—"

"No, no," Malik put one arm around me, "I'm sorry to scare you but he's in surgery though. I saw Brandi when she walked in here and we checked it out and that's where he was in surgery." He said as we walked into another waiting area. "I took her to the surgery waiting room with the rest of his family. God this is so terrible, do they know who did this?"

"Brandi seems to think she knows who it was," I said leaning into him while trying to lower my voice.

"So who is it?" he asked whispering now as well.

"I shouldn't say anything," I said remembering that if I tell him about Lester Black stalking Brandi for the last few years that would lead into the question why? Then that would have to be explained about her rape and I wasn't about to tell all of my girls business like that. Matter of fact most of our family including the girls didn't have as much info about the situation as I did. "Well it's something I don't feel comfortable talking about with Brandi's permission."

He shrugged his shoulders, "okay I understand that and I'm not the nosy type so I won't probe you for info."

"Thanks though," I said touching his arm then shaking my head, "I just can't believe this happening. I mean things had really turned around for the both of them; they were both in church together and everything. You know I'm new to the Christian walk myself, but I just don't understand why God would allow this to happen with the way things have been going."

"It's a learning experience," Malik simply said. "I think God allows certain things like that to shake up what we call "normal life" as we know it be," he said while throwing up air quotes. "In order for us to learn, I think we have to go through those things. Most time the test is all about faith, do we really believe God can do it, ya know?"

I shook my head with understanding, "you know what that's true, but also with the learning experience do you think some things are wake up calls too?"

"Most definitely," he bobbed his head, "sometimes we get comfortable in things that's not our purpose or things that are temporary. I think God has to wake us up so we can be in the place that He wants us to be."

I waved my hand toward him, "preach on my brotha preach on," I said laughing for the first time since this whole thing started. "But seriously you're dropping some real knowledge."

"I'm just speaking what I know," he said, "but I would have never learned that if I hadn't been through it. So we should just thank and praise God no matter what."

"Alright Minister Malik," I said before my phone starting ringing, "excuse me one minute it's Ray," I said looking at the caller id before answering. "Hey babe."

"Hey baby, are you okay?" Raymond asked with a little panic in his voice. "Aunt Lisa just called your mom and she told us what is going on with Jayson and she said that you were with Brandi, so are you okay?"

"Yeah babe," I said closing my eyes thinking about how I would feel if it was Ray in surgery right now. "I'm just sitting here with Malik because Jay's in surgery right now and Brandi is upstairs with the rest of his family, so baby where are you all at now?"

"We're about forty-five minutes from downtown, but we were going to drop RaeLynn over my parent's house and then we were coming up there. So you drove your car right?"

"Yeah I did," I began to explain to him how Brandi and I drove up to the shop together and we saw all of the cops.

"Oh God," he said in a low voice, "you all didn't see anything did you?"

"No baby not at all," I said shaking my head. I looked over at Malik when his *Blackberry* started going off and he quickly went for his pocket. "Jay was already gone in the ambulance by the time we got to the barbershop." I said to Ray as Malik hit my arm and held up his *Blackberry*, "hold on babe I think Malik has something to say about Jay."

"Okay," Raymond said to me. I then heard him began to tell my parents what I had just told him.

"Well Jayson is out of surgery," he began, "everything went good and it looks like it's not life threatening, although his condition is still critical."

"Oh thank God," I sighed heavily with relief. "Hey babe did you hear that? His injuries aren't life threatening." I said now speaking to Raymond.

"Thank God," Raymond responded, "baby we will be there really soon."

"Okay babe," I said very grateful for many different reasons. "Raymond before you go, I just want to say that I love you so much babe."

"I love you so much too Kennede and I'll see you in a few," he said chuckling.

"Okay," I said again and hung up the phone smiling. I looked toward Malik who was looking at me with a goofy grin, "what?" I asked continuing to smile.

"So that was your ex future husband?" his grin now relaxed into a normal smile as I began to blush.

"Yes it was my *future* husband," I corrected him. "Malik, why are you looking at me like that?"

His smile then turned into a serious face, "seriously though Ken, I am happy to see you guys back together. I hope that Michelle and I can be as happy as you too are." He said talking about his new girlfriend Michelle. I've only met her once but she's a cute girl who also works up here at the hospital. It was probably her that gave him all of that info about Jay because she works as a nurse in surgery.

I smiled at him, "you two will get there soon enough trust me," I said then my smile faded into a serious look. "It took me and Ray a long time to get here, even though the first time we married we were happy and in love, but we were just too young. But this time things are a lot different, first off we are grown and now we're not trying to plan a wedding and take finals at the same time. This time we have a child plus we have both lived on our own. The first time Ray was the only one who had his own place while I was just living my parent's house. And we've been through a lot in life together and separately, so now we are really prepared for this."

"True, and also this time everybody is way more mature now too," he said.

"Yeah that too," I chuckled at how young I was the first time and trying to be somebody's wife. "I was only a baby, I had just turned eighteen and Ray was only twenty-one, we hadn't lived for real. Now I'm twenty-five and he's twenty-eight so we are a lot older, wiser, and have experienced some things."

"Yeah you are a lot older," Malik laughed and I hit his arm playfully. "But on the real though, I think that you two were always meant to be together and to be all the way honest, I do think ya'll kind of rushed it a little the first time."

I shook my head in agreement, "yeah we did, I was…" I didn't finish my statement because I was cut off by Brandi walking into the waiting room. I jumped to my feet and rushed to hug her, "how are you doing sweetie?" I asked.

"I'm doing a lot better now that I know that he's not going to die on me right now." She sighed at first as I still held onto her, "I'm just so glad he's not leaving me yet," she forced a smile as I looked at her face and I could see the traces of tears plus her bloodshot eyes.

"I was so glad to hear that he's going to be ok. Malik just got the message on his phone about Jay's condition." I said and Brandi waved at him, "I've been doing some serious praying down here for you all."

"Girl I have too," she looked up, "so I guess *He* heard all of us uh?" she pointed toward the sky.

"Well Brandi I glad to hear that your husband is going to be ok," Malik said walking toward Brandi then giving her a hug. "Hey Ken I'ma call you later, but now I've got to get back to work."

"Alright Malik, and thank you for waiting down here with me," I said giving him a hug before he walked out of the waiting room. "So how is Jay's family doing?" I asked Brandi.

"They're doing a lot better too," Brandi said sitting down and I sat next to her. "Ken he called my phone then hung up," she said catching me off guard.

"What?" I asked with confusion all over my face and voice.

"Lester Black," she said coldly with a blank stare, "the bastard had the nerve to call me and hang up, coward."

"Well, how do you know it was him, did he announce himself?" I asked.

"No Ken he didn't say anything, but I just know it was him," she said as if she was frustrated, then she paused and I looked at her face as tears began to fall again. "There's a police officer that was up there with us when he called, and I felt it was time to let them know who I thought did this. Plus with the description everyone that was at the shop gave, the cops think it's a sure match."

"So what did you tell them?" I asked.

"The truth finally," she said with a sigh, "I told the officer about the rape and how I felt on many occasions that I was being followed by this crazy fool for the last few years, plus how right after Jay and I got married he started to show up at random places again."

I smiled, "I'm glad you got all of that out, but now what are the cops going to do?" I asked, but I wished she could have told Jay everything before all of this took place.

"First they're going to try to find him, then they're going to run some fingerprints they found at the scene just to make sure my premonition, plus the information the guys gave them line up with the facts."
"Woo, that's so good," I let out a loud sigh, "so are you feeling better about this whole thing with Black being that the police are about to catch him?"

"Kennede I'll tell you this," she turned to look into my eyes, "the police better catch him very soon, or at least before I go find him my damn self." She said in a very serious tone while holding up my purse because she left hers in the car due to the fact that she was packing and the security at this hospital searched you before you can enter. But when she held up my purse I knew what she meant, if Brandi saw Lester Black before the police did, Brandi's gun in his face would be the last thing he'd ever see.

22
Brandi

"Beep, beep, beep," the monitors sounded off as they calculated each breath Jayson took. I continued to stare at him as he lay in the bed looking peaceful, although he had tubes coming out of his mouth and nose.

I walked back to the seat I had at his bedside after saying goodnight to Ken and the rest of our family. Almost everyone made their way to the hospital to check on Jay's condition, and it made me feel real good that my family showed up in the numbers they did to show support and concern. Even though it was already dark outside when Jay got shot, Grandmother even broke her no coming out after dark routine to be here with me. Right before she left she offered to say a work of prayer with both our and Jay's family. I tell you that little woman prayed so good and strong we had turned that waiting room into a church service, and there wasn't a dry eye in that room afterwards either. Not only did it make me smile at the support, but for a brief moment I forgot about the person that put us in this situation. Also for just one minute I forgot about what I had just told Kennede about what I'd do to Lester Black if I saw him. But as I returned to Jay's bedside those thoughts of "payback" began to creep back into my mind.

"Baby," I whispered softly then touched the top of Jayson's hand, "I know that you can't respond to me right now, but I hope that you can hear me." I spoke a little louder as tears quickly swelled my eyes then started flowing down my face. "Baby I am so sorry this happened to you, this is all my fault and it should be me laying here in this bed and not you. Baby I swear I am so sorry," I began to sob while trying to apologize to my husband. "I love you so much baby and I know I can't take back what happened, but all I can do is just tell you how sorry I am. And baby I promise that fool won't ever do anything like this to us again. This will never happen to you, me or Jordan or anyone in our family again, and I promise you that." I laid my head right next to Jay's hand that I was still holding onto.

A light knock at the door interrupted my crying. "I'm sorry to bother you Mrs. Hill," the nurse walked through the doors just as I lifted my head and quickly began to wipe away the tears.

"Oh no you're fine," I sniffed then grabbed the box of tissues that was next to me. "I'm glad that you came in here because I wanted to know what the doctor's are saying about his condition."

"Of course you already know that the injuries are not life threatening and he's going to live," she stated and I shook my head in agreement. "Luckily the bullets didn't do any major damage to any of his organs, although he did loose a large amount of blood which was one of the main concerns that the doctors had. But as you are aware we did give him several units of blood during surgery, and if we need to give him anymore blood, you know that's what we will continue to do until we can this young man out of here."

"Thank God," I said aloud looking up toward the sky thinking that the prayer session in waiting room with Grandmother worked. "So is there like a target date that he'll be released on?"

"At this moment with the way that he's progressing it could be at the most maybe three to four weeks, and that's just at the most." She said while she continued to hang a new bag of IV fluids, "but if he shows signs of improvement soon then of course you know he can be released sooner."

I exhaled as I closed my eyes, "thank you again."

"No problem at all Mrs. Hill," the older black woman said while walking to the door, "is there anything that I can get you at the moment?"

"Oh no ma'am, not right now but thanks though, I'll be fine for the time being," I replied.

"Okay sugar," she smiled and began to remind me of my mother. As a matter of fact she looked as if she was around my mother's age. "But you just remember if you need anything at all, just push the call button and either me or someone else will be right there."

"Thank you," I replied again and she walked out of the door then closed it. I turned back toward Jayson and touched his again.

"Did you hear that baby?" I asked even though I knew I wouldn't get a response. "It looks like you are improving baby, I'm so glad that you could be released as soon as 3 weeks or sooner. I just wish that you could talk to me now, I really miss having conversations with you, holding you and you holding me." I leaned in closer, "and most importantly I miss us making love," I whispered with a giggle.

Another light knock came from the door, "excuse Mrs. Hill," the police detective, James Hart that has been working on Jayson's case said opening the door. "How are you doing today?" he asked holding out his hand toward me.

"I'm doing a lot better now that I know that Jayson's condition is improving," I said shaking the detectives hand before sitting back in my seat. "So is there any other news?"

"Well yes and no," Detective Hart said sitting down as my face grew concerned. "We did run the prints on the gun that was left at the scene which was the one used to shoot your husband, and it seems that you were right, it matched Mr. Lester Black. Once we saw the picture we also realized that Mr. Black's photo matched what the witnesses at the scene said as well."

"Okay," I said without emotion because I already knew in my heart it was Lester. Then after Jerrod told me and Ken what the guy looked like, I was certain of who it was. "Well detective I do recall telling you and the other officers who I thought it was, so what's the other news?"

"I am sorry Mrs. Hill that we didn't take your premonitions seriously, but we went to the last known address of Mr. Black and it seems that he wasn't there. But there was a young woman there that informed us that he may have left the city."

"What?" I questioned with wide eyes, "so you're telling me that Lester Black is still walking around here free while my husband is here fighting for his life?" I asked in a very angry tone.

"Unfortunately, yes ma'am," he said looking down at a small notebook, "but it seems the young lady informed us that Mr. Black is somewhere in the Chicago area. So we've notified that police department so we can get this man in custody."

"So tell me this, how do you know that this girl isn't lying about him leaving?" I asked trying to calm myself down, "how do you know that she could be just saying that to throw you all off, which would make it easier for him to come back at me?"

"Well Mrs. Hill, we did take that into consideration as well," he said, "that's one of the reasons I'm actually here. Because we aren't sure what Mr. Black will do, there will be a couple of officers to take you into around the clock watch."

"Like a protective custody type thing?" I questioned. "Yes ma'am something like that," he replied. "There's actually an officer that will be on watch right outside of this door, then there'll be one that will actually follow you where ever you go just as a precaution. It's just in case Mr. Black tries to follow you again, we'll be there and hopefully we can catch him to get him off these streets."

"Okay," I sighed with some relief. "So pretty much until this fool is caught, I'll have an officer joined to my hip?"

"Exactly," the detective said, "but just remember this is all for you and your family's protection. And just to let you know there will be an officer still waiting outside of the door here with Mr. Hill even when you decide to go home. Then once you are home there will be one outside of the house on watch and one in the house with you. As a matter of fact the officer will go in the house before you to check the house to make sure that no one or nothing is in the house that was designed to hurt you or your son."

"Oh we don't have to worry about Jordan being with me right now, our son is just going to stay with Jayson's parents until all of this is over," I explained.

"Alright well okay then, well we're going to keep you protected then," he said with a half smile on his face. "But trust me Mrs. Hill, we're doing all that we can do to try to find Mr. Black and bring him to justice for what he has done to your family."

"I hope that you do," I said very sincerely, "I don't know if I could get into trouble for saying this, but I'll take my chances, because if you all don't find him soon, then I'm going to take care of him myself. And if I have to "take care" of the situation it's not going to be done nicely and you all will be investigating a homi—"

"Mrs. Hill I'd be careful of what you're saying," Detective Hart warned with his hand up. "I understand that you are hurting and that you are upset by what taken place, but I'll advise you to leave Mr. Black up to us."

"No you don't understand what I've been through; you actually have no idea what Lester Black has taken me through," I stood from my seat as tears were filling my eyes once again. "You don't understand how I felt that night when he raped and beat me up like I was just some trash, you don't know I felt after that and I was only eighteen years old and I was scared out of my mind. Then on top of that the fool started stalking me for no good reason," I paused as I started to cry. "And you don't know how I felt living paranoid for the last few years of my life because I just had this feeling that I was constantly being watched or followed. And after all of that, here he goes trying to kill my *new* husband. Jay and I haven't been married a good six months before this idiot tries to take away the love of my life away from me. You can't imagine how I am feeling right now and that's why I want to kill him because he has taken some years of my life away from me by having me afraid to even live like I wanted or as I should live, a free person. So don't tell me you understand how I feel because you don't. Besides have you ever been through any of that? Uh?"

"I...uhm, no ma'am I'm sorry I haven't," Detective Hart said hesitant at first as if he was scared to speak. "I've never gone through that but—"

"So how can you tell me how to react if you don't know what I've been through?" I asked cutting him off. "No let me rephrase that, how can you say anything when you haven't been in my shoes or been through what I've been through with Lester Black?"

"Again Mrs. Hill I do apologize," he tried to sound apologetic, "but all I'm saying is that be careful with making those type of threats. I'm just trying to prevent you from going to jail for killing someone who is on his way to jail anyway, and for a long time." I exhaled hard and fell back into my seat and began to sob.

"I'm sorry Detective Hart," I apologized to him with my hands covering my face.

"Its Okay Mrs. Hill," he said and I could tell without looking up that he was walking closer toward me. I then felt a hand on my shoulder, "again I am so sorry for upsetting you."

"Oh no, its not your fault," I looked up at him and started to wipe my face, "its just that I've been holding all of that in for so long and I'm just so mad at Black and myself for allowing that fool to have so much control for the last few years and I just haven't let out yet, well until now."

"Like I said before, please just leave the justice part to us," he stated. "Trust me, we're gonna get him and make him pay for what he's done to you and your husband," he put his arm around me.

"Thank you," I leaned into him for a hug. "I really do appreciate the work that you and the other officers have done. I pray that you don't hold what I said against me."

"Oh no ma'am, I understand that you are hurting right now and you're very upset," he said pulling away and walking toward the door. "But I do want to introduce you to the officer that will be going home with you and he'll be the one that's in the house with you."

"Okay," I said still trying to wipe away all of the tears while Detective Hart went out of the door, then he returned with a tall medium brown skin guy who dressed in some jeans, t-shirt and a baseball cap. If this was an officer he sure didn't look like your average cop.

"Mrs. Hill this is Officer Irvin Dennison," Detective Hart said introducing the guy that looked like a civilian rather than the police.

"Hello Mrs. Hill it is nice to meet you," Officer Dennison extended his hand toward me.

"Nice to meet you too," I said with surprise on my face, "you don't look like a police officer at all."

"Well Mrs. Hill that's kinda what we are going for," Detective Hart began to explain. "Actually Irvin is an undercover detective. We want to keep it like that to kinda throw off our suspect."

"Oh okay," I shook my head as if what the officers had plan made sense. "That makes much more sense to me now. I really pray that all of the work you all are doing pays off by catching that bastard."

"Trust me Mrs. Hill we're gonna catch him very soon," Officer Dennison said in a very somber tone, "soon and very soon, I promise."

"I sure hope that you all do that," I said as I grabbed Jayson's hand again.

"Oh yes we're going to bust our butts day and night so you and your family can truly feel safe," Detective Hart explained.

"Again I want to thank you so much," I said then I felt my hand tighten. I looked down in surprise and realized that it was the hand that was holding onto to Jay's hand, "Oh my God!" I said aloud.

"Are you okay Mrs. Hill?" Officer Dennison asked.

"Jayson just squeezed my hand," I said with enthusiasm, "he's starting to respond to me," I began to give a slight smile.

"That's wonderful and it's a good sign of his improvement," Detective Hart explained.

"Yes I know and I'm so glad he's starting to improve this soon," I said beaming and squeezing Jay's hand lightly. "Baby I am here with you, I love you," I said then looked up at his face and saw Jayson's closed eyes moving as if he was trying to open them. "I love you so much Jayson and I can't wait until you totally recover so we can get you home." I said to Jay then I looked up at the officers who began to talk among themselves.

I had almost forgotten they were there while I was in my own little world with my husband. I looked back up at Jay then his eyes popped wide open as if someone just called his name.

* * *

It had been about two weeks since Jayson had been shot and Lester Black was still on the loose. Jay had now recovered about seventy-five percent and was close to being released from the hospital. Just yesterday he began to talk to us, he was making full sentences this time and as soon as he started that the police started questioning him about what happen the night of the shooting. During that time the detectives ask all of us to leave the room, so all of us except one of Jay's cousins who is also his lawyer left the room. Mrs. Janet and I took the time to go to the cafeteria to get some coffee and a light snack. When we returned back to the ICU area, the detectives had finished what they needed to do and let us back into the room with Jayson. Mrs. Janet didn't stay much longer after that, she was still caring for Jordan because we didn't want him to be in any danger staying with me.

"Baby I'm glad I can finally be alone with you," Jayson said in a raspy voice after his mother closed the door as she was on her way home. "I need to talk to you about what I told the police."

"Okay baby," I sat in the chair next to the bed and grabbed his hand. "But do you think that you should be doing all of this talking and stuff?"

"It's cool B, the doctor's actually encouraging me to do all this talking so I can exercise those vocal muscles," Jay said squeezing my hand.

"Alright," I smiled at him then I got up and kissed him on the lips gently. As soon as our lips met, I felt butterflies just like it was the first time all over again. "Jayson I really have missed that," I exhaled.

"Yeah me too," he smiled, "and I must say it was pretty nice, I swear I love those soft lips," he lightly kissed me again. "And I also love those *other* lips too."

I began to blush as he smiled, "I love that you love *both* sets of lips," I giggled like a schoolgirl. "And I can't wait until you are well enough to do that again, and vice versa."

"Yeah me too," he said then his smiled faded, "but on a more serious note, I want to tell you about that night."

My smiled now faded and I started to have this uneasy feeling in the pit of my stomach. "Okay baby, I think I am ready to hear this, so what happened that night?" I asked as I exhaled loudly.

"Alright here it goes," he blew into the air and looked up toward the ceiling. "Well actually it all started earlier that day, LB had called me saying that he needed to holla at me about something important. I told him cool, just come by the shop and he agreed. So when he showed up to the shop he had an envelope in his hand, he hands it to me and says, 'these are for you, but I think we should open it up in private.' I grabbed it from him and walked into the office and closed the door. I told him to have a seat while I sat behind my desk and I start to open the envelope. Then he says, 'that envelope contains some information on your wife that you may not know,' I looked at him with a what-in-the-world-are-you-talking-about-look on my face."

"What? What on earth could he know about me that you don't already know?" I questioned with confusion on my face.

"That's the same thing that I said too," I smirked thinking about how sometimes we can think alike. "After I said that he says, 'oh trust me I'm sure you don't know *everything* about the woman you married.' I looked up at him, smiled and then said if you are referring to the time when she was eighteen then yes I know. I didn't want to just come out saying the whole stripping thing just in case he was trying to lie or something."

"Good baby, I'm glad you didn't say anything other than that."

"Come on now baby, I'm not going to sell you out like that," he said, "well then he goes on to say, 'oh so you already know about her days being on the pole?' He asked with a devilish laugh. I said to him, yes she's my wife and I know everything about her. He continued to laugh then said, 'well since you know about her being a *pole dancer* then those first couple of pictures won't surprise you. But maybe you should take a look at the other ones first,' he says with this evil grin plastered on his face." I continued to hold Jay's hand as my forehead was wrinkled trying to figure out what other pictures Black could have on me. "I then threw the envelope down on the desk and said to him, look man I don't know what the hell you are up to but I think you should get the hell out of my office and my shop now before I make you leave here through a body bag. He smirked then said, 'you don't want to make any threats like that with me homeboy, but like I said you need to know that your wife really don't love you like you think she does homeboy.' So I rose up from desk."

"Oh no that bastard didn't say that," I said letting go of Jay's hand. Every bone in my body wanted to rush out of this hospital and track that mutha-scooter down and kill him my damn self. "I swear the police better find his ass before I do, because if I find him there won't be any need for them to prepare a jail cell for him, but they will need to prepare a plot at the cemetery."

"Brandi I know you are upset and I was too, but if you don't calm down I'm not gonna finish the rest of the story because what I've already told you isn't even the half of it."

"Okay babe," I closed my eyes and exhaled slowly then grabbed his hand again. "I'm cool so you can go on and finish now."

"Baby are you sure you're alright?" He asked and I simply nodded my head, "after he said that I laughed and said to him homie you need to leave now because you can't tell me anything about my relationship with my own wife. He reach for the envelope and stood up as he ripped the envelope and said, 'ok you think she loves you?' He asked then threw a picture down and it was of you and it looked as if you were dancing on a stage." My heart was now in my stomach and tears started to make their way to the brims of my eyes. "Then he threw another picture and I saw you on a pole wearing this green looking bikini type thing. Baby when I saw that picture of you I wanted to cry just thinking and knowing what you went through in that place," Jay said sounding like he was getting chocked up.

"Baby it still hurts what I went through in that damn club," I said squeezing my eyes tight as tears made its way to my face anyhow. "I hated every moment I had to work there, and uhm Jay, it's something I should be honest with you about," I pressed my lips tightly together before confessing something that I never told anyone, not even Kennede who seems to know all of my deepest darkest secrets. Well all of the secrets except this one. "Every night that I worked there I would pop pills and take several shots of liquor before I could even step out into that club half dressed to degrade myself."

"Brandi," he sighed and grabbed my hand. Because Jayson didn't have the ability to move anything other than his hands at the moment, he was squeezing and caressing my hand more than usual since he couldn't hold me. Normally during something like this Jay would hold like I know he wanted to do now. "Baby I wish you would have told me all of this, I had no idea what you were going through."

"And I'm sorry for not being all the way truthful, but Jay if I didn't get intoxicated before going out there to do that, I would have probably killed myself because I couldn't have dishonored myself by stripping for strangers for fast cash sober, I couldn't that sober at all."

"You know that makes sense to me," he said and for some reason I felt a little relief. "But anyway LB then says, 'oh yeah right she loves you so much that she slept with me.' By this time I'm fuming and he throws this picture of you two laying butt naked on something."

I let go of Jayson's hand and put my own hands over my mouth with wide eyes, "what? How did he get...when in the hell? Uh?"

"I mean the picture was kind of dark and it was hard to see your face because that part was very dark, but I know your body. Plus I saw your tattoo, and when I saw that heart with JH inside of it on the right side of your pelvis, I knew it was you." He explained and my confused brow went away as I started to think, *did he take a picture of me while he raped me? Or* was it after he raped me? Was I that out of it that I don't even remember anything after the rape? I asked these questions in my head. "When I saw that baby I swear I wanted to break down because I actually thought for a split second that maybe something went down between you two."

"Jayson baby please tell me that you don't believe...baby I would never cheat or—"

"Brandi, baby its cool," he paused and slowly took the back of my hand then lifted it to his lips to kiss it. "Baby I know you wouldn't hurt me like that. And like I said for a *split second* that's what I thought, until I realized after continuing to look at the photo, I saw that you were either sleep or unconscious. So he asks, 'what are you thinking about your little wifey now?' I then said to him, man whatever that ain't my wife and he threw another picture on the desk this didn't show your face at all but I could see your tattoo really good. In this picture it looked like he was licking on your," Jay paused and closed his eyes, then I closed my eyes too and began to cry harder.

"Baby I am sorry, I didn't know all of that happened," I apologized.

"I know you didn't know what was going on baby," he said lifting my hand to his lips again. "Brandi you don't have to apologize, but let me finish. So he then says, 'come on let's face it Jayson, I banged your wife and I have pictures to prove it. So you just need to go on and leave her, so me and her can just be together.' I rushed from behind the desk and grabbed the collar of his shirt then said, that's *my* wife and I don't give a damn what happened in the past but she's mine always and forever. He then put another naked picture of you in my face and said, 'look homeboy look carefully at this one and you still want her?' I loose my grip to grab the picture; this one had you still naked and still looking as if you weren't into what was going on, and your face was still dark, but he had his stuff all in your face looking like you were giving him oral—"

"Oh my God!" I said leaning back in the chair in shock. First off, I had no idea that bastard had took pictures of me while I was out of it, and second I had no idea he was doing all of this other stuff to me taking advantage of my lethargic state. "Are you serious? I...uhm...I have no clue how he did that, baby please tell me you believe *me?*"

"Baby I never questioned you, baby just let me finish this story please." He said, and I just nodded. "So after staring at that picture in disbelief for a minute I sat down in the chair next to LB. He then continues to taunt me by saying, 'so you believe it now?' I glanced up at him without a word then I looked back at the photo and I noticed something that he probably forgot to do. See all of the other pictures had the date blacked out with a black marker or sharpie. But the photo I held in my hand had the date on it in the corner and it didn't say 2008 either. Instead the date or the year said 2003; around the same time that you stopped stripping and at the same time you were only eighteen years old as well.

"It was also around the time that you told me you were raped. I started piecing all of that together in my head while looking at these pictures. I sat quiet for a minute then looked up at him and asked, so how long ago was it when you said you slept with my wife? Was it before or after we got married? He then starts to chuckle and says, 'well after that day I was at your crib and she saw me again, so it was a couple of days after that, but that was our second time though.' And by now I know he's lying so my jaws tighten as I tried to store up all of my energy to beat the hell out of him.

"Oh ok I said, so when was the first time ya'll was together? He smiles then says, 'oh it was back when she worked at the club, man I sexed her up real good in the club,' he had this lying grin all over his face that I wanted to slap off for him. I tried to keep my composer because I was about to catch him in a web of his own lies and he wouldn't be able to get out of it. So I ask him, are these pictures from the first time or second time that ya'll boned? He chuckled again and said, 'man them pictures are from the second time, and it was her idea to take pictures and stuff. It seemed strange to me that she wanted to take pictures since you know ya'll was about to get married and stuff, but you know I took them anyways. And now I'm glad I did so you would have proof of how she really is and I couldn't just see a homie of mine get played by some ole bitch like that.' My jaws tighten even more after he said that."

"No his trifling ass didn't say that," I sat there in shock because of the lies that this fool had told my husband. Then on top of all of that he has the nerve to call me a bitch, oh I was ready to find him and beat his ass down for real. "I'm sorry for interrupting you again," I said but with each word that Jay said that Black said, I was becoming more and more angry.

"It's ok babe, but then he goes on to say again, 'I just had to look out for you, you know?' Yeah but you know something isn't right about this picture though because you said this picture was from a couple of months ago in 2008 right? 'Uh yeah, the day after I was at your place it was uh around then,' he says. Then I chuckle and stood up to go back to my seat behind the desk, so I could get my gun because I was ready to light his ass up. I sat back down then said you know what's funny though, you said this picture as taken a couple of months ago in May of 2008, but over here in the corner it says 03-2003, you see? I turned the photo around and pointed to the corner so he could see the date. His sly grin slithered right from his slimy face and he said, 'oh damn my bad man, but we did take pictures that first time too. I must have slipped one of them in that pile too.' Oh okay I said ready to start target practice on him.

"Let me tell you this little story, I started to say; a few months ago Brandi tells me some disturbing news. My wife informs me that I wasn't the only reason she stopped stripping even though she said she was about to stop anyway because we had got back together. But she tells me that her last nigh at this club after she gets off stage she gets pulled into a dark area of the club and is raped by an unknown dude. While I'm saying this I have my hand on my gun, but I go on to say by the way she tells me what happened and looking at the picture which was taken in the same month she quit, it kinda makes me wonder if that unknown man was you." I gasp and cover my mouth with my hand.

"He starts nervously chuckling and says, 'oh naw man I didn't have to rape her man cause she was *willing* to do me.' I stood up quickly now showing my gun; I rushed in front of his face then I said, for some reason I just don't believe that. My wife wouldn't lie to me like you've been doing this whole time. I put the gun to the side of his face and said, you lying mutha, then I paused, you was that unknown dude that hurt my wife wasn't it you? I questioned. His face then went black and he had the most evil look on it, 'yeah so what? I took it from that bitch!' Baby I swear as soon as he said that I dropped the gun and began to whoop his ass with my bare hands. Somehow in the midst of me beating his ass, he grabs my gun and shoots me that's how I ended up her right now."

I sat silent for about a minute before I burst into tears, "Jayson baby I'm so sorry," I managed to say in between the sobs. "I should have been all of the way truthful with you from the beginning."

"Whoa, whoa wait a minute baby," he said looking at with glossy eyes, "what do you mean you should have been truthful from the beginning? Are you telling me that you knew from the start who it was that raped you?"

"Yes," I said barely over a whisper as I closed my eyes and tears seemed to keep falling. "Not only did I know it was Lester Black or LB, but after it happened he started to stalk me for a few months then it stopped or he stopped "popping up" at the same places that I was at. That lasted up until recently and I started to feel he was stalking me again, and that's the day he showed up at our house with you and all of my paranoid feelings was confirmed."

"Baby I wish you would have come to me," Jay said as a few tears now appeared on his face. "I wish I could just hold you right now B," he said kissing my hand again as I lay my head down on the bed next to our intertwined hands. "Brandi baby look up at me."

I raised my head then he wiped my face, "yes Jayson?"

"I promise you that he can't hurt you anymore, and once I get out of here I will see to it that he," Jay paused and I could see his jaws tightening, "just know that he'll *never* hurt us again."

*   *   *

Furious was the word that came to mind after hearing what Jay had told me about that night. I don't think anyone could even imagine how bad I wanted to track this idiot down myself and do to him what Jay was about to do, but maybe ten times worse. Ever since I left the hospital I've been thinking of ways to shake these police so I could find Black so I could carry out my threats, but after Jayson requested extra security for me plan A was now dead. That's part of the reason I was taking a long hot bubble bath in my whirlpool tub, trying desperately to come up with a plan B to kill Black. As I lay in the tub with the jets soothing my body, all I could think of was what Jay said about those pictures. I closed my eyes tightly trying to take myself back to that night to see if I even remember pictures being taken after Black raped me, but all I could remember was the pain of him entering my body then the pain to my head after he hit my face. Soon after a few more blows to my head I had blacked out, the next memory was being put into an ambulance after one of the club's security guards found me in that closet.

Knock, knock! "Mrs. Hill is everything ok in there?" Officer Dennison asked after a loud knock on the bathroom door which made me open my eyes suddenly.

"Oh...I uhm, yes officer," I said setting up as the water splashed lightly. "I'm doing ok, actually I'm about to get out of this tub now." I removed the drain so the water could go down and I stepped out of the tub to put my terry cloth robe on.

"Okay, just let me know when you're coming out of the bathroom," he said, "once you come into your bedroom, I'll then step out of your door or I can have one of the female officers to come up here to stay outside of your door."

"No you don't have to worry about it," I opened the bathroom door and the officer was standing at the bedroom door entrance. "I don't mind you standing outside the door while I'm getting dressed, not unless *you're* the on that's uncomfortable," I chuckled and so did Officer Dennison.

"No ma'am it won't make me feel uncomfortable at all. I'm ok, but I will say that you are a very attractive young woman, even though I am happily married." He chuckled again, but this time I looked at him with slanted eyes. "I know that you are married too, but that doesn't mean I don't have eyes."

"Okay Officer," I said walking toward my bedroom door, but never keeping my eyes off of him just in case he wanted to be crazy enough to try anything. "Thank you for your concern, but you can wait outside of the door for now and I will be out of here in just a moment."

"Yes ma'am," he stepped out of the door, but he turned around just as I was about to close the door. "I do apologize Mrs. Hill for that last comment because it was completely unprofessional of me. I hope that I didn't make you feel too uncomfortable."

"It's alright Officer Dennison," I managed to give a half smile, "but I would really like to get some clothes on please." He nodded his head and I closed the door, then locking it; I've been through enough to know you can't be that trustworthy of people, police officer or not. Also as a precaution I dragged my vanity chair into my walk-in closet along with my clothes and lotions just in case the officer tried to catch a peek through the cracks in the closed door. "Woo some people. I just hope, naw I don't think the officer would have been that crazy," I whispered a loud to myself as I started to think or rather question whether or not Officer Dennison would have tried to make a pass at me voluntarily or involuntarily. I quickly had to put that out of my mind because everybody isn't as crazy as Black.

I slipped out of the robe and into some oversized black sweatpants with a black spaghetti strapped tank that had a built in bra. After hanging my robe up on the back of the bathroom door, I went back into my closet to put the vanity chair back at the vanity table. Then I went back into the closet again to get a fresh throw fleece cover then I grabbed a couple of pillows from my bed and I headed downstairs to the living room so I could get some sleep. Even though I haven't spent a day alone in this house since the shooting, I just didn't feel right sleeping alone in the bed without Jayson. Sleeping on the couch made me feel a mixture of emotions; one of those emotions was a sense of comfort and protection while the other one I felt he'd be walking thru that door at any minute. Night after night I'd wait on the couch hoping that Jay would really walk in, but each night I'd have to remind myself that Jay was still in the hospital. I'd pray he'd walk in and this nightmare would *finally* end. Unfortunately night after night of that door not opening it let me know that this nightmare is my current reality and in order to see my husband walk thru the door again, it would actually take a few weeks, not the minutes and hours I hoped for while I laid there.

"Okay Officer Dennison, I'm ready to head downstairs now," I said after opening up my bedroom door then he took the covers and pillows from my arm.

"Yes ma'am you may lead the way," he said stretching out his free arm as I began walking down the steps in front of him. "Mrs. Hill I have a question to ask if you don't mind?" he asked from behind me as I stepped down the last step into the foyer.

"Sure, what do you want to know?" I asked stopping to turn around to face him, but he continued to walk toward the living room and I soon followed.

"I mean it's nothing very important, but I am just curious to know why since you've been under our watch that you haven't slept in your own bed." He said putting my covers and pillows on the couch. "But you continue to sleep here on this couch though, and I know it can't be that comfortable."

"Well officer, I don't know how to explain this," I sat down as he took a seat on the loveseat that was across from me. "But I just don't want to sleep alone in that huge bed of mine without my husband, plus I just feel safer being down here with the rest of the detectives. And another thing is that I am hoping that the fool that shot my husband will try something here at the house, and I want to be right here when and if he does so I could get him myself."

"Mrs. Hill I don't think that the suspect is going to try anything with all of us officers and detectives both in and outside of this house." He stated and I looked at him with a blank stare, "besides he wouldn't even get into this house or even close to this house without one of our officers getting him first. So I doubt that you'd be able to get to him before us."

"Oh, I guess it's just wishful thinking because I want to get him," I sucked my teeth then I paused so that I could choose my words carefully. "After all he has done to me and now my husband, I just want him to get justice and pay for what he's done."

"I know and understand Mrs. Hill," he said sitting back on the loveseat. "But just please trust me and the other detectives that are in here to protect you. We're going to catch him either way and we will especially get him if he tries to do anything here at the house, I'm sure of it," he explained as he was referring to the two other officers that were now inside the house with us, Detective Marie Green and Detective Angelo Perez. They were stationed in two different locations of my house; Detective Green was in the back of the house near the garage and kitchen, while Detective Perez stayed in upstairs.

"Alright then Officer Dennison."

"Mrs. Hill you can stop calling me Officer Dennison now, please just call me Irvin."

"Well Detective— I mean uhm, Irvin," I chuckled, "I'll stop calling you that as long as you start calling me Brandi. I love to hear you say *Mrs. Hill*, but you can just call me by my first name though."

"Okay Mrs. — I mean Brandi, it's a deal," he chuckled then stood up briefly to shake on it. "Now you get some sleep please."

"Yes sir," I released his hand and managed to adjust my pillows as I laid my head down. "Oh here you go Irvin, I'm not up to watching any TV right now," I said handing Irvin or Officer Dennison the remote.

"Okay, but go to sleep Mrs. Brandi," he said and that's when I managed to close my eyes.

Instead of dreaming about better days and my husband coming home to me quickly, I was plotting. I was still trying to figure out how I was going to track this fool down and kill him myself. *Ha, I need to just give it up, give up the fantasy of being able to "take care" of Black myself, because in reality I had no idea on God's green earth where this fool was. I don't think the police even really knew where he was at either. So I was just gonna have to let Black go, and give him over to the Lord as hard as it was to try to do that; I just had to. And God while I'm trying to hand Black over to you, Lord I ask that you will make a change in me. Change me to the point that I don't want to see the man dead, but I want him to be caught by the police and justice be served because of what he has done to my husband and what he has done to me in the past.*

As I continued to lay on the couch now half asleep, I heard a lot of commotion going on around me. At one point I could have sworn I heard someone say, "*Has the person been identified yet?*" But I could have been dreaming, I think.

Once I finally opened my eyes I saw my front door open and there was flashing lights that seemed to surround my house. I quickly sat up and saw Detective Green standing near the front door. "What's going on Ms., I mean Detective Green?" I asked now standing, "it doesn't have anything to do with my husband does it? Please tell me there's nothing wrong with Jay." I said beginning to panic for no reason.

"No, no please calm down Mrs. Hill, and I told you before call me Marie," she said putting her arm around me and walking me back to the couch.

"Okay Marie, but call me Brandi," I sat back down and she took a seat next to me, "so are you gonna tell me what's going on?"

"Yes Brandi," she paused, "well we think we may have found the suspect Lester Black."

My eyes grew big, "found?" I questioned shaking my head, "what does… uhm, what do you mean by *found?*"

"Okay you know we've had surveillances over at his apartment just in case he may come back to it," she said. "So tonight we detected movement in the apartment along with a tip from the female that was staying there before. She confirmed that he was back in town and his first stop would be his apartment, and since there was already an officer in the area, we notified them. We also let them know that he could have entered into his apartment home thru the garage which was in the back of the complex." I sat on the couch looking at here in amazement and with butterflies in my stomach as waited for her next words which could be the very end of this nightmare.

"I mean so was it him in the apartment?" I questioned now leaning forward and placing my chin in my palm.

"Well yes and no," she replied while running her fingers thru her jet black. As a side note; the more that I looked at Marie with this jet black hair and light complexion I thought that maybe she was mixed like Kennede, but after speaking to her I found out she was straight up black, it was just the dark hair and light skin made her look really pale. Anyway back to the present situation at hand.

"So what do you mean by that?"

"Okay, Mr. Lester Black was in the apartment but he wasn't alone. There was another young woman in there as well but not the same one that we've been in contact with." She paused and I was confused because Marie was only telling bits and pieces of the story.

"Marie I uhm…I don't want to be rude or anything, but I don't understand why you won't just come out and tell me what's really going on?" I questioned because I was tired of her beating around the bush. "It seems that you aren't trying to be direct with me or something."

"Mrs. Hill there's some information that I'm not allowed to talk to you about when dealing with a homicide," she said in a stern voice.

"Homicide?" I put my hand over my mouth as I began to think the worst because all I could think about was Jayson; instantly I started to feel sick to my stomach. "Marie please be very straight with me right now, but this homicide has nothing to do with my husband does it? Please tell me the truth, please?" I pleaded with her.

She grabbed my free hand and I started to shake, "no Brandi it's not your husband," relief swept over my body when she said those words. "Mr. Hill is safe and sound at the hospital, but here's the story; after we detected movement we gathered a task force to go in and apprehend the suspect. Just as they were coming up with a plan to go inside, they heard gunshots fired from that apartment. Then they rushed into the apartment and found a black female standing in the living room crying with her hand up in the sky and the gun next to her feet with a body in a chair behind her."

"Oh my God," I placed both of my hands over my mouth, "was it Lester Black's body?"

"We think that it is him, so although no family has formally identified the body yet, we—" she stopped talking to answer her ringing phone, "give me a moment," she said to me then stood up and went outside.

"Oh God," I continued to say while shaking my head, "it's over, my nightmare is *finally* over!" I began to sob because part of me felt a huge weight being lifted from my shoulders. Actually it was years of fear and hurt that was now over, "it's over!" I repeated but this time with a smile.

"I'm sorry about that Brandi," Marie came back into the living room. "But I have an important question for you, do you happen to know a Ms. Shayla Love?"

"Shayla Love?" I repeated in a question form before it clicked in my mind who she was, Lovely from the club. "Uhm yes I remember Shayla, but what does she have to do—" I paused, "Oh God, did she do this, I mean did she kill Lester Black?"

"I'm afraid so," Marie replied calmly, "she's down at the station already and she's mentioned your name a few times saying that she did this for you as well as for herself."

"Hold up wait a minute, is she saying that I asked her to do this?" I help up my hand, "Because that's not even so, the last time I talked to Shayla was when we were working at that damn club and her last night there was the last time I talked to her, honestly."

"I know Brandi, because Shayla went on to say the same thing too," Marie said. "She told us that after that night she moved back to her hometown and hasn't been back to Louisville until a couple of days ago. She told us that Mr. Black found her in Paducah, Kentucky and assaulted her after he confessed to a rape and shooting that he did here. When she tried to put him out of her home, he then began to beat her and attempted to rape her too, but he was interrupted by something then quickly left."

"Oh no," I said with my hands back over my mouth again.

"But she came here to Louisville for revenge and well it looks like she got it, in the wrong way though." Marie said as she sat back on the couch next to me, "so Brandi are you alright?"

"Yes ma'am, I haven't felt this much relief in so long. I'm actually ready to go up to the hospital to tell Jay the news," I said with a smile.

"Okay, well that's understandable, but if you want I'll be more than happy to escort you along with Irvin's help." She said. "Even though we're positive it's Mr. Black, we still are going to stay with you just to be on the safe side even up until Mr. Hill comes back home."

"That sounds great to me," I said jumping up, "I'm going to run upstairs to get my tennis shoes and jacket. I promise I'll be ready in like two seconds."

"That's fine you just take your time," Marie said and I quickly went up the steps.

Once I walked into my bedroom I fell on my knees on the side of my bed. "Thank you Jesus that it's over! I'm sorry he had to die, but I'm glad its over for me! Thank you Lord!"

The night of Jayson's Welcome Home Party:

"B, I promise that you are the best wife in the world," Jayson said as he was getting back in the bed at our house. That's right, my boo was finally home, well actually he had been home for about four days, but today we had a welcome home Jayson/Happy Birthday Brandi & Brianna Party. Jayson was released from the hospital on Wednesday October 22, 2008; I wanted to have a party for him that weekend. So my family was like why don't we do it Sunday October 26th which is me and Brianna's twenty-fourth birthday. Also I didn't want to do anything on the actual day he was released because I knew he wouldn't be up for any kind of party that day. Besides I didn't mind sharing my birthday party with my husband's return home party, because Jayson finally returning home was the best present anyone could ever give me.

"Well I try to be the best wife I can be," I laughed and so did he, but I could tell it was probably hurting him to do so. "Oh baby are you feeling ok? Do you need anything right now?" I asked while helping him adjust his pillows.

"I'm having just a little pain that's all," he said trying to get in a comfortable position in the bed.

"Okay baby," I said walking to my side of the bed, "would you like for me to get your pain meds for you?"

"Would you please?" he asked with a half smile, "nurse Mrs. Hill could I get some ginger ale with it too?"

"Yes Mr. Hill, I'd do whatever you would like," I said smiling. "You know as long as we've been together I've never had to play an actual nurse to you like this?"

"I know," he stated and I could tell he was in a lot of pain.

"Okay babe, let me hurry up and bring your meds to you, with some ginger ale and a small snack so the pain meds won't make you sick." I said standing at our bedroom door.

"Thanks a lot babe," he said, "but could my snack be one of those ham and turkey sandwich's from the sandwich wheel? Oh, and could I get some chips with that too?"

"Yes sir," I said while saluting him. I quickly went downstairs but instead of going into the kitchen, I went into the half bathroom first. I had bought this cute red and white nurses uniform from *Fredrick's of Hollywood*, it had the little hat which looked very good on top of my long flat iron hair; I also put on the fishnet stockings that came along with it too. It also had some three and a half inch stilettos that went with it, but I still had to get his sandwich, chips, and drinks so the shoes would go on last. I was able to dress up like this because Jordan was staying with his cousins tonight. The kids didn't have to go to school the next day and his cousins wanted him to stay with them; I'm kind of glad that everything worked out that way so I could take care of my husband like this; I knew Jay would love this too.

"Oh my God," Jayson said looking me up and down with approval when I walked back into the room. "Oh Nurse Hill, I'm not feeling too good at all."

"I know babe," I said sitting the tray on the nightstand on his side of the bed. "Here baby take this now, and try to eat a quick bit so you won't get sick. And you should be feeling no pain temporarily, but I'll continue to give it to you every four hours like it says on the bottle."

"Thank you so much babe," he said after he downed the pills and began to stuff the sandwich into his mouth as if someone was going to steal his food from him. "Nurse Mrs. Hill I need you now," he said after taking another big gulp of his ginger ale.

"Jay," I smiled as he pulled me on the bed next to him, "baby you shouldn't be doing this, trying to pull on me *or* trying to get some either."

"But babe, you don't understand how sexy you are looking in that uniform," he said using his index finger to tell me to come closer to him. I kissed him passionately, "oh come on baby, it's got be something we can do, I mean I'll suffer through the pain."

"Jayson Hill!" I leaned back laughing, "Baby trust me, this uniform isn't going anywhere and neither am I, so just chill out. Once you get your strength back I promise *"Naughty Nurse Hill"* will return," I kissed his lips again, "I promise."

"I'm gonna hold you to it, because you made me a promise," he said with a sexy look.

"Oh I know it's my birthday and I'm the one that should be receiving the gifts, but I have a huge surprise for you though." I said and Jay's face grew concern.

He sat there for a minute then he began to smile, "oh so are you gonna… you know, down there?" I looked at him with a smile and shook my head in disagreement, "okay so what is it then baby?"

"I'm pregnant."

"Pregnant?" he repeated with a confused face.

"I'm thirteen weeks Jay," I said and his face relaxed more and it changed into the biggest smile I've ever seen on his face.

"My baby's pregnant, oh my God I can't wait until that baby comes."

"I know I can't wait either," I smiled hard. "I am so happy that I now get to have a baby with the love of my life," we kissed again and all I could think of was how happy I felt to have my life back.

23
Summer

"Its okay baby, we'll be home in just a minute," Brianna said to a six week old Bianca who was crying in the backseat. "Here you go baby girl." Brianna put something in her mouth that made her stop crying; I couldn't tell what it was because I was driving while they were in the back. We had just come from the welcome home/birthday party for her and Brandi at Brandi and Jay's house.

"Was she hungry or is she wet?" I asked now pulling into Brianna's apartment complex.

"I think it's a little of both, and once we get in the apartment I'll be able to do both," Brianna replied. "And Summer I must say again, thank you so much for volunteering to help me pack or watch the baby; which ever you want to do, I'm glad just to have the help."

"Girl it's no problem at all, we are family," I pulled into an empty parking space. I jumped out of the driver's side and opened the back door to help Bri with the baby. "But girl you know I will do anything for you just let me know what you want me to do, well once we get up the stairs, but do you need me to carry something for you now?"

"Could you please?" she asked then handed me this beautiful pink and white *Louis Vuitton* diaper bag and matching purse. "But right now if you could grab this for me so I can get the baby. Oh and here's the keys too." She handed the keys to me before she put a small blanket over the car seat to cover the baby while we were in the cool air.

"Okay girl," I closed the door after she and the baby was out of the car. "I must say this Louis Vuitton stuff is too adorable."

"Thanks girl, but it was actually one of the gifts that Bianca's daddy gave us during the baby shower." She said behind me because I was trying to open her apartment door. I stopped turning the key to turn to look at her with confusion, "yeah you heard me right, now open the door please, I'm cold!"

"I am sorry," I said opening the door then allowing her and the baby to go thru it first. "So you're telling me this is what Lance's wife brought over to the baby shower?" I questioned as I was sitting the bags on the couch next to Bri who was about to change Bianca's diaper.

"Yep that's what Mrs. Hamilton had in the gift bag when she made a guest appearance at my baby shower." She said laying Bianca on the towel that she had lay on the couch and she proceeded to change her. "But girl the diaper bag and purse wasn't the real surprise; the surprise is what was in the bag."

"Dang girl so what else was it in there?" I questioned, "Shoot I know those two pieces of there probably cost well into the thousands."

"Well there was also a baby carrier and," she paused, "and there was a total of five thousand dollars in an envelope."

"What?!" I questioned. "What I don't understand is why would he do that?"

"Child support," she simply said and I continued to look at her confused. "Girl yes that's what the letter said though; oh yeah he put a note in there basically telling me the money is pretty much to help *take care* of Bianca. Point blank he doesn't want me to take him to child support court because his "happy little marriage," will be ruined or whatever."

"So the money is kind of like a pay off, in a way uh?" I inquired.

"Pretty much, but my baby is not for sale is she? No she isn't," Brianna said now speaking to her daughter as she picked her up in her arms.

I shrugged my shoulders because I didn't know what to think or say about what Brianna had just told me. "I mean…wow. I guess what I'm trying to ask is, did you talk to him at all about the money?"

"Well let me explain something first," she said now reaching in the diaper bag to retrieve a half full bottle. "Like I said he wrote a letter along with the money. In the letter he tries to explain that this money isn't any kind of "payoff" or any "guilt money" to keep me quiet. I guess to clear his own conscience he claims the money is to help take care of Bianca; he also says in the letter that he wants to be in her life as much as he could."

"Wow," I said because I was speechless at what I was hearing. "So did you actually talk to him though?"

"Yeah, I called him after I found the money and he was saying that he was on his way over here anyway. But the crazy thing about it is once he got over here I went into labor, so we didn't talk about it that night. Later on that day that Bianca was born he shows up at the hospital, luckily I still had the money on me; I tried to give it back to him because my pride was talking big time. And my pride told him that Bianca and I didn't need his guilt money, and of course he tried to plead with saying that that wasn't the purpose of the money. Basically he kept repeating himself saying that it wasn't payoff or guilt; but I sat the envelope on the edge of the bed next to where he was sitting, but he got up and tried to convince me that he still loved me and stuff like that. And without grabbing the money he left after I turned him down."

"My, my, my," I said shaking my head in disbelief because of what I just heard.

"Ok Johnny Gill," Brianna said laughing as I joined in with her. "But I know that's a lot of drama for someone so young isn't it?"

"Girl, that's just the way life and love goes." I stated, "But your life I must say, sounds like a straight up soap opera," we began to laugh again.

"Tell me about it," she smiled. "My life should be called, 'The Young, the Old, and the Restless,' starring Brianna Spencer." She chuckled. "Enough about my life with all of its drama, what's going on in your new life and the new love with Amir?" she asked with a grin on her face.

I smiled too at the thought of him, "we're doing really good and I love him so much, but the only thing is that he is celibate."

"Wow, whoa, what?" she asked and I knew she was shocked because she had stopped patting Bianca's back. "So fine as wine Amir is celibate? How do you do it girl? I mean I just didn't know God made men like that, the ones who don't always want what's in between your legs."

"I know girl, and in a way with him being celibate is an inspiration to me," I explained, "but the truth is although I admire his dedication to not have sex until he's married, it is so hard for me to suppress my own sexual feelings and urges. I mean it is so very hard."

"I can only imagine girl, as fine and sexy if I might say that he is, I probably would try to rape the poor boy." She chuckled and I joined in with her laughter.

"Trust me it isn't easy at all especially when he walks around the house with just a towel after he's just gotten out of the shower," I paused for a minute thinking about him in that attire. "And watching the water rolling down each and every perfectly structured muscle in his chest and his biceps….woooo…damn, I'm getting hot thinking about it now."

"Hell, now you've got me hot over here too thinking about it," she said using a free hand to wave toward her face as if she was really hot. "I mean so what do you do in those kind of moments? Cold shower perhaps?"

"Honey I take a cold shower plus use extra ice to put on myself after I get out of the shower," I said now fanning myself. "Between me and you though, if things get too hot for me and a cold shower with extra ice doesn't help, I've purchased a "friend" to help me get over my little *hot spells*."

"Hold up what did you just say?" Bri asked with a sneaky grin on her face, "Are you admitting to me that you have a vibrator?"

"I plead the fifth," I laughed, "I plead it on the grounds that it might—"

"Uh, uh heifer that don't work up in here," she said while shaking her head, "but seriously though, do you have one?"

"Yeah, I actually just got it," I said now blushing.

"Did you go to a store or did you get it online?" she questioned. "Because the way things are looking and how I'm not feeling a man right now, then the fact is that I will *never* touch a woman in any kind of sexual way a sister needs one, so how can I be down?" she asked.

"Brianna you really want one for real?" I asked and she simply nodded. "Well the one I got was through one of those pleasure parties."

"Summer," Brianna said with a devious look on her face. "When did you go to something like that?"

"Well one of my friends had one and she invited me. We really had a great time looking at some of those sex toys and stuff." I explained, "But some of those toys were a little too much for me. All in all I think I would like to host one myself and invite the girls, even though your sister is married now and Ken is close to being married again. I think it would still be a lot of fun though. Not only do they have toys for "self pleasure," they also have some stuff for couples too; since those two are married they would probably enjoy the stuff for the couples."

Brianna turned her nose up as if she was disgusted about something. "Eeeelll, for couples just sign me up with *single and ain't getting none toys*." She said before standing up with Bianca in her arms.

"Bri stop it, don't talk so that about couples."

"I didn't saying anything bad," she said with her nose still up in the air. "I just said Eeeelll to being a couple because I'm just not feeling the whole love and couples thing right now. I've finally accepted the fact that I'll probably be alone, well just me and Bianca."

"Brianna," I simply said as if I was disappointed in her.

"What is it Summer?" she asked. "Look, I'll be right back, I'm about to put my boo-boo down for the night, or at least I hope for the rest of the night." Before I could say anything else, Brianna had already left the living room.

I sat there on the couch a moment before I noticed a box sitting next to my foot on the floor. It was marked "**LIVING ROOM**," so I started to put some of the stuff that was wrapped in newspaper in the box. While I was halfway into the project Brianna walked back into the room, "I didn't know what you wanted me to do yet, and I took it upon myself to start putting this stuff that was sitting on the table in this box." I said.

"Oh that's fine," she walked over to the dining room and grabbed another box. "Most of that stuff is glass vases, candy bowls, and picture frames; you know the stuff that needed to be marked fragile."

"Okay, like I said just let me know what else you need me to do," I repeated again.

"Well if you don't mind, could you get the glasses out of the kitchen and put them in the boxes that are already in the kitchen please?"

"Sure."

"I would do it myself but I'm still having some pain in my abdomen and I can't stand up for a long period of time," she explained. "But if you do that then I will finish what you started in here."

"Like I said I'm here to do whatever you need me to do," I said standing up and making my way to the kitchen. Once I got in there I grabbed one of the boxes that was sitting on the floor that was marked "**KITCHEN/ FRAGILE**" and I began to put some glass dishes in it after wrapping it in newspaper. "So Bri I have something to ask you." I said while working like a busy bee.

"Sure what's up?"

"Before you laid the baby down, you were saying something about being a couple," I began. "I guess my question is have given up on being in love and even being married on day?"

"In a way I guess I have," she paused. And it was so long that I had to look in the living room to make sure she was ok. Once I looked around the corner I saw Bri with her head held down then she began to wipe her face with the baby's blanket that was next to her. I stopped packing and went back into the living room to sit next to her. "Oh Summer you don't have to come in here, I'm fine really I am fine. Just go on back in there and finish packing please?" She said trying to push my arm from her and using the other one to wipe the tears away with the blanket again.

"No I'm not gong anywhere or doing anything else yet." I said wrapping my arm around her anyway, "Bri will you please talk to me because something is obviously going on with you."

She looked over at me with her looking toward the ceiling, "Summer I just don't know how to explain what I am feeling; most times I never have to *talk* it out because I am always writing what I feel down in my journal. It's just easier that way for me."

"Could you at least try to explain what you're feeling to me?" I grabbed her hand, "Bri I promise that what is said right here between us, will stay right here between us, I promise."

"Okay," she took a deep breathe before she started to talk again. "Of course you know how I use to feel about Lance and he really hurt me. I mean it felt like he ripped my heart out, broke it all to pieces then tried to mend it only to pick it apart slowly taking little pieces at time and breaking it all over again and breaking it worse than it was the first time." She paused before she went on to tell me how he had proposed to her the very morning of Grandmother's birthday party and 4th of July celebration; and the day that she met his wife Carla. My heart went out to her as she continued to tell me how Lance would try to justify his love and how he pretty much was lying so he could have his cake and eat it too.

"I will say this, I don't everything but what I do know is you shouldn't give up on love just because of what happened with Lance. I'm pretty sure that you have a true love out there somewhere, but it may be that your true love, or soul mate may not be here in Louisville and we know that it is *not* with Lance."

"You damn right about that," she chuckled mockingly.

"But you are about to make a brand new start by moving to Indianapolis, so let that right there plus that beautiful baby girl that you have in there, let that be your motivation. Most importantly though don't give on that chance of having a true love, and don't let your daughter see you bitter toward men or love for men because the cycle will only continue with her because of what you are dealing with. Because as she grows she's going to be watching what you do and how you handle different circumstances. Trust me I see it all the time at work with the women I talked to who have been in domestic situations, most times after to talking further with them I found out that it started most of the times at home; what they've experienced growing up has followed them into their adult years because they don't know how to deal with the past and let it go. Then trust me that I had more than enough reasons to give up on men and love based on the what I've been through with Damon, but I had gave up on being in love. I wouldn't have found what I have with Amir, and now I am so happy with him. And I can't remember at anytime in my adulthood that I've felt this complete." I smiled becoming misty eyed.

"I know, I must say lately every time I see you, you just seem to have the biggest and brightest glow. And when you and Amir are together like tonight at the party for us and Jay you could just tell that you all are truly in love. And I am so happy for you because you deserve it."

"And you deserve to be happy and in love too," I said as she rolled her eyes. "I'm for real, you never know what's gonna happen once you leave this city. The man of your dreams could be right around the corner from your place once you get up there; shoot he could be right next door. All I'm saying is Bri don't give up on love, because true love can happen, trust me you will know when it's real too."

"Yeah I guess you're right, and thanks a lot for being there for me girl," she laid her head on my shoulder.

"Oh honey hush," I said before we both started to laugh. "I guess you could say not too long ago I was exactly where you are now. But I was afraid of being in love and afraid to let my guard down to allow Amir to love me the right way. I had to do a lot of soul searching along with a whole lot of prayer, and that's why I was able to open my heart to the best relationship I've ever known."

"You don't understand how happy I am for you." She said smiling and I began to smile with her. "The way you just light up when you speak about him just amazes me, but girl what are you going to do while he's away on his business trip?"

"Oh, girl I forgot that quick that we had dropped him off at the airport before we came here," I said pouting like a child. Amir had a business trip for some kind of engineering conference out in San Diego, California; and he was going to be gone all week. Luckily his flight didn't leave until seven this evening so he was able to attend the party and eat a home cooked meal before his non-stop flight to California tonight. "I'm kind of hesitating about staying in that big ole house without him for so long though."

"So how long is he going to be gone?"

"Well the conference starts tomorrow and last until Thursday," I replied trying to remember the details of Amir's itinerary that he posted on the refrigerator before he left. He did that so I would know when his plane landed and the right time to pick him up. "So I believe his itinerary said that he's checking out early Friday morning and his flight will land back here that afternoon around three-thirty in the afternoon or something like that."

"Oh that's the day before I move," Brianna stated, "Summer are you sure that Amir is going to be rested enough to help me move the next day? I know he's going to be jetlagged and I don't want to break the brother down because we're gonna have more than enough people helping me."

"Bri don't worry about that," I waved my hand toward her. "Amir said himself that he'd be okay to help you move, but only on Saturday though. I know you need help loading the truck on Friday and I can do that if Amir is too tired to help. But we definitely are going to help you on Saturday because he has family up there in Indy and we were gonna visit them so he could introduce me."

"Summer," she said in a whining voice, "I just don't want the poor boy to fall out somewhere trying to help us move. Besides I forgot that I hired some professional movers to help me especially with big heavy furniture like the living room and my bedroom stuff. But the movers are only gonna help us once we get there. Hopefully with all of the help that I will have on Friday we can get the truck loaded up. The thing I really need you all to assist me with is the unpacking and straightening everything in the apartment, and while some of ya'll are doing the unpacking someone could keep an eye on Bianca; but that's only if she starts crying."

"Oh well girl that's nothing at all," I waved my hand at her again. "The way it looks you really don't need us to do a lot of labor on Saturday, other than the unpacking part. And I'll do the driving on the way up there so that Amir can rest even more if he want to do it that way."

"Okay Summer," she said slowly as she was looking at me with her eyes slanted, "now changing the subject, do you want to stay here with me if you're scared to stay at the house by yourself? Because five nights alone is a long time and you are more than welcomed to stay here with me and Bianca."

"Thanks for the invitation, but I'd rather be in my own bed and I don't want to get in your way."

"Summer you won't get in my way at all."

"Bri trust me I'll be okay," I grabbed her hand then began to pat it. "I'll set my alarms and stuff, plus Chyna said that she's going to stay with me for a few nights since she and I need time to catch up because it's been so long since we've just set down and talked."

"Okay, well now I feel a lot better knowing that you won't be by yourself."

"I'm glad that you care so much about me, but as long as the Lord is watching over me and ADT is on, I'll be alright." I laughed and Bri gave a light chuckle.

"Alright then Summer," Brianna leaned over to hug me, "I love you girl and I'm going to miss you, Brandi, and Ken so much when I finally leave," she said and I could hear the cracking in her voice.

"Bri, Bri I'm going to miss you too; I mean we've been through so much together growing up and stuff. I'm so grateful to have cousins/friends like you guys." I said chocking up myself, "and you don't know how deep I *really* love you all, and I think that's because I've never had a biological sister, but God blessed me to have best friends who just happen to be my cousins. I couldn't even imagine anything bad happening to either one of you, but I just want to say that I am so proud that you are going to start your new life in a new city with your new baby. I pray that God continues to bless you and that little one in there, I love the both of you so much." I finished my little speech with tears now running down my face.

"Oh girl," Brianna exhaled loudly with tears streaming down her face too. "I'm going to miss you guys too, but just remember that I'm only an hour and a half away. And if you just need to talk please remember that I'm only one phone call away."

I hugged her tighter as we continued to cry, "I am so happy that you've decided to break away from the stress of this city, congrats on your new life! May God bless you and Bianca real good!"

*   *   *

"Dang…baby…" I paused in between the kisses, "Did you….miss… me or something?" I asked Amir as we lay in his bed *trying* to watch a movie, but we ended up in a heavy kissing session.

"Summer you don't understand how much I've missed you," he said kissing me again then stopping for a quick minute to stare at me.

"Baby what is it?" I asked after a few minutes of him gazing into my eyes; him looking that fine and looking at me with those emeralds that he calls eyes made me feel like I wanted to rip off the shirt that he was wearing and let him have *every* single piece of my body. "Amir, why do you keep looking at me like that?" I asked after he didn't answer my first question.

"First off the reason that I keep looking at you like that is because you are so beautiful," he grazed the side of my face with his index finger. I guess since he couldn't move any hair out of my face grazing the side of it was the next best thing. I had cut my hair pretty much as short as Ken's after I took one look at the singer Rihanna's do in the *'Take a Bow'* video and it was over; the next day I was calling Ken so I could get in her shop to get my hair chopped. "Secondly, I'm sitting here thinking about how blessed I am to have the most beautiful woman in the world as my woman and soon to be my wife."

"What?"

"Yes you heard me right," he sat up in the bed and I slowly rose up as well. "While I was away and missing you so much I did some serious praying as well as thinking. One of which was marriage, and I want to marry you; honestly I'd marry you tomorrow if you agreed to do it that soon."

I would marry you tomorrow too, I thought to myself, but what came out of my mouth was, "you really want to marry me?"

"Summer of course I would," he paused, "but one of the reservations that I have about asking so soon is that we've only been official for about four and a half months and I thought maybe it would be too overwhelming for you since you've had so much to deal with this year."

"I mean yes I've been through a *whole* lot of things this year, but I've done a lot of growing as well," I began. "Just in that short time I've began to learn to love myself and now I feel so much better. Then God has blessed me with this wonderful God-fearing man; even with all of the ups and downs I just…I mean if you were to ask me to marry you from this point on, I *definitely* wouldn't say no," I moved closer to him then put my arms around him. "Amir you are too good of a man to let you go that easily."

Our lips met once more, "well I'm glad to hear you say that," he kissed my forehead this time with the biggest smile on his beautiful face. "Now I don't know if you've ever wanted the big proposal in front of your family and stuff."

I scrunched my face, "baby all of that doesn't matter to me and you know I try to think of myself as a down to earth simple kinda girl who doesn't need a big scene."

"Okay well that's good to know," he said standing before he kneeled down by the bed; my heart dropped when he pulled a ring box from his pants pocket. "Summer I can't go on any longer without making some kind of lifetime commitment to you," he said looking into my eyes while holding my hand. "Like I said earlier, you are the most beautiful, smartest, and sexiest woman I know and I can't go another day without making this thing right between us. Most importantly I love you so much plus I feel that you deserve the best things in the world and I want to give it to you or at least die trying." I nervously smiled as my heart raced a mile a minute. He opened he box there was my dream ring, a platinum or white gold marquise diamond engagement ring; I put the hand that Amir wasn't holding onto over my mouth. "Summer Parker will you make me the happiest man in the world and marry me?"

My heart, mind and everything else screamed yes, but my vocal cords just weren't getting the message yet. "Yes, yes baby!" I blurted out before I grabbed his face with both of my hands then kissed him. "I'm sorry it took so long to answer, but I wish to God that I could marry you tomorrow."

"I know," he said placing the ring on my finger then getting up and kissing me again while I began to lie back on the bed. Amir moved on top of me as we continued to kiss which only bothered me some more. "Woo, yeah we need to get married *soon*, because now you've got me wanting you even more." He whispered in my ear before he began to kiss my neck, that's when my eyes went in the back of my head.

"And...uh, with you doing all of that isn't making it any easier for me either." I said trying to compose myself as he kissed me again but this time on my lips. "Okay...uhm, let's pause for a minute," I stopped him then he sat up and so did I, "since you know I have the ring and I'm guessing we'll be getting married pretty soon, so why don't we... you know go on and—"

"Summer," he said moving completely off of me but still sitting next to me on the bed. With the look he had on his face I could tell tonight would be one of those nights that I pulled out my "special toy." I had too much pent up *sexual energy* that needed to be burnt up. "Baby I know that I gave you an engagement ring and all, which means I'm making a promise to you that the wedding ring is on the way. And until we make that *big* commitment before God in the right way I can't do anything like that with you yet." He looked over at me as I sat there pouting, he grabbed my hand, "oh baby trust me, I mean really trust me I want you just as bad as you want me, but I can't disobey God because there is something that God has in store for us, and as much as I love you I can't let my flesh longer. And most importantly I don't want disrespect you or myself in any kind of way."

I looked at him with a question mark on my face, "what do you mean by disrespecting me?"

"What I mean is that you are a lady, a woman, a queen who should be treated as such meaning that no man should approach a woman with the intent of using her body especially if it's not their wife and I'm not going to use you in a way to satisfy my flesh." He started to rub my hand, "and the biggest thing is we are Christians and we're suppose obey the Word, and if it says that we shouldn't do anything if we aren't married then we should pray about these urges; we should ask for strength until we're married. I know it's hard, literally," he looked down then we both started to laugh before he kissed my hand. "But God can't get us through it."

"Well please Jesus help me," I looked up toward the ceiling while squeezing Amir's hand, "so what do you think about a short engagement?"

"Baby I told you I'd marry you tomorrow if I could," he said now pulling me toward him wrapping his arms me from behind. "But I thought maybe you wanted a big wedding with our families then your cousins as your bridesmaids and stuff. But me it doesn't matter," he adjusted me in some kind of way so I could look at his face. "As long as I get to make you my wife I will marry you if it was just me, you, the minister and a witness. But with your big nosy family I'm pretty sure it would be more out again it whatever you want, if you want it big we can do it."

"Amir I really know now that you are the man for me," I turned around some more so that it would be easy to kiss him. "Baby you don't know how much I've always wanted something small and intimate; you know how some girls dream of the big weddings, I was never that type of person, I always wanted just a small dress, only my cousins and Chyna so that's four bridesmaids then the rest of my family and close friends only that's what I've always dreamed." I smiled.

"Well then I guess its perfect small and intimate," he said squeezing my hand, "so what about the date; what time of the year?"

"Another dream of mine, which is probably kind of corny, but I've always wanted was a Valentine's Day wedding," I sat up on the bed all the way remembering what I've always dreamed of because for once my fairytale romance/love was finally about to come true. "I've always wanted to have a wedding around then so I could have a red bridesmaid dress; I told you its kind of corny." I twisted my face.

"No baby it's not corny at all," he shock his head, "I think its wonderful, uhm lets get a calendar to check the date out, hold on I'll get mine." He jumped out of the bed to go to his dresser to retrieve a calendar that was sitting close to it. "Alright, Mrs. Soon to- be-Bryant." He said coming back to the bed sitting across from me this time as I sat with crossed legs like I was in kindergarten.

"Oh I love the sound of that," I smiled so hard it was hurting my face, "Mrs. Amir Bryant, God I just can't wait even though I mean… but you understand."

"Yes baby I do," he said turning the pages of his datebook. "Okay February 2009, oh…hear we go," he said then it looked like his smile was fading.

"Oh no what is it baby?" I questioned with concern.

"Baby it's perfect," a huge smile came back on his face, "February 14, 2009 is on a Saturday a perfect day for a wedding, can you believe it?"

I began to smile even more, "oh my God it's like a total dream come true. I get to marry the most absolutely wonderful man in the world on the day I've always wanted to get married and what do you know the day is on Saturday, I am so excited. Oh no," I stopped cheesing for a minute as I thought of something. "I wonder if the church is booked up with weddings for that day."

"Yeah you're right," Amir's smile had faded by now too, "that is a pretty popular day, but we wouldn't need that buy main sanctuary since we're going to do it small."

"That's true, but we will never know unless we call the church very soon and find out," I said grabbing the pen that was attached to the calendar so I could write down on it to call the church tomorrow. Even though today was Friday I was pretty sure someone would be in the office for a little while on Saturday, or at least I was hoping someone would be in there. "Oh darn, I forgot that we're helping Bri move tomorrow."

"Baby we can just try tomorrow with the info so we can either call before we leave or if we can call on our way, its either or , like I said I'm just glad to be with my boo."

"My boo," I tried to sing the chorus of Usher and Alicia Keys song, "Okay baby I just can't wait, I love you so much," I jumped into his arms and gave him a hug and kiss.

"And I love you too," he said as he lay back while we continued to kiss, but I was now on top of him. *Lord I just can't wait until we can do this.*

"Wow Bri, the apartment is looking pretty good now since we've put most of the stuff up now." Kennede said laying back on Brianna's couch after we had finished getting her living room together while our mother's were helping with both of Brianna's bathrooms and her kitchen.

"Yes it is," she said coming into the room and sitting on the couch next to me. "I really, *really* thank you guys for coming up here to help me; and especially you too B," Brianna said addressing Brandi, "I know with what was going on with Jay and on top of that you're a new mommy-to-be," Bri smiled as she went over to touch her sister's stomach.

"Oh Bri, I had to come help my sister get settled plus there's no telling when I'll see you since you've decided to move away from us," she said pouting playfully for a second before she started to smile. "Then as far as Jay is concerned his mother and father are at the house with him so he'll be okay, but I do think we'll be hitting the road pretty soon since it's getting kinda late."

"Yes we sure will," Aunt Lisa said appearing from around the corner. "So come here baby and give Mama some hugs and kisses, I'm really gonna miss you," Aunt Lisa said to a reluctant Bri who just gave a half smiled before her mom started hugging her.

"Okay Mama," Brianna said rolling her eyes as she held onto to a wide-eyed Bianca with her other arm. "We will miss you too."

"Yeah us too Bri," I said speaking up, "but you know we're still staying here but we're about to go visit some of Amir's people. We'll be right back though."

"Okay sure girl," Brianna waved her hand toward me.

"But before everybody leaves Amir and I have an announcement," I spoke up and Amir came to my side and put his arm around me. I put my hand into my pocket trying to slide the ring on my finger, but it wouldn't work so I just took it out and quickly placed it on. "We're getting married!" I shouted while lifting my left hand in the air so everyone could see the ring as my family reacted with screaming.

"Oh my baby," that was my mother who came rushing over to us with Daddy in tow. "I'm so happy for you baby and congrats Amir, I've always liked you anyway," she chuckled.

"Thank you ma'am," Amir chuckled as well, "and I've always loved her," he said pulling me closer then planting a small peck on my cheek.

"Now you better do right by my baby girl," Daddy said with a half smile as he reached out to hug Amir who now wore a concerned half smile on his face, "but I know you're a good guy and you're not gonna hurt her. Just be warned though if you ever slipped up and hurt my baby girl, not only would you have to deal with me, her big brother Kai would go crazy." Daddy continued to ramble on as if Amir didn't already know about my big brother or the fact that we are so close.

"Yeah he sure would," everyone said in unison and I just laughed. It just amazed me how my family would either say or think the same in some situations. "Okay so have ya'll set a date yet?" Kennede asked.

"Yeah," Amir and I sang as if we were a choir, we looked at each other with huge grins on our faces. "We've decided on February 14, 2009 because I've always wanted the *Valentines Day* wedding and since next year Valentines Day is gonna be on a Saturday it's works out perfectly. And we called the church this morning and we were able to get it for that day, plus we'll be able to catch the pre-marriage class that starts at the first of the year too, since you know in order for us to use the church that's what we'll have to do."

"That's wonderful I am so happy for my baby." Mama said getting misty eyed, "so now its Summer right after Ken and that now means Bri you're gonna be next," everyone turned toward her.

"Dang ya'll give me a minute to get into the city good, but I'm not even feeling the marriage right now," everyone kind of grumbled at her statement but Bri rolled her eyes while wearing this I-don't-care-whatever-kind of smirk. "Alright so weren't all of you all about to leave anyway?" She questioned; changing the subject while trying to get everyone who has now annoyed her out of her apartment.

"Oh *now* she's ready for us to leave when we start talking about that," Aunt Lisa said with one arm around her daughter even though Bri was trying to ease away. "Okay baby you be careful."

"I will ma," Bri said now walking closer to the front door as everyone was giving her and the baby goodbye hugs and kisses on their way out of the door. "You are still coming back right?" Bri asked me since Amir and I were the last two to walk out of the door.

"Yeah girl, I told you we would be back after visiting his people, I mean that is if you don't mind us coming back and staying?"

She shook her head, "oh Summer now you know I don't mind if you all want to stay. I honestly would love to have the company on my first night, there's a lot on my mind that I need to talk out," she said with a serious face; I could tell that when I came back we would probably be up all night in deep conversation, but I didn't mind that at all. "Okay girl, you know I am always gonna be here for you when you need to talk, even when I'm back in Louisville, you can still call me." I said giving her a hug as if I wasn't coming back later tonight.

"Thanks Summer," Brianna said with glossy eyes.

"No thank you for letting me crash here for the night," I said and we began laughing, "but seriously is there anything that you need while Amir and I are out?"

"Uhm…no girl," she waved her hand at me, "I'm gonna feed this little one and put her down hopefully for the night," she crossed her fingers and smiling at her daughter who began to smile back.

"Okay girl, and thanks again, I'll see you later." I said then began walking toward Amir's car; he was already in the driver's seat waiting for me while I was talking to Brianna. Once I got into the car or rather the passenger's seat, Amir was looking over at me with this strange look, "what's wrong baby?"

"Nothing," he simple said at first then stayed quiet while he pulled out of Brianna's apartment complex. It was about 4 blocks down the road before Amir spoke again, "are you nervous about meeting the rest of my family?" he asked referring to his father's side of family; I remember meeting this side once when were growing up, but I didn't know 'The Bryant's' like I knew his mother's side of family. Then again Amir's mother only had one other sibling and their parents lived in Louisville which made it easier for me to meet the small group called a family.

"Well, not too much, I mean it's not like it's my first time meeting your grandparents, it's just been a long time since I met them." I said trying to pay attention to the turn that he had just made so I would know how to get back to Brianna's apartment from Amir's grandparent's house. His grandparent's house was located on the north side of Indianapolis; which was about fifteen minutes away from Brianna, whose apartment complex was right next door to the Colts football training facility. Aunt Regina had pointed that out to us since her husband spent most of his time in that place, I thought it was kind of cool for Brianna to be that close to some famous football players, but the way she was feeling about men at this time, she wasn't too thrilled about the whole idea though.

"Baby are you okay?" he asked breaking my thoughts; that's when I noticed he had reached over to grab my hand. "I mean you were talking then all of sudden stopped and got real quiet."

"Oh I'm fine, sorry about that though," I began, "I was just over here thinking about my cousin and how she's just gotten so cold when it comes to relationships and stuff like that now. I'm just kinda concerned with how that behavior is going to affect her in the long run, you know?"

"Yeah I understand," he stated. "So does she just hate men period or is it even to that point where she's thinking of changing teams?" he glanced over at me with one eyebrow raised.

"OH HELL TO THE NAW!" I shouted then we began to smile looking at each other. "Now hold on I take that back, I don't *think* she would change up on us like that. No she just needs a little Jesus and sometime and the right one will come around or come along, it worked for me and look at what I was going through."

"Well," Amir said before going totally silent. For a minute there I thought that maybe he was trying to either find his way around the dark streets. "Summer I have something I want to talk to you about, but it's gonna have to wait because we're about to pull up to my grandparents house." He said and I noticed that we had pulled in front of this big beautiful older looking home that reminded me of the houses in the neighborhood we grew up in back home.

"Babe what's going on and why can't you tell me before we go in here?" I questioned before Amir opened his door and proceeded to come over to the passenger's side door to open it for me, something he always does for me even if I'm the one driving, he tells me to wait so he can open that door. He says it was something his father *always* did for his mother and he taught Amir to do it for *all women*, especially if it's his wife or girlfriend.

I stepped out of the car and stood in front of Amir, he looked down in my eyes and I felt butterflies because for a minute there I felt him saying how much he loved me just by the way he looked into my eyes. Amir closed his eyes then pulled me into him, embracing him in a way that made me feel light on my feet and I was putting all of my trust in him not to let me go or let me fall. I didn't fall on the ground but fell deeper into the safety of his big strong arms holding onto my body for dear life. I felt moisture hitting my head from above, and for a second I thought that this *mystical* moment that was being shared between us had moved Amir to the tears that was swelling the brims of my eyes. I soon looked up and noticed that it wasn't tears from his face, but it was raindrops or as Grandmother would say Angel Tears.

With my eyes still closed I felt Amir's lips resting on my forehead, slowly I began to open my eyes and was looking into those green eyes. "Summer," he sighed my name in a way that made me feel chills down my spine. "I am so in love with you, I wish you knew just how I feel about you, it's something I can't even describe babe."

"I feel the same," I said and our lips grazed, "is that what you were trying to say before?"

He shook his head, "no but you know nothing else matters anymore, because...I, you know it just doesn't matter." He said and we began to walk up the steps toward the front door, and he was right nothing else matters; if he had said that to the old me I probably would have stressed whatever it was he was going to say at first. But after experiencing that moment we just shared, something I can't explain to anybody else because they would think that we were just crazy and what we just felt was nothing more than lust, but it wasn't lust that I just felt. I'm positive I felt the love of the man that God has designed especially for me and nobody, I mean NOBODY else. Thank you God for such a great gift.

Kennede

"Damn Ken I feel like I'm walking in one of those houses on *MTV Cribs* or something." Malik said as he walked thru the front doors of my new house. We had just moved in Saturday, but I decided to take an extra day off so I could do some more unpacking. "Wow this house is really awesome."

"Thanks Malik," I said trying to keep a smile on my face, "do you want something to drink or anything?" I said grabbing a glass for myself about to get some water from the refrigerator.

"Sure water will be fine if you have some," he said sitting on the stool in the kitchen. "So what was it that you needed to talk to me about?"

My smile faded and I rolled my eyes, "where should I begin?" I questioned but not looking for an answer from Malik. I sat down on a stool that was up against the island that was in the middle of my kitchen, I looked up at Malik because I was directly across from him after taking a sip of water. "Okay well…uhm, it was a couple of weeks ago when we were helping Bri pack up to move, and Ray's ex-wife Shaundie had been calling his phone like a crazy woman. But instead of simple answering her calls, he has been ignoring her because she's heard about us getting married again in a few weeks, so she's *extremely* jealous. The thing about it is that she had a baby in either July or August, and now she's saying that the baby is Raymond's."

"*What?*" he said taking a drink of his water. "Hold up, so when did they officially break up again?"

"They haven't been living together since January," I said with a half smile on my face thinking about that night he showed up on my doorstep telling me that they were separated. "You see that was when Raymond came over and we made love for the first time after he told me they separated," I paused and begin thinking about how even though what we did that night was wrong, it felt so good to have Raymond making love to me again like he did that night, "but anyway, around that same time Shaundie had just found out that she was pregnant and she told Raymond that the baby probably wasn't his because she had been cheating on him with her first baby's daddy."

Malik shook his head, "Lord I told you that you're always involved in *some kind* of drama," he said and I hit his arm. "I'm sorry but I'm just stating the facts, man I could make a fortune off the stories that you tell me about you and your cousins."

"Anyway, when Shaundie had her baby around the end of July, I'm assuming that the guy she thought was the father of her new baby girl was tested and the test came up to be negative," I looked down at my short French manicured nails, "since around the first of October she's been harassing Raymond; trying to make him take a test to see if he's the father, but I didn't know any of this until the heifer showed up at my job the week of Halloween."

"No way!" Malik exclaimed, "Why did she come to your shop?"

I shrugged my shoulders, "I didn't know why then either, when she showed up there I questioned it too; but when she told me the whole story, well what I just told you, and she went on to add that she needed to know who the father of her baby was and since she's already tested who she thought was the father and it wasn't, she wants Raymond tested."

"But I still don't see what that has to do with you," he explained, "why didn't she confront Raymond?"

"She thought *I* was the one holding him back from being tested," I said, "that's when I told her that I had no idea what was going on and he never mentioned that she wanted him to be tested. So when I got off I went *straight* to his condo and proceeded to go off on him and then told him about my visit from his ex-wife. Needless to say he was shocked when I told him that she had *just* left my job; I asked him why he was trying to keep Shaundie a big secret, he then said now that we were about to get married again he didn't want *anything* to try and come between us that could break us up again." I looked up at Malik with a solemn face, "he says that he doesn't want to lose me *ever* again because he loves me too much."

"Okay, I can understand that," Malik stated while nodding his head, but I looked at him now with confusion. "He didn't want you to get upset about something that maybe is nothing at all. I think he's just trying to protect your heart, or that's what my reason for keeping something like that would be. Okay so since all of it is now in the open, did he get tested yet?"

"Yeah he took the test on Halloween," I replied then began to bite my bottom lip, "I finally persuaded him to just go on and get it over with." I paused and bit down my lip harder.

"It looks like you are regretting something," Malik grabbed my hand, "come on Ken, and tell me what's going on."

I held onto his hand as I looked up to the ceiling trying to block the tears that were forming. "I'm scared Malik." I simply responded to his question, "what if that baby is Raymond's baby? I wouldn't know what to do and the results should be here a week before our wedding, what will I do if it's positive?"

"You're going to still marry him," I immediately began to shake my head in disagreement, "why not?"

"How could I?" I put my free hand over my heart, "I wouldn't know how to just *except* that even though I do want to be with him, I wouldn't…" I started to get chocked up as the tears started to fall.

"Kennede," Malik hopped off the stool and came to my side then embraced me. "Look we don't even know if the baby is his yet, so just chill out and try to think positive about the situation. It's a possibility that the baby *isn't* his; just try to think of it that way cause it seems that you've already thought about if the baby is his."

"Yeah but I just have this gut feeling Malik," I said pulling away from him and getting back on the stool. "Believe me I've tried to think that there's a chance that Shaundie could have cheated on Raymond with more than one other dude because when he met the hooker, she was pretty much sleeping around with every guy she could get. That's another thing that I made sure Raymond's butt got tested for every STD in the book because I know how she is, just another hood rat; but anyway like I said, I've got a gut feeling and I've seen that baby so that's why I just have that feeling."

"What? How did you see Shaundie's baby?" Malik questioned still standing in front of me.

"She had the baby with her when she came to my shop," I bit my lip again, "the baby's name is ShaRaye Denise Collins, and I must say the little girl favors RaeLynn a whole lot. You know how my baby girl is the spitting image of her father too."

"Oh," Malik twisted his mouth then he reached out to hug me for a second time, "I know it still looks like things are pointing toward the baby being Ray's, but you are just going to have to trust and believe that Raymond loves you no matter what. If that is the case then your love is going to have to be enough to get you through this and with God's help you can make it."

I nodded my head in agreement, "yeah you're right, 'Lord you're gonna have to help me through this one,' please pray for me too Malik." I looked back down at him after looking up toward the ceiling even though I was still holding onto Malik.

"Trust me Ken, it's going to be okay," he said squeezing me tighter.

"I know it will Malik, but I just—"

"Mommy!" RaeLynn yelled as she busted through the garage door that was right next to our refrigerator. "Hey Uncle Malik," she said running toward us, I quickly let go of him so I could turn my back away from them to wipe my face. I didn't need RaeLynn noticing that I'd been crying because she would start to ask a thousand and one questions.

"Hey look at my RaeLynn," Malik said, I had turned back around in time to see him picking up my daughter in his arms. "Whoa you are getting to be a big girl now," he continued to talk to her as I managed to muster up a smile.

"Hey, hey what's up Malik?" Raymond said after walking thru the garage door. "I knew I saw a car out there but I just didn't know it was you," he continued to talk to Malik as he gave him a handshake and semi-hug like men hug.

"Yeah I just stopped by to see my best good friend," Malik said touching my shoulder, "so how have you been doing Ray?"

"I'm blessed man," Raymond said walking toward me; he kissed my lips then stood behind my stool with his arms around me. "I'm about to marry the love of my life again, and I just moved into this beautiful home, so God is awesome man."

"Yes He is and I was just telling Ken how much I love this house; I told her I felt like I was in one of those houses on *MTV Cribs*," Malik said to Raymond.

"I would do anything for my two favorite girls," Raymond said squeezing me tight from behind, I still managed to keep the smile on my face, even though I felt like rolling on the floor crying.

"I love you too boo," I said looking up over my shoulder at Ray. I really did mean what I said; I did love Raymond with all of my heart too, that's the reason I was marrying him again. That's also why I was hoping and praying that Shaundie made a mistake by saying her baby was my soon to be husband's baby, but when I think it's a mistake I start thinking about what I saw. That baby girl looked just like Raymond and I can't get that image out of my head.

"Oh, ya'll are so cute together," Malik said smiling, "ya'll are making me miss my own woman."

"By the way how is your woman?" Raymond asked.

"Michelle is doing great; I'm actually going to be on my way over to her house once I leave here. Seeing you all acting like ya'll are all in love and stuff got me wanting to be with Michelle. But for real I always believed that the two of you would be back together, ya'll are just made for each other, really I've never met anyone like ya'll, well other than my own parents."

Ray then looked into my eyes as I turned around to look up at him with a smile, "yeah I've never stopped loving this *wonderful* woman here." Ray said wrapping his arm around me making me feel secure.

"I know," Malik said now grabbing his keys, "well you guys I'm going to get out here, I'ma head on over to Michelle's place."

"Okay well I've enjoyed your company," I said jumping off of the stool about to walk Malik to the door. Ray grabbed my hand pulling me back toward him, "what's up?" I looked up at him.

Before he could say anything, RaeLynn came rushing down the steps, "hey Uncle Malik did you see my room yet? Come on up and see it please," she said running up next to him and grabbing his hand.

"RaeLynn, Uncle Malik was about to leave so he'll see your room the next time," I said as Raymond pulled again this time he gave me a hug.

"Its cool Ken, I'll just run up there real quick, if its cool with ya'll?" he asked standing on the last step about to make his way up to RaeLynn's room.

"Okay, RaeLynn don't have him up there all day because he has somewhere to go okay?" I said.

"Yes ma'am, I'll just be real quick, come on Uncle Malik," she ran up the stairs and out of my sight.

"Come here babe," Raymond said wrapping his arms around me as I wrapped my arms around his waist, "I've missed you today Kennede."

Raymond bent down and kissed my lips softly. I closed my eyes becoming consumed by his kisses which made me forget for a brief moment about everything else that was going on in our lives. "Uhm...I," I moaned then kissed Raymond's lips again, "I love you so much Raymond Collins."

"I love—"

"I told you Mommy, did you see how quick that was Mommy?" RaeLynn said coming back down the stairs with Malik just a couple of steps behind.

"I swear you guys, this house is amazing; I took a quick tour of the upstairs rooms and I picked out my guestroom too; the last room on the right side." Malik laughed.

Raymond and I joined in with his laughter. "It's all yours whenever you want or need it," Raymond said to him.

"Come on here boy," I started walking toward Malik and Ray followed close behind me. He was so close to me that I could feel his hand grazing my booty. "Thanks again for stopping by and tell Michelle I said hello too." I said now giving Malik a goodbye hug.

"Thanks for having me and I will tell her that; and ya'll take care too," Malik said giving Raymond that male handshake and semi-hug.

"Yeah you take care too brotha," Raymond said now wrapping his arm around my neck this time.

I smiled waving at Malik as he drove out of our driveway; as soon as he was out of sight I closed the door. Raymond dropped his arm from around my neck and I turned around to face him, he kept smiling while looking at me, "what?" I questioned.

"You are so beautiful Kennede Marie," he said grabbing my hand and looking into my eyes again.

"Why didn't you say my last name, Johnson," I smiled because I knew he was going to say something about me saying Johnson instead of Collins.

"Johnson uh, oh so you don't want Collins anymore?" he questioned walking closer to me, letting his six foot three frame tower over me.

"I didn't say that I didn't want to be a Collins anymore, but until that wedding band is on that finger I'm still gonna be a Johnson." I smiled holding up my left hand while my four carat engagement ring was blinging.

"But you already have this beautiful princess cut diamond engagement ring, four carats and all plus it's platinum," he joked taking my hand and putting it in my face. "Platinum here and four carats princess cut diamond that cost forty-five—"

"Hey, hey that's kinda rude to say to your soon to be wife." I said cutting him off from telling me info I really didn't *need* to know.

"What's wrong? You don't wanna know how much I've spent on your ring?" he pulled me closer to him by my waist. I shook my head, "most women would love to know how much their men spent on them, in a way I guess it shows them just how much they love their women by how much they've spent."

"Well I'm not that kind of woman," I said hitting his arm playfully. "I love you no matter what you've spent; if you spent just ten dollars on the ring, I'd still wear it just as proudly as if you spent thousands." Raymond twisted his face as to say I was telling a lie or something. "What? I am dead serious when I told you that I'm not like most of these women out here."

"You know what you aren't like any other woman I've ever met and honestly that's what I love the most about you," he kissed me slowly and sensually. "That's why I'm about to make you my wife *again*, you are the most beautiful, most intelligent, and the sexiest woman in the world. I can't wait until eighteen days from now when you will become Mrs. Collins a—" he was cut off by his cell phone ringing, but he didn't flinch.

Concern was written all over my face when I asked, "baby aren't you gonna answer that?" He squeezed me tighter then began kissing me again, and by the time we finished his phone had stopped ringing.

"No I was talking to my woman, and whoever was calling isn't as important as you are at this moment," he kissed my forehead. "Like I was saying, I can't wait until December 6th when you become Mrs. Collins." He looked into my eyes, "aren't you excited about being my wife for the second time?"

"Of course I am," I smiled using my hands to stroke his back while I was still hugging him. "I'm probably more excited than you, because eighteen days from now I will be the happiest woman in the world because I have the chance to marry the man of my dreams, my true soul mate, again."

Raymond continued to gaze into my eyes with so much love in his eyes, "I can't wait until that day."

"I know I can't wait either." I looked down at the floor and as my smile faded I looked back up at him, "but I must be honest, I also feel a little nervous too, but about the wedding though."

His forehead wrinkled when he asked, "So baby what are you so nervous about?"

I backed away from Ray so he could see the look that was on my face, the look that said you-should-already-know-why, "Shaundie's baby," I simply replied since it seemed that he didn't know. He lowered his head and shook it at the same time, when he finally looked at me his face showed so much disappointment.

"Kennede," he sang my name while he backed further away from me and started walking toward the couch. I followed behind him as he sat down then rested his head into his hands. "Baby please tell me that she's not going to be an issue for us?"

"She's already an issue Ray," I said sitting down on the opposite end of the couch. "I mean until we get the test that says *you're not the father*, she'll continue to be an issue."

Raymond shook his head is disbelief, "Kennede, baby let's not focus on this please? We're eighteen days away from what is *supposed* to be the happiest day of our lives and I don't need Shaundie's jealousy and false accusations causing problems between us."

I rested my arm on the arm of the couch and closed my eyes trying to hold back the tears once more. "I understand her being upset and jealous because you are a wonderful man and a hell of a father, but baby I have a hard time believing that her accusations are false."

"So what are you telling me...you believe her...uh Ken...are you telling me that you believe that liar Shaundie?" he questioned. I shook my head in agreement as he was shaking his head no. "Why Kennede...why do you believe her?" he begged more than he seemed to be asking.

"Because Ray, I just have this gut feeling that's all," I said not admitting to him what I saw.

"*A gut feeling?* Baby please don't tell me you think she's telling the truth based off *a gut feeling*, Kennede please let's not—"

"I saw her Raymond!" I shouted cutting him off then he looked over at me with a confused face.

"What?"

"I saw her," I repeated this time tears fell down my face. "I saw that baby Ray and she looks a lot like you, have you seen that baby?"

He shook his head no, "when did you see the baby?"

"The day Shaundie showed up at the shop, she had the baby with her and I must say the baby favors RaeLynn a whole lot too, but mostly she looks like you, that's why I have *a gut feeling* Ray."

"I'm so sorry Ken," Raymond said barely over a whisper. "I swear to you if I would have known that...I just...I'm so sorry, but we don't know the facts yet." Raymond moved closer then put his arm around me and I laid my head on his chest.

"I know we don't know the truth yet, but I just know what I saw," I said while wiping the tears away. "And it just seems that—" I was cut off by his cell phone ringing again. "Ray just answer the phone please, I know who it probably is so just answer it please." I pleaded with him then moved my head off of him as he reached into his pocket to retrieve his phone. He looked at the caller ID then rolled his eyes, by his reaction I already knew who it was and I began to shake my head. "It's her isn't it?" I looked over at him.

"Hello?" he answered the phone sounding as if he was annoyed. "So what do you want me to do?" he asked the person on the other end of the phone. I got up from my spot next to him and moved to the Queen Ann chair that was across from the couch.

"Mommy, mommy!" RaeLynn yelled from the top of the stairs.

"Hush girl, your daddy is on the phone. So come on down here to talk to me without yelling, and don't you run down them steps either RaeLynn." I said to my daughter in a loud enough voice so the *person* that was on the phone with Raymond would *know* I was in the same room.

"Yes, yeah it was but was does that have..."I heard him say to the person on the other end of the phone. "Okay but that has nothing to do with you, so what is it that you really want...get to the point please?" I rolled my eyes along with my neck looking toward Raymond; *I know this heifer didn't have the nerve to ask my man who was talking in background*, I thought to myself.

RaeLynn walked slowly past the couch looking at Raymond as if she were meddling with his phone conversation. "Come on here girl and quit being nosy, now what did you want?" I asked RaeLynn.

"I'm hungry Mommy," she sat on my lap with the biggest frown on her face like she hadn't eaten in weeks. "Can I get something to eat please?"

"Well baby, we haven't been to the grocery store yet so I can shop for something to cook for dinner." I explained.

"It's okay Mommy, I have *Lunchable's* that Daddy buy me 'member?" she said wrapping her arms around my neck. "Can my hab it now please?" She asked as she hopped off of me and began pulling my arm. I got up then started walking toward the kitchen.

"No ma'am, *Lunchable's* are for lunch or snack, you'll be hungry in another hour or so," I said as I walked pass the couch cutting my eyes at Raymond while he continued to stay on the phone. "But how about some pizza and chicken wings cause Mommy doesn't feel like cooking because I am so tired, I've been so busy unpacking this big house, so how about that?" I asked closing the refrigerator door.

"Okay Mommy sounds good, can I have pep'roni pizza please?" RaeLynn requested as she tried to get up on the stool. I rushed to her aid to help her but Raymond came out of nowhere to help her.

"I've got her babe, come on baby girl," Raymond said lifting her as I turned back around to get the phone book.

"I'm about to order a pizza and some wings, is there anything special you want?" I asked Raymond with a little bit of an attitude in my voice.

"I'm gettin' pep'roni Daddy," RaeLynn announced grinning very hard at her daddy.

"Okay then, well Ken can you get some cheese sticks too, with the supreme pizza please baby?" Raymond said walking toward me as I sat the phone book on the counter across from our daughter.

"Okay Raymond," I said plainly and he grabbed my arm then pulled me in front of him. "Can you please stop for a minute so I can make this phone call?" I asked while I was picking up the house phone and Ray forced his way behind me grabbing my waist before he kissed my cheek.

RaeLynn sat there giggling at us, "what is it little girl?" her father asked her but he was all up in my ear so I tried to move my head, letting him know that was too loud in my ear.

"You and Mommy always kissin' and huggin'," she laughed and I wanted to roll my eyes but RaeLynn would pick up on it and run her mouth. So I continued to look for the number to the pizza place.

"That's because I just love Mommy so much," he said in my ear. "And there is nothing, I mean nothing that's going to keep me away from being with you all every again." I tried to turn my head so I could look at him, because I knew what he was implying.

"I'm glad you living wit us again Daddy, I missed you when you live wit that Miss Shaundie," RaeLynn said with her face twisted, all I could do was smile. "I don't like her Daddy."

"Well you don't have to ever worry about her again because I'm gonna stay here with you and Mommy until forever!" he said squeezing me. "I mean that Kennede, I love you too much to lose you again," he whispered in my ear.

I started to dial the number to the pizza parlor, "excuse me a minute so I can call this order in please." I said trying to move from his grasp.

"Baby," he begged still whispering, but letting me go reluctantly. Before I could say anything else to Raymond the person came on the other end of my phone. "Hey RaeLynn go on back to your room and we'll call you back down when the pizza gets here okay?" I heard Ray say to our daughter in a low voice.

"Yes Sir Daddy," she said hopping off of the stool and heading toward the stairs.

"Okay thank you," I said hanging up the phone. "The pizza should be here with in forty-five minutes to an hour." I said in aloud the Raymond stood next to me as I turned to face him. "Ray I love you too but it's just hard to deal with the fact that—"

"Baby I know I've mentioned it before, but like I just told RaeLynn I'm not going anywhere because you're the *only* woman I ever want or need in my life," he said cutting me off. "I love you too much Kennede, I mean everything that I said about never wanting to be without you. And I'm never *ever* going anywhere, I'm here to stay."

"Okay," I simply said as I hugged Ray and held onto him tightly. I started to think to myself, *I just hope that I won't have to leave you especially if these test turn out differently than I pray for.*

* * *

Oh my God it's finally here, I thought to myself as I checked the mail for the day and there was the letter from the DNA lab. My heart dropped as I nervously sat the letter and the other mail on the living room table. I sat on the couch just staring at the letter thinking that little piece of paper could change my life forever. *This would be happening to me five days before my wedding…uh perfect timing*, I thought while shaking my head with a sarcastic smirk on my face.

"Kennede, baby where are you?" Raymond called out when he came through the garage door in the kitchen and my heart jumped as soon as I heard his voice. I grabbed the letter and ran into the kitchen, "hey beautiful, I came home early so I could spend a couple of hours alone with you before RaeLynn gets home from school."

"Its here," I said handing the letter to him and shaking throughout my body nervously.

"Whoa…uhm…I didn't expect to come home early to this," he said as his smile faded.

"Neither did I, I mean I was trying to put the Christmas decoration up. I was almost done when I heard the mailman put the mail in box. So come on and open it."

"Okay," he said blowing hard looking up; he then walked slowly to the breakfast table. I sat across from him as my heart started to beat ten times faster than normal. He unhurriedly began to tear open the envelope; then he pulled the letter out and started to read it. "I be damned!" he yelled and slammed the letter on the table startling me.

"Oh my God," I said shaking my head thinking that my gut feeling had come true. "Is she…I mean are you the father?" he picked the letter up and handed it to me upside down.

"Yes it says 99.9% positive that I am the father," Raymond said before I could even turn the paper around to read it myself.

"No, no, no," I repeated over again shaking my head as I read what Raymond had just told me. I put my head on the table and began sobbing. I loved Ray, but now that my fear has been confirmed I didn't know what to feel. God knows I wanted to be with him, but now I don't know if I could deal with Shaundie being my husband's baby-mama; because hearing and knowing about Shaundie she would bring constant baby-mama drama into our lives that I didn't want to deal with at all. On top of everything else she would use that poor baby every chance that she could as an excuse for Raymond to come to see her. And Raymond being a good father like he is, I'm sure he would try to treat this new baby the same way and as selfish as it sounds *I* wouldn't know how to handle it.

I felt a touch to my back so I raised my head to see Raymond sitting right next to me. I moved his arm and stood up trying to get away from him, "Kennede please don't do that to me baby, please baby don't do this," he pleaded and I could see tears in his eyes.

"Please don't touch me right now Raymond," I said now sitting down on the opposite side of him, when I tried to look into his eyes I looked away quickly; I couldn't do it because I just started sobbing yet again. "I can't even look at you right now, I don't...I just don't know if I can *ever* look at you again."

"Kennede...Ken, baby don't do this to me," he pleaded trying to reach out for my hand.

"No, I told you not to touch me!" I yelled this time standing back up and walking to the living room.

"Baby can we please talk about this?" Raymond asked following me into the living room, "baby we can't just ignore this, we're gonna have to talk about this especially since we are only days away from *our* wedding day."

I turn my head around to see Raymond sitting on the couch, "oh my God our wedding day," I paused looking the other way so I wouldn't be looking in his direction. "I just don't know if we should—"

"Ken no, please don't say what I think you're about to say," he said cutting off my statement as he stood from the couch and kneeled down at my side while I sat on the couch. "Ken I swear this doesn't make me want her; baby all I've ever wanted is you. Even when I was married to her all I've ever wanted was you and only you Kennede. I promise this test doesn't change my feelings for you one bit."

"Raymond...I just..." I sobbed titling my head to the side then I began to bite my bottom lip. "I'm sorry baby...but I just can't do it." I stood up from the chair and walked toward the front door because I had to leave this house. Luckily I didn't park my car in the garage today so I grabbed my purse and keys which was right there by the door. "I've gotta go, don't worry about RaeLynn either because I'll pick her up today."

"Please don't leave me Kennede," Raymond stood and came close to the door. "All I can do is just say that I'm sorry baby, we can get through this together, come on baby let's go pray about this."

"I can't do this," I said with my hand on the doorknob. "Oh, and the wedding is off."

"No baby...don't...no baby," he had tears falling down his face, "Kennede I love you so much baby, please let's just talk it over baby, or let's just pray about it, baby please don't leave me Ken." He reached out for me, rolling my eyes upward I gave in and began to hug him as tears kept flowing down both of our faces. "I love you so much Ken, God please help us through this."

I cried harder letting my tears get all over his shirt. I backed away and looked in his red glossy eyes. "I love you too," I said then his face looked relaxed, "but it's over and I've got to go." I said opening the door and started to walk out of it.

"No baby please don't leave me," he pleaded again but I didn't even turn around this time, I just walked out of the door.

Once I got into the car I pulled out my cell phone, "hey are you busy?" I asked.

"No Kennede what's wrong?" Brandi answered my question with a question of her own.

"Can I please come over I need to talk to you right away," I sobbed again as pulled out of the driveway away from my house.

"Yeah sweetie, I'm at home so you can come on over," she said. "So are you gonna tell me what's going on with you now?"

I sighed loudly and simply said, "the baby is his."

"Oh no, okay I get it now," she paused. "C'mon over I'm here for you."

"Thanks a lot B," I said as I made my way to Brandi's house.

"I completely understand and I know first hand where you are coming from," Brandi explained after I told her everything that happen between me, Raymond and Shaundie. "You do remember that my husband has a son that biologically isn't mine, but love has to be enough to keep ya'll together like it has for me."

I shook my before asking, "So...I mean how did you deal with it? I know that you had to be so hurt."

"Yes it hurt me really bad," Brandi looked down, "but when Jay and I got back together I mean, well we got together before I knew about the girl even being pregnant. By the time I found out I had to ask myself, do I love Jay more than my anger toward at this moment? And well you see that now we're married and very happy. Also keep in mind that I am helping to raise Jay's child too, but I've learned to love Jordan just like he's my own son."

"But Jordan's biological mother died during his birth, I'm sorry that she had to die, but Shaundie is alive and well. And if I decided to keep Raymond she's gonna make my life a living hell, acting like the baby-mama from hell!"

She chuckled and I gave a half smile too, "Ken that's when you have to go to God, have you done that yet?" I shook my head, "you've helped me to come to God and if it weren't for your faith sometimes, I wouldn't have the relationship with God that I have now. Don't let your flesh make a decision for you before praying about it first and listening to what God has to say about the situation."

"You know before I left the house that's the same thing Raymond kept on saying before I called the wedding off."

Brandi set up and her face was filled with shock, "Kennede you did what…you serious…you honestly called it off are?"

"Yes I did Brandi I am so hurt, and now I'm going to have to deal with this child and ghetto baby-mama if I decided to stay with him."

"Kennede I'm only saying this out of love, but don't you think you're being a little selfish?" she asked and I looked at her with my nose turned up. "I mean the whole time we've been here the only person that you've mention that is being hurt is you. You haven't mentioned RaeLynn, or what this news might do to her. So how does Raymond feel because he knows that not only does he have to be a father to RaeLynn, but he now has this new baby by a woman that I'm guessing he's doesn't love because he's suppose to be marrying you. But the person who loses the most is that innocent baby, that little person didn't ask to be here, nor did that child choose the parents, but God saw fit to do it that way. And that poor child has to grow up without his father in the same home which means that child will now have what RaeLynn has both real parents in the home."

I relaxed my face then said. "You're right."

"But I'm still guessing because I don't know what Shaundie is up to and I don't know if she's gonna have another husband, but that's not the point. The point is that baby won't have their real full time father in the home, and it's going to make a difference in the baby's life." Brandi paused then looked over at me with her eyebrows raised, "wait a minute, when did Shaundie have this baby?" she asked.

"I think she had the baby at the end of July sometime," I said rolling my eyes, I looked over at Brandi and she looked as if she was using her fingers to count. "What are you doing?"

"So wait a minute, if she had the baby at the end of July that means the baby was conceived in either October or November of last year." She looked at me with her eyes squinted, "when was their divorce final?"

"Sometime in April or March of this year I guess, I don't know Brandi, why are you asking all of these questions about them?"

"Because if my calculations are correct Raymond and Shaundie were still married when the baby was conceived right?"

"Yeah so what, but that is not the point," I said.

"So tell me what is the point then Ken?" she asked and I shrugged my shoulders. "Ken he was married to the girl when she got pregnant, I'm pretty sure you didn't even know a year ago that you two would even be back together. Nobody knew a year ago what would be happening at this moment. For example, if you would have told me last year that this year Jay and I would get married, but months later he'd be shot by the dude that raped and stalked me for years, I would have said 'no way and let me choose another road please.' But if I decided to take another road because I knew what was going to happen in the future, Jay and I probably wouldn't be pregnant now and about to bring our own child into this world." She said rubbing her little pouch, I smiled as she continued, "all I'm saying is Ken God takes us through some tough times to test our faith, you know that because we hear it every Sunday from our pastor. But sometimes in order to get us to the great things we have to go through some bad, but in those bad times we can't give up. And Ken the bad that you're feeling now really isn't all that bad. You just have to stop being so selfish and think of that innocent baby who's gonna be without their father. And you have to support your husband because he's gonna need you more than ever right now."

I began to cry again because the reality that Brandi was painting for me. I guess I was being selfish; the only thing I was worried about was me not having to deal with Shaundie's ghetto acting butt. "You're right Brandi; I am being a little selfish. I just didn't want to have to deal with the ghetto situation with that ghetto hood-rat."

"No you have to stop thinking about Shaundie and support your soon-to-be husband and stand by him to deal with this new baby. And not only him but for RaeLynn too, there's going to be a lot of questions on her part and a lot she's not going to understand either. So you have to be strong for her too, and even if you didn't marry Raymond, you still would have to find a way to tell RaeLynn because that baby is still going to be her sister regardless." Brandi reached out her arm and began to hug me. "Go on back home to your soon-to-be husband and that big beautiful home that you just moved into."

I raised my head from her shoulder, "thank you Brandi for being a *true* friend to me."

"You've been there for me in the past, besides I've already had my dress altered because I've gained some weight due to the baby. So the dress is fitting perfectly now and I'm going to wear that dress as the maid of honor in your wedding even if I have to put a shotgun to your back to make you marry that man." She laughed and I joined in too, "but for real Raymond is a good man Kennede, and I've seen the change in him since ya'll got back together; and I can tell that he loves you."

"Yeah he does love me," I smiled then looked down at my watch. "Oh my God I didn't know it was so late, don't you need to go get Jordan it's after eleven o'clock at night?" I stood up because I told my mother I would be over there to get RaeLynn around nine o'clock, but it looks like I'm two hours late.

"Oh no honey on Monday's Ms. Janet picks him up and takes him to Karate and he just spends the night over her house after that. So I'm okay, but do you need to leave?"

"Yeah but let me call Mama first," I pulled out my cell phone and noticed I had ten missed calls. Most of them were from Raymond, then the last one was from my mother about fifteen minutes ago. "Mama I am so sorry for not calling and leaving RaeLynn over there I swear I'm on my way."

"Calm down Ken, she's okay besides she's already asleep and has been sleep for a while." Mama explained and I sat back on Brandi's couch. "There's no need in waking her up and dragging her out in that cold weather at this hour. So I'll just take her to school in the morning, she has clean clothes and stuff already here. But what I want to know is what's going on with you and Ray? That poor boy has been calling here looking for you and it sounded like he was crying at one point."

I exhaled hard and proceeded to tell my mother the situation; and just like the advice that Brandi gave me, Mama said the same thing, stand by your husband because he needs you more than ever right now. "By the way where are you at anyway?" she asked at the end of your conversation.

"I'm about to leave Brandi's house right now," I said still sitting on the couch while Brandi went upstairs for a few minutes to check on her own husband, who is improving from his injuries by the way.

"Well you go on and leave that girl's house so she can take care of her husband. And you go home to straighten things out with Raymond, like I said before Ken, you all just go to the Lord about it and He'll give you peace that surpasses all understanding."

"Yes ma'am, I love you Mama."

"I love you too baby, be careful going home," she said then hung up.

I stood up while Brandi was making her way down the steps, "thank you so much for being there for me Brandi," I hugged her tightly.

"Oh that's what best friends do, stick by your side, I love you girl."

"I love you too," I said heading toward the door, "pray for me I'm on my way home."

"I've got you, be safe," she said standing at the door.

Once I finally pulled up into the driveway I noticed that it was a little after midnight. "God give me the words to say to Raymond and Lord please give me strength to make it; and give us strength together to go on from here." I said a quick prayer before I opened the front door to our house.

As soon as I closed the door, I heard what sounded like gospel music being played throughout the house. I knew Raymond had to be here, but there were no signs of him in the living room or the kitchen because only the glow from the porch light was in the living room and the only light on in the kitchen was from the overhead light above the stove. I walked toward our bedroom which was right behind the stairs and it seemed as if the music got louder the closer I walked. Sure enough that's where the music was coming from; by the time I reached the double doors of our bedroom, Marvin Sapp's 'Never Would of Made It' was blasting through the speakers of the stereo in our room. I walked in to see Raymond sitting up against the bed in front of the fireplace looking at something in his hands. Tears started down my face as I listen to the words of the song saying, "*I would have lost it all but now I see how you've been there for me…*"

I lightly tapped on the wall next to the door, Raymond quickly turned around, "baby," was all he said and his face seemed to glow; and it wasn't fire that made it glow but it was surprise to see me again.

"Can we talk please?" I asked walking closer to him as he jumped to his feet and laid the picture of me, him, and RaeLynn on the bed along with the other pictures that we had took about a month ago.

"Yes baby I've been praying that you would come back," he hugged me and he began to sob, I began to sob as well. Once I was back in his arms it was like a spark that hit me, I closed my eyes and was consumed inside of his welcoming arms. Right there I had my answer; this was the right thing to do. It felt right being in his arms again because this was my husband and nothing could change it. "Baby I love you so much, I never want to lose you again Kennede, please don't…I… just love you too much." He said squeezing me tighter. The more he squeezed the more I cried because I felt something I've never felt before with another man.

"I love you too Raymond, but I just need to say something really quick," I said and he loosen his grip until he released his arms from hugging me all together. He grabbed my hand and lead me to the chase we had in our huge bedroom. I faced him as we sat down, "let me first say that I am so sorry for acting so selfish. The way I reacted to the news of this baby was very selfish on my part and I am so sorry I don't want anybody else but you Raymond Alex Collins, and I mean that and I felt it just a minute ago."

Tears continued to flow down both of our faces as he started to smile. I took my hand and began to wipe the tears from his face with my thumb, and he did the same for me. "I love you entirely too much to let you go over something like that. So what I'm saying is I am here for you, please let's lean on each other, then we both turn around and lean on the Lord. I'm pretty sure we can't go wrong if we're leaning on Him."

He nodded in agreement, "you are right we need to lean on the Lord more than ever before, right now at this moment," he grabbed both of my hands. "Ken I am so glad you came back because baby I'm scared. I never wanted to be in any type of situation where I'm a father to kids all over the place, but for some reason God chosen to give me another child with my ex-wife," he paused and more tears slowly rolled down his face. "I pray that you forgive me for allowing something like this to happen to us because I'm sure it'll be hard for you to deal with having another child around that's not yours."

I inhaled then exhaled hard, "baby there's nothing for me to forgive you for, because you and Shaundie were married when this baby was conceived," I paused then looked back into his eyes with tears filling in mine. "I love you too much and I ask that you forgive me for over reacting to the news about the baby. Like I said, I'm here for you and you can lean on me and together we'll lean on Jesus."

Raymond squeezed my hands, "okay baby, I need your strength now because I don't know what to do about this new baby. I pray that we can get through this together, like you said leaning on Jesus," he paused. "And as long as we're both leaning on the Lord, there is no mountain we can't climb, no river we can't cross, as long as we have each other and we're both depending on God." I nodded my head as tears continued to flow.

"Baby I just have a feeling that no matter what else comes our way we're gong to make it. And this right here is nothing but the first of many test that we'll have to go through as a couple. This is new for the both of us, and we're just gonna have to learn how to deal with it together." I paused, "because I never want to be without you in my life as my husband. The time that we spent apart was the worst years of my life, but in the process I found God and found my soul mate, which had been there all along." I wiped his face. "I'm glad that you are mine again."

I leaned over to embrace him once again and he squeezed me tightly. Then he started to kiss my neck, then my cheek and moved back a little so our lips could meet. This was the best kiss that felt so good, like it was the first time all over again because the butterflies were flying all around my stomach. "Oh Kennede I love you so much," he said and kissed my lips slowly. "Okay baby I think it's time that we ask for God to be with us." He said sliding down to the floor and onto his knees.

"Okay," I got on the floor right next to him with the biggest smile on my face. He looked over at me smiling as well. "So do you want me to lead us in prayer?" I asked.

"Well as the man of this house, I think that I should lead us."

I smiling so hard, where as some women might go off, but I understand what it means to let a man be a man and Raymond is the man of this house. He provides along with taking care of the business affairs of the house. And he gives me the upmost respect and lets me take care of something's too, but Ray believes that the money I make should be spent on me; he always says that he's the man and he will take care of the house bills as well as the family as a whole. I've got no problems with that at all because he's not beating on me or trying to control me at all, matter of fact he spoils me. He likes being a real man and taking care of his family which reminds me of my daddy and Granddaddy. Those men took care of their families and their women; that's the way the men treated you back in the day and I didn't mind getting that kind of treatment now.

"Go ahead baby, you go on and ask the Lord to bless our household," I said squeezing his hand.

He bowed his head and I followed suit. *"Dear Lord we come to you now first saying thank you for another day that we were able to see. But Lord we come needing you to give us strength today Father, you know what it is that we're dealing with and we need you to please cover us, protect us, and give us your peace, and give us your strength right now in the name of Jesus. And Lord bless our upcoming wedding and marriage. God I pray for strength during the weak moments we may have during our lifetime together, I pray for protection against anything that my try to come against us during our life together. Lord keep us and strengthen us until we leave this Earth to return to you. I thank you in advance for every blessing and for everything that you will do for us and this household. Also Lord bless our daughter that we have together and bless the child that I haven't seen yet and bless the children that are to come with me and Kennede. I thank you again; I ask all of this in Jesus' name. Amen."*

"Amen," I said wiping tears from my face again. "I love you Raymond," I said before I kissed him and began looking up toward the ceiling and said aloud, "and thank you Jesus, I love you too Lord."

25
Brianna

"I hope I'm not too late," I said walking into the church sanctuary with Bianca in her car seat.

"Bri!" Kennede jumped up from the pew and hugged me along with Summer. "Oh my God girl you are looking so beautiful."

"Thank you," I said smiling then I felt a tap on my shoulder, I turned to see my mother, "Mama I've missed you," I turn to hug her and I sat Bianca's car seat on the pew.

"Oh I've missed you too," she said coming to the other side and uncovering the blanket I had over the car seat trying to protect my baby from the cold weather. "And I've missed my grandbaby too," she took Bianca's coat off and picked her up. "Hey my baby, oh my Lord she's getting so big Brianna."

"I know she is," I said then turning my attention to my girls, "so what's up ladies? Hold up where's my sister?"

"Girl you should already know that your other half is always late." Summer said with the brightest smile I've ever seen on her face. Then again I hadn't seen any of them since I moved. "But actually we were a little early anyway, so where was you at on Thanksgiving?"

"Yeah I was hoping to see you and my grandbaby last week," Mama said sitting next to me as I continued to stand.

"Well I just didn't feel like traveling back to Louisville for one day, besides Aunt Regina was hosting dinner at her house and some of the players, coaches, and their families from Jacob's team stopped by so it wasn't like I was alone or anything. I actually had a great time with all of those people."

"That's good, but we really missed you at dinner though," Summer said, "So did you get any numbers from the big *fine* football men?" she asked leaning closer to me.

"We'll talk about that later, we in church now," I said grinning then I felt a hit on my thigh, I looked down and saw Mama looking up at me with squinted eyes, "what?"

"I heard that," she said still looking at me, "you better be acting like the good Christian girl I know that you are. You aren't acting like no football player *hoochie* are you?"

"Ma-ma," I said with wide eyes. "I am a good gir-, no excuse me a good woman." I smiled.

"Alright Brianna," she said rocking Bianca back and forth.

"Brianna!" I head my name from behind me, and I saw my twin sister running down the aisle toward me with Jayson and Jordan in tow. "Oh my God look at you girl, you are looking beautiful," she hugged me tightly.

"Thank you, but if I'm beautiful then it's like looking in the mirror cause we look just alike remember?" I laughed, "but the only thing is I don't have this little pouch right here," I said touching her little stomach.

"Girl I am so excited and I can't wait to get a baby like this beautiful one over here," she walked over to Mama and started to play with her niece. "My God Bri, she has gotten so big since the last time I've seen you all, oh wow she is so beautiful."

"Thanks," I said. "Hey brother-in-law, how are you doing?" I asked Jay as he approached the pew that we had gathered around.

"I'm doing good, feeling a whole lot better," he said sitting down next to Mama giving her a hug then standing and walking to the front of the church where Raymond, Amir, and some other guys were talking to one of the associate ministers of Genesis Church. *I wonder if Sean is going to be here tonight.* I questioned to myself. I was secretly looking forward to seeing him again.

"I'm so glad to see that Jay is doing a lot better, I'm just glad to see all of ya'll." I said smiling

"I missed you on Thanksgiving, but I'm glad that Aunt Regina kept you company," Brandi said.

"Yeah along with a bunch of fine football players," Summer added and I felt a nudge a from Brandi who was smiling when I looked up at her.

"Ooh, it looks like we gonna have a talk later," Brandi said then leaned over. "So that's what is up with this glow around you."

I waved my hand in her direction and plainly said, "oh girl please, but we will talk," I smiled.

"Kennede I must say this house is *absolutely* gorgeous and I'm not hating on you at all," I said raising my wine glass toward her. "Maybe some time soon ya'll can visit me in a house like this. I'm going back to school to become a nurse practitioner while I'm waiting for the center to open."

"That's great Bri and thank you for that compliment, God is wonderful," she said taking a sip of her white wine. "You know what I realized every time that we've had one of these 'last girl's night out,' there is at least one of us who can't drink." Kennede laughed and Brandi frowned while she was lifting her glass in my sister's direction.

"I know, well I'm glad this time I'm able to join in," I said taking of sip of wine smiling.

"So Bri, are you not breast feeding or anything?" Kennede asked.

"No ma'am even though I've tried, but I just couldn't finish the job," I chuckled. "But my baby is getting what she needs though."

"So Ms. Brianna, how's *Naptown* treating you? And what happened at Aunt Regina's house on Thanksgiving with the players?" Summer rambled off a list of questions.

I smiled, "it was good and you already know Aunt Regina can burn, I tried to help her out in the kitchen as much as I could but she wasn't having that. Although honey child there was some big fine football playing men's up in there."

"Okay so did you uhm, hook up with one of them?" Brandi asked with this big grin on her face. "Because the last time you were here you were talking like you didn't want to be bothered with anymore men, so who is he?"

I smiled again, "well I did meet one of them and he is too fine with these long shoulder length dreads, woo he's just too *sexy* for words." I said leaving out the part that he showed up at Aunt Regina's with his girlfriend. But the way he approached me in the kitchen he acted as if he really didn't care about the woman he had in the next room. As a matter of face we exchanged numbers right there in the kitchen and we've been talking almost every other day since last Thursday.

"Ooh I wanna see him," Summer said. "You said he plays for the same ream as Jacob right?" Summer asked.

"Yeah."

"Hold on a minute I've got my laptop right over here, do you mind if we look him up on the team page?" Kennede asked getting up from the couch and grabbing her laptop bag from behind it.

"Yeah he's on the team page, he's a starter and no I don't mind if you look him up because we're only friends for now. We just started talking last week."

"Okay," Kennede said with the laptop in her lap and pressing buttons. "Now what was his name?'

"Oh, his name is T.J. George, six-foot even and two-hundred and sixty-five pounds of fineness with dreads and a goatee that is clean cut and fine!" We all laughed.

"Oh my Lord, Brianna is this him?" Kennede asked and I sat next to her and nodded.

"Yes ma'am that is Mr. George in the flesh, or on the screen." I said looking at the computer thinking about giving him a call later tonight.

"Go on girl, I ain't mad at you," Kennede said.

Brandi and Summer sat on the other side of Kennede, "damn," they both said in unison. "He is too fine for words," Summer said.

"Yeah sis, I ain't mad at you either," Brandi said putting her hand up toward me and I gave her a high-five. "But I must say my sister has taste, she knows how to pick them fine men. Well except for…"

"Don't you say it Brandi," I pointed to her while I was laughing because I knew she was referring to Brian, she put her hands up in the air.

"I'm so sorry Bri, but you know that Brian wasn't your type at all," she said.

"You are so mean Brandi, but I do agree with you cause Brian was a little on the ugly side." Summer commented.

"Oh ya'll ain't right at all," I said as we all laughed again at my past mistake. "So has anyone heard anything from Bianca's daddy or his wife?" I asked and the room fell silent. "Okay guys what's going on, what do you all know that I don't know?"

"Nothing, I'm just surprised that you asked about him," Brandi finally spoke up. "I do see him at work sometimes and he asked me about you a couple of weeks ago."

"He did, really?" I chuckled; I was surprised he hadn't called. "So what did you tell him?"

"I told him that you and Bianca were doing quite well in Indianapolis now. I also showed him the picture of Bianca and he asked if he could keep that one."

"Really?" I questioned with one eyebrow raised.

"Yeah but other than that he hasn't been doing anything else."

"Did you let him have the picture?" I asked.

She nodded then said, "yeah I mean he is the father and besides I could get another picture from Mama because she had some extra ones. I hope it was okay with you."

"Yeah girl I don't care," I closed my eyes briefly and waved both of my hands. "Anyway can we now change the subject?"

"We could but I have one more question about Lance," Kennede stated.

"Shoot for it, what's on your mind?"

"Do you still have feelings for him?" she asked.

I wrinkled my forehead and said, "hell to the naw!" Everyone started to laugh as I smirked, "I've actually come to terms with the fact we won't be together and the only reason we got together was to bring Bianca here." I said probably repeating myself because I remember telling somebody this before. "But actually I've been thinking about sending something I wrote to Lance, letting him know that I'm over him and have moved on with my life. I've now accepted the road that God has me on now."

"Wow, well maybe you should send it to him, but are you gonna send it to his house or office?" Brandi asked.

"Neither, I was going to send it to his email. I still remember his email address, I'm not going to risk anything by sending it to his house. Since I've known Carla, I didn't want to do anything to hurt her, I could care less if it hurt him though, but I couldn't do that to that poor woman." I explained.

"I understand that, it's too bad that Mrs. Carla has a jacked up husband and she doesn't even know it because she loves that man as if he was really faithful."

"Yeah I know," I said looking down. "Okay now can we please change the subject please?" I asked even though I know I was the one who brought him up in the first place.

"Okay then let's change it," Ken announced rolling her eyes playfully. "Well guys please pray for me because as you all know about this new baby of Ray's. Ya'll I'm so scared because this is new for me."

"I understand Ken, I've been there before," Brandi said. "Like I said before when we talked, I'm helping to raise another woman's child, I mean even though she is dead but it still hurt. But you have to trust and believe that your love will get you through those tough times. Trust me it'll get better and with God on your side you can't lose."

"I know," Kennede said looking down. "I mean we prayed that night and it eased up a little, but I still have a little nervousness about it."

"That's normal anytime you step into a new unfamiliar territory it is scary," I said. "When I was about to make my move to Indy, I was nervous and had some second thoughts. But ever since I've moved I just feel so much better, and if I would have stayed here in Louisville, I probably would have been miserable or depressed here. You just have to go with what you feel in your heart."

"Well my heart says that there is nobody in the world that could love me like Raymond. He and I feel so right together and no matter what I just don't want to lose him at all."

"You don't have to lose him Ken, hell you are getting married tomorrow," Summer laughed.

"Right," I laughed too, "like Brandi said the love you two have for each other will see you through anything."

"I love you guys so much," Kennede said reaching out both arms to embrace all of us on both sides. So we all did a group hug. "I'm so glad to have you girls to share things like this with."

"No matter how far apart we maybe, we're always and forever be the best of friends," I said. "I love you all too."

*   *   *

This wedding is so beautiful, I thought standing with the other bridesmaids as Kennede said her vows to Raymond. She looked absolutely stunning, she looked like a winter princess with the sparkling tiara that complimented her new do; Ken had her hair just like Keyshia Cole's hair was in the *"Sent from Heaven"* video. She also had a gorgeous silver and white looking dress, and I must say our periwinkle color dresses were looking good too.

"By the power invested in me," Pastor Williams said about to finish the ceremony. I looked in the crowd where I knew my mother was sitting with my baby, I spotted Mama and Grandmother, but I didn't see Bianca. I looked through each of the pews very carefully on the bride's side of the church, and I found Bianca sitting in the lap of Carla. My knees began to buckle as I almost passed out standing up there thinking, *what in the world is Carla doing here and why is she holding my child?* I looked to the left of Carla and saw Lance sitting next to her. "I now pronounce you husband and wife, Raymond you may salute your bride." Pastor Williams chuckled and the rest of the congregation chuckled too, everybody did but me.

I had to find a way to get my daughter out of Carla's hands before she takes one look at Bianca then at her husband and puts two and two together. Kennede's wedding was the worst time for all of this to come out in the open.

"Wooo," everyone cheered once Kennede and Raymond finally finished "saluting" each other.

"Presenting to you for the first time, I mean the second time, Mr. and Mrs. Raymond Collins." Pastor Williams finished speaking and the happy newlyweds walked down the aisle together after jumping the actually broom that was in between the front two pews. Next to walk down the aisle was the maid of honor, who was Brandi and the best man which was Ray's best friend Donnie. Then it was my turn to walk out of the sanctuary with Raymond's brother Sean who was my first in almost everything and with him looking as fine as he was looking today, I didn't mind being on his arm. And by the way he was holding on to me, I knew he didn't mind having me on his arm either. It had been so long since we've last seen each other and I could tell that he was excited as I was to see him again.

"I must say Ms. Brianna that you are looking beautiful this evening," Sean said after we were in the concourse of the church.

I looked up at Sean who had to be about six-foot-four and with these hills on that probably made me five-foot-eleven; I still had to look up to him. "Thank you Sean and you aren't looking too bad yourself."

"Well you know how I do it," he said playfully dusting off his shoulders. I had to catch myself from thinking *yes I do remember what you do*, because the brotha knew how to put it down. Now see look at me lusting up in the church, now I gotta go repent. "I actually have a question for you, uhm… since we were paired together during the ceremony, how do you feel about being together throughout the reception too?"

I tilted my head and tried to give him the sexiest look I could, "well…" I sang.

"Okay ladies and gents, we need to get the entire wedding party together for pictures," the wedding coordinator announced as the whole wedding party just stood around talking in the concourse. "So what we need is all of the wedding party to do is go toward the chapel and wait until the main sanctuary is cleared out. That way we can do the pictures in there, and remember there will be separate limos that will be taking the whole wedding party with the exception of the bride, groom, and the flower girl. They have their own limo while the flower girl was riding with her grandparents, but once the pictures are done we will get into the assigned limo and had to the reception." Everyone nodded and made their way to the chapel.

"Well alright then, I feel like I'm in elementary school again," Sean commented with our arms still intertwined. "So are you gonna answer my question from earlier, will you allow me to be your escort for the rest of the evening?"

I smiled as sexy as I could while biting the side of my bottom lip. "I sure would love to," I said as we were about to start walking toward the chapel.

"Oh Brianna," I heard a female call my name. I turned around to see Carla coming toward me with my child still in her arms.

"Uh...hey Carla," I said still holding onto Sean. He tried to loosen his grip, but I pulled him closer to me. "Please don't leave my side right now please," I begged in a whisper.

He smiled, "sure I won't leave your side, and I've got you." He said putting his hand on my lower back and I looked at him with a boy-don't-play-with-me look or you'll be getting more than a dance at the reception later.

"Brianna I must say your daughter is so beautiful and you are looking good too," Carla said as I approached her giving her a one arm hug while my other arm was playing with my daughter. "I'm sorry here do you want your baby right now?"

"I would love to hold her, but we are on our way to take pictures. My mom should be coming out of there soon and she has all of Bianca's stuff; she'll take Bianca with her." I explained, "oh I'm sorry, this is my date and Raymond's brother/groomsmen, Sean." I introduced Sean when I saw Lance walking in my direction.

"Hello Sean, my name is Carla and this is my husband Lance," she said as Lance joined her side and he shook Lance's hand after giving Carla a one arm hug too.

"Nice to meet you all," Sean said.

"And who are you again, brother?" Lance asked glancing at Sean before fixing his eyes on me, I wanted to bust out laughing, but I held it in.

"This is Sean; he's Brianna's date and Raymond's brother." Carla said before we could speak.

"Hello to you too Ms. Brianna, how have you been doing?" He asked reaching for my hand which I reluctantly shook, but didn't say any words to Lance. I just smirked while pulling Sean toward me so I could kiss his cheek.

I could tell Lance was burning a hole through my dress as he stared at me and Sean interacting with one another. "But anyway Sean, Lance and

Seasons

I are good friends with Kennede's mother Karen." Carla said before she paused to stare at me and Sean.

"You better stop slipping that hand down to my butt," I whispered in Sean's ear with a smile on my face.

"Oh I thought you liked it, or that's what your body was telling me," he whispered back into my ear, and I could feel someone's eyes watching our every move.

Lance and Carla looked at us in awe; Carla was smiling, but Lance kept looking at me like he was disappointed. I just wanted to crack up laughing in face because I knew it was killing him to see me with another man, and fine one at that or at least I was hoping that's what was going through his mind. "Look at them Lance, they make such a cute couple," I heard Carla say.

"Thank you," Sean and I said in unison then we began to laugh right along with Carla.

"Brianna and Sean we need you two in the chapel ASAP!" We turned around to see Ms. Daniels the wedding coordinator standing at the chapel door yelling at us.

"I'm sorry Carla, Lance, but we have to get going," I said, "I will see you at the reception, yes?" I questioned still holding onto Sean for dear life.

"Of course dear, I might have to grab that baby again once we get to the place," Carla laughed but her husband frowned.

"Okay," I said laughing as well, but I was thinking, *please leave my child alone before you find out something that you didn't want to know.*

"Carla will you give that girl's baby back to her mom, please leave that baby alone so she can rest please." Lance said before Sean and I could turn away completely. I stopped in my tracks and looked back in Lance's direction, he looked a little paranoid.

"Oh it's okay Mr. Lance," I said sarcastically. "Ms. Carla if Mama is willing to part with her grandbaby again, then you can hold her. As a matter of fact you all should sit at the table with my mom and Bianca so you won't have to go so far away from the baby, if you want." I said smirking as Lance rolled his eyes in my direction. At first I was kind of scared about what could happen if the truth is revealed, but after his comment I didn't care about him getting busted.

"That's a wonderful idea, I'll let you all go to do your thing," Carla said, "but we'll see you at the reception, oh here's Bri's mother now." I heard her say. I glanced back to see my mom approach Carla and Lance with Bianca's diaper bag they gave me for a baby shower gift along with the guilt money from Lance. I glanced back long enough to see that Mama took Bianca out of Carla's hand and that's when I smiled.

"So what was that about?" Sean asked opening the chapel door for me. "Was he someone you used to mess around with or something?" He whispered in my ear.

I looked at him with an eyebrow raised. "Why would you ask that question?" I asked.

"Oh c'mon Brianna, Ray Charles could see the tension that was between you and old dude when he walked up," Sean explained and I nudged him. "What? I'm just telling the truth, so did you two have something going?"

"I will tell you this much, but I will have to do some explaining a little bit later too. But there was something between me and *the good doctor* at one point and time." I said and Sean looked at me confused as we sat in the back of the chapel. "Oh that man is a doctor at the same hospital that I used to work at when I lived here, but let's just say that Lance's wife was holding the *something* that is between us."

Sean looked down for a minute then looked back up at me with bewildered eyes. "Your daughter Bianca is the...old dude's?" I nodded, "oh snap so that's old dude's baby." He repeated and I was thankful that he was whispering.

"Ding, ding, ding!" I said lightly clapping with the small bouquet still in my hands. "You are right, but I'll have to explain the entire situation a little later. Because I'm the innocent party over here." He continued to look amazed. "So I guess now you don't want to be my 'escort' for the evening since you know my dirty little secret huh?" I questioned not knowing what was going on in his head, as I hung my head.

"Oh no, I would never do you like that," he grabbed my hand then he used his other hand to raise my face so I could look into his eyes. "Besides I consider myself lucky because I get to escort the finest lady, well next to the bride. But honestly I think you are looking way more beautiful, but that's just my opinion though." he whispered.

"Well no Ken does look beautiful today. Hey don't forget that is my cousin you talking about." I said doing something I never thought I would do by defending Kennede.

"No Kennede is looking good today, I mean she is the bride, but I personally like chocolate any day over French vanilla." I hit his arm lightly, "oh c'mon now Bri don't even play, you know that girl is half white. Shoot her daddy is white," we laughed and I just nodded in agreement because he was right.

"Look at you two over here; are ya'll trying to show me and *my husband* up on the dance floor on *our* day?" Kennede asked breathing hard as Sean and I walked back over to the table after dancing our butts off to John Legend's song, "Green Light."

"Trust me we're not trying to steal your thunder baby girl," Sean began to say to Kennede. "But I didn't know when I asked to dance with Ms. Bri over here how *low* she was going to go."

I opened my mouth wide, "oh how you gonna say that?" I asked hitting him playfully. "You were behind me getting just as low as I was going." I laughed. "You should already know I get down cause we had plenty of practice back in the day, I hope you didn't forget that quick because I may have to refresh your memory later," I smirked with one eyebrow raised.

Sean had a grin on his and winked at me before he grabbed me by the waist and planted a kiss to my forehead. "Naw, I'm just joking, I could never forget my first, besides you are the best dancer I've been with in a while, thanks."

"No thank you," I said as Sean started to walk away but then turned back around quickly.

"Do you want something to drink?" he asked. "I was going over here to the bar if you want something."

"Sure thanks," I said and he went toward the bar. I looked at Kennede who was smiling at me with this sneaking grin, "what is that for?"

"What's up with you and Sean?" she asked still wearing that silly grin. "Ya'll was getting down on the dance floor like ya'll about to *get down* in other places again."

"It's nothing but some friendly dancing," I laughed. "But for real I'm kinda feeling him again, he was my first and now he is still fine and he's single too. The only thing is that I'm living in Indy now and he lives...where does Sean live at now?" I questioned because that was the only thing that we didn't get around to talking about.

"I believe that Raymond said that he lives in Chicago now, or somewhere close it," Kennede guessed while shrugging her shoulders.

"Well where ever he lives, he can always stop in Naptown for a little while to visit," I smiled. By that time Sean returned with a glass of champagne for me in his hands. "Oh Sean, what city are you living in now?"

"I reside in Chi-town, but I do travel a lot back and forth to Indianapolis mostly, and Cleveland, Detroit, you know places like that." He explained.

I smiled with all kind of thoughts going through my head. "Oh," I said, "well you know that I moved to Indianapolis about a month ago?"

"Oh really?" he questioned with his eyebrows raised. "Well I drove here for the wedding and that means I have to pass through Indy to get back to Chicago, would you mind if I stop by to visit you and the baby on my way home?" he asked standing so close to me it almost looked as if we were going to kiss. I could see Kennede out of the corner of my eye wearing this huge grin looking like *The Grinch that Stole Christmas*.

"Sure and for future reference, anytime you come into town for *business*, please give me a call," I said letting my lips graze his ear. "You have my number now, so use it."

"Oh yeah I got your number," he bent down and did the same thing I just did but his lips touched my ear; I closed my eyes and quivered briefly. "So when are you going back home again?" he asked.

"Tomorrow probably after church, probably around one-thirty or so I guess," I said now looking into his face.

"Cool, do you mind if I follow you...just to make sure that you and the baby get home safely." He chuckled.

"Right," I said chuckling too. "But I don't mind if you follow me, just call me so you can meet me at my grandmother's house. Maybe we could go out for a meal or something, well once we get to Indy that is."

He nodded his head, "sounds good to me because honestly I don't have to go back to work until Tuesday morning. Maybe I could stay in Naptown until Monday sometime, I just have to call my usual hotel, *The Westin*." Sean said.

"Or if you want to save a little money, you could stay at my place until Monday," I said moving closer to Sean again. "I mean, I do have an extra room if you want it."

"I would love to," he looked into my eyes and I felt a chill go through my body that caused my body to jerk. Honestly I started to think about those times that we spent together when we younger. "Are you okay?" he asked.

"A cold chill," I simply said then turned my head to see my mother coming in my direction holding Bianca. "Excuse me one moment please," I said to Sean.

"Sure don't leave me here alone too long," he said as he took a seat at the table for the wedding party.

"*Trust me* I won't," I said walking toward my mother. "What's going on here?" I asked my mother. "Hey baby girl," I said now smiling at my daughter who started cooing at me.

"While you were cutting it up on the dance floor, your baby girl was *cutting it up* in my lap," Mama said handing Bianca to me along with her diaper bag. "I love my grandbaby, but this is where Grand-Mama duty stops. So you need to go handle her."

"Okay Ma," I said walking back toward Kennede. "So where are the restrooms at in this place?" I asked her.

"The ones with the changing tables are all the way in the front of the country club," Ken said pointing in that direction. "But before you go, are you about to hook-up with my brother-in-law?" she asked with a grin on her face.

"Maybe," I smiled back at her. "But I do believe we are both two mature adults; I do believe I just turned twenty-four and he is twenty-six, so we're good."

"But what about ole' dude in Indy, the football player T.J.?" she asked. "Aren't you talking to him too?"

"Ken before you start, T.J. and I just met last Thursday, nothing is popping off with us, besides he has a girlfriend anyway," her mouth flew opened in shock. "And Sean and I have been cool for years, since the first time you married Ray. We are just two old friends who happen to have some sexual chemistry; the only thing is will we act on that? Honestly I'm not even trying to go down that road again with another man." I lied. She didn't have to know my business or who I decided to sleep with, hell she would still be in Kentucky while I'm almost two hours away.

"Okay Bri, I just don't want anyone to get hurt," she explained. "I don't want you to get hurt and I don't want you to hurt Sean by trying to play him with T.J."

"Kennede, if anybody is getting played it ain't gonna be me or Sean, okay?" I stated. "Look I need to go change my daughter's diaper, I'll talk to you later." I said walking off and not waiting for a response from Kennede. As much as I loved Ken, sometimes she could be a little noisy and a pain in my behind.

Lance must have followed me to the bathroom because when I stepped out of the door after changing Bianca, he was standing at the door waiting. I already knew that he wasn't waiting on Carla, the whole time I was in the bathroom nobody else walked in there.

"Hello Lance, are you waiting for your wife?" I asked with a giggle.

"No but I wanted to talk you," he said looking around nervously. My guess was that he didn't want anyone to overhear our conversation. "I miss you two, and I don't know your new number since you've moved so I can't get in touch with you."

"I still have the same email address, we could always communicate online." I smiled.

"This isn't a joke Brianna. What if I'm up in Indy and I wanted to see the two of you, how would I get in touch with you?" he asked with a solemn face.

"You still have my cell phone number, I haven't changed that one yet," I said knowing that he was lying about trying to get in touch with me. "C'mon Lance, what is this *really* about?"

"It's about the fact I still want to see you. I want to be in Bianca's life, I want to be in your life." He pleaded. I began to walk over to the lounge chairs. "Please don't walk away from me, Brianna."

"I'm not I'm just going over here to sit down," I took a seat with Bianca in my lap. "My feet are killing me in these shoes."

"Oh okay but I must say you are looking stunning tonight," he smiled. I lost smiled and looked up at him with a boy-please-get-out-of-my-face look. "and when I saw you with your "date" I did get kind of jealous because you were looking so good and he was all up on you."

"Whoa, whoa, whoa," I waved my free hand in the air. "Did you just say you were jealous? Are you serious? How are you going to be jealous of my date, Sean, when I am a single woman?" I questioned with my hand raised and looked down at my bare ring finger, "there's no ring on it, so I'm free to date *any* man that I choose. Besides you are here with your *wife*, you seem to forget that you have one, but I don't anymore." I rose my voice and he quickly raised his hand trying to tell me to keep in down.

"Okay yes I'm with my wife, but things aren't what they seem," he tried to protest. I shook my head and began to laugh loudly. "What's so damn funny?"

"Because you think I'm stupid," I said continuing to shake my head at him. "You think that I will keep falling for your B.S. I'm sorry Lance but those days are over."

"Brianna," he exhaled, "I just want you to give me another chance."

I started to laugh even harder, "you are so funny, another chance? Never! I'll tell you this though, you can have contact with your daughter when she's at the age that she can talk." I spoke with authority as I laid down the rules to him. "I mean you can call for her so she can at least learn your voice. You can have all the pictures that you want, as a matter of fact, check your email tomorrow. I'll send some pictures to you, but as far as anything with me, absolutely positively no way!" I said sternly and his face grew sad.

"Brianna come on now."

"Brianna come on now nothing," I stood up because I was about to end this conversation. "I'm done with this, I'm finished okay? There's nothing else you can say, you'll get your pictures later; other than that, good-bye Lance." I said in the strongest secure voice that I had as I began to walk away from him.

"I love you Bri," Lance said once I was walking toward the ballroom.

I stopped walking then turned around to face him, "stop lying to me and stop lying to yourself." I said in the same strong voice. "You don't love me because love wouldn't hurt and love doesn't have a wife and a mistress on the side. Let's be real for once, that's all I *really* was and that's all I was going to be to you was a mistress, but never again because *I am* wifey material, believe that."

"I know, but come on…let's just," Lance continued to beg.

"Let's just what?" I asked. "No I'll tell you what, let's just end it here and say good-bye to us. You can be in her life all you want, but there is no us, okay? Good-bye Lance, and for good this time." I said and even with hurting feet I swiftly walked to the ballroom before Lance could catch up with me again.

It felt so good to get that part off of my chest, I thought walking into the ballroom with biggest smile on my face. I was now so anxious to get back to my grandmother's house to get my laptop and send Lance the rest of how I felt. I had to end this now and forever because I had a feeling I was about to walk into something new with someone. Or at least I expect it to be Sean, since I'm not trying to be the chick on the side anymore even though T.J. is fine.

"Hey sexy where'd you run off to?" Sean asked as soon as I sat back down at the table with Bianca in my arms.

"I just had to handle some unfinished business." I nodded toward Bianca. "I had to let some people go so I could make room for someone else." I smiled as Sean grabbed my hand and smiled too.

Sunday, December 7, 2008:

"Are you all packed and ready to go?" Grandmother asked as she walked thru the door from church. "Why hello young man, aren't you Raymond's brother right?" she asked Sean who was standing in the living room holding one of my bags.

"Yes ma'am," he said. "My name is Sean," he extended his hand toward Grandmother, but she pulled him into her for a hug and a kiss.

"Baby you are practically family now, so no handshakes instead we hug around here," she said releasing him then taking off her Sunday morning hat off. "Brianna did you go to church this morning or did you skip it?"

"Actually Sean and I, along with Mama went to Eight-thirty service this morning. We wanted to get on the road before two o'clock this evening." I said pointing back and forth between me and Sean.

"Oh so Sean did you ride with my grandbaby from Indianapolis?" she asked sitting down in her living room chair.

"No ma'am, I drove my own car and I live in Chicago," he began to explain. "And since I have to go through Indianapolis to get home, I figured I would be a gentleman and see Brianna and the baby home safely first before I went home." He said leaving out the fact that he was spending a couple of nights at my place before he actually went back to Chicago.

"Okay, so you are a nice guy," she nodded her head with approval. "Uh-uh she needs a nice Christian young single man in her life."

I looked at Sean then rolled my eyes at my grandmother's statement. "Okay Grandmother we are going to get on out of here." I said reaching for Bianca's car seat which she was already sleeping in.

"Alright then suga, but I want to say good-bye to my great granddaughter. And I want to uhm, speak to you in private," Grandmother said pointing at me.

"Well in that case, I'll go start both of our cars up so they'll be nice and warm," Sean said and I handed him my keys. He went to Grandmother's chair to give her a hug again, "it was nice to meet you again Mrs. Spencer, I will you later."

"Okay baby it was nice seeing you too," she smiled as Sean went out the door. "Take a quick seat Bri," she said pointing toward the couch.

"Alright, so what's going on Grandmother?" I asked sitting in the seat she directed me to.

"I know the truth," she simply said and I sat there looking confused before she pointed to Bianca. I looked at her with this I-have-no-idea-what-you-are-talking-about-face, "oh don't look at me like you don't know what I'm talking about. Brian isn't that child's father is he?" she asked looking at me waiting for an answer.

I looked down at my twiddling fingers then looked back at Grandmother, "no he's not," I said in a defeated tone while shaking my head.

"It's that man Lance isn't it?" my heart dropped when the words left her mouth. I looked at her with surprise, *how did she know that?* I asked myself. "I'm right, it is Lance, your aunt's friend's husband."

I lowered my head in disgust when she mentioned it; because instead of seeing him in my mind as a former lover, he was looking more like an uncle figure or something that was far from what he really was, "yes ma'am, but you have to let me explain something first," I tried to protest. "I promise you I didn't know Lance was married to Aunt Karen's friend Ms. Carla in the beginning."

"Are you saying that you didn't know that he was married at all or you didn't know his wife was a family friend as well as my church member?" she questioned.

"Grandmother here's the story, and it's the truth I promise," I began. "I met Lance at the hospital that I worked at while I was here. When we first met I knew nothing about a wife or any kids for that matter. By the second or third date he tells me that he is older than I originally thought, plus he has two kids and a wife."

"Hold on a minute, the Hamilton's have four kids," she said and it turned my stomach to hear her refer to Lance and Carla as *"The Hamilton's,"* like they are some big happy family.

"At that time he told me he only had two kids; I found out at your birthday party that he had four. But after he told me he was married, I kicked him out and told him never to talk to me again," I continued on with my side of the story. I went on to tell her how he begged me to stay with him because he really wasn't happy; and how I thought his wife was this horrible person until I met Carla on at her birthday party; and by that time I was good and pregnant. I even went on to tell Grandmother how he even propose to me the very morning of her party and how totally fooled he had me.

"Shoot he had us all fooled," she said not sounding upset with me. "But I take it everything has ended between the two of you?"

"Oh yes ma'am," I spoke up quickly. "I had written this letter on my laptop I was thinking of sending to him." I went on to tell Grandmother how he had approached me at the reception last night. I paused telling her the rest before asking, "wait a minute, how did you know that Lance was Bianca's father?" I questioned wondering if one of my cousin's or my sister had ran their traps.

"The day that she was born I came back up to your room and the door was cracked and I saw Lance holding the baby." She paused then my mouth flew wide open in shock. "Well I heard the whole conversation even the part about the money." She announced and I just sat there totally surprised.

"Are you serious?" I questioned and she nodded. "You didn't tell anyone else did you?"

"No baby," she reached out for my hand, "your secret is safe with me. I will carry it to my grave." She said, I jumped up and gave her a hug with tears in my eyes.

"Thank you Grandmother," I said holding tightly to her. "I love you so much."

"I love you too baby," she said releasing her arms from around me. "You better go on and get going; you got that young man waiting on you."

"Yes ma'am," I smiled picking up the blanket to cover Bianca's car seat.

"And Brianna, I like that young man out there, what his name again, Sean?" I nodded. "I think he might be the one."

I shook my head then said, "I don't know if there is a one for me Grandmother," I admitted.

"Oh don't speak like that honey," Grandmother stood. "There is always that one for everybody baby, you may not want him now, but if he's the one he'll stick around."

"Okay," I said rolling my eyes then smiling.

"Oh wait a minute Bri, I want to kiss my grandbaby good-bye," Mama said rushing down the stairs and uncovering Bianca. "Bye baby girl, Grandma gonna see you later," she said to a sleeping Bianca, luckily she didn't budge.

"Bye Ma," I said giving my mother a hug. "I will call you guys as soon as I get into town."

"Alright be safe," Mama said as I walked out the front door. "Bye Sean, you be safe too baby." She said to him as he got out of his car.

"Yes ma'am," he said grabbing Bianca's car seat then putting her in my car. "You go on and get in, I'll strap her in and everything."

"Okay," I said getting in the driver's seat then grabbing my laptop. I wanted to send the letter I wrote last night to Lance before I went back home; I didn't want to bring anything old to my new place. I pulled up the letter then highlighted it, then pressed copy. I logged on to the internet and pulled up a page to compose an email, then hit paste. Before I hit the send button, to send my feelings to Lance, I read back over it to make sure there weren't any mistakes and to make sure I didn't leave out any words:

```
Dear Lance,
    I'm writing this to let you know that you did come
across my mind. Those endless nights of making what I
```

thought was love, your sexy smile that ended with your dimples placed in the most beautiful face I've ever seen a man have. I've even been thinking about those times being held by you and wrapped in your arms and how the tears would leave my cheeks to rest upon your bare sculpted chest; like fresh dew in the morning. As I opened up to you about the men of my past and how much hurt they've caused me which was the reason on many nights I ended up laying down my tears on your chest. But now you've been drafted into that league of men; now you're the one that has given me sacks of lies even after I've trusted you to catch the pieces of my fumbled heart. And here you've entered that league but with top honors as MVP. Not Most Valuable Player, even though I trusted you with my heart, which I thought you would treat like it had value. But instead you became the Most Versatile Player; changing the way I viewed this game we played called love.

Unfortunately for me I'm reminded of you every time I look into my daughter's face; it seems that God took a picture of you and crafted her face by your features. So I can't help but to remember you. If things were different you would have been just another memory that I would try to forget; because if it hadn't been for her, your name would never come up in my thoughts or in my dreams that I unwillingly have. Truth be told I've actually moved on form all you've done; all of the lies that you swore you could make good on; and honestly I'm okay now. I'm getting over the hurt, the pain, and everything else you've done. That's the reason I was writing to let you know that I am no longer affected by the things of the past. And my prayer is that God keeps you in perfect peace the same way He's now keeping me. Take care. ~Brianna

"Hey Bri are you ready yet?" Sean asked then I hit the send button. The screen then said, "Message Sent."

With a smile on my face I looked over at Sean smiling, "of course I'm ready to go back home." I closed my laptop then turned around to look in the backseat to see Bianca's wide eyes now looking around with a pacifier in her mouth. I smiled again then said, "alright Bianca we're on our way back home to Indy."

Finally: The End!

A letter to all Readers of Seasons:

Hello to all of those that have just finished reading my first novel, **Seasons**. My prayer is that you've enjoyed the story and that you may have saw either yourself or someone you may know in one of the characters. As the author, I've enjoyed writing this novel for many reasons; I look forward to completing the four part sequel to **Seasons** in the near future. I hope all of those who have either bought this book, or checked it out in library, or even if you borrowed it, will be looking out for the four part sequel which will include a novel that tells the story of each main character from **Seasons**, Kennede, Summer, Brandi, and Brianna. The story is post Seasons; and the first novel of the four part sequel series will be Brianna's story which is titled, **Simply Complicated**. But until the sequel series begins, look for other novels written by *Deanna Lynette*, those novels will be out soon including the next one. **No One but You**, But check out the next page because there's an excerpt from the second novel written by *Deanna Lynette*. Thank you for reading **Seasons** and I hope you enjoy the excerpt from the next novel, **No One but You**.

Sincerely,
Deanna

No One But You

Dyanna

Fine no excuse me, absolutely *fine* was the words that came to my mind the first time I saw Lloyd Bishop about five or six years ago. He was the best man and brother to the groom of one of the biggest, most expensive, and highly publicized weddings I was working on in the early stages of my career. I bet you're wondering what my line of work is; now I am one of the most desired and best wedding planners in the world. My office is located in Miami, Florida along with my home which is right outside of Dade County. Well, back to five or six years ago when the groom of this huge wedding was Lamar Bishop, one of the top Tight Ends in the NFL. I knew that because I was a huge football fan and followed the games very closely. At the time of the wedding Lamar was playing for the Tennessee Titans, but he and his fiancée Victoria Drake, who was a professional tennis player, were planning this huge wedding in the middle of the season while they stayed in Nashville, Tennessee. Okay no problem right? But wrong!

These two wanted this huge wedding to take place not in Tennessee, but on South Beach, and they expected me to plan this while they were gone for the football season. Of course I wanted to throw a fit, but due to all of the trouble I was going to endure planning this wedding they decided to give me an additional ten thousand dollars on top of the fee that I already charged. So with my money in mind, I was *very* willing to do whatever they wanted, because I am always about my money.

Their extravagant expensive wedding was set for the first week in March, but the day I met Lloyd was six months before the big event. When we met it had to be around the middle of September, and I'll never forget that day as long as I live and breathe. I remember that I needed this very important paper signed from the bride and groom before I could start booking one of the venues for their South Beach wedding. They chose to have the wedding on South Beach because they both were natives of Miami, and being that the football season was well underway at the time I needed the papers, which meant I couldn't just go down the street for them to handle this simple task because they were in Nashville and I was in Miami. That was when Lamar and Victoria informed me that Lamar's brother still lived in the city and he'd be more than happy to bring the papers I needed along with other important information by my office.

"Ms. Mackin," my assistant buzzed into my office, "there is a Mr. Lloyd Bishop here to see you."

"Thanks Tessa," I said closing a folder that I was looking through, "please send him right back to my office ma'am." I hung up the phone and opened my file drawer so I could get the folder that was marked '*The Drake/Bishop Wedding*.'

Knock; knock someone tapped lightly on my door, "Ms. Mackin this is Mr. Bishop," Tessa opened the door then stood over to the side as she announced Lloyd's arrival. When he stepped around the corner and stood in my doorway, I wanted to fall out if I weren't already sitting in my chair. Lloyd stood about six foot three or six foot four with the body of a football player, with the thick neck (which is something that I loved), wide shoulders, and not one ounce of fat came through his beige suit. "Is there anything I can get you today Mr. Bishop?" Tessa asked about to walk out of my office.

"Oh no thank you," his baritone belted out as chills went down my spine as if he was speaking in my ear. I started to watch his plump lips as he spoke and I became mesmerized. "You know what on second thought, could I please get some water, only if it's not too much trouble?" he asked then began to smile showing off these perfectly straight white teeth. *Oh my God! This man has dimples too*, I thought. Dimples on a fine man along with his other physically features are a *huge* weakness of mine.

This man was damn near perfect; well to me he was because he had everything I liked in a man. His skin was a beautiful complexion almost like it was a mixture of caramel and milk chocolate blended perfectly together; he was tall like I said before, he was also very clean cut with his sideburns connecting to a goatee and mustache. Even though he wasn't sporting a fade he did have his hair neatly placed in twist like he was starting dreadlocks, which gave him a whole new level of sexiness. Lloyd also showed off a pair of diamond studs in each ear that offset the beige suit, with a white collar shirt that he wore with a beige and red tie. Yes this man was just too fine for words!

"Okay, I'll be right back with that water Mr. Bishop," Tessa said, "can I get anything for you Ms. Mackin?"

"Uh-uhm no thanks," I managed to say after coming out of my trance. "It's nice to finally meet you Mr. Bishop, my name is Dyanna Mackin," I extended my hand toward Lloyd to *finally* introduced myself; and as soon as our hands touched, it was almost like I was being struck by lightening.

"Hello Ms. Mackin," he said taking my hand and placing his lips on the back of it, after he did that I wanted to melt. Those juicy lips of his felt *a lot* softer than I could have ever imaged they would feel, but I had envisioned those lips kissing more than the back of my hand. "It's nice to finally meet this *'Superwoman Wedding Planner'* my brother and future sister-in-law keep telling me about."

"Oh thank you very much, but I'm only doing what I get paid to do," I blushed hoping the red on my cheeks wouldn't come through my warm caramel skin, well at least that's what the *Queen Collection by Covergirl* said my complexion was. "But uhm, Lamar has spoke very highly of you as well, by the way he talks about you he is very proud of his little brother. Now Lamar tells me that you are an attorney right?"

He nodded his head, "yes ma'am I am an attorney. So my brother talks about me like that uh?" he chuckled then leaned back in his chair that was across from my desk. I wanted to slide right out of my chair and onto the floor or into his lap because the way he was sitting in his seat would have been perfect for me to hop right on him, but before I could even think about it further, Tessa busted thru the door.

"Here you go Mr. Bishop," she handed him a bottle of water.

"Thank you so much," he smiled briefly in her direction before his eyes were locked with mine again. I bit my bottom lip because of the way he was looking into my eyes with his beautiful light brown eyes. My mind started racing a mile a minute and I was ready to clear my desk so he could take me at that very moment. "I must say Mrs. Mackin, you are absolutely stunning and I apologize if I keep staring at you."

"Uhm thank you for that compliment Mr. Bishop," I said touching the ponytail bun that was neatly placed in the back of my head. "And you don't have to keep calling me *Mrs. Mackin*, please call me Dyanna. Besides I'm not even married anyway."

"Okay then *Ms. Dyanna*," he chuckled again and I smiled at him, "and please call me Lloyd," he paused then squinted his eyes like he was trying to remember something. "I'm normally not this bold, but let me ask this question first, since you aren't married, are dating anybody or in a *serious* relationship?"

I smirked, even though I was actually stunned by his question, "to tell you the truth," I paused looking down then looking back up at him, "I'm not in a relationship and I'm not dating anyone at the moment." I replied with a smirk still on my face, and a smirk returned on his as well.

"Oh okay, you had me there for a minute," he gave a light laugh while bobbing his head up and down. "So do you mind if I take you out to lunch or dinner some time?"

A smile came across my face, but as soon as I started to think about my busy schedule and about the relationship I just got out of, my smile quickly faded. "I uhm, I would love to take you up on that offer, but uhm," I bit my bottom lip this time trying to figure out how I was going to let this gorgeous creature down easy. "Its just, well let me put it like this, I would love to go out with a man such as yourself trust me I would."

"So what's wrong?" his smile then faded into this serious look that almost looked better than his sexy smile he had been wearing. "I know what it is, you like them ole high yellow dudes and because I'm a *chocolate brotha*, you won't give me the time of day," a smile returned to his face and I started to smile too, "it's because I'm black isn't it?" he joked.

"No not at all, look at me I'm only a shade or two lighter than you. Actually I *prefer* a chocolate man anytime of the day," I suggested with a chuckle, trying to give him my sexiest expression. "But it's that I recently just got out of a serious relationship and I'm really not ready to get out there yet."

"Oh okay, I can understand that," he said.

"Like I said before, I would *love* to go out with you, but it hasn't been two months yet since my ex and I broke up," I explained and he looked so attentive yet concerned. "And I'm just not ready to get back out there in the dating game yet. The next time I start dating again I want to be completely ready, plus with me taking some time off from dating, it will allow me to build up my career." Soon after those words escaped my lips I wanted to kick myself because I could feel that this man could possibly be different than the rest of the men I knew.

"I mean it's cool, I completely understand," he said, but I could see traces of disappointment on his smooth face "I wish things could be different though and this wasn't the case."

"Yeah me too," I looked down feeling some disappointment, "then on top of everything else, your brother's wedding has got me working some *crazy* hours so I can pull off this *lavish* South Beach wedding," I smiled.

"Oh yeah," he snapped his fingers as if something came to his remembrance. He reached into his suit jacket pocket and pulled out a piece of paper. "I almost forgot the reason I was here," he said now looking into my eyes again.

"Yeah I forgot too," I smiled, "but I really need to go on and get that part of the *big event* out of the way," I said wondering for a brief moment how it would be if I did give Lloyd a chance and actually go on a date with him. My body wanted to let him take advantage of me and let him completely rock my world, but my mind connected with my heart that said to use precaution. After this last relationship and the experiences that I've had with men in my past, I just didn't want to risk being hurt again by any man for that matter. "Thank you so much Lloyd for bringing those papers by my office, I do look forward to working with you throughout this wedding."

"Yeah me too, it's just too bad that I couldn't take you out to show you how a *good* man treats a woman." He stood from his seat.

My eyebrows rose, once again I was caught off guard by this fine man but this time it was by his words instead of his looks. "I bet you could show me some things, but just remember the wedding is six months away." I managed to say.

His face showed confusion, "okay that's true, but what does that have to do with *us?*" he questioned.

"Well you see, six months is quite a bit of time Mr. Bishop to get to know someone," I gave him my sexy slanted eyes before saying, "you never know what could happen between *us* in the course of *six months*."